THE STA\ ___ MANUSCRIPT

VINCE WHEELER

M*T*M
PRESS

The Marion/Manville Press

Published in the United States
The Marion/Manville Press, Kansas City
Direct inquiries to: TMMPKC@gmail.com

This book is a work of fiction, and all characters and events depicted
herein are likewise fictitious. Any resemblance of such characters or
events to actual persons or events is purely coincidental.

Trade paperback ISBN: 979-8-9883190-0-9
Ebook ISBN: 979-8-9883190-1-6

Cover illustration and design © Owen Gent
www.owengent.com

Interior book design by Frederickson Concepts

ALSO BY VINCE WHEELER

The Things of Man

Again, and Always, for Pam

Contents

The Books of Stavros

THE FIRST BOOK OF STAVROS
The World in Thirds   1

THE SECOND BOOK OF STAVROS
A Book By Its Cover   99

THE THIRD BOOK OF STAVROS
The Nature of Dreams   151

THE FOURTH BOOK OF STAVROS
Transposition   197

THE FIFTH BOOK OF STAVROS
The Weight of a Black Hole   237

THE SIXTH BOOK OF STAVROS
Symmetry   301

Scriptor Libri

Strangers on a Train   143

Sojourn   189

The Tale of the Nine Years   287

THE FIRST BOOK
OF STAVROS

The World in Thirds

The ego is not master in its own house.

–Sigmund Freud

-1-

I STARED INTO A LIGHT SO BRIGHT *I could see nothing else. A white-hot fire leaving only itself visible.*

I heard a man's voice.

"Read any good books lately?"

"You've got some nerve," I said, "asking me that. I suppose you think that's funny. Who are you?"

"Oh, Leonard, you know very well who I am."

"No, I don't."

"Yes, you do, or you wouldn't have started this conversation."

"I didn't start it."

"You most certainly did. You wanted to speak with me so I could tell you something. Something very important."

I could not imagine what that might be. And I didn't much care. The light—the fire—was hurting my eyes.

"What is this?" I said. "A dream or something?"

"Or something."

"Well, I've had enough of it. I'm going to wake up."

"I wouldn't count on that," he said.

"Why?"

"Because you don't want to wake up. And very possibly, you never will."

"That's ridiculous."

"You may think that. But don't say I didn't warn you."

"Are you honestly trying to tell me that I'm going to be having this supposed dream forever?"

"I didn't say that. I just said you may never wake up. You'll think you're awake, but you won't be."

I could not close my eyes to the fire; I could not turn away. "Look, I'm tired of this. If you have something to tell me—something I actually want to hear—get to it."

"All right, then. But I advise you to listen very closely. And you must remember everything I say. Because I am only allowed to say it once. Only once. Now, I am going to give you the key to the Paisley Codex."

"What? *My god! How do you know that?*"

"Someone told me."

"Who?"

"I am not allowed to say."

"But how could anyone possibly know the key to the Paisley?"

"Perhaps, in time, you will learn the answer to that. But for now, listen. And remember."

I listened. I hung on his every word.

Then I promptly forgot the whole damn thing.

I heard a slew of hard, fist-pounding knocks on a metal door. Lying on my back, I pushed up to a sitting position to find myself on a bed in a cheap hotel room, the drapes drawn against the light of day, the walls and furnishings veiled in shadows.

I did not know this place. Could not remember coming here.

The knocking continued. I threw off the covers and crept to the door. Through the peephole, I saw Ed on the other side.

I cracked the door. "What's going on?"

"Let me in," he said, shoving his way into the room. "We need to get goin'."

"Where?"

"To see the Judge. He's expectin' us."

"Oh, lord, anybody but him."

Ed glanced around the room, taking on a foul expression. "Jesus, they're gonna have to fumigate this place," he said—an allusion, no doubt, to my rather conspicuous lack of hygiene.

I let the remark pass and sat down on the end of the bed, trying to make sense of things.

"I don't get this," I said. "Where are we and how did we get here?"

"We're in a fleabag, asshole."

I swept the long, knotted hair from my eyes. "I can see that."

"We came here after the party. You know, the one where you got shit-face drunk?"

"I don't remember getting drunk."

"Take my word for it, you got that way. We both did."

"But why aren't we at your place?"

"Man, how many brain cells did you kill? Those boys from out of town were watchin' my apartment. Remember?"

I shook my head. "Boys from out of town?"

"The ones I owe the money to," he said, loud and very slow, as if I were dense. "But they had to catch a train. By now, they're long gone." He kicked me in the meat of the calf. "Come on. Get your ass dressed. We gotta move."

My pants lay on the bed. I checked the pockets, finding only a couple of bills and some change.

I panicked. "Where the hell is my money?"

"Those drinks didn't buy themselves. You spent that lettuce, sonny boy."

I had? I certainly hadn't had what one would call a life-changing amount of cash—just enough to make it another few days. Yet I had blown it all but a pittance? On nothing but booze?

I had to wonder.

I looked at Ed suspiciously. "Where did you stay last night?"

"A couple of floors down," he said. "And just so you know, we gotta watch ourselves when we leave. My room happened to come with a real curvy blonde whose husband might be lookin' for me."

"That figures." I got up and searched for the rest of my clothes. "So how am I paying for this?"

"You're not. I took care of it."

When had Ed ever been so generous?

"How?" I asked.

"Credit card."

"You don't have a credit card."

"Yes, I do," he said.

"Since when?"

"Since last night."

"And whose name appears on that card?"

"Well . . ." He laughed.

"Oh, my god."

He shrugged. "Sorry, man. It's what I do."

I had recovered one shoe and was looking for socks when I remembered that I had none.

"This is a nightmare."

"If it is," he said, "it's yours. Me, I'm havin' quite a time." He found my shirt under the bedding and tossed it in my face. "Let's go, douchebag. The Judge awaits."

———◇———

For a long while we moved through the dank city, the sky covered in gray. In places, the streets narrowed beyond reason, cobblestone lanes where the smallest of vehicles could pass but one at a time. The sidewalk too was often wide enough for only one person, constraining us to move single file against the centuries-old stone buildings.

And of course, Ed led the way.

I hated Ed. He was constantly trying to talk me into doing something unscrupulous, and I was forever trying to talk him out of doing something rash. But while I was loath to admit it, the fact was that he looked and dressed and carried himself as I wished I could. And so, even while despising him, I found myself at times wanting to be like him—though only if I could do so without actually having to *be* him. That was where I drew the line.

Eventually our path led to the Judge's favorite café. The Judge, as far as I knew, had no present judicial appointment, though I assumed that at some time he had held such a position. In any event, it was clear that he had vast experience in presiding over matters of human deportment. Of conduct to be praised or condemned.

His honor had seated himself at his usual table near the back. Ed waved off the maître d' and I followed him through the crowd.

The Judge was sipping an espresso, pretending, as we stood before him, that we did not exist.

"You rang, your majesty," Ed said. "So what the fuck is it?"

The Judge continued to all but ignore us. His manner, as usual, was meant to intimidate.

"*You*," he said at last, his voice booming, "the *both* of you, are a disgrace." He snapped his head toward Ed. "You are a reprobate. I want nothing to do with you. Ever! You are the worst of humanity. You would defile a nun. You would steal the last crumb from a starving beggar. You are a pig."

"So tell me how you *really* feel," Ed returned.

Alarmed at Ed's insolence, nearby patrons and waitstaff stopped themselves and looked over; the entire establishment marked a short beat of nervous silence.

"Sit down, you troglodyte," the Judge commanded.

Ed did. Quickly. He knew when to push the Judge, and when not.

"And you, Stavros," the Judge said to me as, quietly, I also took a chair, "you have done nothing to rein in this animal. Made no effort whatsoever to control this . . ." He shot Ed a seething glance. ". . . this lower life form."

"I'm sorry," I said. "I've done a bad job."

"You've done a *horrible* job!" he roared. "You have let him control you rather than vice versa. And that was not our arrangement. You were

supposed to do otherwise. You were supposed to do the *right thing*. But
you have not. And what excuse do you possibly have?"

His glare was unrelenting.

I stared at the floor.

"Your honor, honestly, it's just that I've been so focused on other
matters," I said. "I'm trying to get my life back to . . ." I did not know
how to finish that sentence. "Because I lost so many years trying to . . ."
I *did* know the conclusion to that thought, but found it too painful to
state. ". . . trying to figure out . . . to decipher . . ."

My eyes were tearing. I could not hold it back.

"The Paisley Codex," the Judge said wearily, adding the words I could
not.

Big drops ran my cheeks.

"Pussy!" Ed said.

"Shut up," the Judge told him, his gaze remaining on me. "Perhaps,"
he chided, "you did not work hard enough. Perhaps you might have
given a better effort."

Yes, I thought, perhaps I might have. *Perhaps*. But how? I had worked
every waking hour. For nine years. Attempting to extract some semblance of meaning from a seven hundred year-old hand-written manuscript inscribed with an enciphered message incomprehensible to every
person on the planet.

A career lost. A wife lost. All finances lost.

A life lost.

And I had failed to unravel even a single word. But then, countless
others had tried. And with the same result. The thing was uncrackable.
Eternal gibberish to the human mind.

I wanted no more of it. The mere subject was too painful to contemplate.

Yet leave it to the Judge to give a down man an extra kick.

He regarded me with an air of bland revulsion.

"You are positively hideous," he said. "You know that, don't you?"

I did? *Hideous?* Even Ed, back at the hotel, had not been that direct.

But there I sat, my hair a greasy, tangled thicket that covered my face and fell to my shoulders like clumps of seaweed, my bedraggled beard permeated with putrid specks of food and spittle and forming a long, filthy bib across my chest. And no less indecent, my clothes—the only clothes I owned—were fraught with tears, gaping holes, and off-putting stains in various stages of maturity. I had a particularly noticeable rip in the seat of my threadbare khaki pants which, with no underwear beneath, left my naked butt-skin on display. And what had once been a polo shirt now survived only as a remnant of frayed cloth, the jacket I wore above it so soiled and tattered it looked as though it might have been retrieved from a garbage disposal. My footwear was equally pathetic—mud-soaked canvas sneakers with the soles worn smooth and peeling away, one shoe absent laces and secured to my bare foot with a twist tie from a bread sack.

And beneath it all—though still largely evident to the unfortunate viewer—lay sunken eyes and a physique that could have passed for that of a concentration camp resident.

Then too, of course, there was the stench (which Ed *had* noted)—that, I am sure, being worse even than my appearance.

So—*hideous*...

Yes, I was all of that.

Positively.

"I have no money," I said.

"That can be remedied." The Judge glanced down at his coffee—then up. "I have come into possession of a manuscript."

"I don't want to hear about it."

"Oh, I think you will," he said, taking an advisory tone. "This will be something different for you. Something to get your mind off of the other book. And I would venture to say, it will almost certainly be easier."

"What is it?"

"As I said, a manuscript. Another book. Something I have recently acquired."

"From where?"

"Irrelevant," he said with a finality foreclosing further inquiry on the question.

"Is it old?"

"It may be. As yet, though, it is undated."

"And does this book have a name?"

"None that I know of. But if you can tell me what it says, I'll let you put any name on it you wish. Even your own."

A slight smile creased his face. The Judge did not make such promises lightly. Clearly, to him this was something of great consequence.

"If it's a known script, I can translate it," I said.

"And if it isn't?"

I looked at him warily. "What are you saying?"

"I'm saying that I don't know what it is—although the text may well represent a cipher of some kind."

"Then it's no different than the Paisley," I said angrily. "And I don't have another nine years to waste. Not for you or anyone."

"Do not take that attitude with me," the Judge cautioned.

"Go ahead," Ed goaded me. "You tell him."

"And *you* keep quiet!" the Judge instructed Ed—then leaned in my direction. "Stavros, I will pay you handsomely for this. Forget the Paisley and all the trouble it has caused. Find the secrets of *this* book—this new and most important book—and when you do," he said, raising his now cold espresso in something like a toast, "you may at last find peace."

B Y TRAINING AND EDUCATION, I am, among other things, a linguist and a mathematician. I am also, by gift of nature, a hyperpolyglot—that is, a person capable of learning an extraordinary number of languages. I can, at present, fluently speak, read, and write in twenty-one tongues, and in most others I am proficient enough that one could drop me nearly anywhere in the world and I could hold a respectable conversation in the native speech. I am likewise highly skilled in computer languages—skilled to the point that I am (or at least once was) as accomplished in the encryption and decryption of cyber data as anyone on the planet—although I find the spoken word far more interesting.

For a short time after university, I taught in and otherwise occupied the world of academia. The work was not terribly challenging. I was then called to service by a rather shadowy government agency (an agency, let us say, within an agency, within an agency, etc.) whose job was to intercept and interpret seemingly garbled messages generated by other governments and foreign organizations, such communications intended to be understood only by persons associated with the originating parties. And thus, assigned to a certain Eastern European embassy, I became a cryptanalyst—or to use a description more familiar to the layman, a *codebreaker*. But as I must make clear, to persons in my former line of work, the word *code* is a term of art. Another such term—often confused with *code*, but which means something else—is *cipher*. And the truth is, I did not often break codes. For the most part, I broke ciphers.

Now, to be precise, when we speak of a code, we are essentially referring to the use of one or more symbols, words, or even gestures that work as a kind of shorthand for the purpose of secretly conveying a complete thought, observation, or set of instructions. For example, one wishing to dispatch a coded message might simply transmit the number 6, and to another person knowing the code, this could mean "I'll meet you at noon." Note how the import of the entire communication is expressed by a single digit. This is how code works.

Cipher, though, is quite different. In its most rudimentary form, a cipher does one of two things: it either replaces each character of the *plaintext* (that is, the actual message) with a different character—a method known as *substitution cipher*; or it rearranges the plaintext characters in a way to make the message unrecognizable—a system known as *transposition cipher*. In the modern world of cryptology, extremely complex algorithms applying either or both of these techniques (as well as other methods too convoluted for lay discussion) are regularly used to encrypt and decrypt electronic communications and store sensitive information.

But ciphers have been around for thousands of years and have not always been so sophisticated. For instance, in the ancient encryption technique known alternately as Caesar Cipher or Caesar Shift (a substitution cipher supposedly used by Julius Caesar to outwit his adversaries) each letter of the plaintext is replaced by a different letter some set number of positions up or down the alphabetic line—meaning that if the *shift* were two positions to the right, in order to encrypt a message, *A* would be represented by *C*, *B* would become *D,* and all other letters shifted accordingly. So, using this method—again, with a shift to the right of two positions—if Caesar wanted to say "CROSS THE RUBICON," he would have transmitted "ETQUU VJG TWDKEQP." And that's pretty elementary. Caesar's use of it notwithstanding, it's a cipher that is easily broken—just as many ciphers of other types are, likewise, easily broken.

And by me, codes and ciphers alike were broken. Easily.

But then came something that was, well, not so easy.

Then came the Paisley Codex.

It has been said that the Devil takes many forms. And I don't know whether Satan truly exists. But if he does, then he presented himself to me in the unimposing shape of a book roughly ten inches long, seven inches wide, and two inches thick. A book with a plain and uninscribed leather cover, heavily degraded by its age, and inside, handwritten in iron gall ink, page upon page of characters drawn flawlessly in the script of the medieval Arabic, Greek, and Latin alphabets—the Latin done in capital letters, the Greek in lower case. All such letters being uniformly spaced and ordered line after line in a seemingly arbitrary manner. With no punctuation. No paragraph breaks. No diacritical marks. And never forming a single identifiable word in any language.

The manuscript stretches on, incoherent, for 252 unnumbered pages. The pages themselves are of vellum—that is, calfskin—and have been carbon-dated to the early fourteenth century. So presumably, that is when the book was written. Though of the Paisley Codex, it is folly to presume anything. The book is the embodiment of mystery itself. And to that mystery it offers no transparent clues.

In fact, as far as anyone knows, the book does not even have a formal title. Rather, its working moniker is derived from the location of its discovery during the late fifteenth century at Paisley Abbey, Renfrew-shire County, Scotland—a monastery far older than the manuscript that now bears its name. A historical work published in 1668, McDougall's *Chronicles of the Western Scots*, recounts that the Codex was found at the abbey in a place "most obscure an' leery" (that is, *suspicious*) by a friar associated with the entourage of the visiting Earl of Argyll. Thinking the book valuable, the Earl removed it to his library at Castle Campbell. Not long after the Earl's death in 1493, the next Earl (a son to the previous) sold the manuscript to an Irish collector who, it is said, took it to the European continent.

There is no further surviving record of the book's whereabouts un-til the late eighteenth century, when Swiss historian Gottlieb Emanuel von Haller remarked in one of his diaries that "an altogether strange and incomprehensible book found long ago in the renowned Abbey at Paisley," resided at the library in Bern, where "innumerable great and learned men have attempted to solve its riddle." Over two hundred years would then pass before the next extant mention of the Codex, when, some two and a half decades after the fall of the Berlin Wall, it was announced to have resurfaced in the dusty bowels of the Library of the Hungarian Academy of Sciences in Budapest. How and when the Academy acquired the book is not understood, but accompanying the manuscript was a note referencing both its emergence in Scotland and its time in Bern, confirming that it was indeed the same book described by Haller. And since then, medieval bibliophiles, professional cryptanalysts, linguists, and rank amateurs of every variety have made endless attempts at its decipherment. All for nothing.

Now, as I've said, the Paisley Codex is not explicitly written in any-thing like an actual language, but, with inconclusive results, computer analysis has been repeatedly run on the text to determine whether some or all of its letters appear with a frequency that would demonstrate a representation of some real but *hidden* language. A language whose message is perhaps concealed by the use of alphabetic characters that are intended to signify letters other than those they objectively depict. Or, in the alternative, a message written in the very Arabic, Greek, and Latin characters that appear in the book, but with the letters of that message having been in some way transposed to evade comprehension.

And in case you haven't noticed, I'm talking again about something I mentioned earlier. I'm talking about one of my specialties.

I'm talking about a cipher.

Yes, most certainly, the Paisley Codex is written in cipher. One of the most ingenious ciphers, I would say, ever designed. I believe that within every neuron of my brain—although neither I nor anyone else has been able to definitively prove as much. And the fact is, many researchers have stopped looking for such proof and declared the book to be either the nonsensical work of a madman or an equally nonsensical hoax created by some fourteenth century swindler intent on pawning it off as a document of esoteric import. Yet such claims are pure supposition. Theories without a grain of support. For of the Paisley Codex, all that is truly known is that all remains *un*known. The identity of its author, its place of origin, the very reason for its existence: None of these questions has answers.

When I started with the Paisley, I knew nothing of its history, its infinite complexity. Nor did I care. It was merely a puzzle to be solved, and I was content to examine it via computer. Of course, one might think that given my eventual obsession with the book, I would, at some point, have made a request to the Hungarian Academy for an audience with the actual manuscript—which, by virtue of my position with the agency (that is, when I had such a position), undoubtedly would have been granted. But I never took that step.

And so to this day I have never seen the book in the flesh. And I hope to god I never will. Because to find myself in the physical presence of the Paisley Codex would surely be the end of me.

It has that power.

-3-

*F*OR ALL OF MY ANIMOSITY TOWARD HIM, Ed was nevertheless an old acquaintance and the only person I had left to turn to. For the time being, he was letting me stay at his place. And when we left the café, that is where I thought we were heading. But he soon veered off course, picking up his pace as he led me across a street against the light, the both of us dodging traffic.

"Where are we going?" I asked.

"You'll see."

"But Ed . . ."

He was moving so fast, I almost had to jog to keep up. It was that way for three blocks—until we came to a building in which I knew the Judge had a suite of rooms.

"Ed, come on," I said. "What are we doing? The Judge lives here."

"So he does."

Without further discussion, he took the main entrance. Reluctantly, I followed.

Just inside was a small foyer with a security camera, several rows of locked mailboxes, and a door to the building's interior guarded by a ten-digit code pad. Ed hit four numbers and the door relented.

I was amazed. "You know the code?"

"I know a lot of shit," he said, arrogantly happy. "Let's go."

We bypassed the elevator and took the stairs to the second floor, where we found a dark and quiet corridor with three doors both left and right. Ed went to the last door on the left. It bore, in gold, the number *12*.

"This is his." He jiggled the knob.

"Ed, there was a camera where we came in."

"I wouldn't worry about it."

"Ed, let's get out of here."

"Just hold your horses."

"Ed, it's useless. It's locked."

"Oh, really?"

With a smug expression, he produced from his pants pocket a shiny key that, when inserted in the lock and given a turn, tickled all the pins and drivers.

He opened the door and hit the lights, disclosing shiny wood floors, Persian rugs, and walls covered with prints of fine art. Works by Picasso, Rembrandt, Monet. Something too, it appeared, by Pollack—a thing of incomprehensible paint drizzles.

I was so nervous, I thought I would throw up. "Ed, what the hell are we doing here?"

Leaving my question unanswered, he moved ahead. I trailed behind, and within a short time had discerned the whole of the Judge's apartment: a spacious living room, a well-appointed kitchen, a dining area, two bedrooms, a couple of baths, and a large study. In every room, every item was placed with purpose and precision, and every inch of every room lay impeccably clean. The Judge did not permit disorder, least of all in himself.

We came to a halt in the study. A room with shelves from floor to ceiling—books, some new, some ragged, tightly filling every row. Ed looked along each line of volumes with a furious glare, not finding what he wanted.

"Ed," I said desperately, "he's probably on his way. He was done with his coffee when we left. We can't get caught here."

"We won't," he said with his typical load of confidence.

Dismissing the many books within sight, he turned his gaze to a print hanging on the wall near the back of the room—a crude medieval depiction of two knights riding the same horse, both with tunics and shields displaying a red cross on a white background. Symbols I knew to be of the Knights Templar.

The print seemed irrelevant to me. Yet Ed seized upon it.

"Here!" he said, springing toward the picture and pulling it from the wall to reveal a safe with a combination lock. In the next instant, he began working the dial, slowly turning it next to his ear.

"Ed," I whispered, too scared to speak louder, "he's coming."

He remained oblivious to my concern. And seconds later, I heard a *click*; he opened the safe.

He reached in and pulled out a red, cloth-covered clamshell box with a length and width slightly less than a standard sheet of copy paper. A box custom-made to harbor a rare book.

He opened it just enough to look inside.

"Bingo," he said. "Get one of his briefcases."

"Ed, dammit, what are you doing?"

"Get it, butthead."

I looked around. The Judge had cases of all varieties. I chose a nice black attaché.

"Ed, now tell me, what's this about?"

"Do you have some kind of fuckin' brain disease?" he said, ripping the briefcase from my hand. "It's pretty obvious, ain't it?" He held the box aloft, waving it like an evangelist with a Bible. "I'm gonna take this book."

This was what I had feared from the moment we approached this place. And if Ed could not be dissuaded, the Judge could be counted upon to deal with me in a manner most harsh.

"Now, Ed, why would you want to do such a thing?"

"Man, you are as dumb as the ass your head fits in. You just don't get it. I'm gonna sell this thing. People pay good money for shit like this."

"Well," I said, "maybe. But at this point, we don't know what it says. And it may just turn out to be somebody's idea of a joke. Then it would be worthless."

"But it's *not* a joke, right?" He came close to me, his breath in my face. "Because *you're* gonna tell me what it says. And it's gonna say somethin' real good. Got it, bitch?"

God, how I hated him. But right then, and only right then—and despite what I have said before—I so wanted to be him.

Or anyone.

Instead of me.

*E*D HAD GONE OFF TO DO whatever he did when he did those things he wanted to do without me. And like a babysitter, I sat in his rundown flat with his latest plunder: the Judge's book, in its protective box, now in repose on the cracked laminate of the dusty and condiment-stained kitchen table.

I considered opening the clamshell, but didn't. I picked it up and shook it gently, feeling the weight of the object inside. I did not detect the least amount of sliding or other movement. The manuscript was obviously quite snug in its container. And it struck me that if the dimensions of this box—its length, its width, its thickness—were indeed those of the object it held, then the proportions of its contents were extraordinarily similar to those of another book I knew all too well.

The book that had ruined my life.

The Paisley Codex.

But then, of course, there was only one Paisley, and it lay elsewhere, under lock and key. This book, whatever its attributes, was no doubt very different. Perhaps just as maddening as the Paisley, but different.

Knowing the Judge and his conscientious manner, I thought it probable that he planned to arrange (or perhaps had already arranged) for this presumably fragile document to be placed somewhere with temperature and humidity control superior to his wall safe. In any case, however, for the purpose of my efforts, he had never intended to allow me access to the actual book. Rather, he had been going to provide me a copy on a flash drive. But clearly, since I was now an accomplice to the theft of the manuscript itself, it was all but certain that neither the flash drive nor the work (and desperately needed money) it was to represent would be forthcoming.

I had once had a copy of the Paisley on a flash drive. I had lost it, I thought, at the hospital. Or perhaps they had just taken it away. Or someone had, somewhere. But until it went missing, I had kept it for all those nine years. Nine years that had started with a friendly wager, but that were ultimately filled with a suffocating obsession.

I was well into my time at the agency when news of the Paisley began to circulate. Its discovery in Budapest was covered in various academic journals and, in light of what my colleagues and I did for a living, it was only a matter of time until we agreed to commit to a small pot of cash that would go to whomever among us managed to break the supposedly unbreakable Codex.

At first, for me, the challenge was a mere recreation. But in no time, the fire began to burn. The manuscript was available online, and I downloaded it and placed it on that flash drive—which I carried everywhere, plugging it into any computer handy. Perusing. Surmising. Learning the intricacies of the document. A thing—a cipher—of seemingly unique construction.

I would get it, I thought. I would get it and, in doing so, demonstrate my brilliance to the world at large. Interviews, a book deal, and a speaking tour would follow, all of which would generate a large and enviable sum of income.

Yet I could *not* get it. No one could. But that did not matter. I *would* get it. *I*, the very best in my profession. A master linguist and cryptanalyst. A codebreaker. A *cipher* breaker. *I* would get it. And my coworkers agreed: They all said that I would be the one to crack it.

But still, I did not. Days. Weeks. Months. *Years.* They all passed as I discerned nothing from the text—as did no one the world over. Nonetheless, I continued. It is so humiliating to say, but the book came to dominate my entire life. And I do mean my *entire* life—or, that is, what little life I had.

At the agency, I was heaped with accolades, given a corner office, made head of the division. Yet only months into my attempt at the Paisley I was sacked from my job for neglect of duty. And I did not care in the least. I did care (for a time, anyway) when I lost my wife. And I do care now, greatly—now that she is irretrievably gone and I have come to realize that I have, through my fixation with an old and inanimate object, surrendered everything I once valued and acquired nothing in return. But for years I had no such regrets. Only my blind fascination with the Paisley Codex.

As my downfall escalated, and without money, I engaged in a series of shameful hops between the residences of various acquaintances who pitied my circumstances, sleeping on any available couch, chair, or floor space while spending every other moment staring bleary-eyed at my laptop or scribbling possible interpretations of the text on note pads. Inevitably, though, I ran out of such accommodating persons and became homeless in the most extreme sense. I sold my laptop and had only a computer at the public library by which to continue my work. I ate in soup kitchens. I begged on street corners. I slept anywhere I hoped I could lie down without the police hassling me or being beaten or stolen from by hooligans or other vagabonds. This pathetic state of affairs went on and on like some interminable night terror, during which time reality lost all meaning. I shuffled through the city in a daze, insensitive to the world around, seeing before me only the Codex. Its pages eventually imprinting themselves on my mind so deeply that I no longer required any outside access to images of the book; the manuscript had affixed itself to my very psyche. But even then, it would not release its secrets. It would not speak to me.

Although I spoke to it: *Why do you treat me like this? Why do you torment me? Who has revered you more than I? Who has sacrificed more? Do I not deserve some recompense?*

Yet still, from those pages, not a word.

There was, however, laughter. Oh, yes, the book—that cruel, heartless tome—laughed at me. And the more I pled with it, the greater the joy it took in my suffering. Its cackles filled my head. They split my ears. And I screamed and cursed at the abomination—the *monster*—this thing had shown itself to be.

And that is how I was found by the authorities, late one night, under the bridge I had adopted as my temporary habitation. Shouting epithets into space, threatening violence as the Codex stood before me, as always, laughing mercilessly.

I spent many days in hospital, restrained and heavily medicated for the safety of myself and others. And following that came treatment. I am better now. Though I am still a vagrant, awash in filth. But I have ceased attempting to converse with the Paisley. And I have stopped hearing its laughter.

But here, in this clamshell box, was another book, and I could not help but wonder whether it might have the same vile disposition as its predecessor.

Or worse.

Then too, this was a book on which I could actually lay my hands. And if it were at all like the Paisley, might the mere touch of it deliver the death of a lightning strike? Or send me howling back to a mental ward?

There was only one way to know.

Go ahead, scaredy cat.

Ed, right on cue.

I set the box down. Slowly, I put my trembling fingers under the edge of the top lid.

I started to lift it.

That's right. That's it. You can do it.

I raised it further. I could almost see what lay beneath.

Yet the risk was too high.

I pulled my fingers away, letting the lid fall shut.

I could hear Ed berating me. I put my hands to my ears. Do not listen, I told myself. And do not sit before the thing in this box any longer. Do not even *think* of it.

Let the Judge read his own book.

I felt I had to get completely away from it, out of the apartment altogether, and was leaving when I heard a phone ring—Ed's cell, in his bedroom. He had, as he often did, left without it.

I went back to check the display, afraid of whom the caller might be.

And I was right.

It was the Judge.

-5-

I DID NOT ANSWER THAT CALL. Eventually Ed and I would have to talk to him. There was no way around it. (That damn security camera!) But for the time being, I did not feel the need to subject myself to the predictable barrage of accusation and derision. To avoid even the smallest suggestion of it, I had run from the phone—and the apartment—before a message could so much as *ping* its arrival.

The day remained overcast, but the temperature had dropped. A chilling wind filled the narrow streets, and my shabby jacket was insufficient to ward off the cold. I thought of returning to Ed's. However, it was late afternoon and I had yet to eat anything. I was famished. And whatever food Ed had was strictly off limits to me—as were most of his things.

I passed several restaurants, but they were all somewhat upscale. Their prices, I knew, would not be to my liking, and my appearance and odor would not be to theirs. I finally came, though, to a place that, to say the least, looked a bit less chic. It was small and weakly lit, with about a dozen tables scattered around a concrete floor, none of which were occupied. To one side was a bar, where three men sat drinking in silence. In the back, two others were playing pool.

I seated myself at a table, and from behind the bar (I had not seen her until then) came a woman carrying a paper menu. She was young and slightly built, wearing her thick, dark hair in a chin-length bob that hung straight down past her angular cheeks and, on both sides of her face, curved in precise symmetry under her jawline. In the dim light, much else was left to the imagination, but there was no question that she was very pretty.

"Hello, I am Nina," she said, placing the menu on the table. "Would you like something to drink?"

She was obviously in the habit of using English with customers. There was a noticeable accent, and as with many non-native speakers, she was contraction-challenged. But her diction was otherwise very good.

I kept my head down. "Just water, thanks."

"I am sorry?"

Her slender body in its tight sweater came closer to me, and with it, a scent like something from a garden of flowers.

Clearly, we did not belong in the same room.

"Just water," I said a bit louder.

"And something to eat?"

"Perhaps something small." I glanced nervously at the menu, but in the shadows couldn't see much. It didn't matter. Even here, I knew there was little I could afford.

"Our special today is goulash. It is not bad."

"Really?" I almost looked up.

"I think so," she said. "I had some for lunch and I am still alive."

I went on staring at the menu as she stood above me, waiting—and no doubt wishing to be anywhere other than next to the garbage dump that I personified.

"You know, I wonder . . ." I hesitated, wanting to sink below the table. "Do you have anything lighter? A bowl of broth, maybe?"

"Broth?" Her voice carried a hint of incredulity. But most certainly, she understood. "Yes, I think we have some chicken broth. Are you sure that is all you want?"

"Yes," I said. "That will do."

She walked off.

What a bitch, I thought. She knew damn well I could not afford her goulash. And deriding me about the broth? How typical of such a woman. A woman who looked so perfect. Smelled so perfect. Wore her sweater so perfect. She could go to hell.

She came back with my water. I stared at the wall as she set down the glass, but as she left, could not resist a look at her slender hips, wrapped in form-fitting pants and moving into the darkness with a dancer's grace. So much like the kind of woman I would have once thought obtainable, and who, in my days of hubris, I might have engaged in a discussion meant to lead to something more. But I was no longer that man. I could scarcely remember him.

Soon, she returned again, bringing a steaming bowl, a paper napkin, and a soup ladle.

"Here you go," she said, leaving quickly.

Even in the faint light, I could see that this was not broth. She had brought me the goulash, heavy with meat and vegetables and the smell of paprika.

I knew, of course, that the right and gallant thing was to correct this error. I looked over and saw her standing on the other side of the bar, talking to someone in the kitchen. But then her head turned slightly my way, as if she was furtively tracking me from the periphery of her black bob. And I began to think that this was no mistake.

And I was so hungry.

I delved into the bowl, and by its end was nearly breathless.

A moment later, I smelled again the scent of flowers.

"You did all right with that," I heard, her soft voice beside me.

I sat back, embarrassed and still looking away. "I don't know what to say."

"Say nothing." She took the empty bowl and put another full one in front of me. "Just eat."

Overwhelmed by her generosity, I was about to do as told. But then, unable to deny myself any longer, I glanced up at her, meeting dark eyes and brows, and warm, glossy, smiling lips. On the whole, a quite beautiful face. But even more so, a friendly one.

She left me again and I finished the second bowl. I sat then for some time, waiting for her to return. But she stood forever at the bar, pouring shots for the three men. Checking the cash register. Looking everywhere but my way. She was done with me, I thought. Her act of goodwill was, to her, of no real import. A trivial gift to a charity case.

I got up and walked out, full in the belly but hating the rest of me. Outside, I lingered, facing the street but feeling vaguely unready to move on. In my dawdling, I spun back around and, quite by accident, saw my reflection, repulsive as it was, in the front window of the place where I had just eaten for free.

I nearly recoiled at my appearance. But looking through my image, I could see inside. And there I saw Nina, still at the bar. Watching me and waving kindly.

-6-

I WENT BACK TO ED'S FLAT. He wasn't there, and his phone showed three more unanswered calls from the Judge.

I did not want this situation to become worse than it already was. With no phone of my own, I tried the Judge on Ed's. He answered on the first ring.

"Just what do you think you're doing?" he thundered.

"Returning your calls."

"Stavros?" Expecting Ed's voice, he was understandably confused (although at times Ed and I nevertheless sounded very much alike).

"Yes, sir. I see you've been trying to reach us."

"I most certainly have! You have stolen my manuscript!"

"No, sir, I have not."

"But you are doubtless an accessory. A stooge in the service of that mercurial miscreant. A Renfield to his Dracula." The Judge took a long, fuming breath. "So where is he? And what has he done with my property?"

"I don't know where he is. He's not here. But the manuscript is. It's safe."

"It is *not* safe," he said. "So long as he has any access to it, it is anything *but* safe." Another fuming pause. "Now, you listen to me. You will bring the manuscript to me forthwith or I will have you both jailed for felony theft. Is that quite clear?"

"Yes, sir. I'm on my way."

"You have one hour. No more."

I could not get my mind off of her. And a fool could see it was pointless. Like a fascination with a statue or a picture in a magazine. One cannot effectively love (or be loved by) such things. Nonetheless, the way she had looked at me, waving, giving me her full attention as I stood on the street. And that smile at the table when she had brought me that second bowl. A part of me had started to think that, in some way, she had felt something.

The Judge would not allow it.

You are delusional, Stavros. She was merely being nice—very nice—to a poor, miserable wretch far below her station. You must forget her. As she has, no doubt, already forgotten you.

And if so, who could blame her? Who would want to remember such a dreg of humanity? It must have been all she could do not to run from the sight of me.

I went into Ed's bathroom and looked at myself in the mirror above the sink, meeting the same reflection that had greeted me from that window outside the bar. The very image—the disgusting image—*she* had seen. A figure suggesting an animal as much as it did a man. A creature absent even the smallest vestige of self-respect. How had I allowed myself to become like this? And to stay like this, for so long?

I detested, as I had for days untold, the person I saw. But my animus for myself was worse now than ever. I had become a thing apart from humanity. Apart from anything that could be loved or even tolerated by anyone.

And in my loathing of myself, I assumed an entirely new breed of madness: I rushed to the kitchen, snatched a pair of rusty scissors, and, returning to the bath, began wildly, *vindictively*, cutting my hair and beard. Cutting without a plan. Without a care for the end result. Attacking myself like a lunatic who had discovered misspellings in a book, indifferent to ripping out every page in order to expunge the offending words.

I hacked and chopped and the sink grew high with the strands and clumps of a growth that had spread unchecked through all the years of my obsession and torment. It seemed I could not get enough of it. Of the release that came with watching each disgusting lock fall away.

At last, though, I stepped back, dropping the shears—and looked in the mirror at someone I had seen long ago, but in the time since, all but lost.

I felt my eyes tearing, just as they had that morning in front of the Judge. But these were not, as then, tears of shame and regret. No, I felt something else.

Elation. Ecstasy.

Rebirth.

Hurriedly, I found a can of shaving cream and one of Ed's razors—which he would never have permitted me to use—and finished off my face, clean-shaven. Then, retaking the scissors, I resumed work on my hair, carving out a rough-done look that I thought (though definitely not traditional) could at least pass for fashion in the avant-garde.

And then I went even further: I took off my rags, turned on Ed's shower, and jumped in with a bar of soap. (With Ed, a *real* taboo.) I lathered up from head to toe, rinsed, and lathered again. And again. I scoured myself more times than I bothered to count. But there finally came a point where I felt myself clean. Thoroughly and utterly clean.

I stepped from the shower and gave myself a double scrubbing with Ed's toothbrush. (He would have gone berserk if he'd seen that.) I took a shot of mouthwash too, then gave my fingers and toes a good going-over with his nail clippers.

I dried myself with one of Ed's towels, used one of his combs on my hair, used his deodorant under my arms, and gathered up my old clothes. Putting those clothes back on, however, seemed totally incongruous.

I dropped the rags and, standing naked, considered what to do.

Something occurred to me.

I went to Ed's bedroom and, once there, to his wardrobe, opening the cabinet doors, then the drawers within. Pants, shirts, jackets, coats, socks, belts, shoes, and underwear (boxers *and* briefs) all presented themselves. And all were of a style that I myself would have chosen. These, I thought, could just as easily be *my* clothes.

And surprisingly—unbelievably—they fit. Fit me as if they *were* mine. Ed's physique was so well formed. So full and healthy. Yet here I was, looking virtually the same. A transformation that completely shocked me.

But at once, another shocking thought: the Judge.

I glanced at the digital clock beside Ed's bed. There was still time.

I grabbed the manuscript in its box from the kitchen table and tossed it in the Judge's briefcase, pausing only long enough to slide myself into one of Ed's nicer coats before charging out the door.

-7-

NOW WAIT, I THOUGHT. The Judge was not a forgiving man.
Would he so easily pardon a theft? To his own premises? And by
the same logic, what reason did I have to believe that when I arrived with
the manuscript I would not be met by the police?

Yet on further reflection, I knew there *was* a reason: The Judge was
not lenient, but he was a man of his word. Unambiguously so. And he
had said that legal action would ensue only if the manuscript was not
returned within the hour. So an hour it would be.

Though as he had also made clear, not a moment longer.

Night was falling, the city darkening. For a while, I walked very fast,
then switched to a jog, my feet, in Ed's well-fitting dress shoes, moving
nimbly over the streets and cobbled sidewalks. I passed shops closing
their doors for the day. Restaurants welcoming the dinner crowd. Col-
lections of persons blocking my way here and there. And then . . .

I came to a hard stop at a doorway open to a dark interior. From within
came the smell of beef, vegetables, and paprika.

I could sense the clock ticking.

I went in.

Far different than before, the place was bustling, the tables nearly
filled. I looked about for her—even as it occurred to me that in the
rashness of this detour, I had failed to take something very important
into account: If I were to speak with her, what would I say? That I was
the beggar she had fed less than two hours ago? No, certainly not. I would
need another story. But what? I would have to concoct something.

I hailed a waiter carrying a tray of beers. He ignored me and I lightly touched his arm.

"Is Nina here?"

He acted put out. "No."

"When did she leave?"

"What's it to you?"

I went back outside and paused near the entrance, realizing I had lost valuable time. But just then, down the block, I saw a woman moving away in the direction from which I had come. The same hair. The same hips. In an overcoat with a purse over her shoulder. I nearly called her name, but could not think of a pretext for doing so. And what good would it do anyway, I thought, to approach her on some false excuse? To appear as a total stranger imposing himself on her amid the shadows of a city street? What decent woman would take to that?

And in any event, I had somewhere else to be.

I took several steps in the direction of the Judge's flat, then wheeled about and took a step back toward her. She was walking fast, probably needing to get somewhere, or wanting to get out of the cold. Or perhaps she just did not like walking alone this time of day.

Her form grew smaller and smaller as she increased the distance between us. I stood locked upon it, remembering the smile of her glossy lips, her hair so thick and neatly done. What would it be like, I wondered, to put a hand on her slender arm, and then to her shoulder, and then to the back of her head? To reach into that luxuriant hair and pull her toward me? To meet her body with mine?

To smell again her flowers.

To put my lips to hers.

But in this daydream I had wasted even more time; I had reached, I feared, the juncture where mere seconds had become critical.

I ran down the street in her direction, just enough to see, between buildings, the clock on the church tower in the next block. If it was accurate, I had only two minutes to get to the Judge.

It wasn't possible, I told myself.

But that is what I wanted to believe. Because I knew, in fact, it was *quite* possible. From here, it was a block and a half. In two minutes, I could be there, in the entranceway, buzzing the Judge to let me in.

And yet I found myself rehashing my previous concern: Could there be a chance, no matter how slight, that the Judge was not the scrupulous man I believed him to be? And that even now, the police were at his flat, waiting for me? A trap laid for a trusting fool.

I stood wavering, watching her disappear into the night until the large hand on the tower clock at last moved to the point where my decision was made for me.

I ran for a full block without sight of her, thinking I had lost her. But coming to an intersection and looking frantically in all directions, I saw her, for an instant, across the street as she veered into an alley. I hurried to the alleyway and, watching from the sidewalk, saw her again, a mere silhouette moving down the dark, narrow lane. Moving, it seemed, without the least fear of what might lie there undetected. She then emerged along a busy street, where she turned behind a row of buildings, once more out of view.

Not wanting my footsteps heard, I let a moment pass before I entered the alley and ran its length. As I came to its end, I spotted her waiting at the next corner for a crossing signal. I hung back as she traversed the street to a well-lit park and, keeping her in sight, stood on the corner until the signal had cycled through, allowing a less than suspicious amount of space to develop between us.

There were few others on the green. A couple hand-in-hand. A small group of teens. Two or three loners. All marked by the fog of breath on this cold night. It was a large park with intersecting walkways and a myriad of monuments to forgotten war heroes. Near a metallic horse and rider, the walk angled to her left, and staying on that course through the remainder of the park, she moved into the next city block.

I continued in pursuit—though even as I did, I began to ask myself why I was following this woman. What did I intend to gain? She was beautiful; I was nothing. What worthwhile thing could conceivably come of this?

I could hear the Judge in my head, ordering me to abandon this folly.

But I trailed on. It made no sense. I had seen other striking women. Desired them from afar. And forgotten them. Yet there was something about *this* woman. Something that obsessed me. Obsessed me like alphabetic letters jumbled together on pages of aged vellum, presenting by their appearance no hope of comprehension, but nevertheless holding the promise of a special message.

She (and I) went for another two blocks, where we entered a section of the city that, while well known to me, was, to say the least, not altogether charming. This was my neighborhood, and it was a place no one went without good reason—and certainly, if it could be avoided, not after dark. The great buildings of stone, the stylish and imposing Romanesque and Renaissance structures so popular with the tourists, were not found here. In this place, the buildings were of more recent and functional construction, and far less maintained. Drab and dilapidating shops and tenements for the lesser class. Street-level doors and windows covered in iron bars. Or boarded up.

There was so very little light on the street that, from a half block away, I could scarcely see her. Just enough to tell that she was about to pass Ed's building—or rather, the building that held his flat: a seedy three-story affair with an unlit, recessed entrance set above a rise of three concrete steps. Her route ahead appeared deserted. To the end of the block, there was no one in sight. She walked with her head down against the breeze, her hands deep in the pockets of her overcoat.

Presently, though, a figure—that of a man—emerged from the building's shadowed entrance and moved in front of her, blocking her way. I stopped and watched. A conversation ensued. I could hear voices, but not actual words. She said something loudly, forcefully, and his voice, disarming yet deceitful, came in reply. She took a step to his left, trying to go around him.

At once, with both hands, he took her by the arms, then the shoulders, then, with one hand to the back of her head and into her hair, pulled her toward him. Thrusting himself onto her. I could see her fighting, but not overcoming him as he hauled her up the steps and into the darkness of the portico.

A muffled scream echoed down the block as, already, I was at a full sprint, lugging the Judge's briefcase, its contents seeming to drag on me in an unnatural way, as if the book itself meant to slow me down. But I kept up speed, right to the scene.

And upon arriving, and with no thought for strategy, I took the stairs and brought a shoulder into the attacker. He fell back, separating from Nina. And as she too began to fall, I captured her about the waist and helped her to simply but rather ungracefully sit down, without harm, on the top step of the rise.

The man had been floored, but, undeterred, rose and came at me. As he charged, I hoisted the Judge's briefcase and, my momentum aided by the shifting weight of the object inside, launched one edge of the case directly into his face, hammering his nose, lips, and teeth. His head snapped back and, his body slackening, he promptly collapsed and rolled down the steps, apparently unconscious.

Nina remained sitting on the step. I touched her on the arm of her coat, wanting to (but careful not to) let my hand wander further.

"Are you all right?" I said—knowing her native tongue but, in my excitement, defaulting to English.

She held her face in her hands, trembling and struggling to catch her breath. "I think so." She looked up, her eyes, in the dark, glistening with tears. "You saved my life."

I was about to respond when the man at the foot of the steps struggled, painfully, to his feet. I moved in front of Nina, holding the briefcase at the ready.

In the wake of the blow he had taken—blood running from his nose and mouth and down his chin, neck, and clothes—the person before me was almost unrecognizable.

But recognizable, just the same.

He pointed a finger at me. "You are not in control!" he raged, red spittle flying from his lips. "And the next time I see you, I will kill you!"

Then he ran off, into the night.

Of course, it was Ed.

-8-

*F*LUSHED FROM MY HEROICS, I took her by the arms and gently helped her up.

"Do you think we should call the police?" she asked.

As much as I would have loved to see Ed behind bars, I knew that should I assist in putting him there, he would undoubtedly return the favor by implicating me in the theft of the Judge's manuscript. And in the process, I would be labeled not only as his accomplice, but also, to Nina, exposed as his acquaintance. How bad would *that* be?

"The cops don't usually do much in a case like this," I said to discourage her, "if they bother at all. Look, wherever you're going, I'll walk you."

"You have done so much already. Really, it is not necessary."

"Well, it may be. He's still out there."

As true as that was, I was all too willing to allow the continuing threat to play to my benefit.

She nodded readily. "Stupid of me. You are right. If you do not mind."

"Not at all."

"Nina Benešová," she said, extending a petite hand bound in a leather glove.

"Leonard Stavros."

She told me she lived in the next block over, on the river. We started off, me setting the pace, but walking slowly—protracting our time—as, anxiously, she glanced around the dusky gloom for signs of Ed.

"I wonder if he lives in that building," she said.

"I'm sure he doesn't. He wouldn't be so dumb to attack someone right outside his own front door."

I almost laughed.

"What do you think he meant when he said you were not in control?" she asked.

"Who knows? The guy's obviously a sociopath."

"It scares me to think that animals like that are out running around."

We went awhile without speaking. A man came toward us, approaching on Nina's side. She moved closer to me as he passed, taking my arm. It had been so long since I'd had a pretty girl beside me, holding onto me, depending on me. I found myself walking taller—and even more slowly.

And strangely, with every step, I heard her saying something under her breath, her whispers too faint to be understood. I dismissed this, however, as nothing more than a frightened woman talking to herself, saying a few Hail Marys or some other such incantation.

As we neared her building, the traffic on the sidewalk increased. The lighting did as well. I thought it quite extraordinary how, such a short distance from Ed's, the world could be so different.

"So, Mr. Stavros," she said, "what do you do when you are not saving damsels in distress?"

I was feeling witty. More like my old self.

And wanted also to evade her question.

"*Are* you a damsel?" I asked.

"I think so. Am I not?"

"Well, you're a young woman," I said. "That's one requirement. But are you also unmarried?"

"Is that required too?"

"By definition, to be a damsel, it is."

"Then I am a damsel." She looked over at me. "You know, maybe it is the sound of your voice, but there is something about you that seems very familiar. Have we met before?"

We went another several steps before I answered. "I don't think so."

"I am a waitress. Maybe you have been a customer." She quickly reconsidered. "No, probably not. You do not look like the sort who would go to that place. It is not very nice." She gestured to the apartment building ahead. "This is it."

It was an old stand-alone, three-story structure with a modest but elegant stone exterior. A well-kept remnant of the late 1800s. Its perimeter, like the entire street, was brightly lit.

We stopped and met face-to-face, and it was then, for the first time, that I saw her with genuine clarity. She had, even that afternoon, seemed noticeably younger than me. But it was evident now that she was, at best, little more than half of my forty-two years. Her skin so very smooth and unblemished. As pale as alabaster. A full-on contrast to her dark eyes and brunette hair—that tremendous bob wrapped about her high, dimpled cheeks.

And those thick glossy lips. And her smell. Oh, those flowers!

I thought, as I had earlier, of how I (and just as Ed had done, but so much more tenderly) might move a hand to her arm, to her shoulder, to the back of her head and into her hair. Pulling us together.

Losing myself within her.

She said something that, in my reverie, I failed to process.

"I'm sorry?"

"Thank you so much for helping me," she repeated. "You are very brave."

"And you're very welcome."

"And thank you for walking me home."

"Of course."

There was, then, an awkward silence, me trying to think of something to say that might further prolong things.

Yet here she was, so much younger, and, I thought, probably just wanting to end this.

"I am sorry, but I must go," she said, again extending her gloved hand—which I was afraid I held, between my hands, too long.

"Goodbye, then."

"Goodbye." She turned away.

"Oh, Ms. Benešová?"

"Yes?"

"Where is it that you work?"

I knew that might come off as creepy, but I had to ask. I mean, I couldn't just show up there claiming it was some sort of coincidence. She would have thought me a stalker. And neither would it have been wise to come knocking uninvited at the door of her flat. That might have presented the same impression.

But she had given me the correct name and location of her workplace. She had trusted me enough for that. And trying not to sound too eager, I had told her that I might drop in some time.

I went off into the night, thinking of her, and only her, all the way to the river, to the promenade, and to a bench that held me as the black water went by. This day was over. But I might see her tomorrow. And in time, I told myself (told myself like a man who could promise himself anything), I might even touch her. *Actually* touch her. Not merely her covering—her coat, her gloves. But skin to skin. Her very smooth and pallid skin, from top to bottom.

I was rather astonished that she had in any way recognized me, there being literally nothing about my present appearance that might have tipped her off. I could only assume that, as she had speculated, she had recalled the sound of my voice.

But oddly, the more I thought of it, there were things about *her* that seemed familiar to *me*: The sound of *her* voice. The way she looked. The way she moved. It was, I began to realize, all so very much as I, for want of a better word, *expected*. Almost as if I had met her—fashioned her, some-how—in something like a dream. A dream (if that was indeed what it was) not overtly remembered, but embedded firmly in the subterranean mind, offering an unconscious vision—a feminine ideal—that had now been matched in the flesh.

In a short while, though, as I continued to sit and watch the dark river, my thoughts gave way to matters grounded not in fantasy, but harsh reality: the sting of the hard cold, and the sad appreciation of the fact that the night would be very long and I had nowhere to go. But I had been through many such nights.

If I just had some money, I thought. Something more than the meaningless amount of pocket change with which I had awakened that morning. Ed's claim that I had bankrupted myself on alcohol remained dubious. I still didn't remember that, and it was unlike me to do such a thing. Certainly, in the past, I had far more than once suffered intoxication at Ed's prodding. But never had I spent so much as to leave myself destitute. And now I was not only homeless, but my hunger of the afternoon had returned, and there was little chance on this bitter night that another kind-hearted damsel would come my way.

There were a number of others like me, loiterers, milling about the promenade. One of them, an older man carrying a large plastic trash bag that appeared to contain his worldly effects, sat down beside me on the bench, falling back to rest himself with a mournful sigh.

He looked my way.

"Excuse me, sir," he said, mistaking me for someone of a higher station, "but could you spare a few coins?"

The irony was palpable: This beggar was probably doing better than I was.

"I'm sorry," I said. "I don't have any money."

"No bother," he cracked. "I'll take a credit card."

I was starting to lose the feeling in my toes. I rose and walked down the promenade, thinking that I, too, would have to do some begging. Just as I had during my long illness, my mind infected, as it had been, with the Paisley. I would have no alternative.

Yet after a time it occurred to me that I was not seeing my situation for what it really was. I pictured myself as impoverished and without prospects, but that wasn't necessarily the case. Because in fact I had something of potentially great value.

I had the Judge's manuscript.

Which he was exceedingly impatient to regain.

And that in itself suggested a course of action: I could simply demand payment for the book's return. But such an approach would be both crass and criminal and, I thought, should be avoided if at all possible. It was the sort of thing Ed would do. I was better than that.

Or at least I wanted to be.

No, in the event I could somehow shed the psycho-traumatic hangover of the last nine years and bring myself to face the mind-wrenching challenge of another book, then, without question, the best strategy would be to use that book to make amends with the Judge. I would tell him that I still wanted to work on the manuscript and, at the same time, would return it and extend my heartfelt *mea culpas* for my failure to meet his deadline. Surely, in my great contrition, he would forgive me. He was a man of reason. And after all, he had initially asked for my assistance. All I would ask is that I be allowed to provide it, and for the same fee as before—though a small advance would be nice. (I needed money *now*.) And why wouldn't he agree to that? To something meager up front? Did he want to see his faithful servant freeze or starve to death before the job he had commissioned was finished? (Or even begun?)

Well, yes, I thought, he might. Worse, he might refuse to grant me any pardon at all. However, if he went to that extreme, I would have no choice but to hold the book hostage for payment—or perhaps, as Ed had planned, sell it to an unscrupulous bidder. I knew, of course, that either way, things might backfire horribly. And even if they did not, I would be left with that voice—the voice of the Judge—ringing in my head, chastising me for my moral shortcomings. But desperation is the mother of indiscretion. And as I shivered in the cold of night on the promenade, ethics and illegalities seemed far less important than mere survival.

Still, though, I thought that almost certainly the Judge would show a degree of mercy. If I returned the book tonight, he would stand deprived of his property for no more than a few hours. And its condition had not been altered in the slightest. What was the old adage? *No harm, no foul?* Of all people, a jurist such as he had to understand that.

But if he did not, then he would learn that I was prepared to play by rules even more severe than his own. And those would be the rules to a game in which I was holding all of the proverbial cards.

Yet just as I thought that—and perhaps because of it—I had a sinking feeling. The Judge's briefcase? I did not sense its weight in either hand.

I looked down, left and right. And indeed, I was holding nothing.

I rushed back to the bench where I had been sitting. The case was not there. And the man who had been there was nowhere in sight. But had he taken the attaché? Engulfed in panic, I thought back: When had I last had it? When had I last been conscious of its drag on my arm and hand? On my way here, from Nina's? Or before that, walking her home? I could not recall.

I had obviously had it at the scene of her attack; I had used it to rearrange Ed's face. But after that, there was a blank. I had been so focused elsewhere. So foolishly wrapped up in thoughts of a woman I could never have that I had lost the most valuable item I would ever possess.

In a wild dash, I ran far down the promenade, then back the other way, looking in vain for the bum I had met on the bench. I ran on to Nina's building. There was a directory just inside the entrance listing *Benesova* in *No. 21*.

I did not want to do this, but if she could remember anything, I had to know.

I went to the second floor, to her door, and knocked softly. Then louder. Then with a pounding frenzy. Calling her name. Shouting.

She did not answer.

Which came as no surprise; there was a madman on the prowl.

From behind the door across the hall, a woman said something about calling the police.

I left.

I sped on to Ed's place, convinced more and more that somewhere in the midst of my exhilaration after felling him—within the emotional whirlwind of helping Nina up, clasping her hand, and basking in the glow of my valorous act—I had put the case down and, in oblivion, just walked away. The chances of it still being there, I thought, were slim. Most probably, by now, Ed himself had reclaimed it, and his plan to fence the book was once again in full swing.

However, as I turned the corner down Ed's street, I was met with an alarming scene, the components of which, I quickly gathered, were not at all to Ed's advantage: Two police vehicles, their light bars flashing red and blue, were parked in front of Ed's building. An officer waited on the adjacent sidewalk while three others—two on either side and one behind—escorted a man bound in handcuffs down the front steps. And there was no mistaking who that man was.

I stayed near the end of the block, out of sight, as the police loaded Ed into one of the vehicles and drove away.

-9-

BETWEEN HIS FREQUENT DRUNKENNESS and perpetual neglect-fulness, Ed was forever losing his latchkey and had thus stopped carrying one. He kept the only copy he had left on the frame above his door in the outside hallway. An imprudent practice, to be sure. But that was Ed for you: never a thought for the morrow.

I used the key and entered the apartment, bolting the door behind me. The police had done a number on the place. The contents of every drawer and cabinet had been rummaged through and, for the most part, spilled on the floor. The mattress on Ed's bed had been pulled off and thrown against the wall. The cushions of the couch where I normally bedded myself were likewise strewn about, the couch tipped over. Clearly, law enforcement had been looking for something, and I knew exactly what.

Nonetheless, for a time, at least, my most immediate problem was solved. I doubted Ed would be granted bail, but even if he were, that would not happen soon. So for tonight—and perhaps several nights—I had a home.

I began to think it unlikely that Ed had retaken the briefcase. It was definitely not in the flat, and when the police had brought Ed out, none of them had been carrying anything. Of course, they might have discovered it in the apartment and brought it down before I had come along, but that was the only possibility. Yet if they had found it in the apartment with Ed, why had they not brought both the case and Ed down at the same time?

I had been so incredibly careless, losing it. Consumed, as I had been, so impulsively—*lustfully*—with Nina. Scarcely better than Ed. Choosing mindless passion at the expense of all else.

The voice of the Judge roared in my head:

You are irresponsible beyond words! You were given the opportunity of a lifetime, a chance to start again. And what did you do? You squandered it! And for what?

The Judge, always so superior, forever berating. Never satisfied. He was probably going to throw the proverbial book at Ed. Or would encourage someone to. And if he could find me, I would get the same treatment—unless, perhaps, I could first recover and produce the manuscript. I continued to think that returning it might be good for some measure of amnesty.

But hell. Who was I kidding? We were talking about the Judge here. There would be no exoneration. It was an utter fantasy to think he might grant even the smallest shred of leniency.

I went to the kitchen and made myself a ham sandwich. The ham was greasy and the bread stale; I was too hungry to care. I was thirsty, too, and threw down a couple of glasses of water. I followed that with another sandwich. Ed would not like it, but it was time, I thought, that he entertain his guest—just as he, if in my position, with his infantile sense of entitlement, would have insisted upon.

Suddenly, I was deathly tired. It was the fatigue of a man without an anchor, adrift day long, on edge every passing minute. Never knowing where the tide might take him. Laden with the continual strain of living life beyond his control, at the whim of the world at large.

I was about to turn in for the night when I remembered the key above the door. When I had come in, I had replaced it. Just as Ed would have. Giving anyone with sufficient investigative instincts access to the apartment.

I went out to the hall and retrieved the key, putting it safely in my pocket and rebolting the door.

I was not Ed, I told myself. And soon, under a blanket on his displaced mattress, I fell into a deep sleep.

———◆———

Again, I saw the light. The blinding light of a searing fire. And as always, I could not shut my eyes to it. The flames etching themselves so deeply into my retinae that it seemed I would be left forever with the image of a glaring inferno.

A wave of incendiary heat came like a flood, washing over me, burning my every inch. And in reflex, I started to shrink from the source of the pain—but quickly stopped, holding fast.

Wait for him, I told myself. Listen.

And this time, remember.

But nothing came. I heard only the crackling of the blaze.

I called into the fire: "Talk to me!"

It was useless. I had been given my chance. My one chance—if in fact I had been told the truth. But either way, there was nothing left for me in this place but suffering. Or so I thought.

"Leonard?" A woman's voice.

"Nina?"

"Yes."

"Where are you?"

"Not far away. And yet, I am afraid, very far. What are you doing here?"

"I don't know."

"Well, you must have some reason for coming here. You must want something."

"You," I said. "Always you."

"That is not altogether true. You know that."

"It should be."

"And yet it is not. Even now, you are thinking of the book."

"Yes, but a while ago a man told me he was going to give me the key. The key! But whatever he said, I forgot it. And now I think he may have lied to me."

"Why do you think that?"

"Because, for one thing, he told me that I didn't want to wake up from this dream—or whatever it is. And that I might never *wake up. What sense does that make? It's absurd. The man can't be trusted."*

"Hmmm," I heard. "I wonder."

"And second, he could not have possibly told me the key to the Paisley because I could not have possibly forgotten *something so important."*

"Perhaps, for some reason, you did," she said. "Anyway, why do you not just ask the man to tell you again?"

"He won't. He said he would only tell me once."

"Well, in that case, you will have to get the answer for yourself. But that should not be too hard—if you know where to look."

"But I don't."

"Yes, you do."

"Where?"

She told me. And this time, I did not forget.

-10-

I N THE MORNING, after cooking and eating Ed's remaining four eggs and half pound of bacon, I showered, put on fresh clothes (Ed's, of course) and left the flat. Physically, I had not felt so well in years. But nothing else had changed: The manuscript was likely gone for good.

I wandered the streets for a while, but within an hour found the nerve to return to the same table in the same dark establishment I had visited the day before. Save three men drinking silently at the bar—the same three, I thought, that had been there yesterday—the place was empty. After a time, a man came out of the kitchen to serve the trio another round and noticed me.

"Can I help you?" he said from behind the bar.

"Is Nina here?"

"No."

"Will she be in today?"

"I'm sure she will."

"When?"

He looked at the digital clock above the bar. It was 10:10.

"In eleven minutes," he said.

Smart ass, I thought. "I'll wait."

Minutes later I saw her through the front window, out on the sidewalk, milling around. Off and on she checked something on her phone, but as the clock above the bar hit 10:21, put the phone in her purse and came in. Looking neither left nor right, she went straight to the kitchen—I presumed to clock in and put away her purse and coat. When she came back, she took a spot behind the bar and, almost immediately, saw me. She waved and came over.

"Hello, Leonard." Last night I had been Mr. Stavros. "I thought I might be seeing you today."

I rose from my chair, reddened with embarrassment. "I want to apologize."

"For what?"

"For going to your apartment the way I did last night. I'm sure you thought I was nuts or something, but . . ."

"Leonard, I was not there."

"Oh." That was good news. "Well, anyway, I was outside your apartment knocking on your door and yelling for you, and when you didn't answer I thought you were scared of me. But the thing is, I lost something very valuable, and I just wanted to know if you might have any idea . . ."

"I do," she said with a wry smile.

"You mean . . ."

"Your briefcase. I have it."

The shock of joy that went through me, I cannot describe. I found myself panting, unable to speak.

She laughed at me. "The look on your face!"

"But you don't know how important this is to me." And I wasn't about to tell her. "I thought it was gone. That someone had taken it."

"You should sit down. I will get you something. Coffee?"

I gave her a nod. However, in my muddled state, she was on her way back before I realized I could barely afford what she had offered and would then have too little left for a meal later. And that was a definite concern because there was next to nothing left to eat at Ed's.

Quickly, though, my problem was solved.

"On the house," she said, sliding a mug in front of me. "Do you take it black?"

"I do." I thanked her.

"None of that," she said, sitting beside me with a cup of her own. "And you know why."

I smelled, again, that scent of flowers. And being so close to her. This, I thought, is how it would be if we were a couple.

I found myself pretending that we were.

Do not be naïve, said the Judge.

I ignored him.

"Thank goodness you knew where to find me," she said, "because I knew of no way to reach you." She explained that after we had said our goodbyes outside her building, she had gone in for a short time, then back out. (She was vague as to why she had done so, which made me wonder if she'd had a date.) On leaving her building, she had seen the briefcase standing on the sidewalk, where I had evidently placed it before our farewell handshake. "I knew right away it was yours. Stupid of me to let you walk off without it."

"Even more stupid of me to leave it there," I said, trying my coffee.

"I will not argue with *that*." Her tone, though sarcastic, was attended by a friendly laugh. "Anyway, I was really worried, because I thought there might be something you needed in there. You know, something very important."

A frightening thought crossed my mind: The case had sat unattended for some time.

"Nina, did you look in the briefcase?"

"What do you mean?"

"Did you open it?"

Her eyes evaded mine. "I am afraid I did."

"That's okay."

"But honestly, I was just trying to find out if there was a phone number or an address or something."

"No, no, it's all right," I said. "Just tell me, in the briefcase, was there a box?"

"Yes."

"And inside the box?"

"A book." On her face, a look of wholesale regret. "Oh, Leonard, I opened the box too. I am so sorry."

"Don't be." My fears allayed, I took a deep breath. "I'm just glad to know it's safe. The book, I mean."

I basked in quiet relief as she wrapped both hands tightly around her coffee cup, still nervous that she had committed some great transgression.

"So is this book valuable?" she asked.

"It could be."

"And if it is, will you sell it and make a lot of money?"

Now more than ever, that remained an option. But I could hardly tell her of my scheme vis-a-vis the Judge.

"The book isn't mine. It belongs to, let's say, a client."

"A client? Are you a lawyer?"

I shook my head. "No, I'm a linguist—among other things."

To my surprise, she, a mere bartendress, understood. "You study languages."

"Yes, and I speak many of them." And suddenly—instantly—desperate to impress her, I assumed the braggadocio to which I had been inclined so long ago. "In fact, I speak more languages than you have fingers on your hands and toes on your feet."

"Wow!" She was as awestruck as I had hoped. "How many?"

"Maybe fifty. Maybe more. But twenty-one with absolute fluency."

She appeared, at once, strangely preoccupied, causing me to wonder if she had already grown tired of my boasting. But then, much as she had done as we walked together the night before, her lips moved for a time as she recited something under her breath, the words imperceptible.

"Twenty-one," she concluded, just loud enough to be heard.

The end, it seemed, of a list.

After which she was every bit as attentive as before.

"So what languages?" she asked. "Do you know French?"

"Certainly."

"Tell me something in French."

"Tu as de beaux yeux."

"What did you say?"

"I said you have beautiful eyes."

Proving me correct, her dark eyes widened. And by her expression, she was exceptionally pleased. "What others do you know?"

"Você tem um cabelo lindo."

"What was that?"

"Portuguese."

"And what did you say?"

I was only too happy to tell her: "You have beautiful hair."

I thought she would wet her pants. "Another!"

"One more," I said. *"Hai il viso più bella che abbia mai visto."*

She clasped her hands to her chest. "That sounded so romantic."

"Of course. That was Italian."

"And what did you say?"

"I just told you that you have the most beautiful face I have ever seen."

Though it had been years, I had done this sort of thing before. And it was usually at this point that I would say something along the lines of *So, are you free for dinner tonight?*

But a man without cash cannot seriously pose that question.

And even more to my dismay, Nina lowered her eyes, no doubt flustered as she had begun to suspect that my compliments were more than mere repartee.

Then too, I feared the age difference was also taking its toll.

In any event, the moment was dampened.

"But we're off topic," I said casually, trying to lighten things. "You asked what I was going to do with the book."

She glanced up, showing a renewed interest.

"The answer," I announced, "is that I've been commissioned to translate it—or decipher it. Whatever is required."

Bragging is one thing; lying is quite another. Yet I was now almost certainly engaged in both.

Ed would have approved.

"Decipher it?" she said quizzically.

"Yes, you know, in the event the book is written in a way that attempts to hide its meaning."

She nodded slowly, as if pondering something. "So basically, your client is going to pay you to tell him what the book says."

"Right."

"And do you think that will take a long time? To learn what the book says?"

"I hope not."

"I wonder," she said, with a cryptic smile. "From what I have seen, I think it might."

I sensed she had revealed more than she intended.

"Why do you say that?"

"Well, because . . ." She was not, I could tell, much good at making things up on the fly. "I guess because it is a really thick book."

"And did it seem to you like an old book?"

"Yes, very old."

I looked down at her soft hands on the table. Hands that had, I suspected, with youthful and carefree curiosity, gone where mine had not.

Here, I thought, was a girl with guts enough to pick the apple.

"Tell me," I said, "did you touch it?"

"Touch it?"

I realized I had posed an odd question. I tried to deflect the weirdness of it.

"Yes. Did you put your hands on it? You know, handling an old book like that . . ."

Again, a look of repentance. "I should not have done that. Like when you go to a museum, you are not allowed to touch the exhibits." She dropped her head. "This is horrible."

"No, not really. If your hands were clean . . ."

"They were!"

"Then you didn't do any harm. But you see, not even *I* have touched that book, let alone turned its pages. But *you* have done that? You have actually *turned the pages*?"

As much as I desired this woman—as much as she had filled my every thought since the day before—I now abruptly—and pathetically (and almost hypnotically)—found myself less focused on her than I was on this nameless, lifeless tome upon which I had never laid eyes.

And just as a grave illness may produce, at its onset, only mild and ambiguous symptoms, I felt myself at the insidious beginning of another vile obsession.

"I looked through it," she admitted. "But only a little. I could not understand any of it."

"Was that because it appeared to be written in some language you didn't recognize?"

She shrugged one shoulder, her head angling to the same side. "Frankly, I am not sure that it is written in *any* language. It is more like just a bunch of marks and letters thrown around. Like something a crazy man would do."

-11-

*T*HIS NEW MANUSCRIPT called to me like a siren. But I dared not listen. And no, I seriously doubted that if I touched the book I would be struck instantly dead or insane. Yet I did fear that to follow my impulse to even the slightest extent—to open the book, to run my fingers over its leaves—might very well be no different than a long sober alcoholic handling a glass of liquor, allowing himself a mere sip, and then wanting more and more until the destruction from which he had once escaped was complete.

Nonetheless, I had to retrieve the thing. I had asked if I could drop by her apartment to pick it up. She had said she would be getting off work just before six-thirty and to come by any time after seven. The relaxed timing suggested she was free for the evening. But fat lot of good that did a man without means.

The sky was as gray as yesterday, the air as cold. I went back to Ed's and scrounged through his refrigerator for the few morsels that remained there. At the same time, I also began to think about his money: Where did he keep it? For there, I thought, I might find my own lost cash. Rolled and bound, as it had been, neatly by a rubber band.

I was certain that somehow Ed had illicitly lightened my assets during our supposed drinking escapade of two nights ago—or, if not that, deceitfully coaxed me to pay for his liquor. There was just no way that my finances could have dropped as low as they were now without his nefarious involvement.

I slapped the last piece of Ed's slimy ham on his last slice of moldy bread, choked down the rancid combination, and started to look around.

Where, I thought, would I have put my money if I were Ed? Or perhaps more to the point, where would I have hidden my money if *I* had stolen it from *me?*

The police had tossed virtually all of Ed's belongings to the floor. I searched through every item—through everything that was spilled and the few things that were not—and inspected every dark corner and out-of-the-way space, all without positive results. I began to think that law enforcement, in their zealous search, had very possibly helped themselves to whatever cash they had come across.

But then something Ed had said entered my head: *You spent that lettuce, sonny boy.* Yeah, that was what Ed always called it.

Lettuce.

And where to look for that?

I went back to the refrigerator. There was a plastic bag of thoroughly spoiled romaine in the bottom drawer that I had heretofore disregarded. Now, however, I examined it. And low and behold, at the bottom of that stinking sack I found a roll of bills held tightly by an easily recognized rubber band.

But it was a roll that seemed to have expanded since the last time I had seen it.

I merrily stuffed the wad in my pocket.

The bastard.

I went to the shelf that held Ed's liquor, pulled out a bottle of his best scotch, and poured myself a tall, celebratory shot in a water glass.

"To hell with you, Ed," I said to the walls, slugging the booze in three gulps. I poured myself another, feeling very warm just as I heard the door knob jiggle.

And then, an angry salutation:

"Where's my key, motherfucker?"

There was no way, I told myself. Not this early in the legal process.

Yet the voice was unmistakable.

"Open up, asshole," he said in a kind of comic, sing-song way. "Or else here's fuckin' Johnny!"

I thought he was just dumb enough to break down his own door.

"Yeah, well, come on then," I said, "and you can say hello to my little friend."

"Whatta ya got?"

"Somethin' for your punk ass."

If only temporarily, my bravado had made an impression; from the door's other side came an extended period of silence.

Then: "You know what I told you I'd do the next time I saw you."

"Well, you're not looking at me, are you?" I said. "What are you doing out of jail?"

"I cut a deal with the Judge. He wants his book back, and if I get it for him, I'm a free man. I got twenty-four hours. So where is it?"

"It's not here."

"Then *where?*"

I thought this over carefully: If Ed was handling this mess, then so be it. He had created the problem anyway, and I wanted no part of dealing with the Judge. But could what Ed claimed be true? Would the Judge bend his principles to such a considerable degree? He might, I thought, but only if he deemed the book more important than Ed's punishment. My own father, though very strict, had been that way, the utility of the situation sometimes dictating the extent of his leniency.

But even if the Judge had relented as Ed apparently believed, would I, if I cooperated with Ed to effect the book's return, meet with the same level of his honor's absolution? I thought it logical that I would, but there was certainly no guarantee.

Then too, Ed had promised to kill me.

So . . .

"Ed, look, exactly when do you have to get the book to the Judge?"

"I told you, I got twenty-four hours."

"Yes, but when did he tell you that?"

"What fuckin' difference does that make?"

The stupidity was off the charts.

"Because, Ed, you said you had to get the book to the Judge in a set period of time, and I'm trying to understand when that time started, so that I can then understand . . ."

"Oh, right." Now he was tracking. "I got till high noon tomorrow."

High noon? Lord. No doubt, the Judge, with his flair for the dramatic, had provided that phrasing.

"Okay," I said, "I'll make a deal with you. I'll bring you the book so that you can get it to the Judge by noon tomorrow. I'll give you my word on that. But you will stay clear of me until then. Agreed?"

"Well . . ." He paused, considering my offer. "Agreed. Now, let me in."

"Not yet." I did not trust him in the least. And we were on the third floor. I needed some way to create enough distance between us to allow myself a getaway. "Listen, here's how we're going to do this: You're going to go out the front door of the building. When you get to the street, I'll be watching you from your bedroom window. You're going to cross the street and go east until you see me wave, and when I do, you will stop right where you are. Then I'm going to replace your key above the door and go out the back of the building. You will reenter the building from the front. You will *not* try to follow me. And I will be here, with the book, tomorrow morning. Got it?"

I heard him exhale, frustrated. "Okay. But I'm still gonna kill ya."

-12-

GIVEN WHAT I HAD TOLD ED, I knew precisely what he would do: He would wait on the street until I had disappeared from his bedroom window, then streak to the rear of the building. Consequently, I made my exit from the front. And as I did, predictably, Ed was nowhere to be seen.

I ran east, and then, in successive blocks, zigzagged north, east, and north again. Finally, certain that I had lost him, I slowed to a stroll and moved into areas of the city that I did not know all that well—and where I thought neither Ed nor the Judge would venture. But on that day I was not destined to merely wish and wander; I had money.

In the early afternoon, I stopped at a decent restaurant and ordered oysters on the half shell and a couple of beers. I had not done that (the oysters, anyway) for longer than I could remember. After that, I came upon a part of the river that I had never seen, and for some distance along its shoreline, followed a nature trail. It was a delightful change from my usual slog. And though the sky remained sunless, the temperature grew warmer; the breeze was negligible. Everywhere, people shuffled about in the nicer weather.

Near sundown, I encountered some food carts and bought a soda and curried beef on a stick. This had become the most incredible of days. And still, I had a pocketful of money. Enough, I thought, that I could ask Nina to dinner that night and have plenty left for a cheap room (if I had to sleep alone) and maybe a meal tomorrow. I would, of course, have to formulate a strategy for what I would do after that, but I would have the manuscript—which Ed direly needed. That in itself presented a very interesting possibility: If Ed wanted the book badly enough, why wouldn't *he* pay me for it? I must say, there was a great irony in the thought that the thief himself might have to purchase his own swag to keep himself out of lockup. And of course, if he would not perform to my satisfaction, I could then deal with the Judge and execute my original plan.

As it grew dark, I started back toward more familiar parts of the city. I reached a view of the church tower just as the clock was striking six. From the shadows—at 6:21, according to the clock—I saw her leave work. I followed her to make sure she would be all right. She avoided the street along Ed's place and made it safely home. I waited, then, outside her building, pacing the block up and back until, in the distance, I heard the clock strike seven.

I went to the second floor, to *21*, and knocked politely. She seemed extraordinarily happy to see me.

"Leonard! Please come in."

It had been years since I had received such a welcoming. It threw me, and as I entered could muster only a cloddish *thank you.*

Her apartment was small, much the same size as Ed's. The layout was also similar: In the front was a living area and a kitchen with an oaken breakfast table; to the rear was a short hallway with a bedroom on one side and a bath on the other. The place was far nicer and cleaner than Ed's, though. The furnishings, too, were of a considerably higher quality.

"I will be right back," she said, scurrying to the bedroom and returning with the briefcase. She put it flat on the breakfast table, the latches toward me. "There. You can take a look."

I did not want to seem distrusting—but even more so, did not want to expose myself to the naked manuscript.

"I'm sure everything is in order," I said.

"Well, you never know. I may have kept your very valuable book and replaced it with an old dictionary or something." She laughed at her joke. "Leonard, is it true that you have not actually touched the book?"

"No, I haven't."

"Have you even *seen* it?"

I tried to sound nonchalant. "No."

"Then you should. Right now. Look at it. Touch it. Turn the pages. See if you can *read* it. I bet you can tell me just what it says."

She was enthused.

I strained a smile. "I'd better not. Remember, *clean hands*. I haven't washed."

She pointed toward the bathroom. "Right there."

Suddenly, I did not feel terribly well. But with no other pretext at the ready, I moved haltingly to the lavatory, scrubbing with soap and water longer than necessary while trying to concoct some graceful way out of this. Yet graceful or not, I wanted nothing to do with that book. Not now, at least. If I could smooth things over with the Judge, I would try to deal with it then. But like this? On the spur-of-the-moment? I was wholly unprepared.

And yet, I wondered, why was I so hesitant? Was it even logical? After all, I was a man of languages. One of the most proficient on the planet. A cryptanalyst too. Maybe the greatest ever. And in the other room was a manuscript that, regardless of its complexity, I was quite capable of examining.

And in that same room was a beautiful young lady—the very object of my infatuation—who very much wanted to see me examine that manuscript.

And I very much wanted her to see me do it. And to marvel at my expertise. (Was there any better way to win an evening with her?)

So just what the hell was wrong with me? This was an opportunity only a fool would refuse. And really, how could things possibly go awry? Even if the book turned out to be written in some impenetrable cipher, there was no need for her to know. I could just fake a fascinating decryption; she would be thrilled.

You would lie to her, I heard the Judge say.

I paid him little mind and looked at myself in the mirror above the sink, trying to throttle my anxiety.

You can do it, I told myself. *You'll barely have to handle it at all. And if it starts to get too much for you, just give her some excuse. You forgot an appointment or something.*

Yes, I thought, that would work.

If it came to that.

I dried my hands and, straightaway, reentered the room.

"All right, let's see what we have here," I said, staging an air of confidence.

I seated myself at the table. Nina stood just behind me, to my right.

I released the latches and, opening the case, was greeted by the book's clamshell box, sitting right-side up. I transferred it to the table.

Then as I had done once before, I raised the lid—but this time forced myself to lift it all the way up and over, revealing a dry and cracked leather book cover, unadorned and evidently very old.

My fingers hovered above it.

I stalled.

"What is it?" she asked.

"Nothing. Everything's fine."

Much as yesterday, I felt her waiting for me. Waiting then for a bum to decide on his choice of a meal. Waiting now for what she believed to be another man to show his self-professed brilliance.

Yet the delay of today's man, if allowed to continue, would be by far the worse.

This was silly, I thought. I had amplified this thing into something it wasn't and would never be. This was just another old book. An obscure bag of dusty pages. Nothing more.

And with some effort—as if pushing against a sort of resistant energy—I lowered my hands onto it.

"Do you think it is hot in here?" she said.

"A little. But I'm okay if you are."

Between the briefcase and the open clamshell box, my workspace on the table had become rather limited. I was about to move things around, but she saw the problem and beat me to it, reaching in front of me to remove the case. At which point her warm and sweatered chest met me at eye level, inches away, inviting me to notice—which I did.

Do it! Ed said. *Just reach up and grab those sweet, juicy . . .*

I found it more difficult to disregard Ed than I had the Judge. Nonetheless, as Nina closed the briefcase and set it on the floor, I managed to refocus my attention.

I centered the manuscript in front of me, leaving it in the clamshell.

I drew back the book's rigid cover.

And in that instant, I had the feeling of one who has escaped prison only to see, coming down the road, the warden with an entourage of armed guards.

Before me lay row upon row of Arabic, Greek, and Latin letters, all written in seemingly senseless disorder. Characters I knew well—but of their collective meaning, knew nothing.

With numb-dead fingers, I turned the first page. Then the next and the next. Each leaf of vellum revealing something much like the notes of a song I'd once had, for nearly a decade, stuck in my head. It was all here. Every incomprehensible line. Every symbol in its cryptically appointed place.

It simply was not possible.

I had been summoned once more by the Devil.

Yet this time, he had come in person.

I violently shut the book.

"Leonard," she said with concern, "what is it?"

"Uh . . ." It was hard to form a thought.

"Leonard, what is wrong?"

I rose from the chair, feeling faint, stumbling, catching myself.

"Does the book say something that bothers you?"

At last, I managed a reply: "No." I ground my hands into my eyes. "The book says *nothing!*"

And it never would. *It would not speak.* But it would laugh. Already, I had begun to hear it again—that chortle that if appropriately fed and nurtured by an agonized mind would grow to a chorus of howling cachinnations.

She kept her distance, looking scared and uncertain.

"Tell me, Leonard, what is going on?"

The room spinning, my heart racing, I turned away from her, fighting for control of myself. But wanting, more than anything, to make a wild run for the door. To leave without another word. And to then rip from my thoughts the abomination that lay on her table.

But this was Nina. Had it been anyone else . . .

I turned back to her, bracing myself against the table. Trying, in the wake of this abject impossibility, to think of some way to make myself look larger than the size of the man to which I had presently shrunk.

"It's the wrong book. I've been given the wrong book."

"Are you sure?"

"Very."

"And that is *it?* It is just the wrong book?"

"No," I said. "It's much more than that. But very hard to explain."

It was a thorough humiliation, her seeing me like this. So weak and vulnerable over what no doubt seemed to her some trifling problem. And now, I thought, I was no longer the man she had believed me to be.

"I'm sorry for acting like this." In my state of shame, I took the book from its box, and for a short moment, like a man suffering a fresh and not yet painful burn, was impervious to its influence. "May I leave this here?"

She nodded meekly.

I dropped the book to the table, no longer able to hold it.

I snatched up the box.

"I have to talk to someone."

-13-

*M*Y MOOD, ON THE WAY OVER, changed gradually from one of emotional stupor to a state of stiff mental resolve. And also anger. Great anger.

I stepped inside the foyer and hit the call button for *No. 12*. Within seconds, the stern voice of the Judge came over the intercom:

"I see you. What do you want?"

I looked into the security camera. "I'm bringing you something."

"What?"

"The book."

"Show me."

I held up the briefcase.

"*Show me,*" he demanded.

I opened the case and took out the box, raising it aloft as though encumbered by the weight of an object within.

"Proceed."

There was a buzzing noise and a corresponding *whack* as the door before me laid back its bolt.

I entered and took the stairs to his floor. The Judge, in his lounging robe, opened the door before I had finished knocking and, without a formal greeting, ushered me in.

He shut the door and for a moment stood watching me with a show of surprise.

"My, what has happened to you?" he said snidely.

He referred, of course, to my self-makeover.

"It's pretty simple. I stopped being a bum."

"And how did that possibly occur?"

This was the Judge's game—to ask disparaging questions until you surrendered some answer that gave away your inner thoughts and left you feeling unworthy of your own existence. But that game would not be played tonight.

"I just told you," I said, standing taller than he. "I stopped. Do you have a problem with that?"

I had never in my life spoken to the Judge in such a way. And remarkably, he had no retort, humbly shaking his head as he avoided my eyes.

Yet he would not be intimidated at length.

"The police are looking for you," he said, with an ominous voice. "They have already apprehended your counterpart."

"I know. I watched them do it. And I've talked to him since."

"Then you know that it is in both of your interests to return the manuscript to me. I do assume that is why you are here."

The briefcase at my side, I said nothing.

"Give me the book," he commanded.

I stepped back with an overwhelming satisfaction—and a broad grin—opening the case at shoulder level to let the empty clamshell box fall to the Judge's fine hardwood.

The Judge lurched forward to gather the box from the floor, but discerning its lack of mass, quickly recognized the trick. He did not open the container.

"Where is my book?" he fumed.

"*Your* book?" I said. "Let's talk about *your* book. Where did *your* book come from? You were very vague about that, as I recall."

"And I will be equally so now."

"It doesn't matter. I know where you got it."

"And where is that?"

"The Library of the Hungarian Academy of Sciences."

The Judge's face contorted into an expression of confusion and denial. "That is most definitely not the case."

"Oh, but it is. Somehow you have acquired the very book that you know would be the end of me. That would *finish* me. But how did you get it? *How?*"

I had wanted, as much as possible, to control my rage—an indignation born not only of the constant irritation this person had caused me, but of the belief that he was now literally, sadistically, trying to destroy me. But I could not hold back. My wrath had escaped its cage, consuming me, putting itself fully on display and taking charge.

With an unyielding stride, I advanced on him, just as I imagined Ed might under similar circumstances.

And the Judge was clearly no longer comfortable in his own house.

He stared at me with a look of open-mouthed shock.

"Stavros, you think . . . you *honestly think* that you have within your possession . . ."

"The Paisley Codex."

"Good lord! Have you gone mad? *Again?*"

He began retreating slowly, into the study. I pursued.

"No, Judge. I am perfectly sane and you know it. I have seen the book with my own eyes. There is no mistake. It came from that very safe." I pointed behind him to the Templar print. "Ed took it. And I had every intention of seeing him return it to you. But now I don't think that's going to happen."

I backed him into the far corner of the room. He hovered above the couch as I closed in and, becoming more of Ed every second, punched him with two fingers in the chest, dropping him unceremoniously onto the sofa cushions.

"I will call the police," he said timidly.

"Not from here, you won't."

"Stavros, please, you must listen to me." He was openly frightened, unable to breathe—a reaction thoroughly delightful to observe. "That book is *not* the Paisley."

I towered over him. "Then it is the most diabolical forgery possible."

"It is not that either. I swear to you."

"You can stop lying to me, Judge."

"Stavros . . ." Grasping the impotence of his blanket contradictions, his voice trailed off. "Look, may I reason with you, for a moment?"

I made a show of impatience.

"Proceed," I said, mocking his former directive.

"The Paisley Codex . . ." He stopped, anxiously considering his line of argument—then restarted: "The Paisley Codex, as you know, is one of the most closely guarded manuscripts in the world. One would have to go to great lengths to steal it, and you know, too, that I am not a thief. But even if I were, do you honestly think I would steal the Paisley and, upon losing it, engage the police to find it? I would almost certainly end up incriminating myself."

I remained unmoved.

"On the other hand," he said, "could I *legally* acquire the Paisley? One cannot just go to the Library of the Hungarian Academy of Sciences and check out the Paisley Codex. You know *that* as well. It must never leave the Library. So to legitimately possess the Paisley, one would have to *buy* it. But I, like most people, do not have the means to do that—if indeed the book could even be considered for sale. All of which precludes the very possibility that I have ever had the Paisley, and therefore precludes the possibility that you have it now."

"Then, as I said, it's a forgery."

"But why would one do such a thing? For starters, the cost of making a convincing copy could itself be prohibitively expensive. And what's more, to be taken as genuine, the manuscript would have to be written on unblemished fourteenth century vellum, and, as we both know, there really isn't any of that lying around."

"No, but modern-day vellum could be made to look older than it is," I said. "And unless it was carbon-dated, no one would know the difference."

"True," he acknowledged, "but if the actual Paisley currently resides at the Academy, then who would possibly be fooled?" By now, he had recovered a measure of composure—and with it, some semblance of his hold on me. "I ask you, does it make even the *least* amount of sense that anyone would attempt to replicate the Paisley when the forgery would be so obviously exposed as an imitation? Such a book would be worthless. And in any event, why would I, knowing your previous troubles, request that you conduct work on it? Merely to torment you? I have always tried to help you. To be your moral benefactor."

"You badger me. You harass me. You berate me. You call that *help?*"

"I do my best," he said. "You require guidance. You always have. Without it, where would you be? Well, I can tell you: You would be no different than that degenerate with whom you all too frequently associate yourself."

"Ed and I are kind of on the outs."

"A positive development. But I assure you, the both of you remain in the greatest possible legal peril unless my book is returned by noon tomorrow. And you can forget about any services to be performed for me—or fee to be collected. I simply want my book, the delivery of which will end this matter."

He stood up—daring me to knock him down again—and shoved the clamshell box at me, forcing me to take it.

He had regained himself.

And I had lost my fire. My previously unswerving tenacity derailed in the face of his airtight, self-exonerating logic.

I did not look at him. "What's that book worth to you?"

"I'm going to pretend," he said, "that I did not hear that. But if you persist a second time with such a question, my hearing will improve. Do you understand?"

My threat—the only viable tactic I had left—had landed like a humorless joke. And in the Judge's presence, I felt at once a devastating sense of dishonor. What kind of person was I to have ever considered such a scheme?

Yet I had seen the book, and I knew exactly what it was. That much, he would neither talk nor shame me out of.

I made for the door. "You'll get your book when I figure out what's going on here, and not before."

"Stavros," he said, kindlier than was his custom, "I think you already know. You're just not admitting it to yourself. I presume you've heard of the Law of the Instrument?"

"To a man with a hammer, everything looks like a nail."

"Something like that. And to a man obsessed, as you were—and are—with a certain book, well, every book looks like *that* book."

-14-

I DID NOT RETURN to her flat that night. I took a room at a nearby flophouse, and, the next morning, after a night of fitful sleep—a sleep that brought another incomprehensible dream of blinding fire and scorching heat—showered and headed for her apartment. I realized, though, that I was probably set to arrive too early and decided to while away some time along the river.

The morning light had cleared much of the nighttime vagrancy from the promenade, replacing it with a more upscale slice of citizenry. Up and down went joggers and power walkers, bicyclists, babies in strollers, dogs on leashes, each face producing a fog in the cold air. The sun remained blocked by the continued gray overhead, but there seemed perhaps a chance of a break in the clouds.

I passed the bench on which I had sat two nights before, and had not gone much further when I saw her running toward me in tights, a long-sleeved shirt, and an insulated vest. A stocking cap covering her dark hair. She was intent on what she was doing and didn't see me.

I ran up beside her. "Hey."

"Leonard!" She stopped.

"I was on my way to your place." I held up the briefcase. "To get the book."

She was panting. "I am going there now."

"I wanted to catch you before you went to work."

"No hurry. I am off today."

"Really?" Here was an opening. "Nina, I'm very sorry about the way I left last night. And I want to thank you for keeping the book."

"No need for any of that."

"No, really. I'd like to make it up to you. May I buy you breakfast."

"Well . . ." She did not think too long. "Okay. Where?"

"Anywhere you say."

She named a place that was close by and not too expensive. Just what I would have suggested.

"Can I meet you there in an hour?" she asked.

"Sure. I'll get a table."

"Oh, and by the way," she said before running off, "did you straighten out your difficulties?"

"No, I'm afraid I didn't."

She smiled in an odd way. "I did not think you would."

———⋄———

The restaurant was crowded. I was waiting for a table, keeping the Judge's briefcase company on a bench near the entrance, when she came in. She wore black, knee-high soft leather boots, matching leggings, and a white sweater dress with a cowl neck that ringed and accented her dark hair. Her makeup was so delicately done, I could almost believe she had felt me deserving of a special effort.

The mere sight of her made me sophomorically nervous. I stood, wanting to take her by the hands in greeting, but thought it best to hold back.

"We should have a table soon," I said.

"Sounds good."

We sat on the bench with another couple and the space was tight, permitting me contact with her that I did have to initiate. We were pressed so closely together, I found myself distracted. I could think of nothing to say.

At length, she spoke.

"Well, Leonard, congratulations. You are famous."

"What do you mean?"

"I am sorry if you are offended, but I googled you."

The life went out of me. "That's okay."

I knew, of course, what she had found. The internet was packed with articles and other postings about the Paisley Codex. And given my well-documented obsession with the book, the two of us were often mentioned together. Just query *Stavros* and up, too, would come the Paisley. The lunatic and his unsolvable manuscript.

"I just wanted to see . . ."

"I understand."

She glanced around the restaurant, unsure, I thought, of her next move.

"Leonard," she said, "you are a very remarkable person."

I was taken aback. "Why is that?"

She looked at me, her dark eyes deeply earnest. "Because you do not quit. I read how you spent years trying to translate this Codex thing, and you could not do it, but you would not quit. Even when others said it was impossible or just a big hoax and you were wasting your life, you would not quit. That is to be commended."

"In what way?" I said, less than gracious. "As a monument to futility?"

In a short time, this had all taken such a very bad turn.

"But Leonard, perseverance is a virtue."

"Nina," I said, closing my eyes to her, "you have undoubtedly read some very unflattering things about me."

The headwaiter came over. "Stavros? Party of two?"

———◈———

We were seated and given menus.

It was a while before we spoke again.

"Leonard, I am sorry if I upset you."

"It's all right. Some things in my life are just, you know, very embarrassing."

"Embarrassing only because others do not understand."

"Nina, as you now know, I have issues. Grave issues. I was hospitalized." This, I thought, was the end. So why hold back? "Crazy as a loon. That was me. No use denying it."

"You are better now."

I shrugged her off. "In some ways."

She gave me an intensely sympathetic look. A look so very young and trusting. Much like one I had often seen on another young woman. Years ago.

"Leonard, I have issues too," she said. "I do. And like yours, they are embarrassing. And I do not like talking about them. Because when I do, they make me look foolish. And people laugh."

"I won't laugh."

"I know. That is why I can tell you." She leaned over the table and whispered: *"Arithmomania."*

I had spent enough time in the bowels of academia to know the term.

"You're obsessive compulsive," I said.

"Yes."

"You count things."

"I do."

"Such as?"

"Your name: *Leonard Stavros.* The first time you told me your name, I counted the letters in my mind. Fourteen of them. Seven in your first name and seven in your last. Perfect symmetry. Mentally, I always arrange things that way, with symmetry. It is easy to do that with your name. Still, every time I think of you, I count the letters again and separate them in the same way."

I pointed to a sign near the entrance that had, along its top, words written in the local dialect, and below that, their English translation: *Breakfast All Day Every Day.*

"What would you do with that?" I asked.

"The English? Twenty-three letters," she said immediately, as if she had (and she obviously had) already counted. "In my head, I would break it down to *b-r-e-a-k-f-a-s-t-a-l.* Then the next *l* goes in the middle by itself, and *d-a-y-e-v-e-r-y-d-a-y* after that. That way, it is eleven on one side, eleven on the other. So again, symmetry."

"And you do this all the time?"

"Constantly. All day."

"Do you ever get tired of it?"

"Not too much. I am used to it."

"Do you count anything else?"

"Yes. Everything. Bricks in a wall. Cars on the street. But just to let you know the extent of my problem, while I am counting things, there is one thing I do most often: I count to *twenty-one*. Twenty-one people sitting at tables in a restaurant. Twenty-one settings of silverware lined up on a serving tray. Twenty-one times some waiter goes to and from the kitchen—and that guy," she said, pointing behind me, "is going on seven since we sat down up front."

"So when he gets to twenty-one, will you stop counting?"

"Not necessarily. Because, you see, sometimes I also count backwards."

I tried to reign in my disbelief. "From twenty-one back to one?"

"Right. Symmetry, remember? So I say 'twenty-one' twice. I count up to twenty-one, then I say 'twenty-one' again and start back down. And I may or may not be able to stop until I complete the cycle. So with that waiter—now he is starting on eight—I may have to sit here until he makes forty-two trips."

This explained some things: The words spoken under her breath as I had led her from the scene of Ed's attack—she had not been saying a prayer at all; she had been counting steps. And her arrival at work the next day, exactly twenty-one minutes after the hour—then leaving eight hours later, again, at precisely twenty-one minutes past.

Even the way she had muttered as we sat in the bar yesterday, after I had merely spoken the number: *twenty-one.*

"So you see, Leonard," she said, "you really have nothing to be ashamed of. I am the ultimate kook."

"But Nina, why twenty-one?"

She threw up her hands. "I wish I knew. I guess it is something that got stuck in my head somewhere and I just cannot get rid of it."

The waitress came and Nina ordered eggs Benedict and coffee. I did the same. I didn't really care. This discussion was all too interesting.

I was about to ask another question.

"Leonard," she said, before I could speak, "where do you live?"

I took a long moment. "At present, I'm sort of between lodgings. My roommate and I got into a bit of a tiff, and since the apartment was his and I was just, let's say, subleasing, I left."

She had a look of concern. "Do you have somewhere to go?"

"Sure. I had a room last night."

"But nothing permanent?"

"No, but I'm looking." Yeah, I thought, for a park bench. That would likely be tonight's accommodation.

"There are some openings in my building."

"Really?" I said, as if that were actually an option. "I like your building. I may consider that."

"It is a pretty quiet place. That is what you need, right? Somewhere you can work on your translations without being disturbed."

The waitress brought our coffee. When she left, I could see Nina's lips moving, counting, it appeared, the woman's steps as she walked off. I doubted, however, that the total had reached even twenty-one on the upside before we started yet another subject.

"So," she said, "that problem you had with your book did not get worked out?"

I shook my head. "You didn't think it would. Why?"

"Because when I googled you, besides finding a discussion of the Paisley Codex—which I knew nothing about—there was a link to the book itself. So I took a look at it, and I immediately understood why you were so upset last night."

"You saw, on the website, a certain manuscript you had seen before."

"Yeah, which is supposed to be locked in a fancy library somewhere, not sitting on a table in my apartment."

We talked about the book and its mysterious emergence. She had several theories.

"You know," she said, "it seems to me that the person who wrote this book could have made a copy. Or several copies. And maybe this client of yours just bought one."

This client. I had still not identified him—and didn't intend to.

"No," I said, "it doesn't work that way. There is no more chance that the creator of the Paisley Codex produced a second, identical book than there is that Da Vinci painted a second, identical *Last Supper.*"

"A forgery, then. Perhaps it is a modern fake."

I waved her off without comment. The Judge had covered that one.

"Well then, what else is there? It looks like your client may have stolen it. Or is involved with someone who did."

"I guess that's possible. But I think it's far more possible that he may have just blundered into possession of it without realizing what he had."

"Is he an honest man?"

"That's the thing. He's the most honest person I've ever known. Not the nicest—definitely not that. But honest? Extremely."

The waitress brought our food and we broke off the conversation until she left.

Nina lowered her voice: "So what are you going to do? Go to the police?"

Now, there was a touchy subject. As Ed's (albeit unwilling) accomplice, I had my own legal issues. Thankfully, I had already taken a mouthful of poached egg and ham and could, as I considered my response, simulate the inability to talk.

I swallowed and dabbed my lips with my napkin. "Bringing in the police might be dangerous. I could be implicated."

"But you are innocent."

"Yes, but there are those who might not see it that way." I took a sip of coffee. "You know, we'd all be better off if the damn thing would just disappear."

"True. But you cannot very well stuff it in your briefcase and leave it there."

"Oh, I could," I said, only half joking. "And then get rid of the case. Maybe fill it with cement and throw it in the river." Which might be a fitting end for it, I thought, the wicked tome to never again see the light of day. "The book doesn't serve a purpose, anyway. No one can read it. No one will ever be able to read it."

"But why *is* that?"

"Because the process that is needed to decipher it—the key—is unknown. In seven hundred years, no one has ever come close to figuring it out." I looked at my food. "It can't be done."

"Leonard, are you sure?"

That quickly, my fuse was lit. "Are you *kidding* me?"

She recoiled and, self-conscious, looked around to see who might have heard my outburst.

Still, she was contrite.

"I know, Leonard. You tried so hard. I am sorry to even suggest otherwise."

An apology I did not deserve. I was ashamed of myself.

For a time, we ate in silence. Finally, I couldn't stand it.

"I'm going to tell you something," I said. "You may think I'm even more weird than you already do, but I'm going to tell you anyway."

At the sound of my voice—as though on call—she raised her eyes to me. The innocent beauty held enthrall by the Svengali-like ne'er-do-well.

I could hardly look at her.

"Some nights I have this dream. I'm surrounded by fire. I can't see anything for the flames. The heat is intense. Maybe I'm in hell. I don't know. But sometimes, in that dream, I hear voices. Two nights ago, I heard your voice."

Her face veritably ignited. *"Really?"*

"Yes."

"What did I say?"

"Well, many things, most of which I don't remember. But in the end you told me that you knew where I could find the answer to the Paisley Codex—the *key*. Then you spoke four words."

She raised her dark eyebrows, prompting me to continue.

"You said, 'The answer lies within.'"

She had a sudden look of recognition. Her eyes shifted about.

"What's wrong?" I said.

"I cannot put my finger on it, but I would swear I have heard that before somewhere."

"You have?"

"Uh-huh. Those very words." She laughed uncomfortably. "Or maybe I just remember saying them to you."

"Where?"

"In your dream, of course."

It was my turn to laugh. "You think you were actually in my dream?"

Her face reddened. She managed to smile—though rather ambiguously. "Okay, I will admit, it is not likely. It was a dumb thing to say."

"No, not really. Not at all."

I did not want to embarrass her any further. She was, I thought, afflicted with a brand of youthful silliness she had yet to outgrow.

Nonetheless, the bit of levity had left me feeling better.

"Anyway," I said, "I can't stop thinking about it: 'The answer lies within.' Does that mean within *me*? Or does it mean something else, like within the book?"

The waitress came by. I asked for the check. When I returned my attention to Nina, she carried an almost professorial expression. A look that stood in paradox to the girl—the less than mature woman—I had only moments before assumed her to be.

"Some dreams are meant to help us," she said. "I believe that. Leonard, this dream may be trying to tell you something. Something very important. And I do not want you to think I am some crazy person who believes she can pop in and out of your dreams. Even if I could do that, how could I possibly know enough about the Paisley Codex to give you advice on how to solve it? Anyway, there is no use thinking about that. Because wherever it is coming from, the only thing that really matters is the message itself, which told you where to look for the key."

"Okay, but again, is the dream telling me that the answer is within my own mind? Or within the book? Or what?"

"Why not both? You have studied the book more than anyone who has ever lived. You have *absorbed* it. Your mind has literally torn it apart looking for clues. And if those clues are there, in the book, your subconscious has been at work on them. Constantly at work. All nine years it worked, far below the surface of your conscious awareness. And in that process, it may have found answers. Answers that were buried within the book, and now within you."

"That's a wild thought."

"Leonard, you may have already deciphered the Paisley Codex. You may have already *read* it. And now it is just a matter of bringing that solution—and that information—to the surface. Bringing it into your conscious mind."

"You," I said, "are too smart to be working in a bar."

She frowned. "I went to university for a while."

"What did you study?"

"Mathematics." She laughed, looking almost apologetic. "I like numbers."

"You didn't finish?"

"Not the way I should have."

"What happened?"

She seemed pained by a thought. "Things."

Her soft hand lay on the table within reach. On impulse, I placed mine atop it.

She took hold.

15

SOME YEARS AGO, I met a girl who liked numbers. I was visiting a floral shop to pick up a dozen roses. I was very interested in a certain woman and wanted something to impress her. Of course, I had already impressed her. I was sure of that. But I wanted something to really seal the deal.

This woman I was in pursuit of was lovely. And smart (at least, I thought she was). Smart women, by the way, are attractive to me. And certainly, they must have other things. Womanly things. Those things a man may visibly admire. And hold. And caress. Yet I like it most when those things—those carnal attributes—are blended with intellect. There is nothing quite like it, that intersection of beauty and brains.

Anyway, I went in to get my roses and the young woman at the counter advised there were none. They were all spoken for.

I was miffed.

"I called first thing this morning," I said.

"I am sorry. But I am sure you did not talk to me. What is the name?"

I told her. She looked through a stack of tickets. "There is nothing here for you. I do hope you accept my apology. Someone made a mistake. But this is a very busy day for us."

I had no doubt of that. It was the first of May—what they called, around there, the Day of Love. They had been celebrating it since time immemorial. It made Valentine's Day look like a non-event.

Which, of course, was why I needed the roses.

"Again," she said, "I am sorry."

I believed it. She was sincere. She was genuinely sorry.

And, I must add, genuinely nice-looking. Gorgeous, actually. I had initially been too bothered by the flower foul-up to fully notice. But I was calming down, and I certainly couldn't blame her for the problem. Not with those petite yet rounded hips, and those dark eyes, and the way she packed that sweater.

"Look," she said, "I can understand how upset you must be. Let us try to make it up to you. Just tell me what you would like. On the house."

I was well versed in many things—well, most things, really. But sadly, a knowledge of flowers was not on the list.

"What would you recommend?" I asked.

She looked behind me, seeing several customers waiting.

"Katya," she said to a woman nearby, "can you take the register?"

She led me to a row of display coolers. I followed, watching, discreetly, the swing of those hips. The sway of her arms and shoulders. The way her thick dark hair hung bobbed just above the unblemished, waxen-white nape of her neck. And I could imagine my hands touching those arms, those shoulders. Wandering upwards . . .

"We have some very nice tulips," she said. "We have some irises too, but frankly, I would not recommend them. They are looking a little haggard. And we have many bouquets, most very fresh—those without the irises, that is."

I looked from one cooler to the next, from shelf to shelf, the many flowers mingling beyond my ability to distinguish one from the other. I had by then, however, lost all interest in everything but the girl on display to my right.

"How about this bouquet?" she said, putting a finger near the glass. "It has a mix of trilliums, geraniums, cosmos, and cineraria."

I saw petals of white, red, yellow, and dark violet. There were several flowers of each color. I thought it the most unique bouquet in sight, although I remained unable to classify any of what I was looking at.

"So which of these flowers . . .?"

"Is which?" she said, anticipating my ignorance.

I nodded readily.

"The trilliums are the white ones. The geraniums are red. The cosmos, yellow. The cineraria, purple. Do you like it?"

"I do."

"Good," she said. "I put this together."

"Really?"

"Yes, this is one of my arrangements."

I did not hesitate. "I'll take it."

I gazed into her eyes for a time too long to be considered polite. She blushed, but did not turn away.

"Let me box it for you."

She opened the display and, holding the glass door with her hip, reached in and took the vase with two hands. Seeing the door would slam, I grabbed it as she backed away, easing it shut.

"Thank you," she said, seeming, I thought, a bit more appreciative than the situation required.

I was encouraged.

I followed her back to the counter. My eyes, again, consuming her every move.

And by now, I was utterly craving her. Her luscious hair. Her faultless skin. Her eyes. Her hips. Her breasts. I had an urge to wildly throw myself onto this beautiful thing and indulge my desire with abandon. Yet I knew that such thoughts (and my previous ogling too) were not only vulgar, but counterproductive—the very opposite of the chivalrous touch that would ultimately be necessary. On the other hand, this was not something the reckless hedonist within me understood. His hungers were constant. And because of that, from time to time—this being one of those—I had to deal him a figurative smash in the face.

She set the flowers on the far end of the counter from the other customers, and after pulling a cardboard vase box from a nearby shelf, began inspecting the bouquet. I thought it odd the way she examined every flower, her fingers bouncing in a circle around each set of petals, her lips, as she did, moving silently. Nearly a minute must have passed before she spoke again.

"A couple of these are not right," she said, disappointed.

"What is it?"

"This cinerarium has only twelve petals. And this geranium, four."

"Is that bad?"

"I would not use that word. But let us say that it is not as nature intended. The cineraria should all have thirteen petals. The geraniums should all have five."

"So what happened?" I didn't much care. Anything to extend the conversation.

"Some petals fell off. They had to. Because yesterday when I put these flowers in this vase, every one was as it should be."

"As nature intended," I said.

"Yes, exactly. You see, the genetic code for each species of flower in this vase causes that flower to produce a set number of petals that should never vary. In fact, together, by the number of their petals, these four species represent a segment of a very well-known arithmetical series."

It was right then I quit glancing between her eyes and breasts and focused solely on the former.

"What series is that?"

Her lips tightened. "I should not have said anything. Now I look like a nerd."

"No, you don't."

"Most surely I do. But you see, this flower arrangement is the sort of thing I do to amuse myself. It is hard to explain."

"Tell me about it."

She shook her head. "You would not understand."

"I might."

Knowing now the number of petals on the geraniums and cineraria, I looked down and counted the petals on the others—three on each of the trilliums and eight on the cosmos. For a man of my educational background, the pattern was apparent: I knew precisely what she was talking about.

I was curious, though, how she might explain it.

"Come on," I said. "Try me."

She heaved a sigh of resignation.

"Okay, well, have you heard of the Fibonacci Sequence?"

I withheld a smile. "You know, I may have. It sounds familiar."

"It is a numerical sequence that is embedded almost universally throughout the natural world. Its numbers are evident in the manner in which many trees and plants develop. Certain of the numbers are found in human genetics. They are even found in the notes of a musical octave. Indeed, the sequence roughly suggests a geometric progression of the golden ratio, which is apparent in everything from the spirals in the shell of a snail to the extent of curvature we observe . . ." She squeezed her eyes shut. "Oh, my. You see? I am a *geek*."

I wanted to laugh; I didn't.

"No, no, please go on," I said. "What is the sequence?"

"All right. It goes like this: Starting with *zero*, the sequence adds the number *one* to create the sum of the next number—which, obviously, is also *one*. *One* and *one* are then added to create *two*, and *one* and *two* to create *three*, and so forth, each number thereafter being the sum of the preceding two numbers."

I was a bit awestruck. She had nailed it.

"So one plus two equals three," I said, pointing to the three petals on one of the trilliums.

"Yes."

"And two plus three trillium petals equals five geranium petals."

"Right."

"And the three trillium petals plus the five geranium petals equal the eight cosmos petals."

"Yes!" She jostled her head excitedly, her dark, bobbed hair flopping irresistibly about her face. "You understand."

"I do," I said. "And the five geranium petals and the eight cosmos petals equal the thirteen petals of the cineraria." I tapped the head of a flower. Probably the wrong one. I didn't bother to look.

And neither did she. She could not take her eyes off of me. She marveled at my acumen.

"You really *do* understand, Mister . . ."

"Stavros. Leonard Stavros."

"Yes, Mr. Stavros. I am sorry. You told me before."

"And the next number?" I said. "*Twenty-one?* The eight petals of the cosmos plus the thirteen of the cineraria? What flower might that be?"

"It could be an aster," she said. "They have twenty-one petals."

I glanced at the arrangement. "So why not?"

She laughed. "They are out of season. But if you will notice, the number is nevertheless represented by the total of the flowers in the arrangement—six trilliums and five each of the other three varieties."

I looked hard at this girl. And in the same way—now without blushing—she looked at me. She had lost all sense of diffidence. And we had, in that moment, a kind of connection—a connection beyond sexual, something ethereal—that I cannot and never will be able to explain.

I felt my pulse pounding in my face and neck.

"You know a lot about flowers," I said.

She was taking heavy breaths. "I know more about numbers."

I leaned into the counter, closer to her, catching her sweet scent and the smell of flowers all around. Our eyes remained locked. But very abruptly she broke off and proceeded, businesslike, to assemble the cardboard vase box. She placed the vase in the box and pushed it across the counter.

"There you are, Mr. Stavros. I do hope your sweetheart enjoys it."

"My sweetheart?"

"Yes. And you know the tradition here? On this day you must kiss her under a blossoming cherry tree. That is what we do." She became, then, rather curt. "Thank you very much for your patronage."

She turned and went to the cash register, relieving the girl who had taken her place. She spoke to the next customer. She was done with me.

"No, look," I said, following her. I cut in front of the man she was about to help. "Those flowers. They're for my mother. She's been ill."

A wide smile came to her face. The most welcome smile I had ever seen.

The flowers, by the way, never reached their destination. In fact, as to the woman they were meant for, I never saw her again.

And later that day, under a blossoming cherry tree, I kissed the girl behind the cash register.

16

*W*E LEFT THE RESTAURANT.
    "What time do you have?" I asked.

She looked at her phone. "Just past eleven."

The idea of extorting something from Ed in exchange for the book still had its appeal. He would have done the same to me, and, let's face it, he was in a tough spot and I needed the money. But then, I hadn't really thought such a scheme through terribly well. Shaking Ed down might produce any number of adverse consequences I hadn't even considered. And the Judge would excoriate me for it, in any event.

No, I thought, the sensible thing was to simply do as I had promised and deliver the book to Ed so that he could restore it to the Judge by the appointed hour. That would hopefully end my involvement in this mess. And as for the Judge, whatever he chose to do then would be his problem. I had given him a solid heads-up as to what he had, and should he continue to cast aspersions on my sanity, he would do so at his own peril.

"I've decided to return the book to my client," I said. "Let him deal with it."

"Good for you. That thing is only trouble."

It was starting to drizzle. We walked faster, and as the rain picked up, we were soon running. We kept a hard pace all the way to her building.

At her apartment, I washed my hands in order to handle the manuscript. It lay on her breakfast table where I had left it the day before.

I took the clamshell box from the briefcase.

"You know," she said, "I noticed last night, this book is not made like books are now."

"No, they didn't use glue. Someone sewed it together by hand, with a needle and thread."

She bent down to look along the spine where, in several places, the rotted leather cover had crumbled away to expose the bindings.

"And it is like they have taken a bunch of little books and sewn them up to make one big book."

"*Quires*," I said.

"What?"

"The little books. They're called *quires*. Most books today have them too, more or less. But they're not so obvious."

Her eyes continued to run up and down the spine. "So Leonard, tell me, exactly how did they do all this?"

Oh, boy.

I looked at the clock on the microwave in the kitchen. Time was becoming a fairly serious issue. And certainly, this book was no longer my favorite subject.

But she was hard to resist.

I spoke with some haste.

"Okay, well, first off, centuries ago, books were almost all written on animal skin. And in the case of this book, it's *calf* skin. It's what we call vellum. Which is extremely resilient. Lasts almost forever. And to make this book, the person who wrote it took three sheets of vellum and, with a quill pen, filled them on both sides with text. Then, after that—or maybe before; we don't know—those three sheets were folded to make six leaves of the manuscript. And, there being a *recto* and a *verso* to each leaf—that is, a front and a back—that made twelve pages. And that was one little book, as you call it. One quire. And every quire in this book was done the same way, with exactly twelve pages."

She was fixed upon me, waiting for more.

I talked faster.

"And when it came time to assemble the book, the first quire was put on a device called a sewing frame, and that quire was sewn together along its centerfold with hemp thread. In the process, the thread was also looped around these three leather binding cords that, you can see, are set horizontal to the spine. Then another quire was laid down on top of the first. The two quires were sewn together, and the second quire was also sewn along its centerfold and secured to the leather cords. And it went on like that, one quire after another. And after the last quire was sewn in, the ends of the leather cords were threaded through openings underneath the front and back of the cover and tacked down." Still holding the briefcase and clamshell box, I made a clumsy gesture toward the book. "And basically, that's it."

I looked again at the clock. I had gone on longer than I'd planned.

"That was probably more than you wanted to know."

"No, I think it is fascinating," she said.

To which I honestly thought: *You're kidding me.*

Hurriedly, I put the briefcase on the floor and set the clamshell box on the table, opening it. I made another check of the clock.

I needed the book.

But blissfully ignorant of my deadline, she had resumed her inspection of the manuscript, leaning over in front of me for a better view of the dilapidated spine, where the gatherings of vellum that comprised each quire were most apparent.

I waited.

"Nina, I really need to . . ."

She popped up, smiling and satisfied. "*Twenty-one!* Did you know that?"

"The number of quires?"

"Uh-huh."

I nodded. I knew.

And I could only guess how many times she had counted since last evening.

"I'm sorry, Nina, but I should probably get going. May I?"

She tendered a brief look of apology and moved back.

I spread my hands toward the book, not touching it.

Then, strangely, it was as if I *couldn't* touch it. As if it had a force field of some kind. And yes, even when I had thought this was a different book, I had felt a certain resistance. But now, knowing what lay here—the very thing that had driven me to madness; a thing, it seemed, as lethal as an incurable disease—I was rendered utterly powerless.

She appeared to understand.

"May I help?" she offered.

A set of fears swept over me: Fear of the book. Fear of being unable to deliver it and what would happen as a result. Fear of seeming, in Nina's presence, even more impotent than I had the previous night.

But in short order, I felt something else: Anger. Hatred. An overriding rage against this unholy relic.

And suddenly, I could think only of removing it from my sight.

"This goddamn thing is going in that box," I snarled. "And I'm going to put it there."

I held my breath, and in a flurry—like a person yanking a bandage from a throbbing wound—I took hold of the book, hoisted it, and dropped it into the lower tray of the clamshell.

I shut the box and stared into space.

"You know," I said, feeling her eyes on me, "that really wasn't so bad."

I put the box in the briefcase and made for the door.

"Leonard?" she called after me. "You are coming back, right?"

———— ❖ ————

The rain was falling hard. I ran into the teeth of it, ducking, whenever I could, under awnings for cover. Partway down Ed's block, I crossed to the north side of the street in order to have a better view of his building as I approached.

Across from his building, I sheltered under the entrance to a board-ed-up store front. I had no real plan, and I wondered: How should I do this? Go over, knock on his door, and just hand him the case? No, I thought, too dangerous. Or perhaps quietly put the case by the door, then knock and run? That seemed, at first, a more acceptable option—until I considered the possibility of him lurking somewhere along my line of retreat. Best, I thought, to not even enter the building. But then, how was this going to work if I didn't?

As badly as I wanted to avoid another encounter with the Judge, I began to think I should just continue on to his flat and finish this job myself. But even as I entertained that notion, on the third floor of the building, Ed's bedroom window came open. He poked his head out.

"I *seeee* you," he sang cheerily, his face blue and swollen.

I raised the briefcase and shouted over the rain and passing traffic: "Here it is."

"Bring it up."

"No, you come down."

"Either way, asshole, you know what's gonna happen."

With the rain, there were few people on the street—but no doubt thinking something ugly was in the offing, the handful present began steering away from me.

"There's no time for that," I said. "Look, if you're not going to take the book to the Judge, then I will."

"No, you won't. *I'm* takin' it. And the Judge is gonna pat my head and tell me what a good boy I am."

"Then you'd better get down here and get moving or you won't make his deadline."

He slammed the window. Seconds later, he came out the front of the building and down the steps on which I had, nearly two days ago, knocked him all but unconscious. He was smoking a cigarette and, as he left the bottom step, gave the burning butt a violent flick onto the sidewalk.

He started across the street, through traffic, letting cars stop for him. Despite the cold, he wore short sleeves.

Above the waist of his pants, I saw the butt of a pistol.

"It's all yours," I said, putting the case down.

In the middle of the street, he drew the gun. Some variety of Glock. He leveled it.

Instinctively, I picked up the case. "Ed! No!" I turned to run east. There was traffic passing between us, frustrating his sightline. But at once, he was on my side of the street.

I hit top speed, looking back just as he, following, again raised the gun. I saw a flash and heard an attendant *pop*.

"High noon, bitch!"

Ahead, along the walk, people screamed. Some dove to the pavement. In the street, I heard a car swerve and the sound of a collision.

At the first corner, I took a left, hoping I could get to the nearest alleyway and disappear before he, too, turned the corner. But as I came to the alley, I heard another *pop* and, as the bullet struck the building beside me, saw a chunk of stone turn to powder.

I ran on down the sidewalk, swerving left and right to make myself less a target, the weight of the briefcase wearing on me. But he remained within view, and that alone moved me to greater effort. Eventually, I committed to a stiff right turn and within two blocks came to the park spotted with war monuments that I had crossed the night I had followed Nina. A large, open expanse.

The rain had become even heavier. In torrents, almost blinding. The weather had driven all others from the green. I looked back and saw no one. Then a *pop-pop* told me that Ed remained in chase. I heard yet another blast and saw, just ahead, sparks fly from the metallic ass of a soldier's faithful steed.

I left the park without regard for traffic, wet car brakes locking and horns sounding angrily in the driving hail of water. I was near spent and veritably dragging the case, but knew that quitting would be tantamount to suicide.

I glanced back, seeing in the streaming haze a form still advancing. Gaining, even.

Losing my will by the step, I staggered on. With the church tower in sight, I could, through the rain, just make out the hands of the clock standing on the verge of noon. Then, as I passed the bar where Nina worked, I slipped just a bit—but enough—on the cobbled stones and went down, smacking my knee on the rough, hard surface. Tearing my pants and losing my grip on the case. It went sliding ahead, the wet grime of the sidewalk caking my face. People in the bar were watching, laughing—but I think not so much after I had, in panic and bloodied pain, gathered myself and the case and, with my damaged leg, limped furiously on, my would-be assassin close behind.

I had the sense that Ed may have paused in front of the bar to take another shot at me (and if so, that would certainly have been bonus viewing for the patrons). But then, what I heard might have been only a clap of thunder.

Yet if he had taken that shot, it had cost him time. Clearly, something had. Perhaps it was his own exhaustion. In any event, even trailing an injured man, he had fallen back.

I neared the end of the next block without hearing anything more resembling gunfire. I began to think I might be out of range—or that he was out of ammo—but I was not about to chance it. With the rain slacking, I did my best to increase my speed and crossed the street to the Judge's building.

At the building's entrance, I dropped the briefcase and ran on.

I must have gone forty strides before I looked back and saw Ed reach the entrance. He stopped and brought the pistol up, aiming it just as the bells on the church tower began to signal the noon hour. I could read his lips as he said *Shit!*—then saw him grab the briefcase and hurry inside.

THE SECOND BOOK
OF STAVROS

A Book By Its Cover

Things are not always what they seem.
The first appearance deceives many.

–Phaedrus

-17-

"LEONARD, MY GOODNESS, WHAT HAS HAPPENED?"
Wet, dirtied, and bloodied, I stood outside the door of her flat.
"Have you been in a fight of some kind?" she asked.
"You might say that."
"With your client?"
"More like his associate."
"Did you deliver the book?"
I nodded.
"Then you have done all you can." In a motherly way, she ushered me inside and to the bathroom. "Clean yourself up. Take your time. I will get you some dry clothes."

———◦———

A towel around my waist, I came out of the steamy bathroom and peeked into the living area.
"Nina?"
She was sitting on the couch, watching television. "Yes?"
"I'm not sure what to do. My clothes are in the bath."
"Just leave them. I will take care of them."
"Then what?"
"I told you. I have things for you." She stood and came toward me.
I took a step back.
"Leonard, nobody is watching but me."

I made a silly laugh. "I *know*."

"How is your knee?"

"I cleaned it. It's okay."

She bent down and raised the towel just enough. "Maybe. But a dressing might help."

She was probably right. I had a nasty cut.

"We will get to that in a minute," she said "First, though, come in here." She led me into her bedroom. "There. These are yours."

Laid out on the bed, I saw four pairs of pants, twice as many shirts, various pairs of socks, two belts, a stack of underwear, even a bathrobe. On the floor was a pair of dress shoes and a pair of sneakers.

"There is also a nice coat. You can have that too."

This was far more than an offer to lend out a simple change of clothes. It made me wonder whether she had somehow come to suspect my lack of wardrobe options.

"This is very nice of you," I said. "But maybe I should just use what I need for the time being, until I can get back to my things at the hotel. You know, where I stayed last night."

"Sure."

"So where did all this come from?"

"It belonged to someone who used to live here."

"Someone that lived here with you?"

She made a face that answered in the affirmative. "I suppose you are wondering what happened to him."

"It's probably none of my business."

"It is no secret, though. He left. We were together a long time, and then he left. He did not even bother to take his things."

"I'm sorry." I really wasn't. The guy had done me a favor—in a couple of ways. "Where did he go?"

"I do not know. I have lost track of him. Everyone has. He has totally disappeared. You could look the world over and you would not find him."

"Sounds like a guy with some issues."

"To say the least." She crossed her arms. "I have always thought it would have been easier if he had run off with another woman. Then I would not have to feel so sorry for him."

"So he just left? For no reason?" I could not help wondering whether her numerical disorder might have played some part in the breakup.

"No, he had a reason. He . . ." She seemed to sense my suspicion—and dismiss it. "Let us just say he had his own obsession."

We did not discuss the matter further. She bandaged my knee, I put on the bathrobe, and she encouraged me to rest while she went out for a few groceries. I had intended to close my eyes for only a short time, but given the stress of recent events, fell into a deep sleep on her couch, waking some two hours later to find her sitting at the small desk in her bedroom, looking at something on her laptop.

She saw me and lowered the screen.

"I promise I won't look," I said.

"I am sorry. It is rude to be secretive."

"That's okay."

The head of her bed lay between two narrow, double casement windows, the bottom frames of which stood just below the level of my knees, the windows themselves stretching up another four feet or so. I went to the one on the side of the bed nearest her desk and parted the curtains enough to see gray sky. The rain had stopped.

"Do you mind?" I asked, a hand on the pull cord.

"No, some daylight would be nice."

I opened the curtains and, from our second-story height, found myself looking out from the rear of the building at the river—barges, tugs, and pleasure boats moving along. The far side of the channel was heavily treed and rose sharply to the peak of a hill, tenements and other structures clinging to the slope. The near side, of course, featured the promenade, which extended to my left. Noticeably, however, the broad walkway all but terminated at Nina's building, where, below me, it shrank to a mere sliver of stone and mortar—hardly the width of two persons—as it ran along the building's backside and behind several other dwellings before expanding again beyond.

"Leonard, I have a question for you. And if you do not wish to answer, I will understand."

"Sounds fair."

"In a way, it is about the Paisley Codex."

I most certainly did *not* want to answer. But then, if I had intended to declare the subject of the book off limits, I should not have been so willing to discuss it that morning. And I'd had my own questions to her about the former owner of the wardrobe I had inherited.

"Whatever you want to know," I said.

"All right, it is this: How does someone like you go about trying to figure out something like that? Something that is—what is the word?—*encrypted*. I mean, I read online that you used to be like a spy or something. And that you broke all sorts of top-secret codes."

"Codes," I said, "and ciphers." I thought it best, however, to avoid confusing her with technical distinctions—and even more so since she had been kind enough to compare me to James Bond.

"Okay, so how do you do it?"

"You mean just in general?"

"Uh-huh. Like if somebody handed you an old book like the Paisley Codex and it was all in some kind of code, how would you go about trying to break it?"

I sat down on the foot of the bed and she turned around to sit on the side of her chair, facing me with great expectation. I didn't really know what to tell her. It had been so long since I had cracked anything—code or cipher—and in the interim I had been through so many varying states of confusion and mental decay, I feared I had lost the ability to even explain the process.

For a few seconds I sat quietly, just hoping in her presence to convey something intelligible.

"All right." I took a deep breath. "Let's say you have a piece of text—or a book, as you say—that you know is written in some kind of code. And you don't have the key—that is, the rules for decoding the script." I looked down at my hands, my fingers jiggling about faster than my thoughts. "If that's the case, then you have to ascertain the key through a method known as *brute force attack*—which is really nothing more than trial and error. One starts by making assumptions. And at the same time, one looks for patterns consistent with those assumptions."

"Assumptions," she said, making a mental note. "And patterns."

Her unprompted response struck me something like the welcome feedback from a student in a lecture hall.

I felt my confidence slightly on the uptick.

I took another breath. "Yes, now, let's pretend that your book is written using just the Latin alphabet—the same alphabet that's used for French, English, Spanish, and literally over a hundred other languages. But as we know, it's also written in code—or better yet, let's call it a *cipher*," I said, unable to help myself. "And because of that, the letters of the text are arranged in a manner that doesn't appear to make sense. We call that version of the text—the encrypted version—the *ciphertext*. But of course, hidden in the ciphertext is a message, and that message is called the *plaintext*."

"Ciphertext," she repeated, very intense. "Plaintext."

Once more, the listener validating the lesson.

And with that, my worries continued to subside as, increasingly, I felt myself conversant on this subject of which I had once held mastery.

"Let's also pretend," I said, sitting up straighter, "that we don't know the language in which the plaintext is supposed to be understood. And the letters of the ciphertext include no diacritics or ligatures of any kind that might give us a clue. So the plaintext could *be* French. Or English. Or Spanish. Or any one of those hundred-plus languages. Still with me?"

She nodded, ready for more.

"But we have to figure out which one it is or we won't have any idea how to formulate the plaintext message. And that's where we have to start making assumptions and looking for patterns. And one method of looking for patterns is called *frequency analysis*."

She spoke the words under her breath. But after, her lips moved on silently as, most probably, I thought, she counted and symmetrically bisected the collection of letters involved.

"And to explain what I'm talking about," I said, now rolling with full force, "let's say that we make an assumption that the plaintext is in French—at which point, to check our assumption, we need to understand the patterns inherent in the French language, such as how frequently each of the various alphabetic letters tend to appear in written French. Then we conduct an analysis to see whether our ciphertext uses its letters with corresponding frequencies. If it does, then we know that the plaintext might be French. After that it becomes a matter of trying to determine whether the ciphertext can actually be decrypted to say something in French."

"How do you do that?"

"You analyze the text to determine the method of cipher that's being used." I smiled learnedly. "And where cipher techniques are concerned, there are two that are most commonly applied: In one of those techniques, the letters in the ciphertext are the same letters that make up the plaintext—but the letters have been shuffled around in order to hide the message. We call that a transposition cipher."

Again, she spoke under her breath.

"The other method is what we call a substitution cipher, which is where the letters in the plaintext message have been left in their proper order, but have been replaced by other letters."

She looked bothered by something.

"Wait," she said. "If it is a substitution cipher and all of the plaintext letters have been replaced by other letters, how would you ever know the language of the plaintext? I mean, you said you would know it was French because all the letters would appear with the sort of frequency you would expect in that language. But how could that be true if all the letters were replaced?"

Not a terribly smart question, I thought. But then, she was a total novice.

"Because," I said, "if we're dealing with a simple, straightforward substitution cipher, the characters that make up the text of the cipher—that is, the letters of the ciphertext—will appear with the same frequencies as their counterparts in the plaintext. For instance, the letter *e* is the most commonly occurring character in the French language, and, of course, we know the frequency with which it tends to be used in French. Likewise, all of the other characters used in French also have known use-frequencies. However, we may have a ciphertext in which some letter other than *e* appears with the same frequency as does *e* in written French. And if the other letters of the ciphertext appear with frequencies that can be matched to those of the various other letters used in the French language, then we know the ciphertext may be hiding a plaintext message meant to be read in French. Does that make sense?"

She nodded again and, by her expression, appeared to understand. But I had vastly oversimplified. No discussion of bigram frequencies, trigram frequencies, unicity distance, or other concepts that might wrench the mind of one cryptologically uneducated.

"So have you done this frequency analysis on the Paisley Codex?" she asked.

I felt my face constrict. "To an extreme."

"And did you actually *try* French?"

"Are you kidding?" I said, now somewhat less the jovial professor. "French. English. Gaelic. Scots. Welsh. German. Romanian. Russian. Farsi. Catalan. Hebrew. Berber in all its variations. Literally every language in use during the fourteenth century in the entirety of the British Isles and the European continent, as well as the Middle East and North Africa. Nothing correlates. Nothing."

"But it has to translate into *some* language."

"Very clearly, it does. And with three alphabets, quite probably more than one." I struggled to remain outwardly calm even as my insides had begun to boil. "But solving the Paisley is a much more complex proposition than what we just discussed—and for many reasons. And one of the biggest of those reasons is that the text has been engineered in a way to make frequency analysis impossible."

"But you said that is how you would do it." She seemed let down. "By making assumptions. And looking for patterns."

"*Yes*," I said emphatically. "And I'm telling you, I have tried that. Over and over. And here and there, patterns *do* emerge. But regardless of whether one analyzes a random section of the book, or a single quire, or a single page, the text divulges no *extended* and *consistent* pattern. Which for all practical purposes makes it utterly resistant to frequency analysis. It simply doesn't work."

"But how can that be?"

"Because . . ." I had to force myself to go on. "Because *someone* . . . some . . . *person* . . ."

Oh, that person! A person whose name I did not know. Would *never* know. This obfuscator—this goddamn *scriptor libri*—who had tormented me some seven centuries beyond his own grave.

"The man who concocted this book . . ." I took a heavy, wavering breath. "That son of a . . ." I broke off, barely restraining myself. "He did something very devious. He took all of the characters used in the ciphertext—the characters of all three alphabets—and synchronized their frequencies to the point that almost every letter appears with virtually the same frequency as every other."

She rubbed her forehead. "But how could such a thing ever make sense? Surely, there is no language anywhere in which all of the alphabetic characters are used with the same regularity."

And this woman had gone to university?

"*Of course not*," I snapped. "Which obviously means that a countless number of the characters that appear are not actually part of the plaintext."

"Then what good are they?"

My god, the thickheadedness!

"They're no good at all! Not to me! Not in the least!"

At once, I caught myself—raving like the madman I wanted to believe I no longer was.

Then too, I was rudely shortchanging her intellect, which, despite these recent deficiencies, I knew to be quite above standard.

I took another deep breath and (albeit with some difficulty) a softer tone.

"Nina, they're simply extra letters. They're what we call *nulls.* Worthless information. Stuff that's intended only to obscure—to confuse people who don't have the key, and to prevent them from *discovering* the key. And the Paisley Codex is full of nulls. They have been put there specifically to confound frequency analysis and to otherwise complicate and frustrate the decryption process. In fact, there are so many nulls that they may even exceed the amount of text that is actually intended to mean something."

"Nulls," she said to herself. The once aspiring mathematician, she looked at me with a faint smile. "Things of zero value."

"That's right. Those are nulls."

She gazed past me, out the window—seeming lost in thought—then brought her eyes back to meet my own.

"I think it must have taken a genius to create the Paisley Codex."

I spoke reluctantly. "I think so too."

"And do you envy him? That man?" She smiled again. "Or *woman?*"

Why had she asked such a thing? How *could* she? *Envy?* Never!

I did not answer; I smoldered.

There was a protracted silence.

"Leonard," she said, "I have an idea. I will make dinner, and then we will go out."

"Go out?" The phrase passed my lips like words from a language I hadn't learned.

"Yes, you know." She leaned forward, clasping her hands. "Go *out?* Have *fun?*"

I had not had fun in so long.

"Oh, Nina, I don't think so. It takes . . ."

"What?"

I churned with embarrassment. "Money. It takes money. And I . . ."

"You are waiting on payment from clients," she said.

"Something like that." I was flat broke.

"Then you can owe me." She closed her laptop and jumped up, heading for the kitchen. "How about goulash? I have everything we need."

For a moment, I feared she had expressed her own hidden message. But no, I thought, there was not the least possibility. I bore no resemblance to the person she had served two days ago. I was no longer that man.

I hoped.

"Goulash would be wonderful," I said.

"Want a beer?"

I sat on the couch drinking a Dreher, watching the news as she prepared the meal. I turned down the volume as the anchorman reported a certain story: *"This afternoon, in a scene straight out of the American Wild West, an unidentified armed assailant pursued a would-be victim down city streets and through Soldier's Park, firing as he went. The bullet-laden chase lasted for over a mile. There were apparently no injuries."*

I ran my fingers over the dressing on my knee.

-18-

*T*HE CLOTHES SHE HAD PROVIDED fit even better than Ed's. But I could not comprehend why their former owner had run out on her the way he had. Just leaving without a trace. Clearly, she had cared for him. What was wrong with such a person?

We ate at her small breakfast table and carried on talk that was, by and large, likewise rather small. Yet the mere fact that I was speaking with her in this domestic setting filled me with a kind of euphoria. I felt myself vital in her presence; she treated me as if I were, to her, someone of significance. A man of exceptional abilities. It had been so long since a woman had given me such deference. And this woman, so beautiful.

"I am not going to count the stairs as we go down," she said as we left her flat. "I am not going to count anything at all tonight. I promise."

"I'll watch your lips."

"You will not have to," she said. "Because when I am talking with you, I cannot count. And we will be talking. The whole time."

"About what?"

"About all the things we are going to do together."

She took my arm.

Before the Paisley, my wife and I had gone out often. There was a club district not far from where we lived and we went there almost every week. On occasion I saw certain of my co-workers there.

My wife knew I had a government job, but due to the nature of the work, I could not give her any real specifics regarding how I spent my time. I had simply told her that I was an "interpreter" of communications and other documents originating from foreign agencies, some of which involved national security. But she had focused more on the *interpreter* part of the description (which, for her own peace of mind, I had not discouraged) and had come to believe that my days were consumed by the process of translating bland administrative dispatches and records.

"Leonard," she had said once over drinks at our favorite place, "you should try for something more. You are far too talented."

"I do very important work."

"Yes, you do, very surely. But with all of your expertise, I cannot believe you are happy."

"*Can't,*" I said, correcting her.

"What?"

"Remember, use the negative contraction: *Can't.*"

She rolled her eyes. "Fine. Can'ut."

"No, it's *can't.*"

"Can't!"

People looked at us.

I tipped my head back and laughed. "There you go. See, it's not so hard. You can do it."

"I have told you, I did not . . ." She stopped herself. "I *didn't* learn that way."

I put my arm around her. "And now you're learning another way. The way people actually speak English."

"Leonard, I do not . . ." She stopped herself again, then went on stubbornly: "I *do not* care about that. The subject is your work."

"I wish it weren't. Let's talk about something else."

"You never want to talk about your job. You know, I really think you hate what you do. I wish you would look for something different. Something that excites you."

"You excite me."

"Leonard, please be serious." As I stroked her neck, she tried to hold back a giggle, but couldn't. "Besides, there is no money in the excitement I provide."

We both laughed.

"I don't care about money," I said.

"Me neither. Just us. And you."

I moved my hand to the back of her head, my lips toward hers.

"Okay, enough," she said, pulling back. "Public displays are crass."

We both knew that was not necessarily her opinion—particularly after a couple of drinks.

"How about private displays?" I said.

"Much better."

"Then we'll have one. Later."

She laughed again, warmly, her breath on my neck as one of my colleagues approached.

"Sponge!" he said.

At the embassy, I had been given the nickname because of my affinity for soaking up languages. Carlo Marino rarely called me anything else.

"Hey, Carlo," I said.

He stopped at our table. He had a nice girl on his arm, but I would not have traded mine for his.

"Spongie, boy," he said, "you are the most goddamned . . ." He laughed so hard he snorted. He was more than a little drunk. "Oh, that beautiful little trick you pulled off yesterday with those bastards and their so-called unbreakable . . ."

"You mean those blocks that came in around noon?" I said, cutting him off. Carlo was one of those that, once he got a measure of alcohol in him, you had to watch. "Yeah, that was interesting."

My wife had experienced Carlo before. She had looked away from him as he neared the table and was ignoring our exchange. And Carlo's date, as drunk as he, was plainly not on board mentally.

"Oh, man, I'll tell you, those boys in Tel Aviv," he said, "they were impressed."

"Carlo," I whispered, taking him by his coat lapel to bring him closer. "Loose lips."

Glazed over, he nevertheless understood.

He grinned and bobbed his head. "Sponge, you are the model for us all. You are the best of us."

Carlo and his girl continued on across the room. My wife had heard his parting words.

"See, Leonard, you are the best. Even he says it."

One strives to be humble, but it was true: I was, in fact, the best at what I did. I had known it for some time. And everyone agreed. Young as I was, I had become, already, a legend. A veritable rock star in the intelligence community.

And the truth was, I liked my job. My wife only thought I didn't because I spoke so little about it, and when I said anything, made the work sound altogether boring. I could have safely told her more than I had, however. I would not have violated any rules by giving her a very general but more genuine description of my responsibilities. Then she would have understood things much better. But as I have intimated, I did not really want her to understand. The codes and ciphers that crossed my desk, as well as the foreign data bases into which I regularly hacked, frequently held the plans for all manner of assassinations, terrorist plots, malevolent foreign alliances, genocide, and even nuclear conflict. And it was my job—and that of my co-workers—to discover those plans before they came to fruition. I do believe it would have been unsettling for my wife to go to bed at night had she been aware that all that stood between such villainy and the end of life as we knew it were the cryptologic skills of the man lying beside her. I did not want her to have to live with such thoughts in her head. I loved her too much.

We had another drink and some hors d'oeuvres. As we finished, the club fired up its dance floor, strobe lights flashing. A deafening bass beat starting in sync.

"I have been thinking about . . ." she said, her voice lost in the music.

"What's that?" I asked. I felt her hand creeping up my leg.

"That private display you mentioned that we would have later," she shouted in my ear. "I have been thinking about that."

"And what are you thinking?" I shouted back.

"I am thinking it is *later*."

"Später ist meine Lieblingszeit," I said, putting my arm around her tiny waist.

"Stop showing off," she said. "My German is not so good."

"'Later is my favorite time,'" I translated.

Our eyes met. We both smiled.

I paid the tab and we taxied home. She took a shower. I went to the study. I had been there on my laptop for some time when she came in.

"Hey, I am waiting on you," she said, "What are you doing?"

"Just checking out something that came up at work."

"What?"

"Nothing much. Just this old book that's been posted online that everyone's betting they can decipher."

She looked over my shoulder. "An old book? Do you people really have so little to do?"

"No, we've got plenty going on. This is just for fun. You know, a distraction."

"Oh, so that is what you are looking for," she said. "Leonard?"

"Huh?" I glanced back at her.

She lifted her nightie all the way to her neck. *"Distraction?"*

I wish I could say that I chased her to the bedroom and never looked back. The week before, even the day before, I would have. But not that night. Nor any night after.

"Go on," I said. "I'll be right in."

By the time I closed my laptop, she was fast asleep.

N INA SUGGESTED A CLUB she had been to a few times. It was far across the city, but we took the Metro and were there in half an hour. It was a big place that was known for a laser-light dance floor that flashed ever-changing colors.

There was a cover charge at the door, which, of course, as with the Metro tickets, Nina paid. The guy who took her money gave me a disparaging look. She saw it and gave him one of her own.

"How rude was that?" she said as we went in.

I felt myself afire with embarrassment. "I should have told him that I'm your father and we're celebrating my birthday."

"My *father?*"

I wished I had said nothing.

"Well, as I'm sure you've noticed, there's a bit of an age difference between us."

She looked at me as if I were joking. "What are you talking about?"

"The fact that you're very young and I'm . . . older."

"Leonard, that is nonsense. I am sure we are closer in age than you realize."

The club was filling up, the crowd mostly upscale twenty-somethings. We were lucky to get a small table near the front. Before long, the place was crammed to capacity and, by necessity, Nina and I sat close together. The dance floor had not yet been activated and, rather than music, the sound of voices—talking, shouting, laughing: a full cacophony of human sound—filled the air from every side. An unaccustomed discord to my ears. It had been so long since I had been part of such a scene. I felt like an island castaway, lost for years and returned to a world scarcely remembered. Uncertain how to behave.

A waitress came and we ordered drinks. I asked for water, but Nina wouldn't hear of it, so I went with scotch. She ordered wine.

"Make it a double," she told the waitress, pointing at me.

"You shouldn't spend money on me," I said.

"I said you would owe me. I am keeping track."

"You don't have to. *I'll* keep track."

She laughed. "Leonard, you are funny."

"I'm not trying to be."

"Oh, Leonard." She touched my shoulder in a sociable way. "You do not owe me anything. We will have a few drinks. *Fun*. Remember?"

I sat quietly, the crowd around us growing more and more raucous, awaiting the music. I wanted to speak to her, but just as in the restaurant that morning, could think of nothing to say. Perhaps, I thought, I no longer knew how to talk to a woman. Or worse, the age gap was so considerable that, in our few conversations, we had exhausted the extent of our shared interests.

I mulled over the second possibility, not wanting to believe it. Yet we sat in a silence that went on and on, neither of us uttering a word as she continually looked about the room—most likely, I thought, for persons with whom she had more in common. She had said we would be talking constantly. What had happened to that? No doubt, she had hit the same conversational wall as I had, and like me, had started to feel the discomfort in this situation.

Or had she felt it even before we sat down at this table? That comment she had made: . . . *closer in age than you realize.* Ridiculous. False flattery in the extreme.

You have deceived yourself, Stavros, the Judge admonished. *Filled your mind with the silly romantic notions of an older man for a younger woman.*

I'm only forty-two.

And she is . . . what?

I don't know.

Yes, you do. You said it yourself: Very young.

It was a hard truth. And yet there was another: Her generosity. Taking me into her apartment. Clothing me. Feeding me. Now buying me a night on the town.

Would any woman show such benevolence but to a man in pitiable circumstances?

Stavros, you blind idiot!

What was wrong with me? It was obvious. She *did* know—she *had* to—that I was the same pathetic bum she had fed two days ago.

And I was still her charity case.

At once, it seemed that all of the feelings I had previously had for her were exposed to me for what they had really been—the unrequited affections of a forlorn man for an unattainable beauty. She was not really my girl. She had never intended such a thing. She was merely showing me a nice time. Then she would be gone. But that was as it was meant to be. I didn't deserve her. I didn't deserve anyone. I had lost, long ago, the one I had been truly meant to have. And I belonged now only to the lesser of humankind, to the freezing streets, to lonely days and nights.

"Are you ready to dance?" she said at last.

I looked over at her, her dark eyes alight.

I did not want to dance. I was not going to.

"Nina . . . I don't . . ."

"What?"

"I don't know how to dance."

She laughed me off. "Yes, you do."

"Not very well. And my knee's pretty stiff."

"Look at me," she said, leaning toward me so much I found myself leaning back. "Right here." She pointed to her eyes.

Reluctantly, I went along. She locked onto me with a kind of comical, hypnotic stare, pretending to scan my psyche.

"Ah, yes, I can see him," she said, giggling. "He is in there, all right."

"Who?"

"Your other self. Your party animal. And he wants to come out and play."

I was feeling older and more foolish by the moment. I considered excusing myself to go to the bathroom and just leaving. But then she would have to return home alone, and that would not be safe, nor what she deserved. No, I thought, I couldn't just desert her.

I had done that to someone before.

The waitress brought our drinks. Nina paid the tab and, straightaway, drank her wine in a series of gulps.

"Leonard," she said. "Your scotch."

I took an obligatory swallow.

"No, no. Drink more. Drink fast. It is almost time. And when it starts, we go."

"Go where?"

She laughed once more. Laughed, I thought, at an old man's confusion.

In veritable defiance, I chugged the rest of my drink, and as I finished, a sound like the siren of an approaching fire truck overtook the room. At the same time, the lasers of the dance floor stirred to life, quickly becoming an ever-richening swirl of red, yellow, and blue. And as the clamor and lights intensified, the throng around me rose and shouted as one, and with that shout, from the speakers, came the maniacal cry of a single voice: *"Let's do it!"*

Like an attacking force, the music came in a thunderous, pounding rush. And in the next instant (I was not even conscious of standing up), I found myself on my feet with Nina springing toward me, airborne, requiring me to catch her about the hips as she wrapped her legs around my waist, her arms around my neck. Everywhere, women were doing the same to their nearest male, each man packing his prize to the dance floor as a sultan might a concubine.

"Tradition!" she yelled in my ear as, with no apparent alternative, I carried her into the hail of light, now spinning all colors of the rainbow.

On the floor we were pushed together by the mass of persons on all sides, her front pressed tightly to mine, the look on her face one of frenzied release as she twisted with abandon. It was the same everywhere. In all of those around, there seemed a relentless urgency, an overwhelming need to free something painful and long festering. People jumped and twirled, screamed and whooped. The entire floor seemed to drop and rise with the collective rhythm of the unbridled mob.

And in the midst of it all—amid the din and the flailing bodies and the whirling, dizzying shots of light—I became aware of something I had not thought possible.

I was dancing.

And as the beat of my own dance became one with the wild pulse of the others, I felt my reservations wither. The Judge was rendered mute. And I was left to harness, to the extent I chose, that which was left of me in the absence of his overriding control.

The mind-hammering tempo of one song became the next and the next, each bringing, it seemed, an increase in volume and brilliance of light until reaching a pinnacle of raw sound and luminosity. A mix of perfect chaos. And somewhere within it all, Nina took my hands and put them to her waist, guiding them up and down, from her underarms to her supple hips. She then turned and, with her back to me, found again my hands and pulled me toward her, my arms around her, inviting me to go where I wanted as she writhed and the separation of her hips ground hard against me and I against her, her head swinging side to side, her short dark hair swinging with it. I let it douse my face. Smelling it. Losing myself in it. Holding her as if she were all that would ever matter.

Sweat dripped from every part of us, and in the shifting vortex of colors, I could see, all around, dancers likewise soaked and glistening. Each, in the stuttering of the lasers, revealed in flash after flash, and each, in the interim between each flash, hidden. In the strobe effect, the couple next to us seemed to bounce as if, in unison, riding a pogo stick in slow motion. And in the same flickering I saw a woman nearby swinging her blouse in the air, her large, wet breasts bouncing in her brassier as a man standing on his hands flipped onto his feet to grab her and pull her to the floor—much to her apparent happiness. And winding slowly through the middle of the crowd, snakelike, was a train of revelers bound by hands on hips, singing the words to the song that played.

But it was far across the floor that I saw *him*. A man, like others, dancing without restraint. Yet unlike every other man, with more women than he needed. One hand up the blouse of a woman to his left, another up the blouse of one to his right. Groping them both—to *their* happiness. And a third woman, with an active hand, helping him below his waist while, even as he cavorted in decadent bliss, his eyes searched the room for still another partner.

Of all the gin joints in all the world, I thought.

Goddamn Ed. Having the time of his life.

I took Nina by the shoulders, turning her so she would not see him. I put my lips to the side of her head.

"I need to leave," I said.

She could not hear me. I spoke louder, repeating myself.

She was disappointed. "What is it?"

"There's a man here who wants to kill me."

"*What?*"

"I just saw him."

"Leonard!"

"Just be cool."

"Has he seen you?"

"I don't think so."

"Then we should go. Now."

We hurried from the floor and gathered our coats.

———— ❦ ————

Hand in hand, we ran for the Metro, neither of us speaking on the way. When we reached the station she turned loose of me and looked me in the eyes, panting and shivering.

"Leonard, you are in trouble."

"No, I'm fine. It's just that guy. I need to avoid him."

"Are you some kind of criminal?" She appeared ready for bad news.

"You know I'm not."

"But that man. Why does he want to hurt you?"

"Because I wouldn't let him have his way. It's a long story."

Her dark eyes conveyed a dread of what might result from further questions.

She dropped her head and shook it with a violent confusion, strands of her bob sticking to her cold, sweaty cheeks.

"Leonard, I do not know what to make of all this. This man tonight. And all the trouble you had with the book. There are clearly things you are not telling me." She looked up with a dire, teary expression. "But whatever you may be hiding from me, there is something I cannot hide from you. Not any longer. Something I feel about you. About *us*. And I hope you do not laugh at me."

"I never do."

She let out a breath. "Leonard, I feel . . ." She glanced off nervously. "I feel, somehow, that we have known one another much longer than we have been together. That night you saved me, I told you how familiar you seemed to me."

My stomach turned over. "Nina, we had never met before. I swear."

"Yes, but I still have the *feeling*. And even stronger now than then. It is as if that night I was calling for help, and I realize now that it was you I was calling to. Like I was in some kind of nightmare and I knew only you could make it stop."

At a loss for what to say, I went with something far too flippant. "I thought *you* were the one that lived in *my* dreams."

She stared at me in a way I first took for resentment, but realized that what I saw was merely the reflection of what was, for her, a genuinely alarming notion.

"Or maybe we are having the *same* dream," she said in a kind of epiphany. "Together. We were dreaming that night. And we still are."

Silly, girlish absurdities. The wine, I thought, had gotten to her. And the stress of the moment.

"Nina, how could such a thing ever happen?"

"Because maybe, somewhere, we are desperate beyond reason. Desperate to be together. But something lies between us. And this is the only way."

There was an odd, out-of-place smell in the air. Smoke. Something burning.

I touched her hand and she seemed at once to become very weak. She fell into me, her arms about me. I held her tightly. "Oh, Leonard, I wish we were home."

The train came. There were few riders. We took a seat in the back, away from the rest. As we settled in, a sudden change came over her. She became enlivened and her former concerns seemed to disappear in a wave of careless, youthful excitement.

She slid close to me, laughing in a celebratory way.

"That was so much fun," she said. "Did you have fun?"

I looked at her marvelous lips. They were not moving. Not counting. But even then I thought: *twenty-one.*

Which was the age I was starting to feel.

I took her by the arm, my hand moving up to her shoulder, then the back of her head, grasping her thick hair, crawling through its luscious resistance as I had so long fantasized.

"Yes," I said, "I had fun."

I started to pull her in. The effort was needless. We kissed as the train began moving. And as our speed increased, she threw off her coat and straddled me, each of us breathless and pushing into the other as the train rolled on.

-20-

WHEN I AWOKE, the bedroom was dark save for the light from the screen of her open laptop. She sat at the desk in a long-sleeved nightshirt, with a pencil and notepad. From the drawn window curtains came no sign of daybreak.

She heard me stirring in the bed and turned around.

"Go back to sleep, Leonard."

"Why?"

"Because you have not had much rest."

"Neither have you." I sat up. "What are you doing?"

As best I could, I focused on her screen—full, as it was, of rows of brownish thumbnail portraits. The many pages of an aged book. Images I recognized.

She started to close the laptop.

"Don't," I said. "You did that yesterday. Why do you keep looking at that?"

Seeming remorseful, she let her chin fall against her chest. "Because I want to help you."

"Nina, the one way you can help me is if neither of us ever sees or talks about that thing again. Understand?"

She kept her head down. "Leonard, I am sorry."

"So never again?"

Suddenly—and explosively—her emotions went in reverse. She raised the screen and glared at me. "No, we are going to look at it, and we are going to talk about it."

I dropped back onto the bed. "Nina, I don't know how you think you could possibly . . ."

"Forty-two," she said.

I thought for an instant she was referring to my age—but then, we had never discussed the actual number of years.

"Have you ever counted how many lines there are on each page of the Paisley Codex?" she asked.

I stared at the ceiling. "Nobody cares about that."

"Well, maybe someone *should.* There are two hundred and fifty-two pages in this book, and on two hundred and ten of those pages there are exactly forty-three lines of text. But on the other *forty-two* pages—pages that appear here and there in no regular sequence—there are *forty-two* lines. What do you think about that?"

"Nothing." The number of lines for every page of the Codex was well known, and no one who had earnestly studied the book had ever thought such details to be of significance. "Nina, it's handwritten. It just turned out that way. It's a coincidence."

"Oh, really? Leonard, whoever wrote this book was clearly a master calligrapher. Right? I mean, the characters are all precisely drawn. They are precisely spaced from one another. And the top, left, right and bottom margins are precisely the same on every page. So why, when it came to spacing the *lines* on forty-two pages, was that master calligrapher so *imprecise?* Why did he leave just a *tiny bit* more space between the lines on those pages so they each end up with one less line than all the rest?"

I made no reply.

"There can only be one explanation," she said. "Those forty-two pages were done that way intentionally. Because those pages are somehow special. Do you not agree?"

I closed my eyes.

"Leonard?" She wanted a response.

I gave her none.

"Leonard!"

"You said I needed rest. Leave me alone."

"Well, I am not going to."

"Suit yourself."

I heard a long, aggravated sigh. "Leonard, help me. Help me help *you*."

"I already told you how you can help: Quit doing this." For a time I lay still and said nothing, quietly disturbed as she persisted with her laptop. "Nina, come to bed."

"Not now. I am too distracted."

I raised myself up to see, on her screen, an enlarged image of a page from the Paisley, her finger moving left to right as she counted characters.

Always counting.

"Nina, you're wasting your time."

She ignored me completely. "This whole book is just one letter after another. There have to be words here—encrypted, of course—but there is no way to tell where one stops and the other starts." She drew closer to the screen. "Many of these letters I do not even recognize. Like I am sure that the first letter on this page is a lowercase Latin *u*. But then the second and third letters are Arabic, and I have no idea what they are." She glanced back at me. "So what are they?"

Realizing I was doing exactly that which only minutes ago I had essentially sworn off forever, I crawled across the bed to examine the screen.

"The Arabic characters are *siin* and *kaaf*," I said over her shoulder. "They're roughly equivalent to *s* and *k* in Latin script. But let's go back to that first letter you mentioned. I hate to burst your bubble, but that is not a lowercase Latin *u*. It looks the same, but in fact it's a Greek letter. It's a lowercase *vita*, as it's pronounced in Greek—or as most of the world *mis*pronounces it, *beta*."

She was incredulous. "How is *that*? I know most of the Greek alphabet, Leonard, and *beta* or *vita*, or however you say it, is always written in both upper and lower case more or less like a capital Latin *B*."

"It is *now*. But the Greek letters in this book were written in the fourteenth century, and some of those letters were formed differently then than they are today."

"Yes, but how do you know whether this letter that looks like a lower-case Latin *u* is *not* a Latin *u* instead of what you are saying? I mean, you said yourself they look the same."

"Because in case you haven't noticed, in this book, all of the Latin characters are written in capital letters, as opposed to the Greek characters, which are all written in minuscule—that is, lowercase." I reached out, indicating various spots on the screen. "See? That way you don't get confused between the two alphabets, like you just did."

With a frown, she conceded. "Very well. You are the expert. But you know, I have been thinking: Each one of these letters makes its own sound. So why not put those sounds together to try to make words? I bet if we did, they would say something in *some* language."

"Undoubtedly, they would. But so what?" I was trying not to get worked up again. "Nina, you can find letter combinations all over this book that can be spoken to sound like individual words in various languages. But those combinations are as random as the words that form in a bowl of alphabet soup. They convey nothing intelligible."

"But Leonard . . ."

"*No*," I insisted. "The book cannot be understood phonetically. Many have tried that. *I* have tried that. It's useless."

The room's light shifted as she went to another page, which, given her beginner's grasp of the material, surely appeared no different to her than the one before.

"Okay, maybe that was a bad idea," she said, not the least put off. "But all of this *has* to mean something, and there *has* to be a way to read it. You believe that, Leonard. You will *always* believe it."

I went to one of the windows and parted the curtains. It was indeed still dark. I looked down at the river, its black water glistening in the lights along the promenade and lapping against the absurdly thin strip of walkway that hugged the building two stories below.

"All these letters," she said. "They may seem, as you say, like a bowl of alphabet soup, but we both know that someone put all of them there for a reason." She expelled a short breath, suggesting a secondary thought.

"Except, of course, the nulls. The letters that mean nothing." She looked back at me. "The ones that are just there to fake us out."

I found myself surprisingly impressed. She was, despite her limitations, a good student.

"That's right," I said. "The nulls. But even *they* are there for a reason. Everything in the Paisley is there for a reason."

"You mean even the number of lines per page?"

She gave me a wink.

I awoke again much later, feeling her next to me. I dozed awhile, and when I next came to, heard the shower in the bathroom and saw, from the amount of light in the room, that the day was well under way.

There was the sound of a blow-dryer, after which she entered the bedroom naked.

"Nice," I remarked. I had once known another woman like that, unafraid to show herself.

"No sense hiding it now," she said, going to her wardrobe.

I went into the bathroom and, with the door open, called across the hall. "Do you have any razor blades?"

"And you are asking because you just looked in the mirror and saw the rebirth of Cro-Magnon Man?"

"Something like that." I had not shaved since my evening of revelation at Ed's. "Do you like beards?"

"No," she said categorically.

She stepped into the bath with a handful of bills.

"Here," she said. "Get what you need. Blades. Shaving cream. You know, manly stuff."

"Nina . . ."

"Don't argue. Just get enough to make do for the time being—until, of course, you can get back to your things at the hotel." ("The hotel," it seemed, had become something of an implicit joke.)

"But you're giving me too much."

"I doubt that. How about deodorant? How about cologne? How about anything that makes me want to do this?" She smiled and lightly thrust her bare self into me.

"I'm going to get some money and pay you back."

"Forget it. I will not take it." She returned to the bedroom and began dressing. "I have to get to work, but . . ." With her arms through the straps of her bra, she stopped before hooking it and opened the desk drawer. "Here is a key so you can come and go. And there is a shop down the street where you can get the things you need. Go out the front of the building and head north. From the first intersection you come to, it is two blocks further on, on the northeast corner."

I was in the shower when she left. While I dried myself and dressed, I glanced repeatedly at the clock by the bed—until it hit 10:21.

As I was about to leave, I noticed that she had left the desk drawer partly open. Visible were a number of pens and pencils, some metal paperclips and rubber bands, a handheld calculator, a clear glass paperweight, a hairbrush.

I pulled the drawer out a little further. Near the back lay a Bible with a white cover. Too curious to resist, I picked it up and flipped through its pages. Maybe a dozen of them had been dog-eared, but overall the book did not appear to suffer from overuse. In the front, written neatly in blue ink, was an inscription:

> *On your confirmation—*
> *"By Grace alone*
> *Through Faith alone*
> *On the basis of Scripture alone."*
> *All My Love—*
> *Papa*

As I closed the Bible, I realized that something had been rolling around in the drawer—an object disturbed by the removal of the book.

It was a plastic pharmacy bottle, the kind one gets with a prescription, but there was no identifying label. Inside were half a dozen round, white pills. And against the back of the drawer were two more identical, unlabeled bottles, both full of the same thing. She had quite a supply of something here, but I assured myself there was good reason for it.

As near as possible, I put the Bible and bottles back as I had found them and shut the drawer.

Her laptop lay on the desk, her notepad beneath. I honestly felt a bit guilty for snooping through the drawer, but this was different.

I slipped the pad out from under the laptop. The top sheet was blank, but I knew that trick: In my time at the agency, I had developed a practice of never writing on the first several sheets of a tablet, burying my notes under the unblemished pages to keep them confidential and give the illusion of an empty pad. And just as if she had learned the ploy from me, she had skipped three pages, and then, on the fourth, penciled a concise list:

> *Paisley Codex—3 sheets/6 leaves/12 pages/21 quires*
> *Brute Force Attack/Assumptions/Patterns*
> *Ciphertext/Plaintext*
> *Ciphers—Transposition/Substitution*
> *Frequency Analysis/Nulls*
> *42 lines/42 pages*
> *"The Answer Lies Within"*

My god, I thought, she was genuinely serious about this. And genuinely serious about helping *me*.

Not that it would ever do any good.

But who could not love such a woman?

There was no other writing on the pad. I put it back as it was, with the laptop above it, and left the flat.

The street was blindingly thick with a strange late morning fog. I wondered for an instant if it would burn away and finally bring the sun. But only for an instant. Because, in fact, I did not much care. The fog, the cold, the smell of the damp pavement all stood unnoticed in the presence of the only thoughts my mind could seem to hold.

Thoughts of a woman I had known only four days.

I walked into the mist, unable to see more than fifteen meters ahead. Persons moving toward me emerged from the haze as though materializing from another dimension. Vehicles were heard, but even those with headlights on remained invisible until just before passing by.

At the first intersection north of Nina's building, I crossed the street to the east, then crossed to the north. I had gone almost to the next intersection when a long black car with tinted windows pulled up from behind me and stopped along the curb ahead. The front passenger-side window came down. The driver, a massive, head-shaven man in a dark suit without a tie, leaned toward me and spoke.

"Get in," he said.

I took a step toward the vehicle. "Me?"

"Uh-huh. You. Get in."

"No thanks." I turned to go back in the direction from which I had come, but had taken only a handful of strides when another hulking man in matching attire—a twin image to the one in the car—came out of the fog, blocking my way.

About to retrace my steps in a second retreat, I looked back to see the first man approaching.

"The Judge wants to see you," he said.

I SAT IN THE BACK OF THE CAR with one of the goons ahold of my coat sleeve, the other at the wheel. The two were indeed identical in every respect.

"What's the deal?" I asked.

Neither of them answered. They did not even appear to hear the question.

"So does the Judge have some problem with me?"

They continued nonresponsive, though in view of my circumstances, my inquiry was clearly superfluous.

We stopped in the alley behind the Judge's building and I was escorted in through the service entrance, the large men bookending me, each ahold of an arm and daring me not to keep pace.

We took the elevator to the Judge's floor. The door to his flat was unlocked. One of my chaperons opened it and I was conveyed to the study, where his honor sat in the middle of the room in a Louis XVI side chair, sipping a cup of tea.

He acted perversely happy to see me.

"Good morning, Stavros." He rose from his seat and, with a gesture toward his vacated chair, spoke to the man on my left: "Protos."

Of course, I recognized the Greek—but it seemed more an adjective than a name.

Protos: First.

The giant walked me over and, despite my attempt at compliance, spun me round and shoved me into the chair.

And upon changing my perspective, I saw the room's additional occupant leaning arrogantly against a bookcase in the corner, a toothpick
hanging from his mouth and a length of rope coiled in one hand.

Ed. With his face still a blackened and scabbed-over mess.

"What's *he* doing here?" I was indignant. "He chased me with a gun.
He tried to kill me."

"I am aware of that," the Judge said, placing his cup and saucer on a
shelf alongside a row of aged volumes. "Fortunately for you, he is a poor
shot."

"And will you be as lucky? He'd like to see us *both* dead. Then he can
do whatever he wants."

"He was doing that already, thanks to your ineffective regulation." He
gave Ed an ambiguous look. "But I do believe he is now under restraint.
And he has proven his fealty."

"How? By bringing you the book? Because he really didn't . . ."

"Fuck the book, asshole," Ed chimed in. "I brought him *you*."

I was making no sense of this. *"Me?"*

"Oh, yeah," Ed said. "You've been on the lam, thinkin' you could
dodge us. But I've seen you around with our little girlfriend, and I found
out where you two have been playin' house."

Our girlfriend? I was steaming. "He attacked that girl!" I started to
stand—and was quickly reseated by Protos.

The Judge tendered a regretful nod. "A poor choice on his part. A
very poor choice. But as I have said, he has atoned. The same, however,
cannot be said for you, Stavros." He signaled to the other behemoth,
who had remained standing near the room's entrance. "Teleftaios," came
the summons.

Again, Greek. But the reference was inverse to the other.
Teleftaios: Last.

The apparent second-born stepped forward. Ed tossed him the rope.

"Wait," I said, panicky. "What are you doing? That's not necessary."

"I shall be the judge of that," said the Judge, smirking at his pun.

Protos held me by the arms, forcing my hands behind the chair, and as his brother began winding the rope around my chest and the chair's medallion back, I felt the rising of a cold fear that built with each tightening loop of the cord. Clearly, something very bad was on the verge.

"This hurts." I was unable to keep my voice from shaking as the rope, through my coat, bit into my arms. "You have no right."

The Judge was amused. "No *right?*" He moved directly in front me. "Where do you think you are, California?"

"*California!*" Ed said, joining the levity. "Good one, Judge."

The Judge glanced at Ed, rolling his eyes.

"Come on, stop this," I said. "Why are you doing this?"

"Quit playin' dumb," Ed said.

Behind me, a knot was being tied, and as I felt myself firmly anchored by the tug of brawny hands, a sense of dread overtook me to the point that, without intelligent thought, I blabbered a string of screaming and all but incomprehensible pleas for help—which ended abruptly with a slap to the side of my head and the insertion of a rubber ball into my mouth, courtesy of Protos and Teleftaios, respectively.

There was a high-pitched ripping sound just before a strip of duct tape was drawn across my lips by Protos, securing the gag.

"You whine like a little girl," Ed said, greatly enjoying himself.

The Judge motioned to his beefy minions, and so prompted, they crossed the room, picked up the couch, and carried it to where he stood, setting it behind him.

Our positions separated by only several feet, the Judge sat down, facing me—ready, it seemed, to become very upset.

"Stavros," he said, "there are many respectable people in this building. People who must not be bothered. People who *will not* be bothered. And I would hate to see them bothered. Particularly with the vociferous protestations of one such as you. So may I trust you to speak in a more decorous manner?"

He sought a mere bob of my head.

I gave him nothing.

My eyes darted between the Judge and Ed—the latter grinning like a bloodthirsty medieval peasant come for the thrill of an execution—and then to the twins, standing behind the couch, impassive, awaiting their next command.

God, how I hated all of them.

"Perhaps you do not *wish* to speak," the Judge said. "But if so, you will find it rather difficult to mount a defense of yourself."

A defense, I thought, to what?

"Shall I convict you incommunicado?" the Judge asked.

I looked past him, intending only to avoid his glare, but finding instead the Templar print that concealed his safe: those two frugal knights riding the same horse.

The Judge followed my eyes. "Do you like my picture?" he taunted. "The picture that covers the very place where my book *formerly* reposed?"

Breathing heavily, choking on the ball, I did my best to convey disinterest.

"Ah, the Templars. You know of them. Of course you do." He rose from the couch. "The Templars!" he announced with theatrical flair. "Brave knights of the Crusades. Knights who gathered a vast fortune. The greatest treasure in history. Gold. Jewels. Holy relics beyond comprehension. Yet they hoarded their plunder. Gave nothing to their king, Philip of France, save usurious loans which worked an onerous burden on the Crown." Bending down to me, his voice turned to a veritable whisper: "But they would pay dearly for their avarice. Hundreds were arrested. Scores of them tortured. Dozens burned at the stake. They could not escape justice, Stavros." His glowering face hovered before me. "And neither will you."

I found myself needing more air than my nostrils could provide.

"Would you like less of *this?*" the Judge asked, stroking the tape that covered my mouth.

My obstinacy had been in vain. Time, I thought, for a different approach.

I nodded.

"And will you be a nice boy?"

I gave another nod.

The Judge stepped back.

Ed stepped up.

"Allow me," he said, gleefully snatching the tape from my mouth.

I spit out the rubber ball. *"God dammit!"* Part of my upper lip had gone with the adhesive.

The Judge was apathetic. "That is a shame," he said, dropping back onto the couch. "But you will be civil now, won't you?"

Blood ran into my mouth and down my neck.

"Sure," I said. "Whatever."

"That is appreciated." He took a solemn posture. "And now, Stavros, we will speak on the subject of the book. *My* book." He hit me with a grim stare. "Where is it?"

I thought it a trick question. "What do you mean? You have it."

"I do not."

"Well . . ." I could not imagine where he was going with this and felt myself about to nervously ramble. "All I can tell you is that *I* had it, in *your* briefcase, and *he*," I said, flicking my head toward Ed, "was chasing me down the street with a gun. And just before the clock on the church tower struck noon, I dropped the briefcase in front of this building, and I saw *him*," I gestured to Ed again, "pick up the briefcase and carry it in. But are you saying you didn't get it?"

"The briefcase, I received," the Judge said. "Just as the last bell struck midday."

"What about the book?"

"That is the question you are here to answer."

"But I told you. It was *in* the briefcase. I put it there."

"Is that so? And just what book would that have been?"

"You know damn well what book," I said, belligerent.

He feigned disappointment "Oh, Stavros, you're not going to start with that again, are you?"

"I'm telling you. It was the Paisley."

He let pass a pregnant moment, then, in the spirit of the humorless persecutor he personified, hung his mouth open in a poor and noiseless imitation of a man laughing.

Of course, Ed laughed for real. He was doubled over.

The twins remained silent, expressionless.

"Stavros," the Judge said, "you really are quite delusional."

"I have a witness," I said.

"And that would be?"

As I had the night before upon entering the club with Nina, I had spoken and wished I hadn't. But this was a far worse mistake.

"Who?" he demanded. "A name. Give me a name."

He waited.

I was not about to answer.

"You are a liar, Stavros."

"I am not."

He came closer—closer than before—inspecting me, my face, my eyes. Peering into my very soul. Much as Nina had done in jest. But there was no jesting here.

This inquiry was of deathly consequence.

"Interesting," he said at last, pulling away. He had, it appeared, seen something worthy of note. "But let us not debate trifles. I must know only this: Whatever book you *think* you had, what did you do with it?"

"Okay, I will say this one more time." I spoke slow and emphatic: "I put it in your briefcase. Which I dropped at the entrance to your building. And he," I said, with another head-jerk toward Ed, "took it in."

It was not the desired response.

The Judge stood up, looming over me. Simmering. "Stavros, I assure you, I most certainly did not receive what you claim to have delivered."

"Then that's *his* doing."

"*How?* You admit that the noon bells were ringing when he entered the building with the briefcase. And I heard the last bell ring just as the case arrived at my door. An interval of mere seconds."

I rolled my head about in confusion, my hands and arms numb from their awkward position and the bindings that held me.

And ever so slightly, the room was spinning.

"Well, he must have *done* something," I said. "He must have had a duplicate briefcase waiting in the foyer."

Out-and-out guesswork, to be sure—of which the Judge was wholly contemptuous.

"Do you really believe he is that clever?" He glanced at Ed. "That is not even conceivable."

"Yeah," Ed agreed, "it's not conceivable."

Once more, the Judge rolled his eyes.

Then erupted.

"I will hear no more of this! What happened is beyond all doubt! *He*," his honor boomed, pointing stiffly at Ed, "only gave *me* what *you* gave *him!*"

I was feeling more and more unwell, groggy and sweating profusely, my shirt, beneath my coat, sopping wet.

I found it hard to hold my head up.

"I did not bring you an empty briefcase," I muttered.

"And I did not receive one," the Judge answered.

That caught my attention.

"Then what was in it?"

"A book, of sorts" he said. "But it is a book that makes for a very quick and uninteresting read, given that all of its pages are blank."

I raised my head. I thought perhaps I had misheard. "Blank?"

The Judge ground his teeth. "*Blank*."

I could not even begin to find the logic in this.

"Are you saying you think I erased your book?"

The Judge threw up his hands. "Are you as big an idiot as *he* is?" His eyes darted in Ed's direction. "No! I'm saying I have an entire book of pages that have *never been written on.* Two hundred and fifty-two pages of *spotless* vellum. *Virgin* vellum. *Medieval* vellum, it looks like to me. And hey, I'm the guy who said none of that was lying around." He let go a kind of whacky, edge-of-sanity cackle. "Boy, was I wrong about that!"

The shock of the Judge's outlandish claim had served to restore my flagging state of consciousness. I ran my tongue over the oozing gap in my upper lip, the sting of the wound rousing me further.

"But Judge," I said, "two hundred and fifty-two pages? That's the same as the Paisley."

"Well, I'll be," he replied, sarcastic. "What a coincidence. Yet am I amused? Not in the slightest."

"But are you sure . . ." Thinking better of it, I went full stop.

"Sure of what?"

I shook him off, saying nothing. However, as usual, he was a step ahead.

"I believe you were going to ask," he said, "whether I am sure that, instead of a blank book, I don't really have the Paisley Codex—a question through which you might very well seek to expose me as a liar and a thief, or, at a minimum, prove *me* a lunatic. Was that to be your query?"

"It seemed worth exploring."

His fury ongoing, he went to where the couch had been and, from an end table, picked up a book with a dilapidated leather cover. He brought it over and held it in front of me.

"What does this look like to you?"

The cover was unmistakable. The cracks in the leather just as I knew them.

"It looks like the Paisley Codex," I said.

"Really?" He sat down on the couch and opened the book at random, tilting its interior toward me. "And what is this?"

It was indeed aged vellum—or looked like it. "Two blank pages."

"And this?" he said, turning a leaf.

"Two more blank pages."

He turned another leaf. And another. "Need I continue?"

Ed let out a small laugh. The room, though, was otherwise achingly quiet as, from outside the building, I heard the faint sound of traffic—persons going about their day, altogether ignorant of the desperate confrontation that transpired within these walls.

"Judge," I said, "look, I don't know what's going on here, but I give you my word. The book I left here yesterday is the same book that came out of your safe."

"*The Paisley Codex,*" he said, as if enraged by the name itself.

"Yes."

"Then let's just say it was!" he bellowed. "Or better yet, a Guttenberg Bible! Or the original copy of the Egyptian Book of the Dead! But in any such case, it would nevertheless have been a *written manuscript.* And yet now you tell me that a book covered in ink from start to finish has somehow mysteriously become . . . *this?*" He flipped through the unmarked pages. "This worthless collection of calf hide? How did that happen? *How!*"

I was supposed to answer that? He might as well have asked me to explain the nature of the Universe.

I could only shake my head.

His patience spent, he gave a wave to Protos and Teleftaios. Directed by his eyes alone, they moved to either side of me.

He was in complete control. His power over me had never been greater. And while he had inflicted physical pain—and was poised to inflict more—his supreme method of punishment came, as always, in another form: Intimidation. Accusation. Reprimand.

Derision.

"This book," he said, holding it before me, "is as vacant and pointless as you are. It is the story of your life, Stavros. All blank pages. *Useless* pages. One after the next. Just as you have lived your days."

I looked at him as I had once faced my own father.

A whole year out of school, just hopping from country to country?
That's the idea.
You've got to be kidding me!
I'll learn more languages that way.
You speak six already.
And I want to learn six more.
Why? So you'll have a dozen ways to say 'I can't find a job?'
I have a talent.
Indeed you do, boy—for avoiding reality.

The Judge examined me with a look of revulsion—a mere lead-in to another round of scorn-filled condemnations: "What a waste you are, Stavros. You are nothing and always will be nothing. Forever an empty book."

I mustered my last ounce of defiance. "I'm not going to listen to you anymore."

His minions came closer, eager to correct me, but he raised a hand, halting their advance.

"Oh, but you *will* listen. Just as you have *always* listened." He stood and moved within a foot of me, my eyes unavoidably meeting his. "Now, I will ask you once more, and once more only: *Where is my book?*"

He pierced my very psyche. Bound as I was, I could do nothing against him; I could tell the court no lies.

But then, I had none to tell.

"You have your book," I said.

Expressionless, he pulled away. "So I do." He looked to the twins. "Untie him. Let him go."

"*What?*" Ed was incensed. "I thought you were gonna . . ."

"Shut up before I put *you* in that chair. He has told the truth."

But what *was* the truth? I had told the truth as I knew it. The Judge had recognized that. Yet that accounted for nothing in the way of explanation. A written book—a priceless manuscript—had somehow become *un*written. Just how, I wondered, had that come about?

I had fully expected the Greek twins to dump me unceremoniously in the alley from whence they had dragged me in. But they had, rather courteously, walked me to the front entrance and, without the slightest violence, released me. From there, I had sorely wanted Nina's comfort and had thought of dropping by her work. But I knew that would not be smart, sporting, as I did, the lack of a full upper lip and the otherwise bloodied and disheveled look one tends to present after a mob-type abduction and rough-up.

Avoiding even the proximity to Nina's workplace, I went north and then west until reaching the store she had recommended, where I bought the toiletries I needed, then returned to her apartment. There, I took a look in the bathroom mirror to assess my lip, at which point I concluded that my blood-stained white button-down shirt would simply have to disappear. My coat had a couple of stains as well, but its material was dark and didn't show the discoloring unless one examined it closely. I could get rid of the shirt in the dumpster out back, I thought, and she would never know. I also had an idea for an excuse about the lip.

I pitched the shirt, then quickly shaved and, for the second time in hours, showered. The ordeal with the Judge had drained me. And Nina, the night before, had drained me. I felt, in every respect, all of forty-two years.

And when I lay down on her bed, I thought still of *forty-two*.

Forty-two lines. Forty-two pages.

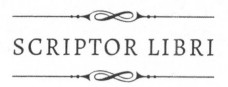

SCRIPTOR LIBRI

Strangers on a Train

THE RINGING OF THE TELEPHONE came like the knock of an unwanted visitor. I pushed myself across the bed and grabbed the receiver.

"Hello?"

I heard a loud, shrill beeping noise. My wake-up call.

I parked the receiver and swung my legs to the floor, standing with a drowsy lack of balance. The room about me smelled as cheap as it was. But from the expense check the company had sent, I had saved quite a bit by staying here, which left more for meals and other necessaries.

I went to the window and parted the curtains. In the sky, the early morning light exposed a thick cover of billowing clouds.

I began to prepare myself for the day.

I waited in the reception area for over half an hour. I was offered coffee, soda, and water, all of which I turned down, too concerned I might spill something or need to go to the bathroom.

Finally, a pretty young woman with short dark hair came out.

"He will see you now," she said.

I was shown to a large office with a striking view of the city. A man behind a big desk rose to meet me.

"Mr. Edwards," I said, shaking his hand.

"Good to see you. Have a seat."

I did so as the woman left, shutting the door behind. Edwards watched her leave.

"She's a nice one, don't you think?" he said.

"Yes, she is," I agreed, much too politely for what he was suggesting.

Even with the door closed, his eyes remained for a time in the direction of her departure.

"So how was your trip?" he asked.

"Uneventful."

"And I assume you found satisfactory accommodations?"

"I did."

"Good. We're glad you're here." He picked up a single-page document from the papers on his desk and ran his eyes over it. "You know, something in your resume here really jumped out at me. Do you actually speak twenty-one languages?"

I smiled proudly. "Twenty-one with fluency. And many others with just a tad less. But I'm always working to improve my repertoire, so to speak."

"Very impressive. You know, as a company that does business worldwide, we are in constant need of people who can interpret not only conversations, but just as importantly, documents. And if you were to work with us, we would need you to function closely with our legal team to translate agreements, memoranda, and the like. A lot can be lost in translation, as they say, and we need people who won't allow that to happen."

"I'm sure that would not be a problem."

He looked at his wristwatch. "Mr. Richter should be along any minute, but he won't be able to stay long. He has a board meeting at nine. Would you like something to drink?"

"No, thank you."

"You're sure?"

"Yes, I'm fine."

"I think I'll have something."

He punched a button on the console of his office phone. There was a single ring. I recognized the young woman's voice: "Yes, sir?"

"I need a bottle of water," he said, "as quick as you can get it here." He punched another button to hang up, showing me a sly, double flash of his eyebrows. "Watch the way her tits bounce when she walks fast."

The girl with the dark hair who had shown me in knocked and, upon invitation, entered, dashing to Edwards's desk with the water. She performed as advertised.

"Anything else, sir?" she asked innocently.

He answered with a devilish grin. "Not just yet."

She left and shut the door.

Edwards was quite inspired. "Man, T and A! What do you think?"

There was no denying, he had a point. But before I could respond, the door again came open and in walked a man who I knew from his picture on the company's website to be Richter, the branch manager.

I stood, smiled, and extended my hand. He gave me a cursory shake. I waited for him to take a chair before returning to mine.

There were no pleasantries.

"Mr. Stavros," he said, "I have reviewed your resume, and it is obvious to me that you are an extremely bright person with unique abilities. In particular, with your aptitude for languages, you have precisely the credentials we are looking for."

"I'm very happy to hear that," I said. "I strongly believe that I can be an asset to . . ."

"But I do have a question," he interrupted. "Your resume lists no work history following your government job, which covers a period of many years. Are we to assume that since you left that job, you have not worked at all?"

I was careful in my reply. "I'm sorry to have given the wrong impression. No, I was working during all of that. Quite intensely, in fact."

"May I ask where?"

"I was self-employed."

"Doing what?"

I wanted to tell an outright lie, but thought there was too great a chance that he already knew the answer.

"I was attempting to decrypt a very old manuscript," I said. "It's written in an extremely complex cipher that no one has ever been able to read."

"Were you under contract with someone regarding this manuscript?"

"No, but had I been successful, the financial reward would have been substantial."

"Hmmm," he uttered, seeming to reflect on the merits of my pursuit. "So I take it that your efforts were ineffective."

"That is unfortunately correct, sir."

"And have you given up on this, shall we say, 'quest?'"

I spoke with conviction: "Yes. I'm through with it. Definitely."

"What a pity," he said. "So much time and nothing gained." He rose. "Well, I apologize for rushing off, but I have other business. I'm sure Edwards would like to chat with you some more, though." He gave Edwards a look. "We shall be in touch."

———◇———

I was waiting for the train when the call came in on my cell phone.

"Hello?"

"Stavros, this is Edwards."

"Yes."

"I want to thank you for interviewing with us today, but I'm sorry, we've decided to go with another candidate."

I was slow to speak. "All right."

"Again, I'm sorry. As I said, your resume is very impressive."

"I suppose the fact that I spent nearly a decade without a real job didn't help." No harm, I thought, in saying it now.

"Mr. Richter did feel that was something of a drawback. But with your qualifications, it really wasn't the deal-breaker."

"What was?"

"I probably shouldn't say this, but it was the way you responded to his last question."

"You mean whether I have given up work on the manuscript?"

"Yes. He was aware your answer was not candid."

"Well . . ." I felt a sudden and fierce resentment toward this man who had so casually judged me. "How could he possibly know?"

There was a pause on the other end. "He knows. He always knows."

It would be a long trip back. And long days lay ahead. I had thrown all of my hopes into this job and had no other prospects. The small amount of money I had left would be gone within a few weeks.

But how could Richter have been so sure I was lying? Who was he to determine such things? Even now, I felt I had told him the truth—or at least been as truthful as I could. Yes, maybe I did want to return to the Paisley, but that did not mean I would. He was not a fair man, this Richter. He had not given me a chance to prove myself.

Through a light rain, the train passed planted fields and grassy meadows, forests and villages, then ascended to the mountains, snowy peaks towering at every turn. My disappointment did not wane, but in time I found my thoughts drifting. And one image kept coming back to me: that girl with the dark hair. She had been stunningly beautiful. And had I gotten that job, we might have seen each other often. We might have even become friends. Or something more. I closed my eyes and thought only of her. What it might be like to hear her say my name. And to touch her on the arm, and then the shoulder. To feel her thick hair and pull her toward me.

I heard a deep voice. "Excuse me, sir."

I realized I had been dozing and opened my eyes to see a tall, older man with neatly-combed white hair standing in the aisle. He wore a black clerical suit and a white tab collar.

"I'm terribly sorry to disturb you, but I was wondering if this spot is taken," he said, gesturing to the seat beside me. "It's the last one in this car."

He spoke in Czech, a Bohemian dialect; I answered in kind.

"No, please sit."

"Thank you."

I surmised that, during my slumber, there had been a stop I had failed to notice. I asked the man his destination and he inquired as to mine.

"Traveling for pleasure, I hope," he said.

"No. Business."

"What is your line of work?"

I frowned.

"That's bad of me," he said. "It's wrong to pry."

"No, it's all right. The truth is, I don't presently have a line of work. I'm between jobs. I was interviewing today."

"I do hope it went well."

"I wish I could say that it did. But I didn't get the position."

He appeared disappointed, almost as if he'd had some stake in the outcome.

"I'm sorry, son," he said. "But I'm sure your time will come."

He crossed his arms, lay back his head, and closed his eyes. There was something, however, that was bothering me.

I had to ask.

"You know," I said haltingly, "I apologize, but . . ."

"What is it, son?" He did not open his eyes.

"It's just that your voice sounds very familiar. Have we met before?"

"You really think we have?"

"Yes, I do."

"Are you of the Lutheran faith?"

"No."

"Then I doubt we have seen one another at Holy Communion." He chuckled, his eyes still closed. "Perhaps we should explore the issue further."

I assumed we would. Nonetheless, he fell silent and sat seemingly asleep as the train crested the mountains and we began a slow descent. We were gathering speed in the lowlands when he spoke again, abruptly turning my way, eyes opening wide.

"Read any good books lately?"

THE THIRD BOOK
OF STAVROS

The Nature of Dreams

Dream delivers us to dream,
and there is no end to illusion.

–Ralph Waldo Emerson

-22-

I WAS ON THE BED, asleep, but awoke as she entered the flat. I looked out from the bedroom.

"Hey," she said, breathing hard from the stairs. She dropped her purse on the breakfast table and spread her coat over the back of a chair. "We are getting a lot of snow."

"Really?" I went to one of the bedroom windows to see, in the evening dark, flakes swirling like insects about the streetlights. The promenade was covered in white.

The clock by the bed read only a quarter till six.

"You're early," I said.

"With the storm coming, it was dead. I could have left even before I did."

And no doubt she would have, I thought, had she not been compelled to wait until twenty-one minutes past the hour.

Entering the bedroom with frozen sparkles in her hair, she took the hairbrush from the desk drawer and went to the mirror in the bathroom, giving her tousled bob several strokes. "So what did you do today besides sleep?"

She laughed at her joke.

"Looked for a job."

She was taken aback. "You *have* a job."

The translation thing. She was a true believer.

"Yeah," I said, "but I think I need to supplement that with something that pays more often."

She came back to the bedroom and left the brush on the desk. "So did you have any luck?"

"Not really. I was wondering if there might be something where you work."

She shrugged. "We could use some help in the kitchen. But that would be so beneath you."

"It would just be temporary." I came toward her, intending to give her a kiss.

"Leonard, your lip!"

I had forgotten. I covered it with my hand.

"What happened?"

"You won't believe it."

"That could be." She was already skeptical.

"Well . . ." I paused for an uneasy giggle, but had my excuse ready. "I got those supplies we talked about this morning, and I slipped in the bathroom while I was shaving. I nearly fell, and as I was catching myself, I did this." I touched the wound.

"With a *safety* razor? Leonard, how is that possible?"

"I'm just incredibly clumsy."

She appeared to accept that. "So you are. And did that happen *before* you went job hunting?"

"Uh-huh."

"You obviously made a great impression."

———◇———

We ate frozen dinners from the microwave. There was no use going out anyway. The snow was shutting down the city.

I should have been ferociously hungry; I had eaten nothing all day. However, the events of the morning had squelched my appetite. And it was not merely the stress of the Judge's interrogation that had affected me, but even more so, the continuing question of how a priceless book could literally erase itself. In what world could that happen?

Yet in the end, even the Judge himself had seemed to agree that it had.

I poked my fork around in my uneaten food.

"Are you okay?" she asked. "You are not talking much."

"I'm sorry."

"Are you bothered by something? Not getting a job?"

"No, not that."

"Then what?"

Clearly, for conversation, the matter of the disappearing manuscript was off limits. There were too many facets to that I dared not get into.

Nevertheless, I needed to advance something.

An alternate topic presented itself.

"I had another interesting dream this afternoon," I said.

"Was I in this one?"

"I think you were. But that wasn't the remarkable thing about it."

She seemed disappointed. "Did I say anything even slightly profound?"

"Not this time—that I remember, anyway."

"Did someone else?"

"I don't know. Maybe."

"Did you see the fire again?"

"I didn't."

"Then why was this dream so interesting?"

"There was a man in it who I thought I knew," I said. "And it was really just his voice. I was sure I'd heard it before."

"Where?"

"In another dream, a few days ago." Then I said another one of those things I wished I hadn't: "He told me he was going to give me the key to the Paisley Codex."

She was about to eat her last bite, but stopped the fork halfway to her mouth. "And when did this man say that was going to happen?"

"Well . . ." I had no choice but to go on. "He said he was going to tell me right then. And I don't remember what he said next, but it hardly makes a difference."

"Why do you think that?"

"Because I don't *know* the key to the Paisley. So how could I dream it?"

Her loaded fork landed loudly in her plate as, exasperated, she slapped a hand to her forehead.

"Leonard, what is *wrong* with you? Did you not listen to me in the restaurant yesterday? Do you not understand? You may very well *know* the key. You may have already *read* the Paisley Codex. It could all be right there in your subconscious. And if it is, then this man has appeared in your dreams to try to help your conscious self extract it."

"Whoa," I joked. "You mean somebody *else* found their way into my head?"

Another thing I wished I hadn't said.

She bristled. "I never claimed I was really in your dream, Leonard."

"You also never really denied it," I said, making things worse. "And last night you proposed we were dreaming *together*."

"Which I am sure you thought was even *more* whacky."

"I'm not saying that."

"You do not *have* to." She clenched her teeth.

Clearly, it was time to get off this subject.

"Okay, I'm sure this voice is just something I dreamed up. Basically just me talking to myself. And through the voice, I told myself that I was going to give myself the key. But so what? There is absolutely nothing in any of that to suggest that I actually *have* the key."

She looked ready to throw something. "Are you *shitting* me? You. Do. Not. Listen!" she said, with each word banging on open hand on the table. "'The answer lies within.' You *do* have the key. It is *within* you."

Where before she had spoken to possibilities, she now sounded utterly sure of herself.

And, of course, livid.

"Nina, you're just speculating."

"And you are hopeless!"

She abruptly stood and plucked her fork and plate from the table. Like a penitent child, I followed her to the kitchen sink.

"Nina, come on. I'm sorry. I'm not totally dismissing your theory. But if I know the key, then why don't I *believe* that I know it? And why can't I remember it?"

She put her fork and plate in the sink and faced me as though I had asked a dumb question.

"Because you do not want to remember."

"Why the hell not?"

She turned on the tap. "You punish yourself, Leonard. You punish yourself."

I awoke in the night to find myself in bed alone. She had all but refused to speak to me after our disagreement and had gone to bed angry. I thought perhaps she had eventually become so disgusted by having me in her immediate proximity that she had moved to the couch.

A faint illumination shone through the bedroom curtains—the lights along the river reflecting themselves in the massing snow. The gleam effect made the room just bright enough that I could see the open bedroom door. I got out of bed and shuffled into the hall across from the bath. It was darker there, and the remainder of the apartment lay in near obscurity. I turned toward the couch, expecting—and hoping—to hear her sedate breathing, but did not.

My heart sank. Had she left?

Just then, I heard a sigh and the sound of a shifting human form.

"Leonard?" she said softly.

"Yes?"

"I am over here."

My eyes were adjusting. I could see the outline of her head and shoulders above the far side of the breakfast table.

"What are you doing?" I said.

"You are not the only one who has dreams."

I located the chair across from her and sat down. The wooden seat was as cold as the air around. I shivered in my boxers.

"Did you have a nightmare?"

"I guess you could call it that."

"About what?"

"About us."

"That was a nightmare?"

"No. The nightmare began when I realized that something was going to happen to us. Something very bad. And there was nothing I could do. Only you could stop it."

"How?"

She didn't answer. I heard her sniffle and take several sharp breaths. She was crying.

"It's cold out here," I said. "Come back to bed."

"I will." Very soon, she calmed herself. From her silhouette, she appeared to be wiping her eyes. "Leonard, that dream you have when you see the fire. What do you think that is about?"

"I don't know."

"But what *is* the fire? And why is it there? Does it threaten you?"

"I suppose it does, in my dream anyway. Why?"

"Because in my dream, I spoke to you about it. I spoke to you just as I am speaking now, at this table, with the darkness between us. And I spoke almost as if I were another person entirely. I knew things about you, and us, and the book, and the fire. Things I cannot remember now. And I told you that I was here to bring you a message. A very grave message—that you must *cross* the fire. That you must go through it. That doing so was your only hope. And mine."

Feeling then a cold beyond that of the room, it struck me:

Only minutes before, I had awakened from the same dream.

23

*T*HE STORM HAD SUBSIDED. Daylight had come. But the city remained at a standstill. Over a foot of snow had fallen and it would be some time before humanity would again hold sway over the elements.

She sat at the desk in the bedroom with her laptop and notepad.

"I just learned something very interesting," she said as I awoke. "Several things, actually."

"What?"

I sat up and, at once, felt my pulse rise; she was looking at the damn book again.

"For one," she said, "remember when you told me about how the Paisley Codex was made? About how there were these things called *quires*, and how each quire was made with three sheets of vellum, which became six leaves and twelve pages? Remember that?"

I sighed heavily. "Yes."

"Well, there is something about those numbers—*three, six,* and *twelve*—that is quite noteworthy."

"Sure. They add up to *twenty-one*," I said. "Your favorite."

"Yes, that is obvious. And as you know, that also happens to be the number of quires in the book—which is also very interesting. But that is not what I am getting at."

I rolled out of bed and made for the kitchen. "Do we have any eggs?"

She went right on.

"Leonard," I heard from the bedroom, "tell me something: The word *quire*. What is its origin?"

I opened the refrigerator. There were no eggs. Nor much of anything else.

"The word is from Middle English," she said, answering herself, "but is derived from the Latin *quaterni*. Which means a collection of four."

This was getting worse; she had done research.

I shut the refrigerator and flopped onto the couch as she appeared from the bedroom.

"Four!" she repeated, holding up an identical number of fingers. "And in medieval times, a gathering of vellum sheets in a book was called a quire because they typically used *how many* of those of sheets?"

I looked away.

My answer was a mere concession: "Four."

"Uh-huh," she said, cocky, "which would make *eight* leaves and *sixteen* pages. But somebody did not like those numbers. Somebody liked *three*, *six*, and *twelve*."

I did not want to continue this, but my arrogance could not help itself.

"Yeah," I said, "and in the same way that four sheets will always make eight leaves and sixteen pages, using three sheets will always result in six leaves and twelve pages. The numbers simply become a foregone conclusion depending on how many sheets are used per quire."

"But the number of sheets, leaves, and pages per quire in the Paisley Codex deviates from the norm, and there is clearly a reason for that."

"Such as?"

"Perhaps it is a clue. Something that is there to be noticed if you just look for it. Like the forty-two pages with forty-two lines. Perhaps we are being told that these numbers are part of the key."

"And perhaps we're not."

"Well . . . perhaps."

"So what about *twenty-one?*" I said, leading her on. "That could be part of the key too."

"And I think it is. If the other numbers refer to the key, then so does *twenty-one*. But its significance is independent of the others."

"How so? Nina, it's the sum of . . ."

"You mentioned that already."

"But how can you possibly say it's somehow separate from . . ."

"Because *twenty-one* does not follow the geometric progression—or as you might also call it, the *pattern*. The sequence starts at *three*, which is doubled to yield *six*. And *six* is doubled to yield *twelve*. So, logically, *twelve* would be doubled to yield *twenty-four*—that is, twenty-four quires. But that did not happen. Rather, despite the fact that *three*, *six*, and *twelve* add up to *twenty-one*, the use of twenty-one quires breaks the progression. Therefore, we must make the *assumption* that the number *twenty-one* has been employed for a reason unrelated to the other numbers—although there is a nice symmetry about it since *twenty-one* does first suggest itself as the total of the sheets, leaves, and pages in each quire, and then appears a second time as the total number of quires in the book."

She broke into a grin, supremely sure of herself. But where she felt elation, I felt the very opposite. I had been on her side—on that rollercoaster of conjecture—so many times. And I was not about to take another ride.

I had had my fill.

"Nina, I hate to break it to you, but all of that is bullshit."

I barely had the words out before her look of satisfaction became a show of anger to match what I had seen the evening before.

"You are just saying that because you want me to give up."

"Yes, and you *should*. Nina, please listen. You have no training or experience in what you're trying to do. And you may think these numbers you've picked out have some special meaning, but no one on the planet agrees with you. Yeah, it's true, centuries ago, quires were *usually* constructed with four sheets of vellum. But some had five. Or six. And some had *three*. So these numbers in the Paisley that you attach such importance to mean nothing. No more than any other book of that period. And even if they are somehow important, the manner in which they should be used to unlock the cipher is undoubtedly more complex than an amateur such as you can possibly imagine."

Offended, she spoke as if to mock me: "Oh, you think so?"

"Yes, I do." I rose from the couch. "I'm sorry to insult you, but I cannot stand to see you go on like this. It is futile! You don't have even the slightest idea what you are up against. The greatest cryptanalysts in the world have tried every conceivable approach to solving this manuscript, and they have all given up."

"Which is precisely why none of the greatest cryptanalysts in the world have ever *read* this manuscript," she said—then looked at me curiously. "Or have they?" The width of the room between us, she directed an index finger between my eyes. "Well, maybe just one."

My god. Her crazy hypothesis.

She returned to the bedroom and I sat back down on the couch. I was tired. I had awakened only minutes ago and was already tired. She had worn me out with her stubbornness. Then too, I had slept poorly. The previous day's double dose of inexplicable enigmas—first the vanishing book, and after that our respective dreams (or had there been only one?)—had roiled in my head through the night.

The apartment was no warmer than it had been hours before. I went to the bedroom, put on pants and a shirt and, for want of anything else to do, sat on the bed behind her. She had resumed her work at the desk. She ignored me, quietly paging through the manuscript. Then abruptly, she stopped and stared at the screen, deep in thought before suddenly returning to the first page of the book, where she began counting under her breath and, as she did, alternating between tapping her finger on the screen and writing on her notepad.

I had to ask. "What are you doing?"

"Making . . . an . . . assumption," she said, tapping and counting between each word. "Looking . . . for . . . a pattern."

Whatever she had in mind, she was as deadly serious as I had ever seen her.

I was despondent.

"Nina, for the last time, I'm begging you. Quit this. There are so many other things we could be doing. *Together*. You can't imagine how pointless this is. Trust me. I *know*. It's just an old book. It's not worth it."

"It might be," she said, "if you would do your part." She held her finger in place on the screen and looked back at me, disappointed. "I thought you would."

"I never told you that. I never said anything like that."

She turned back to the screen and spoke to me over her shoulder. "Go play in the snow, Leonard."

Her instruction was, at first, not altogether clear.

"I mean it. Get out of here."

24

*I*N A SIMILAR WAY, my wife had tried to help me. Early one morning, not long after I had more or less abandoned my job (and not long before my job abandoned me) she had entered the study as I sat on the couch in jeans and a t-shirt, running through the Paisley on my laptop, my flash drive hanging from the USB port.

"Did you call in sick?" she asked.

My eyes were locked on the screen. "Yes."

"Leonard, you cannot keep doing that. They will not stand for it."

"I *can't* keep doing it, and they *won't* stand for it," I said, correcting her. "Are you ever going to start speaking real English?"

"I will if you go to work today."

"Not today."

"Then tomorrow."

"We'll see."

"But Leonard, you are hardly ever there. They are going to get suspicious—if they are not already."

"I doubt that. And frankly, there's been so little going on down there, they don't even need me." There was a nice big lie. "Anyway, I think I'm close to beating this thing."

"I hope. Because we both know that you cannot keep this up for much longer. And if you lose your job, we are going to have a very hard time."

I looked up from the screen. "That's ridiculous. After I've cracked this book, I'll do a speaking tour. I'll write my *own* book. We'll have everything we need."

She came over and sat beside me.

"We have everything we need *now*." She spread her hands broadly in a gesture that was clearly meant to reference more than just the room in which we sat. We indeed had a lovely place: an upscale two-bedroom suite with a large living room, a dining area, a full kitchen, two baths, and, of course, this spacious study with shelves of books from its ceiling to its finely polished hardwood floor. "And by the way, I know that you *are* needed at the embassy. Very badly. I have found out what you really do there."

"You have?"

"Yes. The hacking. The codebreaking."

"Who told you?"

"The spouses, the significant others, they all talk. They told me everything—or as much as they know. Leonard, one of them said that if the world of cryptology were Goddamn City, you would be Batman."

"They meant Gotham City."

She winced with embarrassment. "Well, whatever. I did not think that sounded right. But I do know what it means. It means you are one of the most important people they have. Maybe one of the most important people in the world. Surely you know that."

I nodded matter-of-factly.

"I wish you had told me," she said.

"If I had, would you love me more?"

"No. Leonard, my love for you is complete. It always has been. I am just disappointed that you were not honest with me. But even with that, knowing this makes me so very proud of you."

She waited for me to say something.

I looked down at my laptop.

"I used to think you did not like what you did there, at the embassy," she said. "But do you? Do you like it?"

"Yes."

"Then why are you doing *this* instead of *that*?"

"I don't know. I suppose because right now my mind won't allow me to do anything else."

"Then we must find a way to break you free from this . . . this *thing*," she said, thrusting a finger at my screen.

"This won't be over until I've read the book."

"Then you *will* read it," she said. "And I will do whatever I can to help you. And I *can* help. I am not an idiot, Leonard."

She was a doctoral candidate.

I shook my head. "Look, I appreciate the offer. Really. But I'm not sure what you could do or where you would even start. You have no training in linguistics."

"Why is that necessary?"

"Because the book is written in three different alphabets—Greek, Latin, and Arabic—so the language component is obviously complex."

"But if it is some kind of code . . . "

"It's *not* a code. It's a cipher."

"All right, *cipher*," she said, annoyed by the distinction. "And if it is a cipher, then there must be a mathematical aspect to it. And I just happen to be a mathematician."

"And so do I—among other things."

"Yes, but why cannot . . . I mean *can't*. Why *can't* we work together?"

She awaited my approval.

"I'll think about it," I said.

She sat anxiously for another moment, then got up and went to the master bedroom. I heard a drawer open and the shake of pills in a bottle. She had been taking a lot more of those recently. But her father was ill, and with the trouble I was causing, who was I to criticize?

She returned to the study.

"I have to go to class," she said. "But when I get back, I will start on this. I will devote myself to it. I will help you. I *promise*. But you have to promise me something."

"What?"

"That you will go back to the embassy no later than tomorrow."

"No."

"Then the day after."

I did not answer.

She looked unwell. "Leonard, please do not do this."

But I did. I did it because I was stubborn. And selfish. And wholly obsessed. And so smugly fixed in my belief of self-invincibility that I could not even contemplate the possibility of failure.

And soon, my job was gone. And with it, our swank apartment. We moved to a tiny one-bedroom flat along the river where I did nothing every day and all night but the one thing I should not have. And though I had refused her wishes, she nevertheless immersed herself in the role of my assistant, doing everything within her power to enable my efforts. She studied the manuscript. She offered thoughts and suggestions. She refined my raw and often misdirected notions. But there came, of course, a time when she at last believed the Paisley to be impenetrable—a lost cause—and for her own sanity, put it aside.

Certainly, though, I did no such thing. I kept on, the same as before. I kept on for days and weeks even as she begged me to stop. Then as she simply tolerated me. And then as she withdrew from me and I saw her only as she left at the start of each day and returned at its end. We barely spoke. Eventually, money became short and she had to give up her doctoral pursuit. She took menial jobs to support us. Yet even then she did not throw me out nor so much as hint that we should separate. Rather, one day, I simply wandered away. I was too ashamed to even say goodbye.

Some time later, word got around that her father had died. He was a well-known and greatly respected man and I had loved him like my own father. (More, actually.) In my disgrace, I watched the graveside service from afar, no one knowing I was there. And for many nights after, very late, I found myself across the street from the building in which we had made our final home, stopping there as I imagined her asleep in our bed. Wanting to run my hands through her thick hair. To kiss and hold her one last time. And knowing she was lost to me.

-25-

*I*THOUGHT IT WAS PROBABLY SMART to stay away as long as I
could. I decided to trek to the small store she had directed me to the
day before. I was still carrying change in my pocket from the toiletries
I had purchased there, and thought that if the place was open, I might
surprise her with something for breakfast. Maybe that would put me
back in her good graces.

The sidewalk in front of Nina's building had been largely cleared of
snow. On down the street, however, the walks were either half shoveled
or not at all, and with virtually no traffic, the intersection crossings
remained piled high, all of which made traveling on foot something of a
challenge. Happily, though, while businesses along the way were mostly
closed, I found the store open.

I bought a Danish and two coffees and had enough left over for a
dozen eggs. The clerk put the coffees in a paper carrier and put everything
in a plastic sack. Other than the two of us, the store was vacant. I hung
around for a while, talking with him about the weather, letting time pass.
When I left I thought about taking a longer way back, but, under the
conditions, knew the going might be uncertain. And it was damn cold.

I went back the way I had come. And quickly.

As I approached Nina's building, I saw a man loitering near the entrance in a gray hoodie, his head covered. I had crossed the street and was
perhaps thirty meters away when I recognized him: It was Ed.

I slowed my pace, then stopped, leaving plenty of space between us.

"What the hell are you doing here?" I said.

"The Judge wants to talk to you."

"You know, I've heard that one before. I think I'll pass."

"It's not that easy."

I gathered resolve. "We'll see."

"I mean it, Stavros."

"So do I. I'm done with him. And you."

"No, you're not. You know that. We're all in this together."

"Oh, bullshit. You're in this for yourself. You always have been." I glanced around. "And just how stupid are you, coming here? She might see us."

"You mean our girlfriend?"

"*My* girlfriend," I said. "As you'll recall, your approach wasn't particularly to her liking."

"Well, maybe I'll try again."

"If you do, *I'll* kill *you*. Now get out of my way."

"No. Sorry."

I held my hands up to my sides, the plastic sack in my right. "What? Are you going to try to shoot me like before? In broad daylight?"

"Not unless you push it," he said. "You fucked up my face. I fucked up yours. That's good enough. For now."

"Fine. Then leave me alone."

He looked off and let out a deep, foggy breath. "I can't. Like I say, the Judge . . ."

"Screw the Judge!"

Suddenly more frustrated than afraid, I started toward him, pressuring him to yield.

He did, wilting as I passed.

"Stavros, come on. He says it's important. He says there's some weird stuff goin' on."

I stopped and looked back, feeling bigger than before. "Meaning what?"

"He'll tell you himself. He understands it. I don't. Look, he's not gonna to mess with you. He gives his word."

"No, *you* do. And I don't trust a bit of it. Now, if you don't mind—and even if you do—I've got someplace I'd rather be."

He held up a hand to implore that I remain. Against my better judgment, I indulged him.

He pulled out a cell phone. As he dialed a number, I became more and more nervous, afraid that somehow Nina, only a flight above, would discover us.

"It's me," he said to his receiving party. "He's right here."

He handed me the phone.

"Hello?"

"Stavros?" It was the Judge.

"Yeah?"

"I must talk to you at once. It is of the utmost importance. Come to my flat."

"Are your boys going to tie me up and slap me around?"

"No, there will be none of that. That is behind us. I have something I must tell you. It is extremely urgent. It involves all of us. Will you come?"

"I don't know," I said, insolent. "Probably not."

I tossed Ed the phone and went inside.

I came in to find her at the breakfast table, her laptop still open to the Paisley. She was now working from two notepads.

"Any progress?" I said.

"I did not think you cared."

A surly response. In my time away, nothing had changed.

"I picked up a couple of coffees and a Danish," I said, removing them from the sack. "Some eggs too."

"We had coffee." As before, she was alternately looking at the screen and writing on one of the pads. "You could have made those here and saved the money."

"Sorry."

And of course, the coffees were cold. They were also in Styrofoam. I poured them into ceramic cups and put them in the microwave.

I placed a hot cup in front of her.

"No, thanks," she said.

"Would you like some Danish?"

"No."

So much for good intentions.

"Leonard," she said, not looking up.

"Yes?"

"Put the eggs in the refrigerator."

I ate half of the Danish and watched television from the couch while she continued at the table. Even assuming the bar would open, she was scheduled to work the late shift, so it seemed likely she would be glued to her computer and notepads for at least the remainder of the daylight hours. To my surprise, though, in the early afternoon, she shut her screen.

She rubbed her eyes and glanced over at me.

"How could you possibly have done this for nine years?"

I took the question as rhetorical. "You'd better eat something. How about eggs and Danish?"

"All right." She sat for a moment longer before going to the bedroom. "On second thought, no. I will eat later."

I turned down the volume on the television and literally within a minute could hear her breathing heavily, dead asleep on the bed.

I flipped through channels for a while, but found nothing of interest. The same proved to be true with her stock of reading material, of which there was next to nothing: no magazines, and the only book within sight was a text on stochastic processes resting on the bottom shelf of the television stand. I pulled the book out, immediately recognizing the names of the two authors printed on the cover. From years past, I knew them both personally. However, I also knew them each to be about as dry as the Atacama Desert and imagined their book would be no different. Without reading a word, I replaced it under the television.

That left only one thing for me to do.

I turned off the TV and went to the breakfast table, standing over her notes. On one pad, laid out in neat rows and columns, she had covered the top sheet with Latin script, the next sheet with Arabic, and the next with Greek. The Arabic letters were not particularly well formed—more clumsily sketched than written—but since she had no understanding of those characters, such was to be expected. Nevertheless, knowing the Arabic system as I did, I had no trouble recognizing the letters as she had fashioned them.

As for the second pad, this was the one I had discovered the day before. The top three sheets were still blank, and on the fourth page, of course, were the notes she had made from our conversations. But now the several pages that followed, formerly empty, had been filled: The first three displayed, in three columns on each page, an extensive list of six-place numerical groupings, each sequence including the digits comprising the numbers *3*, *6*, *12*, and *21*. Starting with *112236*, she had apparently run through every permutation of those digits. Many of these combinations (more than I bothered to count) had been circled. And on the third page of this exercise, at the bottom of the list in all caps, she had written a lone word: *SYMMETRY*.

I ran my eyes up and down those three pages, the same six integers repeating themselves, each arrangement only slightly varied from the one before. And seeing those numbers so configured, I began to sense something eerily significant about what she had done. I had veritably laughed at her, but could it be that somewhere deep in my past—in those now blurry and all but forgotten years before my final breakdown—I had experimented with these numbers in this very way?

Not likely, I told myself. And yet . . .

I went to the next page, where, on the left side, she had rather haphazardly scribbled most or all of the numerical permutations she had circled on the pages before—but with a twist: After each six-digit series, the same series had been copied in reverse, creating a palindrome. (There it was: Symmetry). On the other side of the page, she had listed, vertically, all of the letters in the medieval Latin, Arabic, and Greek alphabets. Curiously, surrounding each letter column, like swarms of insects, were literally hundreds of dots where she had repetitively pecked her pencil on the paper. (Counting something?)

After that came a sheet of calculations in which the four original numbers—*3, 6, 12, 21*—were, in all ways possible, multiplied among themselves, with each resulting product then being divided by the sum of its individual digits. The quotients yielded by these computations were then, in subsequent pages, subjected to a variety of additional and more complex calculations. But to what intended end, I had no idea.

At any rate, I had to admit that in *all* of this—in everything she had set down here—I had a vague but persistent notion that somewhere during my long insanity I may have well tried something along the same lines. Regardless, though, I had to give her credit: She had (and impressively so) launched her own rather intricate brute force attack, the preliminary results of which, I suspected, were represented by those pages of Latin, Arabic, and Greek characters on the other pad. Of course, it was impossible to think that a person of her rank inexperience could make even the smallest inroad toward solving the Paisley—and if this method had indeed been used by me, then it had already been proven ineffectual. But on the outside chance that she might be onto something new, I could not help myself from wanting to understand it. And that might be possible, I thought, by examining the book itself and attempting to match the letters her method had apparently rendered with the positions of their counterparts in the manuscript. Presumably, then, a pattern would emerge and I could extrapolate the formula by which her letters had been selected.

However, I had no immediate way of doing that. For where I had once known the Codex with perfect recall—able, in my mind, to see every page, every line and letter in its place—since my crack-up, those keen mental pictures had faded, and my memories of the book had become little more than those of a disordered, jig-sawed mix of symbols.

Which, I reminded myself, was a good thing.

Nonetheless, I stared at her closed laptop, knowing very well what I would do if I had her password. But like an addict with no hope of gaining a fix, my abstinence was assured for lack of access.

Then again, I thought, if there was merit in her process, there could be something legible right here, among the characters on this tablet.

And if so, Leonard Stavros might become the first person in seven hundred years to comprehend the incomprehensible.

I looked away from the notepad. I had sworn that I would not do this. Over and over I had promised myself—and many others—that I was finished with this self-destructive project.

But then, I wouldn't actually be looking at the book. Just alphabetic characters written on ordinary paper. Would that really be such a transgression?

And what was there to be afraid of anyway? Surely the Paisley could not harm me, could not mock and laugh at me, from this otherwise common notepad. I would merely be playing a game with letters. Nothing more.

Yes, I thought, I could do this and almost say I hadn't.

And besides, she was neither a cryptanalyst nor a linguist. She needed my help. She *wanted* my help.

I would be doing her a favor.

Hurriedly, I sat down at the table and centered the tablet before me. I was literally giddy with expectation. But sorting through the page of Latin letters, and then the Arabic, I found nothing.

Suffering a bit of a letdown, I went on to the third page, where at the beginning of the first line, in lower case, stood the fourth letter of the Greek alphabet: *delta*—which she had shaped quite nicely. The letters that followed, though (while also well done), produced nothing coherent, and I was about to give up on this endeavor when my eyes, trained by years of examining encrypted text from all angles, ran instinctively from that first-line *delta* down the column of letters that lay immediately below. And there, in the vertical, I found something that seemed, well, let us say, of note:

$$\delta$$
$$\iota$$
$$\kappa$$
$$\alpha$$
$$\sigma$$
$$\tau$$
$$\eta$$
$$\varsigma$$

Dikastís, it said.

Judge.

I wondered at this. What were the odds? Slim, I thought. Indeed, *incredibly* slim that those letters would inadvertently line up that way. Yet wasn't this the very sort of thing I had warned her of? The fallacy of deriving substance from the chance assemblage of a few characters? Well, yes, I thought, it could be. But it might also be something more: A trace of intelligent expression. A message amid the alphabetic mayhem.

Whatever its import, though, it was but a single word, standing alone. The rest of the page—horizontal, vertical, and diagonal—was complete gibberish.

Still, it was *something*. And because of that, I thought perhaps it might be worthwhile to go back and recheck the first two pages. But as I began that process, I felt a lingering unease that left me uncentered on the task at hand. That word: *Judge*. It was all too disturbingly apropos. And did I really want to continue with this anyway? Almost certainly, there was nothing to be gained. This would be a dead end just as every other attempt had been. And it was not healthy for me in the least.

I got up and paced about the small kitchen and living room, then went into the bedroom, to the window nearest the desk. Listening, for a while, to her gentle, measured breathing and looking out at the river. On both sides, ice grew from the shoreline. But traffic continued to pass easily down the open channel between. A barge hauling pipe came from the west, its bow stamped with a set of numbers.

2121.

I felt a chill sweep over me. Even before I saw the tug coming from the east.

With *42* on its wheelhouse.

And near the ice on the river's far side, three ducks came in for a watery landing. They were joined a moment later by exactly six more.

Then one, two, three . . . *twelve* more birds (starlings, I thought) dropped en masse and perched in a line on the tug's port-side railing.

. . . He says there's some weird stuff goin' on.

I looked over at her, still deep in sleep, her tender beauty in perfect repose. Here, I thought, was the only person left for me. The only person in the world. I did not want to leave. And in fact felt, for reasons wholly unknown, that I should not leave.

But I did. I left a note on her desk. *Be back soon*, it said.

That, however, would not be the case.

-26-

I ENTERED THE FOYER of the Judge's building and buzzed his apartment. As I looked into the security camera, I heard the release of the latch on the door to the building's interior. I took the stairs to his floor. His door was open. He stood just inside.

"We're in the study," he said.

He led me there, where I found Ed drinking a beer while sitting backwards on a side chair—indeed, the very chair in which I had been held hostage the day before.

"May I offer you something?" the Judge asked.

I touched a finger to the raw skin on my lip. "What's the best you've got?"

"I have a Chateau Lafite Rothschild, vintage 1996."

"What's that run a bottle?"

"Some fifteen hundred American dollars."

"I'll take it in a plastic cup."

Ed laughed as if it was the funniest thing he had ever heard.

The Judge did not flinch. I sat at one end of the couch as he went to the kitchen. I heard the pop of a cork. Shortly, he returned.

"Here you are," he said, handing me a sixteen-ounce chalice of polystyrene, half filled with red wine.

I guzzled it.

"I'll have another," I said.

Again, no reaction. The Judge went back to the kitchen and returned with the bottle, handing it to me.

"My compliments," he said, reclining on the other end of the couch.

I examined the label. "Man, this really *is* Lafite." I drank straight from the bottle.

The Judge casually crossed his legs. "Stavros, do you like that wine?"

"It's terrific."

"And what if I told you that it isn't really what you think?"

"Somebody sold you fake wine?"

"No," he said. "Not fake wine. Not wine at all. In fact, *nothing* at all."

"I don't understand."

"Allow me to elaborate." He glanced at Ed, but the latter, involved in finishing his beer, did not reciprocate. "Yesterday," he said to me, gesturing to Ed's chair, "you sat there. And you sat most uncomfortably."

"That, I did." I took another hit of Lafite.

"And the issue was the book that you had somewhat hastily dropped off in front of this building the day before—which you swore was the same book that had been taken from my safe—the pages of which were all blank. But upon examining you . . ."

I corrected him: "Viciously interrogating."

"As you say," he conceded. "In any event, near the end of our encounter, I realized something. Or rather, I realized several things. First I came to understand that, strangely, although the book you delivered here had nothing written in it whatsoever, I could not truly remember whether the book from my safe had been any different. In fact, I could not remember anything about the appearance of that book at all."

I took another drag on the bottle. But smallish. A fifty-dollar shot.

"Gosh, Judge," I said. "Dementia?"

"I do not think so. The evidence points elsewhere, which I will explain presently. But as for the book from my safe, not only was I unable to recall either its contents or its general appearance, I also began to understand that I did not even recall *acquiring* the book. Nor did I recall actually putting it in my safe. And I still don't."

Ed let out a belch.

"Clearly," I said, "you've got a bad memory."

"Really?" The Judge cast a wry smile. "Then tell me this: I have heard from your associate here that you and he awoke in a cheap hotel several days ago. Do you recall how you got there?"

"No."

"And where were you the day before?"

I pointed at Ed. "With him."

"What did you do?"

"We got drunk."

"Do you remember doing that?"

"Not specifically."

"How about *generally?*"

"Well . . . no."

"Then how do you know you got drunk?"

"He told me," I said, again indicating Ed.

The Judge turned to him. "And what do *you* remember?"

I sensed the question was something the Judge had rehearsed with Ed before my arrival.

Ed shrugged. "I don't remember anything."

"You don't remember getting drunk?" the Judge said, leading him.

"No."

I looked at Ed, incredulous. "But you said we got drunk. Why did you tell me that?"

"I don't know." He stared at his empty bottle. "I thought we did, but I don't know *why* I thought that."

"And you said we were at that hotel because there were people in from out of town. You owed them money, and they were watching your apartment. Remember?"

"Yeah, I thought they were."

"Were they?"

Ed looked at the Judge, then me. "I guess not."

"So why did you *tell* me that?" I said, raising my voice.

Ed threw up his hands. "Hey, asshole, I don't know!"

The Judge intervened: "I'm afraid he does not fully comprehend this situation. But he did not intend to mislead you, Stavros. His belief about what you did the day before you woke up in the hotel, and why you were at that hotel, is no different from my own belief that I had purchased a valuable book and put it in my safe. I believed I had done those things, but when it came to actually examining the basis for that belief—when I searched for genuine memories of those activities—there was nothing there. So it's very apparent: I have no *memory* of those activities because I never *engaged* in those activities."

And for this I had taken those Greek letters on Nina's tablet as an element of some supernatural summons?

I laughed and had another belt of wine. "Judge, you're crazier than I ever was." I pointed at Ed. "You too."

"No, Stavros," the Judge said. "Hear me out. Please."

Well, what the hell, I thought. I'd come all the way here on a nasty day. I had nothing else to do. Then too, maybe I wasn't concentrating all that well on what he was saying; this Lafite packed a wallop.

I set the bottle on the floor.

"Okay," I said. "I'm all ears."

He leaned toward me. "We must examine this from a logical perspective. And let us start at what I perceive to be the beginning: the hotel. To your knowledge, had you ever been there before?"

"Never."

"And did you have any idea why you were there?"

"No, but *he* told me . . ."

"Let us put that aside for now," the Judge said. "You woke up in this strange hotel. And after that, did anything else happen that seemed out of the ordinary?"

"We came to see you at the café. That didn't seem unusual, I suppose. But then we came here and Ed had the code to get into the building. And a key to your flat. And then he cracked your safe. And all of that seemed, you know . . ."

"Preposterous?"

"Sort of."

"Because idiots such as he," the Judge said, giving Ed a look, "typically possess neither the resources nor the abilities necessary to do as you've described. True?"

I nodded in agreement.

Ed, reluctantly, did the same.

"And are there any other, shall we say, *oddities* that you have noticed?" the Judge asked.

Those Greek letters would probably qualify, I thought. And the numbers on those boats. And the birds in their groups of three, six, and twelve. Yet those events, while seeming to create, as a whole, a series of mystical indicators, could nevertheless each individually be taken as sheer fortuity.

There was, however, one thing that did not lend itself to such an interpretation.

"The book from your safe turned out, at least for a while, to be the Paisley Codex. That was certainly peculiar. But then, according to you, I was hallucinating." I gave him a sneer. "So that didn't really happen. Right?"

He exhaled sharply, suggesting his answer would not be so straight-forward as my question.

"A hallucination? Yes, that was my assumption when you came here three nights ago. But as you may recall, it was not necessarily my conclusion at the close of our meeting yesterday. Today, however, I find myself back on the side of my initial inference, and I shall tell you why."

He adjusted himself on the couch.

"Let us assume," he said, "for the sake of argument, that you are right. Let us assume that the book you saw—the book taken from my safe—*was* the Paisley Codex, and that said book was in fact the very same book you returned to me. If so, we have the following scenario: A priceless manuscript appears ostensibly out of thin air, its posses-sor—myself—completely unaware of its contents. Enter, then, an emp-

ty-headed fool," he said, referencing Ed, "who suddenly and unaccount-
ably obtains the powers of a cat burglar extraordinaire and gains access to that manuscript. The book then falls into the hands of another
man—you—who returns it to its original holder—me, again—only for
all concerned to find that the pages of the book have been magically
wiped as clean as if they had never been touched by a drop of ink. Now,
Stavros, I ask you, in what world might all of that occur?"

As to the book's bizarre modification, I had, of course, already pondered the same question almost verbatim.

"I honestly don't know," I said.

"Then perhaps you can tell me this: Very simply, where are we? What
is this place?"

"What do you mean?"

"This location. This supposedly very old and large city. What is it
called?"

"It's . . ." I stopped to think.

"Excuse me?" he said, highlighting my uncertainty.

"We are . . ." I was just a little drunk, I thought. I would remember.
"We are in . . . well, Europe. Central or Eastern Europe."

"And the *city?*"

I could have named half a dozen. But just possibilities. None for sure.

"You don't know, do you?"

It was true. I had not, until then, even thought about it.

"Well, don't feel bad," he said. "Neither do I. Nor, for that matter,
does anyone else."

"That's ridiculous."

"You think so? Ask anyone on the street where you are and they will
merely laugh. Or ignore you. Or change the subject. And try to find out
by other means. Call information. Look for a phone book. A street sign.
Listen to the radio. Watch television. You will find nothing. And do you
know why? Because we are *not* in Europe. We are not in a city. We are,
effectively, *nowhere.*"

"Judge, we have to be *some*where."

"And in an illusory sense, you are correct. But *only* in that sense. Because this is not the real world, Stavros."

"Then what is it?"

"A state of mind, I would say. One of those elusive and involuntary mental experiences in which the illogical becomes commonplace." He paused, looking between Ed and myself. "Which is to say, a dream. Or just as likely, some similar condition of altered consciousness. A drug-induced delusion. Or a psychosis, perhaps." He smiled knowingly. "And are you not predisposed to just such a disorder?"

The Judge was indeed slipping, I thought. For here I sat, feeling wide awake. A witness to the apparent materiality of the room, its occupants, the city outside.

And yet hadn't I somewhere, not long ago, heard echoes of the very thing his honor was now asserting?

. . . you may never wake up. You'll think you're awake, but you won't be.

Nina, too, had proposed something along these lines.

I picked up the wine bottle—a very solid bottle—and jiggled it, watching, through the dark glass, the liquid slosh inside.

I was supposed to be imagining this?

"This doesn't feel like a dream," I said. "Or anything of the kind."

"And how would you know?"

"I know how a dream feels, Judge. *And* how it feels to be psychotic."

"Do you? Really?"

"Well, *yes*. I've had dreams I remember very well. And as for my insanity, I remember much of that too."

"But as you say, those are *memories*. And is a memory of an experience genuinely the same as the experience itself?" He shook his head rapidly. "Most definitely not. Let us take the case of a dream: A dream, just as real life, is truly experienced only during its occurrence. The dream is *felt* only when we are within the dream itself. And upon awakening, we are left with mere fleeting fragments. Inferior scraps of sensations and images. It is upon the basis of those poor recollections that we form our perception of what it was like to have the dream. Yet when we were within the dream, our perception was undoubtedly different. When we were within the dream, we embraced the dream totally. And it became, in every respect—if but for a short time—our only reality."

I made a scoffing sound. "A short time? Judge, if we're in a dream, it's a dream that has lasted for several *days*."

"So you think," he said. "But in the course of a dream, cannot mere seconds *seem* like days?"

"But . . ." I was fighting this. "Look, Judge, since I woke up in that hotel room, I've *had* dreams. Real dreams. Now how could that happen if *this* is a dream?"

He came close—closer than I had ever seen him—to something approaching actual laughter. A snicker that did not audibly escape his lips.

"Dreams within dreams?" he said. "Dreams like Russian nesting dolls, each wrapped within another? You think that impossible?"

"I think it unlikely."

"Yet *unlikely* occurs, does it not? And it occurs most frequently within this realm of the fantastic in which we now find ourselves."

The Judge was not one to speak without thinking. Not one to put forth unsupported theories. He had considered the evidence. And what he had said, he thoroughly believed.

He had made his ruling.

I was not, however, constrained to accept it. His opinion, right or wrong, held no bearing on the facts—whatever they might be.

Still, he had, as always, made an impeccable case. The *oddities*, as he had called them, were too numerous to dismiss. Yet even so, there was one more—that dream Nina and I had shared just the night before. I had taken it for something unearthly, proof of some bond between us that transcended natural laws. But had I merely shared a dream *with* a dream? A figment of love and beauty borne purely of my own loss and longing?

I refused to believe that. But as with the Judge, my convictions would not alter the truth.

I took a long draw on the bottle, but tasted the wine noticeably less than before.

And then, at once, as if a fog had lifted, the buzz in my head was gone. Gone as if I had not taken a single swallow.

I let the bottle drop to the hardwood floor, spilling its remaining contents. The liquid spreading over the flawlessly varnished wood. An apparent mess in the making.

"Does that concern you?" I asked the Judge.

"Not in the least," he said. "It is nothing. It did not happen."

I stood up, feeling sober but unsteady, like a man awaiting judgment for a capital crime.

"If you're right," I said, "what happens when it ends—this dream, or whatever it is?"

The Judge took a deep breath. He pursed his lips. "I think you know. It disappears, this place. It evaporates. Disintegrates. And its memories—if there are any—will be like the past-life memories of a man reincarnated, lost to his former self and circumstances. All of it gone, save for a smattering of torturing, nebulous recollections that his mind cannot ever quite grasp or make sense of."

"But I like it here!" Ed said, dropping his beer bottle in mimic of my own display. "I want it to go on!"

"Yet it will not," said the Judge. "Our time here runs short. Such is the nature of dreams. And delusions. And reality itself. Such is the nature of everything."

I felt a renewed madness coming on. To think that everything around—buildings, streets, the very clouds in the sky—could be wiped away. And with it, Nina. Lost to me as surely as if I had killed her.

Unless, of course, she had been right that night in the Metro station—that somewhere, somehow, we dreamt together. Dreamt the same dream of one another and all that surrounded us in this transient world.

A beautiful thought—even, as it now was, arising between states of denial and bargaining.

"Dreams can be revisited," I said.

"Perhaps," said the Judge. "Though not by force of will."

"We may have to see about that." I made for the door.

"You don't look well," he observed.

"And why," I said, "should that matter?"

I headed for Nina's flat. The day's light was on the wane and the sky, as always, lay veiled in clouds. Never, since I had awakened in that hotel, had I seen the sun.

If this place had a sun.

Perhaps, I thought, I had failed to dream one.

A man came toward me on the sidewalk, the snow between us trampled to an icy trail. I hailed him to a stop.

"Sorry to bother you," I said, "but could you please tell me where we are? What city?"

He laughed and went on.

Just after, I was about to pass Nina's place of employment. It was open for business. I went in.

"Excuse me," I said to the man behind the bar, "do you have a phone book?"

"No."

I looked down the bar. Three men sat there. The same three I had seen before. Each staring ahead in an apparent stupor.

"Could I ask you all a favor?" I said.

They did not acknowledge me.

"I wonder if you—any of you—could tell me how to get to Vienna?"

They did not acknowledge me.

"Or Budapest?"

They did not acknowledge me.

"Nuremberg?"

More of the same.

One then raised his full shot glass. The other two followed suit. All three drank in sync. Their empty glasses hitting the bar the same way.

And after, all three remained with eyes forward. In perfect silence. Motionless. A sort of catalepsy in trio.

I glanced at the clock above the bar. It was after six. How could that be? Night had fallen. More than two hours had passed since I'd left the Judge's flat.

Yet hadn't I arrived here only moments ago?

I went out to the street. There were few people. I started up the snow-packed cobblestone walk. The clock on the church tower came into view, its long hand a tick away from 6:21.

And in the next instant, I saw her hurrying toward me in her heavy coat. Walking fast, then breaking into a run. She checked her cell phone and ran faster, her dark bobbed hair rising and dipping with each stride. Her smooth white cheeks flushed from the cold.

Her lips moving. Counting every step.

The sight of her left me forgetting everything I feared. Everything I *knew*.

I shouted her name, rushing to meet her.

But as I did, a haze gathered between us, ever thickening. Her form becoming less and less perceptible. Withering to a blur. A distortion. And all around, the shapes and shades of the city ran together like the figures and colors of a wet painting under a fiery heat.

SCRIPTOR LIBRI

Sojourn

I CLIMBED DARK WOODEN STEPS on an old and narrow staircase that wound like a corkscrew. A steep incline. Wobbly rails. The structure creaking and swaying, unbuttressed, it seemed, by any means of support.

Reaching the top, I stood on a small landing, facing a closed door. I knocked.

A friendly voice: "Come in."

I opened the door. The room was windowless but well lit, the walls papered with a flowery yellow pattern that enhanced the sense of illumination. Directly ahead, he sat behind a desk in his black cleric suit, his full head of white hair nearly the same shade as his collar tab.

He smiled as he looked up from the pages of an open book and removed his reading glasses.

"Ah, Mr. Stavros. From the train. So nice to see you."

"Hello, pastor."

"Please sit."

The chair opposite his desk creaked like the staircase, but was surprisingly comfortable.

"How did you manage to find me?" he asked, closing the book.

"I'm not sure. I just sort of ended up here."

"Why do you think that happened?"

"I suppose because I wanted to speak with you about something."

"And what would that be?"

"I don't know. I've forgotten."

It would do no good to say otherwise, I thought. Whether he had actually given me the key or whether he had lied, he would not entertain the subject further. He had made that clear.

Unless, of course, he let something slip—which during a lengthy conversation seemed a possibility.

"In any event, I'm happy you came," he said. "And I trust you have had some luck with your search for work?"

"No, I haven't. No one wants me."

"I'm very sorry."

"Thanks. But I guess it's probably what I deserve."

He looked at me curiously. I lowered my eyes.

"Why do you say that?" he asked. "Have you committed some crime?"

"Not technically."

"But a transgression nonetheless?"

"Yes. Many."

"And could that be the reason you wanted to see me?"

"As I've said, pastor, I don't remember."

He gave me a dubious grin. "Well, perhaps if we discuss other things, you will recall."

There passed an uncomfortable silence during which I felt the inevitable question coming. I decided to head it off:

"Read any good books lately?"

He glanced down thoughtfully at the volume he had been looking at when I entered. "As a matter of fact, I have. A sort of history. It concerns a very interesting man by the name of Ferrante da Rimini. Have you heard of him?"

The name had a familiar ring. "I think I have. But I can't remember how. Italian, I assume?"

"Italian by birth, but a citizen of the world. He was one of the great men of his time—although, sadly, his legend has not survived."

I racked my brain. I was sure I knew of this man, but beyond the name, could recollect nothing.

"What was the nature of his greatness?" I asked.

"Things you would appreciate. For instance, he spoke countless languages. In fact it was said that he could fluently speak every language known to the western world before the time of Columbus."

I leaned forward. "Impressive."

"Indeed. But there is more. This man, Ferrante, also had unsurpassed mathematical talents, not to mention legal, literary, and diplomatic expertise. And with such skills, he was, even from a young age, much sought-after in the courts of Europe. He went from monarch to monarch, providing his services to the highest bidder. He became relatively wealthy. And this will further interest you . . ."

He paused.

I slid to the front of my chair.

"He had unparalleled command of codes and ciphers," he said.

"A cryptologist!"

"Yes. The field of *secret writing*, as it was then known, was in its infancy. But all the better for Ferrante, a genius in any era. Employ him to draft a cipher and its message would be impenetrable. Hire him to decipher what was thought indecipherable and he would reveal the plaintext straightway. Such things were, for him, the play of a man against children. And it seemed there was no intellectual task that was beyond him.

"But," he added, "while Ferrante's abilities left him perfectly suited for the world of Machiavellian politics, in utilizing those abilities he necessarily placed himself among the sort of amoral individuals who occupied that world."

I chuckled at the pastor's phrasing. "He fell in with some bad people."

"He most certainly did. And perhaps the worst of those was King Philip of France—Philip the Fair, as he was laughably known. Ferrante attached himself to Philip for several years in an advisory capacity, during which time Philip did some of the most awful things you could possibly imagine. And it was in the midst of those events that Ferrante made his exit from France and quietly returned to his home country, ending up in the Republic of Pisa just as tensions were reaching a boiling point between King Robert of Naples and the emperor of the Holy Roman Empire, Henry of Luxembourg—who was then also in Pisa with his army and threatening all of central and southern Italy.

"But of course, Ferrante's reputation had preceded him, and upon his arrival he was immediately employed by Emperor Henry as one of his highest counselors. At that same time, the emperor was preparing to march south to face Robert, and though he had made previous efforts to negotiate peace with Naples, he nevertheless directed Ferrante to travel ahead and make a last attempt. And thus began what became known as the Great Dialogue of the Lower Peninsula, which occurred in the year . . . Oh, I can't remember. Let's see, it was the fourth year of Robert's reign . . ."

"1312," I said, literally without thinking. "And the month was June."

"Why, Mr. Stavros, I do believe you are correct! I must say, for someone who professes to know so little about this man, you have amazing recall for the events of his life." He flashed another dubious grin.

"Frankly, I don't know how or where I learned such an obscure fact."

"Well, perhaps you can remember another: There is a woman involved in this story. A woman who was living in Naples at the time Ferrante arrived there. She served as King Robert's chief advisor. Do you know her name?"

I looked about the room. I shrugged my shoulders. "I have no idea."

Clapping his hands a single time, he tilted his head back and laughed softly.

"That is actually the right answer. Because *no one* knows her name. Not her real name. And it is said that no one then knew it either. Likewise, just exactly how she came to Robert's court was also something of a mystery. And where she came from, a mystery as well. Some said she was Greek. Others said she was Turkish, or Persian, or Arabian. But no one knew for sure. And with good reason, because she could speak, fluently, every one of the languages of those cultures. Indeed, it was said that she could speak every known dialect in Europe, Asia, and North Africa."

"Now that *is* impressive," I said excitedly.

"And yet that was only the half of it. As with Ferrante, she possessed consummate skills in the arts and sciences. In fact, in most all things intellectual she was not only Ferrante's equal, but—if it can be believed—his superior. Of course, in the fourteenth century, for a woman to hold such a position in a royal court was unheard of, and her male counterparts were angered to no end. But given her abilities—not to mention that she probably had the highest IQ of any person living at the time—that was a risk Robert of Naples was willing to take.

"But I have left out an important detail," he said. "And it is an element in a story such as this that seems almost obligatory."

Again, from me, a wholly reflexive response: "She was beautiful."

"Precisely, Mr. Stavros. She was beautiful. Dark eyes. Raven hair. Olive skin. A flawless, womanly figure. She was the desire of every man in Naples. But nonetheless, it was not for her appearance, but rather for her cerebral talents that this otherwise nameless woman came to be known in the court of Robert as *La Bella Mente*."

La Bella Mente.

Silently, my lips and tongue moved over the syllables.

"The Beautiful Mind," said the pastor, translating. "It fit her perfectly. In time, though, the sobriquet was shortened to a single word: *Bellamente*. And as I've inferred, in this woman, Ferrante would meet his match. But while one assumes that he may have been initially put off by the prospect of being outdone by her, things between them soon became a sort of good-natured contest. And with that, passions began to grow.

"The negotiations lasted some two weeks. The emperor had sent many emissaries, but Ferrante took the lead on his behalf—as did Bellamente for King Robert. And while the talks were initially somewhat unremarkable, it is said that by the end of the fourth day, Ferrante had started to pick up on certain strange mannerisms on the part of his female adversary. The repeated batting of an eye. The abrupt flinching of her head. The multiple stroking of one hand with a finger of the other. This went on for some time until Ferrante, in his own genius, came to understand that this woman was actually sending him signals! A kind of code meant only for him, which he was meant to unravel and use in turn as a secondary form of communication with her. And naturally, that happened. Oh, the private thoughts that must have been exchanged between them as representatives from both sides and even Robert of Naples himself looked on. All ignorant of what soon became, to Ferrante and Bellamente, only marginally a negotiation between royal rivals, and for the most part, the playful banter of would-be lovers."

"Seems like a relationship destined to fail," I said.

"Maybe. And had Robert or anyone else in the room picked up on any scent of romance between the two, they would have both suffered horribly. But then, one must consider the faculties of the parties involved. These were two people with unique problem-solving abilities. And some time after the negotiations broke down—and with war about to break out across the Italian peninsula—they indeed solved their problem: They absconded from Italy. Together.

"And a most interesting thing," he said, "is that before the day they covertly met and left the country, they had never uttered a spoken word to one another other than in the formal proceedings at King Robert's court. On the other hand, in the weeks that followed the conclusion of the negotiations at court, many official messages had been exchanged between the two, each ostensibly relating to continued discussions between their principals. Yet buried within each message, by way of an ingenious cipher only Ferrante and Bellamente could perceive and understand, were other messages. Esoteric messages that had positively nothing to do with diplomatic relations."

"Love letters," I said.

"That, yes. But also an interchange of information and a planning of the strategy they would use to escape the tyrants by which they were both employed."

"And did they live happily ever after?"

The pastor's face fell to a sad expression as his aged right hand brushed back and forth across the cover of the old book on his desk.

"What do you think?" he said.

"I'm sensing there were difficulties."

He gestured in the affirmative.

"So what happened?" I asked. "They were no doubt privy to all sorts of state secrets. Did the emperor or King Robert—or both of them—hunt them down?"

I laughed a bit nervously at my suggestion. The pastor joined me, but with half a heart.

"No," he said, "they left Italy without incident and made their way west, finding, eventually, a place where they could live in peace. And for some time, they did—and they did so in the relative bliss of persons who each believe that they have found their ideal mate. And it would seem they had. But their immense harmony was not to last. Something came between them."

"Religion?"

He laughed, more expressive than before. "No."

"The plague?"

"No."

"Adultery?"

He frowned, dismissive. "Of course not."

"Then what?"

"A book."

I felt a sudden souring in my stomach. "What kind of book?"

"A book that came to obsess Ferrante. A quite vexing kind of book. The kind of book that is, generally speaking, not meant to be read, if you know what I mean." He smiled in way I thought unseemly. "Do you know of such a book, Mr. Stavros?"

So great a fury went through me, I could not stay seated.

I leapt to my feet. "You know about me."

He nodded slowly. "I do."

"But how? And why have you told me this story? To punish me?"

"On the contrary," he said, "you punish yourself, Mr. Stavros. I merely want to help you."

"Really? By driving me mad with regret?"

I stomped to the door.

He remained seated. "We both know why you came here, Mr. Stavros. We have no secrets between us."

"We have one: the thing you said you would tell me."

"Which I did."

"But why can't you just tell me again?"

"I don't make the rules, Mr. Stavros."

"Then who does?"

"You should know."

"This is pointless."

I jerked the door open and started down the stairs.

He called after me. "Mr. Stavros, please do not leave like this. You will not easily find your way back."

"I'm not coming back."

"Mr. Stavros!"

THE FOURTH BOOK
OF STAVROS

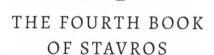

Transposition

*Why, thou hast put him in such a dream
that when the image of it leaves him
he must run mad.*

–William Shakespeare
Twelfth Night

-27-

"MR. STAVROS?"

The voice seemed to come from far away. I tried, but could not answer.

"Mr. Stavros?"

Now it sounded closer. I parted my eyes enough to see a human face with an impossibly bright light all around it, making it hard to discern the person's features. I started to shield my gaze but found my arms fast at my sides, each restrained at the wrist. My legs too were powerless, immobile, held down at the ankles.

I realized I was flat on my back. I struggled to raise my head, but was too weak. At the same time, I felt further restrictions: straps coming from under my arms and passing over the front of my shoulders and behind my neck. There was one across my middle as well, tightly binding my torso.

I struggled to loosen myself.

"Easy, Mr. Stavros," the voice—a man's voice—said.

I shut my eyes and ran my rough, dry tongue around my mouth and lips. "Some water?"

"Maybe. Are you going to be nice?"

"Judge?" I said. The bastard had done it again, I thought. Tied me, this time, to some kind of table.

I again tried opening my eyes, but remained all but sightless from the painful, surrounding glare.

"You'll be nice to us?" the man prodded.

No, I decided, it was not the Judge. But nonetheless a voice I recognized.

"Just some water."

"You'll be nice?"

"Yeah, whatever."

"Let's get him out of this," I heard from the same man, sounding tired and less than sympathetic.

From several directions came the noise of ripping Velcro, and with it, a body-wide release of pressure. My hands and feet came free, then the rest of me.

The man who had spoken took my arm and, with his other hand behind me, helped raise me to a sitting position on what I found to be a hospital gurney. My eyes still hurt from the light of the room, but I was gradually bringing things into focus and could see that the man assisting me wore gray slacks and a dark, long-sleeved polo. Behind him, dressed in white pants and a white shirt, stood a huge man with a shaved head. A small crowd, all wearing navy blue hospital scrubs, stood further back. I too wore scrubs, though of a distinguishing color from the others.

"Mr. Stavros," the man in the polo said, "do you remember me?"

I had begun to. "You're my doctor." I was weak and felt that without his support I would fall back.

"That's right. And it's a shame we had to do this. But you became very upset. And because of that, it was necessary to restrain you. And to medicate you. You gave us no choice. Do you understand?"

"How long was I out?"

"About six hours."

"It felt like six days."

I put a hand to my mouth, running my fingers over my upper lip. Something, I thought, should be wrong there. Something that should sting for lack of skin. But I sensed no such thing. I also had a knee that I thought should be scraped and bruised, but felt uninjured.

As my eyes further adjusted, I saw the room in full: Walls painted butter-yellow. No windows. No furnishings.

An older nurse with hair dyed brown and permed unattractively brought me water in a small plastic cup. I drank it quickly. Ah, like wine, I thought. I could almost taste it—a fine Bordeaux.

Lafite?

"May I have some more?" I asked.

"Yes," the doctor said, dispassionate.

The nurse brought me another. I drank it slower than the first. When I finished, the doctor pulled me toward him, forcing me to swing my legs over the side of the gurney.

"I was upset?" I said. "Why?"

Giving no answer, the doctor motioned to the big man dressed in white—an orderly (I now realized) with whom I was, regrettably, quite familiar. With an unceremonious jerk, the two of them whisked me off the gurney and into a wheelchair.

The doctor turned his back on me.

"Try to get some rest," he said.

The orderly took me down the hall to another room. My room. It had a single bed with a vinyl mattress cover. A small wooden desk with a matching chair. A half bath with a plastic curtain for a door. A narrow window set behind an iron mesh screen. Nothing else.

The orderly hoisted me from the wheelchair and onto the bed, then left with the wheelchair, leaving the door open. He would be watching, though. He always was—as if I were the only patient on the ward.

A short time later, the badly-permed nurse came with a pill, which, in my weakened condition, I took. I usually faked it.

"May I have some paper and a pencil?" I asked.

"I don't know. I'll have to talk to the doctor."

"I need it as soon as possible. I have to write something down before I forget it."

"I'll look into it."

She did not sound eager to help. I could not remember for sure, but I thought she might have been among those recruited to strap me to the gurney some six hours previous. In any event, I did recollect that it had taken a multitude to tie me down. I had been a very bad boy—though still, I could not recall why.

Later, feeling somewhat recovered from my ordeal—and having seen nothing more of the nurse—I went to my doorway and poked my head out. Down the hall, the orderly was seated in a chair against the wall.

"Hey, baldy," I said, "I was supposed to get some writing materials."

"I don't know anything about that."

"Could you check?"

"No. Go back to bed, Stavros."

"It's the middle of the afternoon."

"Like the doc said, get some rest."

"Fine!" I said, exasperated. "I'm going to tell everyone what an asshole you are."

He laughed. "You do that."

I drew back into the room. The Judge was waiting.

"They won't even give me paper and pencil!"

"You don't deserve it," said his honor. "You make the staff here miserable with your constant outbursts, demands, and name-calling. You're the worst patient on the ward."

"Thanks for your support."

"Don't mention it."

I paced the room. "I have to write down those numbers. I can hardly remember them as it is."

"Numbers? What numbers?"

"The numbers that someone . . ." I strained to recall. "A *woman*. With dark hair. She gave me the numbers."

"I do not believe I met her."

"I did," said Ed, from behind me, with a wicked chuckle.

I spun around. "Who let you in?"

"I'm like a bad penny."

"You sure as hell are."

I sat down on the bed, silent for a time. Thinking.

"Stavros," the Judge said. "These numbers. What were they?"

I barely heard him.

I looked up at Ed. "Do you remember her name?"

"I never *knew* her name."

"And I've forgotten it," I said. "I can't really remember her face, either. But she was beautiful. And kind. And very smart. She told me things about the Paisley. Things she had figured out about it. And as I say, it involved numbers. Numbers that could solve the cipher."

"Stavros, *again*," the Judge said, impatient, "what were the numbers?"

"I remember one for sure," I said. *"Twenty-one."*

"Blackjack!" Ed cried.

The Judge cringed. "And what else?"

"Uh . . ." Oh, lord. I'd had others before the nurse left. That bitch. Toying with me. "God, these drugs they give. I can't think." I buried my face in my hands. "I'm forgetting everything. The whole dream—or whatever it was. Except for you two. You were both there. You made my life a living hell."

"Your memory is pathetic," the Judge said. "The worst ever."

"Will you please say something *constructive?*"

The bald orderly appeared at the door, his massive shoulders filling the doorframe. "Hey, Stavros, can you keep it down?"

"We're having a conversation," I said, unapologetic.

He looked around the room. "Seems pretty damn one-sided."

"Just leave us alone."

"As you were," he said, walking off with a crooked smile.

The Judge glowered at the retreating orderly.

"Well, then," he said, "in the interest of productive thought, allow me to throw something out." He motioned towards Ed. "Could it be that in his boundless stupidity, he has stumbled onto something? That is to say, the number you recall, and the card game. Could they in some way be connected?"

I shook my head. "I don't think so."

"Yes, but let us explore further: What wins at Blackjack? An ace and a face card, correct?"

"Or any other combination that adds up to twenty-one."

It is truly amazing how the human mind works; I had not even finished that sentence before I had it.

"*Three* plus *six* plus *twelve*," I said. "*Twenty-one!*"

"The numbers?"

"*Yes! Three! Six! Twelve! Twenty-one!*"

"Stavros!" the orderly called from the hall. "I told you. Keep it down."

"*You* keep it down!" I yelled back. "Don't you see?" I said to the Judge. "*Three, six,* and *twelve* correlate to the number of sheets, leaves, and pages in every quire in the Codex. And the book has twenty-one quires."

"And is that all?" he asked.

"No, there's more. A lot more. I'm sure of it. But this is a start."

Excited, I sat very still for a moment, then darted into the hall, toward the dayroom, the orderly in chase.

"Stavros, stop! Stavros!"

At the entrance to the dayroom, I dodged a staggering old man and a younger woman, evidently comatose, in a wheelchair. I took a hard right around the latter, scuttled past the television area, and landed at the nursing station.

The nurse sitting behind the protective glass had seen me coming. It was of little comfort that she was the same hideously-haired woman who had ditched my request for pencil and paper.

She did not look happy. "What is it?"

The orderly came up behind me.

"I'm sorry," he said to her, out of breath. "He just bolted."

"I need to use one of the computers," I told her. There were two for patient use in a small room within view of the nursing station.

"I'm sorry, Mr. Stavros," she said, it being obvious she was not, "but you don't have computer privileges."

"I did before."

"But then you became upset. The computer upset you. I'm sure you remember."

At once, her reference to the computer triggered a vague recollection: I had, that morning, felt a great distress in the computer room. But the cause?

And then it came to me: It wasn't the computer. Not at all.

It was *them*.

"Now listen," I said angrily. "I know full well what is going on here. The doctor, or you people on staff, or *somebody* has been blocking my access to what I need to look at online."

"Mr. Stavros," the orderly said, placating, "come on, now. Come on. Let's go back to your room."

The nurse stood. "Mr. Stavros, no one has blocked anything. You have simply been unable to find what you are looking for. It has happened repeatedly, and it has repeatedly upset you, and it has gotten worse every time until, this morning, you lost control of yourself. And because of that, you no longer have computer privileges. The doctor has withdrawn them."

"But I can finally solve the Paisley. I have new information. If I can just use the computer."

"Mr. Stavros . . ." She hesitated. "This Paisley thing . . ."

She did not finish. She knew better. But I knew what she wanted to say. The same thing I'd continually heard from all of them.

Liars.

The orderly put a hand on my shoulder. "Come on, Mr. Stavros. Let's take a walk."

"You are all working against me!" I raged. *"Why?* Why do you do this? You know I can solve it. You *know* it."

The nurse pressed a red button on her desk.

I turned away and unleashed a stream of expletives in French. Seconds later, I felt members of the staff closing in. Then the doctor appeared.

He, as the nurse had been, was less than thrilled at my presence.

"Is there a problem, Mr. Stavros?"

I cut loose with another string of obscenities fit for a Parisian cathouse.

"What are you trying to tell me?" he asked.

"I guess you don't understand French," I said.

"Quite the contrary, I know it very well. *Je pense que c'est toi qui ne comprends pas.*"[1]

"Look, I've told you before, I speak twenty-one languages. Fluently."

"Well, perhaps French isn't one of them," he said, flippant. "Now, if you would like to go over and watch television, that would be fine. If you would like to return to your room, that would also be fine. But you will have to move away from this area."

He signaled the orderly with a dip of his head.

"Here we go, Mr. Stavros," the orderly said, leading me away. "What'll it be? Would you like to go back to your room and talk some more with your friends?"

<hr />

It was long after lights out. I lay in bed, waiting for the next time—it was supposedly around the top and bottom of every hour—that a nurse or tech would come by and aim a flashlight at me through the small window in my door. A door, by the way, that could not be opened from the inside (there was no knob), reducing the room's occupant to a mere zoo animal. A thing locked in, meant only to be observed.

But what they hoped to see, honestly, I did not know. I could hardly have killed myself with a desk and chair. And while my bed sheets and the bathroom curtain no doubt presented a method of baneful conduct via strangulation, I had never, to my knowledge, displayed even the slightest suicidal tendency. Maybe those who looked in were just curious whether I was playing with myself. But that was not something I ever did.

Well, at least not on the hour and half hour.

The Judge had not spoken for some time. His voice startled me.

<hr />

1. "I think it is you who does not understand."

"They don't believe you, Stavros."

"About what?" I said.

"About anything."

"Yes, they do. They know the truth."

"You're sure of that?"

"Absolutely. They're all just putting on. It's obvious. Didn't you see how the doctor acted when I spoke French to him?"

"No," the Judge said, "*he* spoke French to *you*."

"Oh, really? If that's true, then why didn't I understand him? *I* speak French."

"Perhaps you don't."

"What do you mean?"

"What you said to him was nonsensical babble."

"The hell it was!"

"I wouldn't get worked up, if I were you," he warned. "Do you want them in here?"

I lay quietly until the light again came to the door and left.

"What they say about the Paisley," I whispered, "it's ridiculous. A fool could see through it."

"So you claim. But then, you're crazy."

"No, I'm not."

"Crazy people always say that."

"As do those who are sane."

"A valid point," he conceded. "Nevertheless, you are clearly crazy."

"How's that?"

"Because you see me and talk to me," he said. "And him."

He referred, of course, to Ed—who, from across the room and scarcely visible in the feeble nightlight from the hallway, smiled and jiggled his fingers at me in the manner of a silly, infantile salutation.

I shut my eyes and rolled over, mentally stretching for those remnants of her that were left to me: A jumble of feminine eyes, lips, and cheeks. Thick dark hair cut in a bob that hugged her face and bounced when she moved. Soft, nubile skin. Delicate curves and projections. All features which, despite my grasp of each one individually, I could not assemble into the whole. The full picture of her lost along with the myriad of sights and sensations from the world that had surrounded her—though, I thought, all still very possibly lodged somewhere within my psyche.

Or then again, had those images left my mind forever? Gone because I did not deserve such pleasures, but had earned, through my transgressions and ill-placed desires, only the solitude of this locked room. In this cold and hopeless house of detention.

I pulled my pillow close to my body, hugging it gently as if holding her petite and flawless form. I recalled we had lain together in just this way. She had whispered my name, warm and impassioned. I had spoken hers in return. The two of us caressing one another beneath the covers, all thoughts beyond our embrace forgotten.

I lay awake for several more tours of the night's watchperson. And when at last I slept, I dreamt of a great, blinding fire.

-28-

*E*ARLY THE NEXT MORNING, I was taken down the hall to the men's washroom for a shower. After breakfast, the doctor came to my room for his daily visit. He sat on the desk chair, I on the bed.

My shadow—the lumbering, head-shaven orderly—loitered outside the door.

"I hope," the doctor said, "that we can find a way to have a discussion without you becoming agitated."

"I'll try."

"That would be appreciated."

The doctor seemed in a somewhat better mood than the day before. Less curt in his manner. Though I had yet, this new day, to cause him any difficulty.

"So," he said, "do you have anything in particular on your mind this morning?"

"Yeah. I want my computer privileges back."

He cleared his throat—a stalling tactic that, even in my short time here, I had come to recognize.

"Mr. Stavros, I think it would be best if you did not use the computer again for a while. You've had a number of unfortunate situations develop related to your searches."

"Well, I'm not looking at porn."

"I understand."

"And I'm not stalking anybody."

"I understand that as well."

"And I wouldn't need to make any searches at *all* if you would just give me back my flash drive!"

"Mr. Stavros . . ." The doctor paused as the orderly peeked in. The doctor waved him off. "As we've discussed in previous sessions, there is no flash drive."

"Well, there *was*," I said. "And I know that because I had it with me when they brought me here. And I know *that* because I had not let it out of my sight for *nine years*. And on that flash drive is a copy of the Paisley Codex, as well as my painstakingly written notes, and *I* know that *you* know *exactly* what I am talking about."

He shook his head, appearing disappointed—but clearly faking it. A vain attempt to continue his pathetic subterfuge.

The bastard.

"Mr. Stavros, I swear to you, this flash drive . . ." He stopped himself, exhaling forcefully in a further show of play-acted emotion. "But more so, this entire matter of the so-called Paisley Codex . . . I will tell you, Mr. Stavros, as I have before, that we have thoroughly checked, and there is no such . . ."

"Another *lie?*" I said. *"Another? Really?"*

"Mr. Stavros . . ."

"No!" I said, staring down his pretended look of innocence. "I don't want to hear it. Now listen, I am a reasonable man. And all I am asking for is a fair chance to study the Paisley without interference from you and the hospital. And perhaps this little scheme you are trying to pull off is understandable. Certainly, I'm here because the Paisley has driven me here. Thus you are reluctant to allow me to view it. And so you take my flash drive and you block my access to the manuscript online. But my only hope to get better, doctor, is to *solve* the Paisley. To *decipher* it. To *read* it. And by preventing me from doing that, you are actually making me worse. And doesn't that violate your oath? That you are doing harm to me?"

Damn right, I thought. Now I had him.

"We must surely talk of all of this in depth," the doctor said. "And I want to do that."

Finally, he was coming around.

"But," he said, "there is one thing I would like to discuss first, if we might."

I threw up my hands and dropped them as if to grudgingly sanction this newly proposed topic.

The doctor again cleared his throat.

"A man came here yesterday morning to visit you. You were, of course, unavailable."

"More like tied up."

"Yes, well . . ." More throat clearing. "This man said he knew you. That you were friends. And that you had worked together."

"Where?"

"At a local tavern."

"A *bar?*"

"That's correct."

This was amusing. "Doing what?"

"I suppose the sort of things employees at a tavern do. Serving drinks. Some short order cooking."

I erupted with laughter. "Oh, that is good! How did you come up with that?"

"I did not *come up* with anything, Mr. Stavros."

"Then *he* did," I said. "Because I have never, in my entire life, worked in a bar. As I've told you, my last job was with . . ."

"The agency." He sounded like a man wearily finishing a sentence he knew too well.

"I am one of the foremost linguists in the world."

"So you have said."

"I speak twenty-one languages. *Fluently.*"

"So you have also said."

God, I was sick of this!

I jumped up and made for the door. Starting out, I met the gaze of the orderly, six feet ahead.

"Everything okay, Mr. Stavros?" he asked, calm, but ready for action.

"Just dandy," I said. I turned back to the doctor. "How can you keep doing this? Is there no end to your deceptions? Your fabrications?"

"I do not deal in such things, Mr. Stavros," he answered coldly. "Only the truth." He held up a slip of paper. "Here is the man's name and phone number. He wants to hear from you and I think it might be good for you to speak with him. Perhaps then you will understand things better. Or at least open your mind to the possibility that certain things are not as you believe."

"Such as the *possibility*," I said, moving toward him, "that I do not speak French?"

In the room's far corner, Ed was laughing, the Judge observing with interest.

The doctor remained seated. I loomed over him, the orderly closing in behind me.

"You're referring to the incident yesterday at the nursing station." The doctor's tone was almost conciliatory. "I apologize for that. I think perhaps I was simply unable to interpret what you were saying."

"My French is excellent."

"And apparently mine is not—although I like to think otherwise. Tell me, when I tried to speak it yesterday, could you understand anything I was saying?"

I did not respond. I went back to the bed and sat.

He persisted. "Mr. Stavros, did you understand me yesterday? *Avez-vous la moindre idée de ce que je dis maintenant?*"[1]

I shook my head. "As you say, your French is not very good."

———⋅◦⋅———

1. "Do you have any idea what I am saying now?"

"You're making a fool of yourself," the Judge said.

"I don't want to hear it."

"Your choice. But if you ever want to see your computer privileges again, you'd better start acting a little less delusional."

The doctor had moved on to his next patient; I sat on the bed staring at the phone number he had given me. And the name written above it: *Carlo Marino.*

I tried to remember: Had he married that blonde? The one I had seen him with that night in the club? I thought he had. Yes, that's right. He had. And she hadn't wanted to take me in, the drunken ditz. I had only asked to stay for a week. Then again, I'd had the reputation of one who would ask for a week and stay for a month. Or more. So in fairness, it was rather hard to criticize her.

Carlo had been far from the most talented at the agency. And I had not seen him in so long. But working in a bar? Impossible. The whole story was. No, this phone number had nothing to do with Carlo Marino, and if I dialed it, I would speak with no such person.

"Still, you might call," the Judge suggested, "just to see who answers, and what they have to say."

That wasn't a bad idea, I thought. There would be nothing lost, and perhaps, by way of investigation, something gained.

I went down the hall and through the dayroom to the nursing station, the bald orderly tailing me ten steps behind. One of the nurses at the station (thankfully, not my perm-haired nemesis) was expecting me and directed me to the courtesy phone on the wall at the far end of the ward's main hall. The orderly stood at the hall's other end, watching me as I dialed the number. The second ring produced an answer.

"Forty Thieves."

"Excuse me?"

"Forty Thieves Bar and Grill. Can I help you?"

I had never heard of the place.

"May I speak to Carlo?"

"This is him."

I was struck by how much this person sounded like the Carlo I had
known. But then, wasn't that a necessary part of the ruse?

"This is Stavros," I said.

"Sponge!" He seemed overjoyed. "Hey, man, I thought it was you!
Great to hear from you. How are you doin', buddy?"

The reference to my old moniker left me fumbling.

"Well . . . I'm . . . fine."

"Good. We're all thinking about you."

"I appreciate that."

"I came around to see you yesterday."

"I know. They told me."

"So when will you be getting out of there?"

"I don't know," I said. "Do you happen to know how long I've been
in here?"

"Seriously?"

"Yeah, I've sort of lost track of time."

That was true.

"Well, let's see. It's Tuesday. And they took you out of here last Friday
afternoon."

"You say they took me out of *here*," I said. "You mean where you
work?"

"Where we both work."

"And how long have I supposedly worked there?"

"Sponge, man, you know, it's been like nine years."

"All that time? Just working in a bar?"

"Yeah. This bar. The Forty Thieves. You don't remember?"

I was wholly incredulous. "That's absurd. Look, if I've been working
at a bar for nine years, what about the Paisley Codex?"

"The what?"

I moved on. "All right, tell me this: Why do you call me Sponge?"

"Because, you know, you're always wiping down the bar. You're obsessed with it."

"Are you shitting me?"

"No, really, Sponge, it's true. You always do that."

I had heard enough.

"Look, I speak twenty-one languages. *Fluently.* I *soak up* languages. I am a *sponge* for languages. That is why I am called Sponge. And I have *never* worked in a bar."

"But . . ."

"You flunked the test."

From down the hall, the orderly noted my distress. He began to advance.

"Oh, man," I heard from the phone—a less than convincing lamentation. "Leonard, what's happened to you?" A long silence. "Look, I'll come see you tomorrow. I'm so sorry about this. And, you know, about everything."

"Sorry about *what?* You said they took me out of the bar on Friday. Why?"

"You mean you don't . . ."

"Why?" I demanded.

"Well, if you don't remember, I'm not gonna . . ."

"Tell me!"

"Sponge, man, your wife, she . . . You know. You *know.* I'm not gonna say it."

"That was years ago," I said.

I was certain of that—although, strangely, I could not quite recall how it had happened.

"Sponge, no. It wasn't. It was just last . . ."

"Oh, yes, it was," I said. *"Years ago.* And I don't care if you're Carlo Marino or who you are. Don't come see me. Ever."

I hung up the phone and went back to the nursing station, baldy in tow.

The Forty Thieves? Did such a place even exist?

I wondered.

From her chair, the nurse I had spoken with before gazed up at me through the heavy glass.

"May I see a phone book?" I asked. "I want to check a number."

She had a funny look. She turned to the other nurse at the desk. "Do we have a phone book?"

The other nurse shook her head. "I don't think so."

"You're kidding," I said. "A hospital without a phone book?"

They shrugged in unison.

"Surely you have one somewhere."

They said nothing else and went on with their work as if I had ceased to exist.

-29-

*T*HIS WEB OF DECEIT had grown to incredible proportions. From the time of my arrival here, I had not only been lied to about the Paisley, but an attempt had been made to refute virtually everything I knew about myself to be true. Yet all done, I had thought, in the name of treatment. They were trying, I had told myself, to break down my psyche. To pull my mind away from the death grip of the Paisley by persuading me to deny its very existence—and to deny, for the same reason, that I was the type of person—the linguist, the cryptanalyst—who could even conceivably undertake such a quest as the decipherment of the mighty Codex.

But pretending to bring in someone with whom I had worked at the agency? Telling me that a man I had known to be a highly trained cryptanalyst was no more than a common barkeep? That had taken the ruse to a new and wholly preposterous level. And I could no longer believe that this monstrous ploy was in any way for my own good. No, something else was afoot. Something diabolical.

And I had to ask myself: Was this even really a psych ward? Or was this hospital setting nothing more than an enormous façade, all created for some ulterior purpose? Clearly, at the very least, my doctor and certain of the staff were not what they purported to be. But perhaps the same was true of some of the supposed patients. Or all of them. Perhaps, among every person here, I was the lone outsider. The sole fish in the tank to be watched and studied.

Yet regardless of the extent of the conspiracy, why such a machina-tion in the first place? And who *were* these people? And what did they want from me? Information of some kind? Something dangerous I had learned at the agency that had become buried within my subconscious? Something they intended to extract by any means necessary?

But I knew I could beat them at this game—now that I had begun to understand the scope of it. I had the wiles to do it. Still, I feared I had taken a misstep by telling the imposter on the phone not to come to the hospital; his mere appearance would have revealed the hoax.

However, it then occurred to me that even if this pretender should present himself, my so-called doctor would nevertheless tell me that, due to my delusional state, I simply did not recognize this person. Either that or (just as likely) this man portraying Carlo, with his obvious inability to pass himself off as my acquaintance, had never been intended to show himself anyway.

"So if you are right about all this," the Judge said, "regardless of how you had responded to his offer to visit, the chances are good that he would never have come here anyway. And even if he were to do so, it would be under circumstances controlled by *them*. With their thuggish orderlies and drugs and bands restraining your every appendage. Circumstances under which they might very well compel you to admit the truth of their lie."

"So you're finally seeing my side of this?"

"Not entirely. But let's just say I'm keeping an open mind."

"That's very nice of you," I said, none too sincere. "But *if* I'm being played by these people—and I know I am—what should I do?"

I had largely put the question to myself, but the Judge—ever the ardent counselor—presumed to answer.

"For one thing, take charge of your situation," he said. "Do not wait for this possibly fictitious Carlo Marino to come to you. Or for this purported doctor to tell you again that this man you believe to have been your colleague at the agency works as a mere plier of alcoholic beverages. In other words, launch your own investigation. Off site."

"*Off site?* You mean leave the ward?"

"Precisely."

"And go where?"

"I'd suggest you start with the Forty Thieves."

"Fuckin' A!" Ed said. "Let's get some whiskey!"

"Guys, that place probably doesn't even exist," I said.

"Then so be it," the Judge said. "If it doesn't, you've undeniably exposed their scheme. On the other hand, if you do locate an establishment by that name, the scheme will be equally exposed if you arrive and find neither Carlo Marino nor anyone there who knows you."

As always, the Judge had plotted a logical course of action. Except for . . .

"One thing," I said. "You do realize, don't you, that we can't get out of here?"

"And why is that?" he said, scoffing.

"Because they've thought of everything. You can't get out a window. The ones that aren't covered with iron mesh are unbreakable and can't be opened. And the fire escapes all have an alarm that triggers as soon as you hit the exit bar—and then the door won't open for thirty seconds. In that time, they'd be all over us."

"Insurmountable obstacles, to be sure," he said. "But are there not exit doors in the main hall?"

It was my turn to scoff. "Yeah, and they're locked."

"By what means?"

"Electronically."

"And those doors are unlatched . . . *how?*"

Of course, he knew the answer.

And so did I.

"With a keypad," I said.

His honor gave me an unflinching stare. "And who among us calls himself the great codebreaker?"

———◦———

Located at one end of the main hall, the ward's principal entrance and exit was a wide double-door affair suitable for wheeling through carts and gurneys. Patients, whether traveling vertical or horizontal, were always brought in and out through those doors, which, as with both the day-room and the adjacent cafeteria, lay in full view of the circular, glassed-in nursing station. At the hall's other end was a single door that accom-modated staff only and which, I assumed, led to some fairly immediate connection to the world outside. That door, too, could be seen from the nursing station, but was watched less than the other areas.

In a corner of the dayroom that afforded a view of the single door, I sat in a chair and pretended to read a magazine.

"Group in five minutes," a nursing tech said, passing by.

I waved to him and went on with my business, waiting for one of the staff to use the door. The keypad was on the door just above the handle, and, like a cell phone, its twelve buttons were laid out in four rows, with buttons numbered *1-2-3* comprising the first row, *4-5-6* the second, and *7-8-9* the third, while in the fourth row a button labeled *0* lay between a key on its left marked with a star and one on its right with a pound sign. On a typical code-lock door, the two non-digit symbols were, I knew, used only for programming purposes or to confirm entry of a code sequence—but never as part of the sequence itself. As also typical of such devices, the pad in question would emit a beep for each button pressed. Four beeps always sounded just prior to any person opening the door to leave the ward.

Within a short time, a tech went to the door. Being right-handed, and with the keypad situated on the door's right side, she stood to the left of the pad, and thus from my vantage point—which was to her left and somewhat behind her—I was unable to see the pad as she entered the code. Nonetheless, the slight but noticeable motion of her arm as the four beeps were heard suggested that the first button she pushed was likely on a row above the second, that the second button was directly below the first, and that the third and fourth buttons were both to the left of and on the same row as the first—although I could not discern whether the entry of the latter two digits required the striking of separate keys or were, instead, inputted by punching the same key twice. In any event, assuming my observations were correct, it was evident that the first two digits of the sequence must be either *2-5, 5-8, 3-6, 6-9,* or *8-0,* and that even accounting for the possible use of repeat numbers for the third and fourth digits, there were but eleven four-digit combinations to consider.

No more than a minute later, a second tech came along. He too was right-handed, but the perceptible movement of his arm between his pressing of the third and fourth digits betrayed, I was sure, a sequence in which those two keys were not the same, but rather, the fourth was to the right of the third—which, that quickly, narrowed things down to a mere two possibilities.

And that is how it is done: The making of assumptions. The study of patterns.

Codebreaking.

Now, I thought, if only a lefty would show up and clinch the deal.

It was time, however, for my group to meet. The door I was watching opened and the therapist who ran both the morning and evening sessions came in. I hated these get-togethers, but showed up in order to avoid being hassled. And given what I was planning to do, it was important today, more than ever, to dispel suspicion by giving the appearance of cooperation.

The meeting, as always, was held in the dayroom. I sat with five other patients in a loose circle along with the therapist—a kind of touchy-feely lady who was forever urging us to tell our darkest secrets and insisted that we conclude each session with a kind of figurative clusterhug.

"Today we're going to start with a fun little activity," she said. "I want everyone to think of two things about yourself that are true, and one thing that is not. Then we'll go around the circle and each of us, one by one, will tell those three things, and the others will try to guess which two of the three are true and which one is false. Two truths and one lie. Everyone understand?"

"For god's sake," I bemoaned under my breath.

I was sitting next to the therapist. She turned my way.

"Mr. Stavros," she said, "would you like to go first?"

Punishment for my big mouth.

I reminded myself: *Cooperate.*

"Sure, I'll go."

"What are your three, Mr. Stavros?"

"I used to work as a cryptanalyst—that is, a codebreaker—for a government agency," I said. "I now work as a bartender. And I can speak twenty-one languages fluently. There you have it."

The fat guy beside me spoke up: "I don't think you know how to play this game."

"How's that?" I said.

"Because you just told *two* lies and *one* truth."

"I don't know about that," a woman from across the circle said. "I think he's lying about all three."

"What?" I was incensed.

"Hey," the woman said with a shrewd tone, "nobody speaks twenty-one languages. So that's obviously a lie. And the government codebreaker thing sounds like complete bullshit. So that leaves the bartender thing, and the fact is we're all sitting around in regular clothes and you're wearing scrubs, which says to me that you have no decent clothes of your own. And why would that be? Probably because you have no job and came straight off the street."

"You're saying I'm a bum?"

"Now, now, Mr. Stavros," the therapist said, "she's only trying to deduce which . . ."

"No, she isn't," I said. "Look, I did exactly what you wanted me to do. I told two true things and one lie. And what she's saying about the way I'm dressed demonstrates *exactly* which statement is false."

"I don't get it," the fat man said.

I fired off a condescending stare. "She identified the fact that I apparently have no suitable clothes other than what the hospital has provided, which implies that, yeah, I'm no bartender, I *am* a bum. Which means that the other two statements . . ."

"Maybe you freaked out and got naked in the bar and they carted you away like that and you just don't have any friends to bring you clothes," he said.

"You're rather cynical," I remarked. "What are you, a lawyer?"

"You can make that guess when it's *my* turn."

"I've already guessed."

"So what's wrong with being a lawyer?"

"All right, all right," the therapist said cheerily. "Anyone else want to chime in before we vote on Mr. Stavros?"

No one spoke.

"Very well, everyone. Let's find out the consensus."

There was none.

The rest of the session was absolute misery. But as it ended, I saw the therapist making some notes.

With her pen in her left hand.

"Will you be staying for lunch?" I asked.

She looked at me as if I had three-heads and had just invited her to the high school prom.

"No, Mr. Stavros," she said. "I must be on my way. I have other appointments."

Discreetly, I followed her until she veered toward the door through which she had entered. I remained at a place in the dayroom where I could observe her egress. As she reached the door, I watched her left index finger as it pressed the first two keys of the code. And being at once supremely confident of my conclusion, turned away before she pressed the other two.

———◦———

"So how are we gonna do this?" Ed asked.

I lay on my bed, looking at the ceiling.

"Lunch is served in ten minutes," I said. "We fall in with everyone heading to the cafeteria. Then when the opportunity presents itself, we break for the door."

The Judge was visibly bothered. "Seems too simplistic. They'll be after us immediately. And none of us has any idea what awaits us on the other side of that door. No, I think we must do something to provide ourselves more of an edge."

"You know," I said, "you're right. Plus that orderly's going to be dogging me like he always does. That'll make it even harder."

"Why don't you kick him in the nuts?" Ed proposed. "If you catch him square, he'll be down till dinner."

I shook my head. "I don't think I have it in me to do that. Not just totally unprovoked."

"Then *I'll* do it," Ed offered.

"Yeah, but even then, we'd have the others to deal with. Like the Judge says, we need to find some way to give ourselves a leg up."

I closed my eyes for several minutes, thinking.

"Lunch," I heard from the doorway.

The big, bald orderly stood waiting.

I sat up. "Okay, give me a minute."

He moved away and I looked at Ed and the Judge. An idea had occurred to me.

"I've got it," I whispered. "Just follow my lead."

I went into the bath to get my toothbrush. Meanwhile, the hall was filling with a troop of lunch-goers ready to be led to the cafeteria. I waited until they were fully assembled, then dropped to the floor and crawled on my stomach halfway beneath my bed. I was so positioned when my escort reappeared.

"Stavros, what are you doing?"

"Looking for something."

"What?"

"Don't worry about it."

"We're waiting for you."

"Just go on."

"You know I can't do that. You're going with me. Now get out from under there."

I continued to lie prone and stretched one hand further under the bed as if to reach for something.

He grew more impatient. "Stavros, come on."

"No, I need this."

There was grumbling from outside.

"Go on. We'll catch up," the orderly said toward the hall. "All right, Stavros, last chance. Now move your ass."

"Not until I find it. It rolled under here."

"What did?"

"My pencil. I told you yesterday I needed a pencil. So I got one."

"Where?"

"The nursing station."

"They gave you a pencil?" he said, disbelieving.

"No, I stole it. And it's really sharp."

"Okay, that's it."

He grabbed me by the ankles and dragged me out. As I emerged, I acted as if I had found what I sought and curled myself into a ball, holding the object tightly to my chest with both hands. He came at me straightaway, intending to pry the thing from me as I lay defensively on the floor. But he had no more taken my wrist when I abruptly brought my hands apart and made a move as if I were about to stab him with what, in the heat of things, he took for a spike of pencil lead. He flinched and released me, and in the next instant I tossed my bogus weapon—the toothbrush—to the far side of the room. On instinct, he started for it. And as he did, I leapt to my feet, sprang into the hall, and slammed the door.

And he was trapped. Just as I had been. Every night.

Stride for stride, Ed and the Judge ran with me to the dayroom, where I saw, just before we dived to the floor, two nurses and a tech inside the nursing station, the nurses working on papers while the tech monitored the lunch crowd filing into the cafeteria. We crawled commando-style past the station before rising and sprinting for the single door in the main hall.

With a look of bewilderment—then astonishment—one of the nurses spotted me at the door, her attention drawn by the beeps of the keypad as I punched the four buttons that I *knew* would work.

And they did.

3-6-1-2.

At the nursing station, there was wholesale chaos as I threw back the door and Ed raced through.

"Fuck me, bitches!" he cried, the Judge and I close behind.

-30-

W E FOUND OURSELVES IN A HALLWAY with offices on either side, most of the doors open, persons within looking up as we ran past. A man in a lab coat came around a corner and, startled by us, stepped aside even as he held up a hand to signal that we should stop. "Hey! Hey! Hey!" he said as we passed him and turned to go down the hall from which he had come—a corridor leading to a skybridge that hung but a story above the street.

Entering the skybridge, we darted around a woman going our direction wearing street clothes and an ID lanyard, and at the end of the crossing nearly collided with a man and a woman—both wearing scrubs and lanyards—who emerged one after the other from a revolving door, neither seeming to know what to make of us.

We spun through the revolving door and found ourselves in a parking garage. I looked back through the glass of the door to see a security guard and a gaggle of staff from the psych ward dashing toward us across the skybridge.

"To the stairs!" the Judge said, leading the way to the nearest end of the garage.

I moved past him and shoved the metal door open. We entered the stairwell. Ed and I started down.

"No, no!" the Judge said. "Up! Go up!"

The directive confused me, but I complied, as did Ed, and we hurriedly accompanied the Judge up two flights of stairs to the next level of the garage, where he called for a halt.

I went for the door handle, but he took me by the wrist, holding my hand back. He put a finger to his lips and we stood unspeaking as we heard the door on the level immediately below come open and those in chase noisily pour into the stairwell, their feet clanging on the metal landing and stairs. But not approaching. Rather, receding until, on the level below that they had entered, there was again the sound of a door opening as the group, en masse, made its exit.

"They saw us enter this stairwell," the Judge said. "But they assumed we went down, to the street. That's where they're looking for us."

"What do we do?" Ed asked.

"Follow me."

The Judge led us out of the stairwell and toward the stairs at the other end of the garage, the three of us walking at a brisk but less than suspicious pace. An SUV went by. Its driver, a woman, was on the phone and failed to so much as glance our way. The level was filled with parked vehicles, but as the SUV disappeared, all was quiet.

"So we take the *other* stairs?" Ed said.

I too thought that to be the plan. But Ed had no sooner spoken than the Judge stopped short of the stairwell and looked about with a concerned expression, evidently reconsidering.

"I think we should not," he said. "They've found nothing on the street, and now they'll be splitting up and ascending both stairs simultaneously. The stairways will then be watched while a search is conducted of each successive parking level, all the way to the top. If we are anywhere in this garage, there will be no escape."

Already, I heard a bustle from the floors below. Loud voices and, from both stairwells, the swinging and closing of heavy doors. Within seconds, they would be on us.

I noticed a single elevator near the door to the stairs. The Judge saw it too.

I knew what he was thinking.

I rushed over and hit the down button. Several long moments later, the elevator dinged, and as its doors opened, so did the doors to both stairwells. We threw ourselves into the car just as the mob entered the garage. I punched the button for the ground floor and we pressed to the back of the car as its doors closed. I prayed we had not been seen—and that below, none of our pursuers were lying in wait.

The Judge was optimistic.

"Two floors to freedom, gentlemen," he said.

Without an interim stop, the car dropped to ground level. Coming off the elevator, I saw no sign of the posse and located an exit to the street. There was a hard rain falling.

I was, of course, wearing only scrubs and house slippers.

"Sorry," the Judge said to me, "but we dare not waste another second. We must go."

We launched into the storm.

Ed ran ahead of us. "Come on, you assholes!"

I had a flash of déjà vu: A wild sprint through driving rain. A desperate run for life against death. Yet it seemed Ed and I had reversed roles—that *he* should be chasing *me*.

But just when and where might such a thing have occurred?

Probably never, I thought. And nowhere.

We had gone almost a block before the Judge called ahead to Ed, who paid no heed.

"Tell that idiot to stop!" the Judge said.

As instructed, I yelled through the storm.

Ed looked back and slowed his pace, allowing us to catch up.

"Gentlemen," the Judge said, "we don't know where we're going. We must get directions."

I had a sudden inspiration: I would do him one better.

I ran into the street and, in ankle-deep water, hailed a cab. I leaned on the passenger door and the cabby cracked the window.

"Would you please help me?" I said.

"What's the deal?"

"I'm Dr. Stavros, from the hospital. I'm chasing a dangerous psychiatric patient and I know where he's headed. Can you take me there?"

"Where?"

"A bar called the Forty Thieves."

The cabby had a look of recognition. "Oh, for sure. Get in."

We crammed into the back seat, me in the middle.

"Good thinking, Stavros," the Judge commended.

It had indeed been a stroke of genius, my scrubs providing the perfect cover.

"Sorry we're so wet," I told the cabby.

He looked at me in the rearview mirror, greatly amused. "Ha! Queen's English, huh? *We* this and *we* that? Hey, forget about it. I've seen worse happen on that seat."

We went maybe a mile and pulled curbside on a busy street.

"This is it, doc."

"I can't thank you enough," I said, sliding out. "Look, I'm very sorry, but I left the hospital with nothing. Come around tomorrow and I'll give you the fare."

"Naw, forget it," he said. "You get that bastard."

"I will."

"Say, you want I should call the police? Just for backup?"

"No, I can handle it."

"You da man, doc!"

-31-

SO IT DID EXIST, this place. But I had never been here before. I was certain of it.

The cheap, faded sign that read *Forty Thieves* had curved Arab swords on either end, their blades angled up and inward. And above the sword on the right, helping form a sort of inverted exclamation point, was the large, badly painted head of a bearded man in a turban with wicked, cartoonish eyes, wholly ready, it seemed, for some violent or lecherous act.

"Come on, boys," Ed said. "Let's party."

He charged in ahead of the Judge as I held the door.

The interior called to mind something I had perhaps seen elsewhere: The space was small and dimly lit. To the left was a bar. To the right, a few tables on a concrete floor. In the back was a pool table.

The place was about half full. Men and women—mostly working people—having lunch, and some a few drinks.

I went to the far end of the bar, passing, along its length, three men who sat evenly spaced from one another. A young woman behind the bar—tall with long blonde hair—acknowledged me with widened eyes.

"You're soaked," she said.

I nodded. "Do you know me?"

"What do you mean?"

"Do you know who I am?"

"I'm sorry, sir. I don't."

"Have I been here before?"

"No, sir. Not that I know of."

"And have you ever seen me before in your entire life?"

"I'm pretty sure I haven't."

"I knew it!" Elated, I slapped the bar. "You see?" I said to the Judge. "They made it all up."

The woman looked at me curiously. "Made what up?"

"Nothing."

"Man, will you quit foolin' around?" Ed said. "We gotta get some hooch."

The occasion did seem to call for it.

"How about a shot of scotch?" I said to the woman.

She held up a jigger-size glass. "Like this?"

Ed gave me a big smile.

"Please," I said. "And I'm very sorry, but I'll have to owe you. I drove my car through a patch of high water about a block from here and flooded the engine. I got so flustered, I ran off without my wallet."

She appeared a bit wary of my excuse.

"Well, okay," she said, "I can give you one. But could you go back for your wallet as soon as the rain slacks up?"

"Sure."

She put the glass on the bar and, without asking my preference, poured me a scotch—a cheaper brand.

"So what are you," she asked, obviously noting my scrubs, "a doctor or something?"

"Yeah, I'm from the hospital." I extended my hand. "Leonard Stavros."

She did not reciprocate the gesture, as a look I could not quite interpret—an expression perhaps born of confusion (or was it dread?)—spread over her face.

"Pardon me," she said, leaving the bottle on the bar as she went quickly into the kitchen.

"Are you gonna drink that or not?" Ed said, eyeballing my scotch. He sensed nothing amiss.

The Judge, on the other hand, flinched about with concern, and I had a nervous feeling that it might be best to depart this establishment. However, before I could fully consider things, another woman—older and hard-looking—came out of the kitchen, my bartendress veritably cowering behind her.

The woman, ill at ease, stared at me for several pregnant seconds.

"Hello, Stavros," she said.

"Who are you?"

She shook her head with a look both dismissive and aggravated. "What kind of question is that?"

"One I expect you to answer."

Clearly, she did not intend to.

She surveyed the surrounding clientele and lowered her voice. "Just what do you think you're doing here?"

"Having a drink."

"Do you have any money?"

"As I told the woman behind you, I left it in my car."

"You don't have a car."

"How would you know?"

"Stavros, you worked here for nine years. I know."

"Nine years?" I laughed derisively. "Yeah, right. They told you to say that."

"Who did?"

"You know very well. You're in on it. Everyone's in on it. Except her." I glanced at the tall blonde. "She doesn't know me."

"Of course not. I hired her yesterday."

"I suppose she's my replacement?"

"Well . . . yeah. I had to have somebody. And from what I've seen, it's going to be awhile before you're able to work again."

"From what you've *seen?* What is that?"

"Do I have to spell it out for you?" She cast another uneasy look. "You know. The breakdown. Screaming and throwing things at people who don't exist. I can't have that in here."

I looked at Ed and the Judge. "Either of you remember that?"

They shook their heads.

This had gone far enough.

"Lady, that is an absolute crock! You know damn well I have never before set foot in this place and that you and I have never met. And yeah, I *did* have a breakdown, but it happened under a bridge. And I was *not* yelling at people who don't exist. I was yelling at the Paisley Codex."

"What the hell is that?"

"A book, as if you've ever read one." I could not stand this woman. Just another fake. Another phony. Insulting my intelligence.

"Look, we both know you're not supposed to be here," she said. "Don't make me call the cops."

I ran my eyes around the room, disregarding her.

"I mean it," she said. "Just drink up and get out. Go back to the hospital."

I swilled the scotch and, with finality, returned the glass to the bar with a smack.

"Yeah, daddy!" Ed reveled. "That is some good shit!"

"I'm afraid this excursion has, at best, yielded mixed results," the Judge said. "We should indeed be leaving."

I withheld any show of concurrence. Nonetheless, I agreed. This place was dangerous.

I moved away from the bar, knowing exactly what I was going to do: Get to a public library, find a computer, and google the Paisley Codex. Then, free of my persecutors, I would resume my work.

"Don't try to follow me," I told the woman. "Nobody had better follow me."

Her features softened. "Stavros, listen to me. You need help. Let me call someone."

"That's what you're supposed to do, right? It's what they've *told* you to do."

"Oh . . . Leonard . . ." It seemed a strain for her to use my given name. "I do want you to know that I feel for you. We all do. After last week."

"What about last week?"

"You know, your wife . . ."

"Not that again," I said angrily.

"I'm just saying, I understand what's caused all this . . ." She searched for a word. ". . . *craziness*. But so much of it is your own doing. The way you treated her. And what happened after. What you *let* happen. I hate to say it, but it's true. And if you're ever going to get better, you've got to face up to that."

Crap, I thought. All crap. A play staged for the benefit of one.

"I've had enough of this charade," I said. "You are a liar, and my doctor is a liar, and God knows how many others. And by the way, *he's not here*."

"Who's not?"

"You know."

"No, I . . ."

"Carlo Marino," I said. "He's not here."

"I sent him to the bank."

"No, you didn't."

"I sure as hell did."

"Describe him," I said.

"Do what?"

"Describe Carlo Marino." I waited. She was dumbstruck. "Just as I thought. You don't know him. You've never met him. Because he doesn't work here and he never has."

"Stavros . . ." she said sadly. "Leonard . . ."

I looked at Ed and the Judge. "Mixed results my ass. Let's go."

As we made for the door, a man came in from the rain. He wore jeans and a Harley-Davidson t-shirt. He had a sleeve of tattoos covering each arm.

"Sponge!" he said.

Carlo Marino.

THE FIFTH BOOK
OF STAVROS

The Weight
of a
Black
Hole

Knowing yourself is the beginning of all wisdom.

–Aristotle

32

*T*HE OLDER WOMAN CALLED THE HOSPITAL as, in the throes of abject shock, I sat quietly at a table, waiting for them to come. Ed pestered me repeatedly for another drink, but I ignored him. And as Carlo sat with me, telling me how things were going to be all right—how I was going to get better—I could not quit staring at his arms, his tattoos. The whole of each appendage covered in a red, blue, and yellow mass of swirling teardrops. An unmistakable design. A pattern in paisley.

He told me he had once worked at a local casino. He had dealt black-jack with those arms. And that, he explained, was how we met. I had sat at his table for several evenings in a row. I'd had a winning streak and told him he was good luck. But while I had been an enthusiastic card player, I was not a terribly skillful one. I had, at one time, he said, accumulated through work and investment a rather large sum of money. I'd had a nice house too. But I had eventually lost it all at the tables. And now, whenever I came into a few bucks, I would lose that as well. I couldn't help myself. I was obsessed with games of chance. I played a little of everything, but mostly twenty-one. At least, that's what Carlo said.

He also said that, for a short while, he and I had owned this very bar. Been partners. The place had long been known as the Forty Thieves, but we had wanted to rename it. We had planned to call it the Forty-*Two* Thieves—the two additional brigands being, naturally, Carlo and me. But changing the sign was too expensive. Everything was. Carlo had quit the casino to manage the place, but he was not much good at it; he could not lay off the booze. And of course, I could not lay off the cards. Bankruptcy had ensued. And for the vast majority of the past nine years, we had toiled in this place as mere workhands, at the beck and call of others. A couple of hamsters running on a treadmill.

Funny. I did not remember any of it. But as Carlo told it, it had the sound, the *feeling*, of authenticity. And resigned as I was to the persuasive effect of his story, it seemed it was time, finally, to capitulate. To give up those grandiose visions of myself as the great conquering hero of cryptology, the great suffering hero of the Paisley Codex. To give up even the notion of the Paisley as an object of the real world. The truth, I was learning, was far more mundane. And tragic.

I returned to the hospital as the epitome of compliance. There, I stumbled to my room without a sound. I was given a sedative, which I readily took before falling into bed. I wanted to lie down and never rise again. To sleep and never wake.

"Stavros," the Judge said, as I faded off, "we're still here."

"I know."

"I'm very sorry. We both are. Perhaps there are times when the lies we believe should be left unchallenged."

I was awakened the next morning by the nurse with the god-awful perm. (Definitely a form of sleep disturbance.) She took my vitals and left, after which my usual orderly (none too happy, I was sure, after my previous day's escapades) came by to escort me to the showers. I declined and told him I wished to skip breakfast as well. Nevertheless, a short time later, a tech brought scrambled eggs and buttered toast on a paper plate, along with orange juice in a paper cup. The meal then sat on my desk, untouched, as the orderly paced back and forth past my open door—I supposed as a precaution against me trying to slit my wrists with the dull-tonged plastic fork I had been provided.

I was sitting on my bed when the doctor came. The orderly removed the uneaten meal and the doctor sat on the bed beside me. If I could have wished him away, I would have been tempted to do so. However, I told myself that here, next to me, sat my best hope for recovery.

I felt his eyes on me, but did not look at him.

"How are you?" he asked.

"I don't know."

"I heard you took a little trip outside the ward."

"Yeah."

"I also heard that you may have experienced something of a breakthrough."

I hesitated. "I guess you could call it that."

"Please tell me about it."

"I think you know. I went to the bar. It was all like you said."

"And do you understand, now, who you really are?"

"Not entirely. But I guess I'm beginning to understand who I'm not."

"So you're not someone who broke codes for some government agency?"

"I suppose I didn't."

"And you do not speak multiple languages?"

I paused for a long sigh, trying to think of a single intelligible phrase in any foreign tongue. French? Italian? I supposed I had learned a line or two to impress women. But I could not remember. And Greek? I knew a few words there. But then, my grandparents had been immigrants. What little I understood I had undoubtedly learned from them.

"I speak English," I said. "Really nothing else, I suppose."

"And this book you have talked so much about?"

"The Paisley Codex."

"Yes. Do you now accept the fact that it does not exist?"

Tears welled in my eyes as I realized that among all of my apparent delusions, this was the one I could least endure the loss of. Even with everything I had discovered the day before, I could not completely shake the idea—the *belief*—that this alleged product of my imagination had, for nearly a decade, dominated my life. Could a mere fantasy evoke such an undying conviction?

And such anger? And regret?

But according to Carlo, I had long been fascinated by old books. Particularly those of the medieval variety. He said that, back when I could afford such things, I had even owned a highly prized volume from the thirteenth or fourteenth century. A book written in some language I could not read.

He told me I had sold it to pay the rent.

"Mr. Stavros," the doctor prompted, "again, my question: Do you accept the fact that this book does not exist?"

I shut my eyes and shook my head. "I suppose it's . . . *likely* that it doesn't. But . . ."

"But what?"

"But if the Paisley doesn't exist, then why am I here? I remember it laughing at me. Driving me mad. It's to blame for *all* of this."

"No, Mr. Stavros," he said, matter-of-fact, "it is not. Your belief in this book and its effect on you is a mere confabulation—your mind's way of shielding you, psychologically, from the pain of having to deal with the true cause of your disorder. There is no such book."

"But I can see it. I can see every page."

Yet I was spouting a fiction and I knew it. I could *not* see it. And it was becoming more and more evident that I never had—not as the image of an actual, material object, anyway. The Latin and Greek alphabets? Yes, I knew them—at least, their modern-day versions. But Arabic? I could not think of a single letter.

"So even though you acknowledge that this book is probably nothing more than a mental fabrication," the doctor summarized, "it nevertheless continues to seem very real."

"Yes. In a way."

"And are there other things—things like the book, that you suspect to be illusions—that likewise seem real?"

"What do you mean?"

"For instance, do you see any persons other than you and me that are here now? Within this room?"

Lord, I did not want him to think me any crazier than he already did. But clearly, he knew. No doubt the staff had passed along their observations.

The Judge and Ed watched us from the room's far corner. I made eye contact with them and then, for the first time, looked at the doctor.

The jig was up.

"Yeah, there are two others here."

"Do you think I can see them?" the doctor asked, glancing around.

"No."

"Why is that?"

"Because they come from inside me. From my own mind."

"Are you quite certain of that?"

"Yes."

The doctor was laudatory. "You are gaining insight, Mr. Stavros. Tremendous insight."

"Maybe. But I can still see them."

"Yes, for now. But knowing they are not really there is half the battle. Because having that knowledge will allow you to ignore them. And once you begin doing that, I believe you will find that they make fewer and fewer appearances. Eventually they will disappear altogether, and you will be rid of them."

I thought about that—never seeing them again—and a kind of panic came over me. As if the last connection I had to my former self—the self I knew—was about to be severed.

I found myself breathing heavily. I felt lightheaded. "I'm not sure I want that to happen."

"You mean you don't want them to go away?"

"I don't think so."

"Why not?"

"Because then I'll be alone."

"Oh, now, Mr. Stavros, I'm sure you have friends."

"I don't know." I couldn't think of any.

"What about Mr. Marino?"

What about him, indeed. I did not think him the kind of person I was likely to fall in with. But then, what did I really know of myself? My *true* self?

"Yeah, I guess we're friends. Acquaintances, anyway."

"Why, certainly. And there are always new friends and acquaintances to be made. I'm sure that when you're feeling better, you'll make friends right here, on the ward."

I tried to think of what life would be like without Ed and the Judge. I could not imagine it.

"But you see," I said, pointing to the corner, "I'm just so *used* to them. Used to having them with me."

"I ask you, though, Mr. Stavros, what good are they? How can they possibly help you?"

"I don't really know how to answer that. But good or bad, they're part of me. They make me who I am."

"Or who you *think* you are," he said, lifting one eyebrow. "But isn't that what you wish to change? Isn't that why you are here? To rid yourself of certain mental and emotional baggage? To excise such malignancies from your psyche? And very surely, these persons who appear to you are deadly cancers upon your well-being—though I would venture to say they always have been. Only much worse now than before."

"Before?" I said. "Before what?"

"Before this condition of yours arose."

"And what condition is that?"

"Something very complex," he said, "and very rare. A disorder the profession has come to recognize as *shattered psyche syndrome*."

"Shattered psyche syndrome?" I pondered the term. "That sounds almost made up."

"I assure you, Mr. Stavros, it is not. It is very real. And the two persons you see—or think you see—in this room conclusively demonstrate its applicability to your case. Because when taken together with the element of your central self—that is, the person who now sits before me: the *ego* of Leonard Stavros—the three of you in fact represent the manifestation of this condition. A condition involving the separation of the individual elements of your aggregate psyche. Your *collective self* broken into its fundamental Freudian triumvirate, if you will. A classic presentation of this particular psychosis."

"But what has caused this . . . shattering?"

"A single, mind-wrenching event. Something so repugnant to your sense of self that it acted like a bomb, splintering the components of your psyche into a triad of distinct personalities."

"And this event—what was it?"

"You don't recall?" he said, with disbelief.

"No."

"Nothing, for instance, that may have happened in the recent past? A tragedy for which you blame yourself, or feel that somehow, had you acted differently—perhaps more courageously and less selfishly—you might have prevented?"

I shook my head. "People keep bringing up my wife. First Carlo, then that woman at the bar yesterday. But that was *years* ago. I mean, they acted like it wasn't, but it was."

The doctor's gaze left mine and he stared ahead—at first solemnly, but then nearly smiling as if contemplating some darkly amusing secret.

"It *was* years ago," I said. "Right?"

He stood up to leave. "You have a long way to go, Mr. Stavros. A *very* long way. We'll talk again tomorrow."

33

*T*HE DAY WORE ON. Later that morning I suffered through another group session. As sick as I now knew I was, I still could not fully see the point of it. But just as I had with my doctor, I told myself that my participation was somehow for the best. That maybe somewhere in the midst of these seemingly inane mental exercises I would start to become something other than the hopeless, talentless, directionless washout I had so recently learned myself to be.

After lunch, of which I ate very little, a tech came by my room with some clothes that she said Carlo had dropped off for me. They did not look at all familiar.

"Where did he get these?" I asked her.

"I assume from where you live."

"And where is that?"

She referred me to the nursing station, where I inquired as to my residence. I was told that my admission records showed an address for a certain "hotel" that, upon further inquiry, I discovered to be more or less a flophouse for quasi vagrants. The nurse I talked to had no information as to how long I had lived there. At any rate, I finally had some regular clothes, which, Ed observed, might cause the fat lawyer in group to retract his insinuation regarding my lack of friends.

Yet I could not bring myself to care. That lard-ass could screw himself. After this, he would probably go back to his wretched, workaday life. But I did not have even that. For me, this was it. Right here. The end. Crazy Town.

Midafternoon there was a lady in the day room conducting a painting class. There was some arts and crafts thing like that going on every day about the same time. I had never joined in and did not do so on that occasion. I went to my room and lay on my bed.

"If you ask me," Ed said, "this whole thing is bullshit. There's not a damn thing wrong with you."

"There's *everything* wrong with me."

"Alas, that would appear to be the case," the Judge concurred.

"Yeah, I know," Ed allowed. "I was just sayin' that to make you feel better."

"Well, you can save your breath," I said. "There is *nothing* that can make me feel better."

"How about a blow job?" Ed suggested. "Like from a super model? I bet that would help."

"Shut up," I said.

"Yes," the Judge chimed in, "do shut up."

Ed shut up. They both did. Leaving me to examine my situation.

Okay, I told myself, be honest. *The end?* Was it *really* that? Here in this bin of loonies? No, I thought, it was not. At least, not necessarily. That had been sheer melodramatic conjecture. No doubt, I would have a lengthy stay in this place. Yet almost certainly they would let me go. Eventually. (Wouldn't they?)

But go where? To do what?

The answer to the latter question seemed straightforward: Cured or not, I would live out my life—a life sentence, as it were—as the real Leonard Stavros, loser extraordinaire. A fate beyond dismal. And that was most definitely not conjecture.

I had lost everything. Everything I had ever considered important. Or had I? No, no. Wrong again. Of course I hadn't. One cannot lose that which one has never had. My wife, I had genuinely treasured. And her passing, so long ago, had undeniably imposed a great cost on me. A thing very real. But all else of which I now felt myself deprived—those things which had existed only through my wrong but unwavering belief in them—had been nothing more than the underpinning of a pathetic fantasy. The wishful components of a person I had wanted to be, but never could.

And yet that fleeting dream of a different Leonard Stavros—oh, that had been such a fine, false truth! A vision of a man superior in will and intellect. An unrivaled cryptanalyst. An incomparable linguist. And the great enemy of the Paisley. Suffering, through it all, the torment of unending failure. But there had been a reason—a reason supplied by the merciless test of the Codex—to go on working. Fighting. *Living*. As the near broken man of still golden talents, I had bravely refused to succumb to my nemesis.

But that nemesis, a mere fiction, had now faded as quickly as its adversary. It had been revealed as less, even, than a windmill. It had become nothing. And with its disappearance, the man who had once gone tilting at its pretended challenge had himself all but vanished.

⸻◦⸻

I ate dinner with the patient population, but, as usual, kept to myself. After the meal there was a movie being shown in the day room. Something light, comedic, and absent any reference to death, insanity, or otherwise disappointing events. I took a pass on the film and returned to my room. I was sitting on my desk chair, staring at a wall, when my orderly came to the door.

"Hey, Stavros, you okay?"

"I don't know. Why?"

"You seem a little, let's say, less animated than usual."

"I'm just tired."

"You ought to go watch the movie."

"You gonna make me?" I could hear, in my voice, the tone of Ed.

"No. Your choice."

He moved on. I called after him.

"Yeah?" He looked back in.

"You don't have a twin brother, do you? One that works here?"

"Why do you ask?"

"Because every day you're trailing me from the minute I get up in the morning to the minute I go to bed at night. Nobody works that many hours. Makes me wonder if there are two of you."

As if to validate my supposition, he pressed a vertical finger to his closed lips.

I had only been joking. "There *are* two of you?"

"Keep it under your hat. Or else."

"Or else what?"

"Or else I'll tie you to that chair and rough you up."

Just before lights out, a tech came by with my nighttime medications, which, as always, included a sedative. I took the pills and lay down in bed. The tech turned out my light, left the room, and closed the door.

I quickly dropped off to sleep and saw, again, the fire, flames leaping before me so intense that when I awoke, I was met by a blazing afterimage that faded only gradually to the dark of the room. I felt as if I had slept for several hours, yet with no clock for reference, had no way of knowing.

Within minutes I heard footsteps in the hall. In the small window of my door, I saw the light of a flashlight and the silhouetted head and shoulders of a man. He turned the light directly on me and, apparently satisfied with my condition, went away. He would, I thought, be back in thirty.

It was strange; I was not drowsy in the least. I lay still for a while, hoping to return to sleep. But no, I was wide awake. Could it be that sedative had been weaker than the night before?

I sat up and put my legs over the side of the bed, feeling the cold tile beneath my bare feet.

"Judge?" I whispered.

There was no answer.

"Ed?"

Nothing.

I thought about turning on my room light to check on them, but decided against it; the light would shine through the window into the hall, alerting the night crew. Of course, a light on for only a short time would likely be ignored. But why risk creating problems for myself?

I sat on the side of the bed, in the dark, for some time—fifteen minutes, I figured, but no more—when I again heard footsteps approaching. Quickly, I lay down and half covered myself with the sheet just before a beam of light once more entered the room, focused upon me, and was extinguished.

Then the same footsteps, receding.

So, they had doubled their checks on me. In a way, that was quite ironic: They believed I was now more of a danger to myself than when, only yesterday, I had been so deluded as to imagine myself to be an entirely different person.

But then, perhaps *this* person—the man lying in this bed—*was* more dangerous. Because this man had nothing left to lose. Not even his self-respect.

It occurred to me that I should not have given in so easily. That I should not have so tamely fallen into that chair at the Forty Thieves and awaited my captures. Rather, I should have run back into the rain, raging against everything they insisted I believe. Then kept running, living my charming lie, on and on. Forever. Always to be that other man. That tortured but heroic possessor of singular intellect, ambition, and acuities.

But it was too late. I had consumed and digested the tangible evidence of the reality they claimed was mine. And without evidence to the contrary, there was no possibility of ever again seeing the world any other way.

I heard more footsteps in the hall—but treading lighter than before. They stopped at my door. I readied myself for the ubiquitous beam of light, but none came.

There was a moment of pause as I wondered what was happening outside. Then, a rapping at the door. Three slow, distinct knocks, as if the sequence had some encoded meaning.

I spoke just above a whisper: "Hello?"

There was the sound of something sliding on the floor, under the door.

I started out of bed in a hurry, but taking stock of the weirdness of this development, quickly restrained myself and crept warily to the door's window. I could see nothing but the shadowy darkness of the hall. Underfoot, though, I felt my toes brush atop what had been slipped into the room and reached down to find a piece of paper, folded in half. Guiding my fingers around the edges, I gauged it to be the size of a standard sheet of copy paper.

I put myself closer to the door. "Who's there?"

There was no response. Whoever it was had evidently moved on.

Yet what had been left behind? Almost surely this was some sort of message. But damned if I was going to wait till morning to find out.

For a second time, I chose against the light in the room. As a slightly preferable alternative, I went into the half bath and pulled the curtain closed.

I flicked the light switch and, as my eyes adjusted, saw notes scripted in pencil. A woman's handwriting on a lined tablet page:

> *Paisley Codex—3 sheets/6 leaves/12 pages/21 quires*
> *Brute Force Attack/Assumptions/Patterns*
> *Ciphertext/Plaintext*
> *Ciphers—Transposition/Substitution*
> *Frequency Analysis/ Nulls*
> *42 lines/42 pages*
> *"The Answer Lies Within"*

-34-

I N THE MORNING, as soon as they let me out of my room, I went to the nursing station and tapped on the glass.

Nurse Perm-Disaster looked up from her paperwork.

"I need to talk to someone who works the night shift," I said.

"Anyone in particular?"

"Yes."

"Who?"

"I don't have a name."

"Man or woman?"

I was having a hard time hearing her over the noise in the adjacent dining area; the kitchen staff was setting up for breakfast.

"Woman, I think."

"What does she look like?"

"I don't know."

Her eyes moved in an arcing motion. "Mr. Stavros, why do you want to speak with this person?"

"It's confidential."

She shook her head. "I'm sorry, but if you have an inquiry regarding the night personnel, I'll need to know the nature of it before I can help you."

"Look, I don't need your help. I want to talk to *her*. How about if I just leave her a message."

"And how would I know who to give it to?"

"Just find out who knocked on my door last night."

"I believe I already know the answer to that, Mr. Stavros."

"Oh? Who was it?"

"No one," she said. "No one knocked on your door. That's not something we do."

"Well, *she* did. And I'm not trying to get her in trouble. I just want to ask her something."

"Mr. Stavros, honestly, there is no one to ask. The tech that was on hall duty reported no irregular activity during any of the rounds he made. *He*, Mr. Stavros. There was no one else conducting checks last night."

"Maybe she was here, at the desk."

"Then she wouldn't have been conducting checks."

"But I'm not saying she was making *checks*. At least, not on me. She came after the tech had already . . ."

"Mr. Stavros," she said, speaking over me, "you were heavily sedated last night. Is it possible you were dreaming?"

"Absolutely not. I know what a dream feels like."

She gave me a cold stare. "Do you, Mr. Stavros? Do you really?"

I lay on my bed, passing the folded tablet page under my nose. The paper carried a recognizable scent—a *lovely* scent—but I could not place it.

"Okay, I'm calling bullshit on that bitch nurse," Ed said, shuffling in.

"Me too," I agreed. "Definitely."

"Count me for a third," the Judge declared.

"She doesn't know anything about what happened last night," I said. "She works days. She wasn't even here."

"She was probably home alone," Ed said, "chuggin' a bottle of wine and cryin' over that fuckin' hairdo. I swear, I want to turn to stone every time. Man, snakes are comin' outta that fuckin' thing."

"Exceptionally well phrased," the Judge commended, "in a way."

"And nice touch with the mythological allusion," I added.

Which was not like Ed at all.

Was he evolving?

I unfolded the mysterious page of notes and reexamined it.

"Who could possibly have written this?" I said.

"Who?" the Judge inquired. "Is that your question?"

This altogether unnecessary call for me to confirm the obvious should have aroused my suspicion that the Judge was setting the stage for something—but it didn't.

I answered with a gullible nod of my head.

"Well, let's consider the issue." He looked over my shoulder at the paper. "What I see here references your imaginary book, the Paisley Codex."

"It does," I said.

"And we also find a reference to *three sheets, six leaves, twelve pages, twenty-one quires*—all of which follows your belief in the manner in which the book was constructed, does it not?"

"Yeah."

"But you simply made that up."

"That's what they tell me."

He tapped the paper "And what's this about *forty-two lines* and *forty-two pages?* More of the same?"

"It's a little fuzzy in my head, but as I recall, there were supposed to be forty-two pages of the book that had forty-two written lines. All the other pages had forty-three."

"Of what possible significance was that?"

"I don't remember."

"Nevertheless, you made that up too. Correct?"

"I guess I did."

"So all of that being the case, who, other than yourself, could possibly possess such albeit bogus information?"

"I don't know."

"Well, have you told anyone?"

"About the Paisley?" I said. "Yeah, my doctor. Some of the staff. You've heard me talk to them about it."

"But what about these numbers? The quires, the pages, the lines, et cetera? To whom have you related such specific details?"

"No one I can think of."

The Judge unloosed a snide expression. "Then your question is answered."

I was slow to grasp his meaning, and when it hit me, was none too happy.

"Now wait a minute! You think *I* wrote this?"

"Who else *could* have? You admit that the Paisley Codex is nothing more than a phantom existing exclusively in your own mind, and that its particulars are known only to you."

"Yeah, but you're forgetting that someone—a *third party*—slid this paper under my door."

"So you say. But perhaps your psychosis is such that you were hallucinating. That no one knocked on your door. And that you yourself created this message and merely brought yourself to believe otherwise."

"But how would I do that? They won't even give me a damn pencil."

"Yet that is a recent development. A consequence of your violent outburst. Previous to that, you had access."

I shook the paper. "Does this look like my handwriting?"

"Most decidedly, it does not," he acknowledged.

"And you call yourself a judge."

I had overstepped. He smothered me with a glare.

"Stavros," he admonished, "I am a man of reason. And as a man of reason, I am merely examining the most likely—and I must say *overwhelmingly* likely—contingency. And if you too were a man of reason, you would understand that." He paused, allowing his rebuke to gain full effect. "Now certainly, the handwriting does not match your characteristic script. But without question, someone with intimate knowledge of the Paisley Codex wrote this message, and I assure you, it was not I. Nor was it he." He made a gesture toward Ed. "In fact, I doubt he even *can* write."

Ed's top lip rose in a sneer.

"So you see," the Judge concluded smugly, "there is but a single possibility."

"But the handwriting . . ."

"Such a thing can be altered. Particularly by one in a state of delusion."

I could not accept it. As mentally unstable as I might be, I knew I had
taken delivery of this paper, nothing more.

"Fine, then," I said. "You believe whatever you want. But I know I
didn't write this. And even though I don't remember telling anyone
these things, I clearly did. I told someone and forgot."

The Judge paced the small room with a self-righteous stride as I again
ran the paper beneath my nose, sniffing its sweet fragrance.

"This paper," I said. "It has such a nice smell. Perfume or something."

I raised it to permit the Judge a whiff.

"Flowers," he said.

———⋄———

The doctor came by at his usual time. There was no mention of the
matters we had discussed the previous day. He probed, instead, into
more standard psychiatric themes, initially touching on my self image
growing up and the relationships I'd had with my parents and siblings.
For me, these were painful subjects. Though I had not seen them for
over a decade, I had twin brothers several years older than me. They had
always been a rather brutish pair. In their youth, they had excelled at
sports, but shunned intellectual pursuits. As I had done the opposite,
they had teased and bullied me to no end—and to his discredit, my
father had far too frequently encouraged them. My mother too had done
little or nothing to dissuade my mistreatment. And so I had passed my
formative years under a constant threat of persecution, while those in a
position to judge my tormenters had all but sanctioned their behavior.

The conversation then moved to the early days of my marriage. The
doctor showed great interest in the association I had developed with my

in-laws, and in particular with my father-in-law—a familial connection that, as a source of emotional consolation, had easily surpassed that of my often disparaging, more demanding and less-forgiving parents. We talked for some time on that topic, and afterward the doctor advised that the information I had provided would prove very useful in my treatment. However, he no doubt left the session more satisfied than I, since, aside from memories of my interactions with the few persons we had discussed, I still had no recollection of how I had lived my life even more than a week ago. Where the subject had concerned such things as my academic and employment record, I had simply told him what I thought he expected to hear.

I was much more participatory in group that morning, but largely for my own amusement. Speaking up—even saying foolish and irrelevant things—helped pass the time far better than sulking in silence. And I could tell, in the process, that I was gaining credibility with the therapist. Perhaps, I thought, she would put in a good word for me with my doctor. (Maybe I would even end up getting a pencil.)

After lunch, I went to my room and, upon entering, saw that I had left the folded piece of tablet paper on my bed, in full view of whomever might darken my door. That, I told myself, had been quite careless.

On reflection, however, I recalled putting that paper in my desk.

I opened the drawer. Yes, there it was.

And this one?

I unfolded this new sheet. There was handwriting—and a scent—that matched the previous note.

Tonight, it said. *12:21.*

As always, it was lights out at ten. And as always, a tech came by with my medications—which, on that night, I only pretended to take. I lay down in bed and spit out the pills as soon as the door closed. I expected a flashlight-wielding visitor some fifteen minutes later, but by the time he arrived I thought it had been about twice that long, causing me to wonder if I had been taken off of special watch. After marking what I thought to be another thirty minutes until the next check came, I decided that was the case.

I cautioned myself against falling asleep, but with my level of anticipation, realized that was not even a possibility. Of course, I knew there was really nothing of substance to be gained here. The Paisley was sheer make-believe, and whoever had passed those notes to me either intended to make sport of my mental failings or was as sick in the head as I had been. But either way, my curiosity was on edge. There was something strange afoot, and I had to learn the gist of it.

So as not to raise the suspicions of staff prowling the hall, Ed, the Judge, and I maintained strict silence. We observed the 11:30 and midnight checks, and a short time after the latter I pulled my legs from under the covers and sat on the side of my bed, waiting.

It came, I was sure, at exactly the appointed minute—three knocks at the door.

I drew near, ready to accept any new message that might be sliding my way, but there was nothing. And I could discern no silhouette in the window.

"Are you there?" I said.

For a moment my question hung unanswered. Then, a quick whisper: "Yes."

I had been right. It was a woman.

In the veritable blackout of the room, I saw the Judge's mouth agape. I gave him a self-satisfied look before pressing myself to the door.

"Do you have anything for me?" I murmured.

"Yes."

"What?"

"Words of encouragement."

Already, she was talking nonsense.

"Why did you give me those notes last night?"

"For the same reason. To remind you of your work. And to urge you to continue."

"My *work?*" It seemed like a bad joke. "I don't *have* any work. I'm a . . . or *was* a bartender."

"You are nothing of the kind. You never have been."

"But they've told me . . ."

"Do not listen to them. Listen only to me." I could hear her breathing rapidly, desperately. "And you must listen well." Two more frantic respirations. "The book is *real*. And you are truly the man you thought yourself to be. And these people who hold you here and tell you otherwise are all liars."

This woman was clearly not on staff.

"That's ridiculous," I said. "They've shown me how wrong I was about myself. About everything. They're trying to help me."

"They are *not*. They are trying to sap away every ounce of the person that is really you. And in the end, to destroy you."

"Why would they do that?"

"Because there is a part of you that *wants* to be destroyed. And if you stay here, that is what will happen."

"But even if you're right, I can't possibly escape."

"Of course you can. You did before."

"Yeah, but they've changed the door code."

"No, not that. The other time."

I did not understand and pulled back from the door, thinking I should end this conversation. But I had to ask.

"Who are you?"

"They are coming," she said. "I must go."

"Tell me!"

Suddenly, it sounded as if she were choking. Then came a series of muffled coughs.

"I too see the fire," she said.

"In a dream, you mean?"

I heard the scuffling of her feet. She was gone. But just before, an answer:

"It is not a dream."

-35-

THE NEXT MORNING my doctor wanted to discuss the days leading up to my breakdown. I had, of course, no memory of any of it, but rather than admit that, tried to invent a narrative sufficient to both sound believable and keep the conversation moving. I was unable to do so, however, where things concerned my wife. Although the doctor had been previously elusive on the subject, now, just as others had done, he openly maintained that her loss had been recent, and that this had somehow factored into my situation.

"Tell me, Mr. Stavros," he said, "do you feel at all to blame for what happened?"

"Frankly, I don't *remember* what happened, so how could I possibly feel responsible for it?"

"You don't believe your actions may have precipitated her misfortune?"

"As I've said, I don't remember."

"So you don't feel that there was something you could—or should—have done to help her?"

"Same response."

He shifted disagreeably in my desk chair. "Your subconscious is blocking these memories, Mr. Stavros, which is interfering with your ability to grieve and suffer."

"*Suffer?*" I said. "I'm suffering now. Every minute."

I did not understand this. Certainly, he was the doctor. But how I might benefit from the imposition of further anguish was lost on me.

And his ambiguities had grown tiresome.

"Look, if you know what happened to my wife, why don't you just tell me?"

He shook me off. "Perhaps in time you'll learn that for yourself. And time is something we have here in abundance, Mr. Stavros."

From his last statement, he seemed to derive a sort of mysterious pleasure, as if he had told a joke only he understood.

I was getting fed up with this guy.

Fortunately, though, we were done: He rose from the chair, signaling the end of our session—but then appeared to have an afterthought.

"I've been told that you inquired yesterday at the nursing station about someone who you thought knocked on your door in the middle of the night."

"Yeah."

"Did you see this person?"

"No."

"But you thought it was a woman?"

"I really don't know."

"The nurse you spoke with advised me that you identified this person as most probably female," he said. "You must have had some reason to believe that."

"I guess maybe I just assumed."

"You didn't speak with this person?"

"No."

"And she hasn't returned?"

"No."

"Not last night?"

It was almost as if he knew.

"I didn't see or hear anything last night," I said.

"Well, if something like this happens in the future, do report it." He started to walk into the hall, but stopped. "The nurse you spoke with also told me that you wanted to get some kind of message to this person. What's that about?"

I looked around nervously and shrugged. "Just to tell her—or whomever—to quit knocking on my door."

"And that's the *confidential* message you wanted to convey?"

———◦———

"I don't know about that doctor," I whispered, gazing into the empty hall. "He's kind of an asshole."

"*Kind* of?" Ed said. "He's been a dick from day one. You should kick him in the balls."

"That's your answer for everything."

"And perhaps, in this case, it is appropriate," the Judge said. "The man advocates for my very demise."

"Mine too," Ed added.

I opened my desk drawer and pulled out the two pages of tablet paper, running them past my nose. It had become a habit. Breathing in that scent of flowers. A scent whose intensity seemed to never wane.

I replayed, in my mind, the peculiar conversation of the previous night.

"That chick was jerkin' your chain," Ed said.

Which was indeed one explanation. But why, I wondered, would anyone do such a thing? Clearly, at some now forgotten time, I had told this woman of certain "facts" related to the Paisley Codex—and also, apparently, something of the imaginary persona I had created for myself. Yet an attempt to prey on me by reference to my former delusions could, at the very least, only serve to agitate me, or, to the other extent, provoke a return to my prior level of psychosis. Needless to say, though, there was no tangible gain to be had in either outcome. So whoever my visitor had been—whether a member of the hospital staff (a possibility I had essentially dismissed) or some patient wily enough to escape her room after hours—she could not conceivably profit from her actions.

Unless, of course, she was bent on my downfall simply for the purpose of revenge. (But in retaliation for what?) However, if that was not her motive, then either this woman was just some lunatic out to satisfy her own deranged sense of amusement or a person so psychopathic that she had adopted my now abandoned fantasies.

All of which made for a fairly messy list of speculations. All equally probable.

Or improbable.

Yet while I was accounting for such feasibilities, there was, unavoidably, one more to consider: That she (whoever *she* was) had told me the truth. That the Paisley *did* exist. That I genuinely *was* the person I had believed myself to be. And that they really were out to get me in this godforsaken place.

And the fire. She said she had seen it too—which, in some incomprehensible way, seemed to bolster her credibility. But did it? Really? How could she have possibly been a witness to the mental images of my own sleep-state? Rather, wasn't it far more likely—veritably certain, in fact—that in telling her of other things, I had also divulged my recurring dream? And that her claims of the Paisley and all else were as false as mine had been?

Still, though, I wanted so much to believe her. And to believe that we shared, if not a dream, at least a common vision.

"I warn you," the Judge said, "it is better not to contemplate such things. Before long, you will again have yourself believing in that beastly manuscript and everything that goes with it."

He was right, I feared. I did not dare go back in that direction—tempting though it was.

I went to the window and looked out through the iron mesh. A light rain was falling. No sign of blue sky.

"Well, one thing's for sure," I said. "That woman, whoever she is, gave me those notes about the Paisley, and you were completely wrong about me having anything else to do with it."

"I will concede the point," replied his honor—typically unapologetic. "You were merely the recipient."

I went on studying the gray overcast.

There was something else she had said. It had me thinking.
"So what other time did I supposedly break out of here?"

In the wake of my conjecture, I wandered the halls, the day room, the dining area, observing women, listening to their voices. Weighing the possibilities of who among them might be her. But not one raised my suspicion in the slightest.

I was oblivious to the remainder of the day, mindlessly sitting through group in the late morning; eating lunch, then dinner, without tasting a thing; returning to evening group even less engaged than I had been earlier. I passed through it all like a man in a trance.

Without thought for doing otherwise, I took my bedtime medications and fell fast asleep, dreaming of fields of blooming, fragrant flowers. Their colors and sweet perfume crowding my faculties until, abruptly, the vivid mix of blossoms faded to the black of the waking space around me. But the scent remained, very strong—and even as I felt myself leave sleep further and further behind, very real. The room steeped in an overwhelming floral bouquet.

And then, another smell: The odor of smoke. Of something afire.

I was struck with panic, fearing that somewhere in the building—perhaps within the ward itself—a disaster was in the making. Yet from outside my room came no sign of crisis. I heard no alarms or sirens. No shouts or screams.

I did sense within the room, however, an irregular presence.

The voice came in a faint whisper, all but inaudible.

"Leonard," she said.

-36-

I ASKED THAT to which I already knew the answer.
"Is it you?"

"Yes."

In the darkness tempered by the dim nightlights from the hall, I could just make out the shadowed silhouette of a small human form in a long-sleeved nightshirt, sitting in the corner between the wall and the desk, her knees drawn up to her chest.

I glanced at the door. It was shut.

"Look, whatever it is you're doing here, how do you think you're going to get out?"

"There is a way," she said. "There is always a way."

The smell of smoke remained. Her respirations were labored. And with each effort came a wheeze like the sound of a rusty gate.

"I do not have much time," she said. "This will be our last meeting here. Perhaps our last ever. It is up to you."

"What's that supposed to mean?" I sat up. "Who *are* you?"

"Who are *you?*"

"I'm a goddamn mental patient!" I shrieked under my breath. "I'm nobody. Nothing."

"Yes, here, in this place, that is true. But that is what you wanted. You wanted to be nothing. And you came here to be nothing. To be *less* than nothing. And to deny your true self and all that is part of it."

"I *came* here?" I was incredulous. "Lady, you don't know shit. I was brought here. Against my will."

"*No*," she said, unbending. "That is what you tell yourself. But this is all of your own making." Her voice shook with emotion and gave way to a chain of hacking coughs. "Oh, Leonard, I am so disappointed in you. In what you have done to yourself. You have given up."

"I have no reason to do anything else."

"Another denial of what you know, deep within, to be true."

"All I *know* is that for some bizarre purpose, you insist on pestering me about a book that doesn't exist."

"But I have told you that it does. And that you are precisely the person you once thought yourself to be. If I could somehow make you believe that, what would you do?"

Against my better judgment, I answered. "I'd do . . . anything. Anything to . . . I don't know. I don't know what I *could* do. Not in this place."

I heard steps in the hall and quickly lay down. A flashlight shone through the window, spotlighting me, but not sweeping the room.

The steps moved on. She had not been seen.

It was some time before I felt it safe to speak again.

"They'll check your room and find you missing."

"I am not a patient."

"So you *are* on staff?"

"No."

"Well then, where did you . . .?" There was a larger issue. "Just tell me: What do you want from me?"

"I want you to believe in yourself again."

"Those were false beliefs."

"That itself is false and you know it. You *know* who you are, Leonard. You always have. Even the last time we spoke, after you had left me to spend your days and nights wandering the streets, you still knew."

"*Left* you?" I could not fathom what she meant. "And when, supposedly, was that?"

"Some six months ago. And when you went away, I thought I would never see you again. But . . ." She broke off for an arduous, rattling breath. ". . . only a week ago you came into a small bar, tired and hungry and homeless. With no money. I had just started working there. You were shocked to see me. Do you remember?"

"Not in the least."

"Try," she said. "Try to remember. I gave you food. Goulash. And you talked of many things. You told me you had been hospitalized for a time, apparently in a place much like this. And you talked of your hardships on the street. But mostly you talked of the book. And I could tell you were very despondent about something. Something more than your immediate circumstances. And after some prying on my part, you told me that you had received a vision. That the book had spoken to you."

An obvious lie.

"That could never have happened. The book would never have said anything. It would have laughed at me. Nothing more."

"Oh, so you remember *that*," she said, as if catching me at something. "You remember the book laughing at you. The book you claim is not real. Or was it laughing *with* you, as you laughed at yourself? Another means of furthering your misery."

"I don't know what you're talking about. You're just making this up. The way you made up those notes you gave me."

"I made up nothing."

She stopped—interrupting herself with a fit of coughing so violent I was afraid the staff would come to investigate. Her convulsions went on at length, and for a time, after they had subsided, she sat speechless, struggling to recover.

She cleared her throat.

"I wrote down exactly what you told me," she said. "The most elemental concepts you believed were necessary to decipher the manuscript. I wanted to understand, so I could help you. Help you to end the madness. And for many months I worked beside you, matching your efforts. But I could not match your obsession. Nor your will to push on in the face of what seemed a hopeless task. And so you went on, without me." She coughed again, her lungs crackling. "Leonard, tell me you remember."

"I . . ." This all felt so wrong. My doctor would not approve. "I'm sorry, but I don't. I don't remember any of it. And I don't want to hear any more about it."

I heard her exhale sharply, frustrated.

"But you must remember *something*. Your flash drive? The one with the copy of the book? And that carried your notes? You kept it with you always."

"Another imaginary thing I told you about."

"No. I have *seen* it. I *used* it. *We* did. *Together*. And when I saw you in the bar that day, you still had it. But you said you no longer needed it. That you had developed perfect recall of the book. Of its every page. And you told me then how the book had laughed at you for so long. But that it had finally stopped. It had talked to you. And that it had at last disclosed its secrets to you."

I rolled toward her, my eyes on her shadow. "Its secrets?"

"Yes. It gave you the key to the cipher."

"Why would it tell me such a thing?"

"As compensation for your lengthy and faithful service. For your utter devotion to the exclusion of all else."

I pushed myself up and sat on the side of the bed. "You're saying that I actually told you what *it* had told *me?*"

"Yes, Leonard. You did."

"Do you swear?"

"Do you *remember?*"

"I do not."

Though suddenly—irresistibly—I found myself wanting to.

And it occurred to me that within the information she claimed to possess there might conceivably lay a hint as to the origin of my many fantasies. Perhaps even something that might light the way toward a cure for my entire psychosis. And given those possibilities, did I not have sufficient justification to continue this discussion?

I thought I did. Still, I knew that such an exercise was potentially dangerous. The Judge himself had cautioned against yielding to this very temptation.

I spoke haltingly: "All right. I want to hear one thing—just one thing—the book said to me."

I could see her shifting about. With some difficulty, she again cleared her throat.

"Very well. One thing: It told you something you had suspected from the beginning—that the numbers found within the structure of the book—*three*, *six*, *twelve*, and *twenty-one*—are to be employed as the basis for the key. To begin the process of decryption, the six individual digits that make up those four numbers must be placed in a specified order and then reversed in sequence to create a palindrome of twelve numbers. A perfect expression of reflective symmetry."

"Symmetry," I repeated. There was, I felt, an odd and inexplicable sort of importance about the word—and I felt, also, that somewhere in my past that same word had held an importance to someone else. But to whom and why, I could not recall.

She sat in silence, my request satisfied.

I could not help myself.

"Tell me a second thing."

"Just as you thought, the book contains many nulls. However, the twelve-number palindrome, when applied repeatedly to the text in linear fashion, over and over, line by line, serves to winnow out the useless letters. It is a simple counting exercise: For every number of the palindrome, one counts, from left to right, that same number of letters. When the count reaches the number itself, the letter on which the number falls will be a null. The individual numbers of the palindrome themselves add up to *thirty*. Thus, twelve nulls are identified for every thirty letters of text. In this way, the relevant letters, which are otherwise indistinguishably scattered among the nulls, are also identified."

What she had described rang in my head like a bell.

"It's a transposition cipher," I said excitedly. "And fairly simple."

"Perhaps. But there is more."

Again, she sat quietly.

And again, the allure was too much.

"Go on," I said.

"After the nulls have been removed, the remaining letters are to be assembled, left to right, in the order in which they appear in the book. The resulting text, however, will nevertheless continue to look like gibberish. This is resolved by a process that initially involves the same palindrome that was used to identify the nulls. The twelve numbers are paired, in sequence, with the first twelve letters of the text, then the next twelve, and so on. The number assigned to each letter reveals how many positions back up that letter's alphabetic order one must go to find the replacement character to be used for that letter. What did you call this procedure? A *something* shift . . ."

The answer came on impulse.

"Caesar," I said readily. "A Caesar Shift."

"Yes, that is it. So if the ciphertext letter is a Latin *d*, and the key number is *three* . . ." She took a long, wheezing breath. ". . . then *d* should be replaced by the letter *a*."

I felt strangely patronized. "I know how a Caesar Shift works!"

"Of course you do, Leonard," she said.

I was literally panting, exhilarated by the depth of the method she had described.

"Remarkable," I said. "A substitution cipher buried within a transposition cipher. Two levels of encryption. But seven hundred years ago? It stretches all credibility."

"Yet there is more."

"Impossible."

"No, Leonard. You told me yourself: The letters identified by the Caesar Shift are *still* not the characters of the plaintext. A series of calculations involving the original numbers—*three*, *six*, *twelve*, and *twenty-one*—must be made in order to obtain additional numbers which are then used as the key to a second shift. This second shift, however, is cross-alphabetical. It converts each character ascertained by the first shift to a character of one of the other two alphabets. These, ultimately, are the plaintext letters."

"That is preposterous."

"And yet . . ."

"No!"

"Yes." She paused, resting her voice and lungs. "Even when the plaintext letters are at last revealed, they must be rearranged using a second symmetrical permutation of the original numbers—a second palindrome. Once this is done, each letter, in order, is assigned to its own alphabet, at which point—after appropriate word spacing and punctuation are determined—the text becomes legible."

"In what languages?"

"Medieval Latin, Quranic Arabic, and Byzantine Greek. All of the Latin passages are read first. Then, at the end of the Latin, one reads the Arabic portion in the other direction—Arabic, of course, being read from right-to-left. Following that, the direction of the text is, naturally, reversed again for the Greek."

I sat for a time in shock.

I shook my head without feeling the motion.

"My god," I muttered. "this is the work of a maniac. . . . Multiple encryption levels. A multi-lingual plaintext. The complexity is beyond belief." I looked into her dark corner. "And I actually told you all of this?"

"Just as I have told you," she said. "I *swear*."

Yet still, I did not remember.

But even so, the image of the Paisley, so recently reduced in my mind to a scarcely perceptible haze, was returning to focus, its cracked leather cover no longer a blurred fantasy, but, once more, seeming solidly the product of centuries.

And with this apparent return of clarity came an inescapable thought.

"So if what you say is true . . . If I was really given these secrets—the key to every step in the decryption process—then I undoubtedly must have . . . I mean, did I . . .?"

I was almost afraid to say it.

No, I *was* afraid.

I sat mute, mustering the courage to finally put the question:
"What did I do?"

"You read the book, of course."

Something like a surge of electricity passed though me, arresting, it seemed, the very pulse of my heart. I shook with a violence I could not control. I wept tears without constraint.

Tears of bliss. Of relief.

It went on—*I* went on—as if I were the only person in the room. A kind of party for one. I pounded the bed. I wanted to shout. I jumped to my feet and whirled my bedsheets about, tossing them to the floor.

Then abruptly, I stopped.

A book that talks? Was that possible? And even if it were, what triumph lay in being given that which should have been earned?

But no, I thought, books do not talk. Though, on the other hand, I was undeniably a madman. And a madman may hear things others do not. For him, a book may laugh. It may even speak. Yet it is the insightful lunatic who understands that the voice he hears is in fact his own. And if the Paisley had indeed assumed a voice, then clearly I had provided it. Its laughter, too, had always been mine. I had been both instructor and student. Heckler and victim.

Which meant only one thing: There had been no cheap receipt of information; the book had not told me anything.

I had told myself.

Because I, alone, had solved the Paisley.

I had beaten the son of a bitch!

I punched the air double-fisted. I clenched and gnashed my teeth, making a growling sound.

"I did it!" I screamed in a whisper. "I really *did it!*"

"Yes, Leonard," she said. "You did."

"*I* did."

"Yes, Leonard. You. And *only* you."

"It must have been the most spectacular brute force attack in history!"

"And the most relentless. You never gave up."

The celebration, though, began to fade. For another question remained, and as with the one previous, the weight of the answer (whatever that answer might be) made the asking all the more difficult.

I took a trembling breath of the room's stuffy air and sat back down on the bed, facing her dark profile.

"What did it say?"

"The book, you mean?"

"Well, what else? Yes, the *book*. What was its message?"

She did not reply straightaway. "You did not tell me."

"What the hell? I told you everything else. Why wouldn't I tell you that?"

"Oh, Leonard . . ." A further hesitation. "You so very desperately wanted to."

"But . . ."

"Leonard, I am so sorry. But you had forgotten. Forgotten everything you had read. Even the very subject matter. As I said, you were in great despair."

I was slow to grasp the import of this, my mind perhaps unwilling.

"Okay," I said, "so I forgot. Big deal. Back when we talked about all this, I knew how to read the book. Right? And now, so do you. *I told you.*"

"You gave me only generalities, just as I have given you. Nothing more. You were not able to. You had forgotten how the key numbers were to be arranged, and how the computations were to be made. All of it."

At once, I began to feel a deathly loss of balance. As if I had endured a momentous climb to the top of a high tower and now stood on its edge, about to plummet its length.

"But I must have written it down. Some of it, at least."

"You did not. You were wrapped in inspiration. A revelation through which you were, for a brief time, given perfect intuition. Perfect understanding. You wrote down nothing."

The room whirled about me. I shut my eyes against the spinning shadows and was overcome by such a sickness that I thought I might very well collapse and retch myself into nothingness.

"All that work," I said. "All a waste. Everything I've done. A waste."

"Only a fool would believe that."

"But it's gone. I've lost it."

"Then regain it."

"How?"

"How do you think? Where could the answer possibly be? Within the book? Or within the man who read it? Or *both*? And are you not the master of both?"

I? The master of the Paisley? And of myself? I so wished that to be true. Yet even after all she had told me, I remained without any hard evidence on which to pin such hopes. I was, at best, something like a man in the grip of dementia, hearing stories of the person he had once been. A person with whom he no longer had the slightest association.

Then too lay the possibility that this portrait she had drawn of me was nothing more than a ride in a pumpkin that had never been a carriage. There was no way to be sure.

"I don't know who I am."

"You are Leonard Stavros," she said firmly, loudly—almost a proclamation. "The greatest cryptanalyst in the world. Do you not believe that?"

"I want to."

"Then *act* as if you do. *Think* as if you do. And be that person—again."

The room had grown stifling. I was sweating heavily. Beads running my skin.

I dropped onto my back, staring at the dark, blank ceiling. Exhausted. A heaviness on my chest.

"Before he died, my father told me that a man who hates himself will never please himself," she said. "That he will not allow it. When he said that, he was talking about you, Leonard. *You.* You left me because you loathed yourself. And that day we spoke in the bar, despite my pleas for you to come back to me—to come *home*—you would not, because you *still* loathed yourself. And you loathe yourself even now. These walls around you, the people here, everything both inside and outside of this place—it is all built of your own self-disgust."

"It seems real to me."

"And the Paisley Codex does not? But you will not find it here. It does not exist here. You have removed it."

"*I* did?"

"Yes, Leonard. Your world, your rules."

I pushed myself up as far as I could, but found myself so drained, I could do little more than half rise, the bed itself seeming to possess an almost overwhelming force of gravity.

"What are you saying? That this is some kind of dream?"

"In a sense, it is. Call it, though, a *sleepless* dream. A *waking* dream. The kind of dream one has when all thoughts and feelings of reality are put aside and the mind falls in upon itself like the weight of a black hole from which almost nothing can escape."

"Can't I just wake up?"

"Not from here." The smell of smoke grew stronger, the room hotter, virtually ablaze. "Not from here, ever."

I felt an increasing stupor. I could hardly form the words: "So how do I get out of here?"

"There is a way. You know it already. And you know also where you must go then."

"Where?"

"As I have told you before," she said, "through the fire."

I lay baking in the heat, sopping in sweat, trying to move, but unable. "What is the fire?" I asked.

Her voice trailed away like a dissipating vapor.

"It is what separates us."

-37-

COME MORNING, I found it hard to wake. The night staff claimed to have discovered me during the early hours in an agitated state and, out of alleged necessity, administered a booster of my bedtime sedative. In a dead sleep, I had missed breakfast, and when I finally arose, was led zombie-like by my orderly to the men's washroom for a shower, which I intentionally took cold. The shock of the frigid water revived me, and even before I had toweled off, found myself fully focused on thoughts of the previous night's visitor.

Back in my room, we spoke in whispers.

"I know what I'm going to do," I said.

Ed flashed a wicked smile. "I think I like it."

I looked at the Judge. "You?"

He was adamant. "It is a positively horrible idea. Most likely, you will only be making more trouble for yourself. And us."

Ed and I exchanged glances.

"I think we have to take the chance, Judge," I said. "It's a calculated risk."

"But Stavros, absolutely nothing this woman told you has been verified. Regardless of her intentions, she may only be leading you deeper into psychosis."

"Maybe," I said. "But if she's right, and we stay here, we're finished. This could be the only way out."

"It is unadulterated folly!" the Judge declared. "I stand most firmly against it."

I looked at Ed again—then both of us at the Judge. "You're outvoted."

———————————

The doctor sat on my desk chair, his legs crossed; I lay supine on my bed, his Freudian captive. The usual preliminary pleasantries had been exchanged.

We entered the meat of the session.

"Mr. Stavros, a few days ago, you told me that you saw other persons in this room. Specifically, there were two. Do you recall that?"

"Yes."

"And may I ask, are those persons here now?"

I raised myself to check the room's far corner. "They are."

"Very good," he said. "I would like to know more about them. For instance, do they have names?"

"Yeah, more or less."

"And what are they? What do you call them?"

"I don't think that's important."

"Well, Mr. Stavros, unfortunately, I think otherwise. Now, to make this easier, let's just approach whichever of these parties is the more gregarious. You know, the one who is most outgoing. Surely he . . . Or is it a *she?*"

"No, they're both of the male persuasion."

Ed had a nice chuckle. The Judge remained staidly unamused.

"Very well. So which of you is the most sociable?" the doctor asked, looking aimlessly about the room. "Will you be friendly and tell me your name?"

I felt as if I were attending a séance.

Ed spoke up: "Pudden Tame."

"What?" I asked.

He told me the same.

I told the doctor.

He was dubious. "That's his name?"

"Of course it isn't, you ass," I said, channeling Ed. "And by the way, what's *your* name?"

The doctor acted taken aback. "Mr. Stavros," he said, "as we've discussed in the past, our time together will be more productive if we behave in a civil manner."

"Don't evade the question, doc," I said, sitting up. "Now, let's hear it. Your name."

I had hit upon something. Seconds passed as he squirmed in his seat like a little boy caught being naughty.

"You know very well what my name is. Now . . ." He cleared his throat, his old stalling tactic revisited. ". . . I want to go back to . . ."

"No, no, no." I swung to the side of the bed and slapped my feet to the floor, facing him eye to eye. "In my entire time here, you have never told me your name. And I have never heard anyone here call you by a name. Do you even have one?"

My orderly, who had been lurking outside the door, moved to occupy the threshold.

"We okay in here?" he asked, glaring at me.

"What's *your* name?" I said.

He continued his glare—without an answer.

In fact, it seemed he had none.

And right then, I began to feel a greater assurance in what I was about to do; the ruse I suspected was on the verge of being laid bare.

"So," I said, "you're both afflicted with the same problem. I'm so sorry."

The doctor examined his wristwatch. "Mr. Stavros, we need to get back on track here."

"In a minute," I said. "But first, tell me something: *Where are we?*"

With a puzzled expression, the doctor glanced at the orderly, then back at me. "You mean where are we in the course of this session?"

"No, that's not what I mean, and you know it. Let's try again: Tell me the name of this hospital. Or better yet, the name of this city."

"Are you saying," he asked, "that you no longer know where you are?"

"No, I'm saying I have *never* known."

My reply appeared to stir within him a measure of delight, as though he had found a new cudgel with which to increase my torment.

"Well, that is rather disconcerting," he said, holding back a derisive smile. "So tell *me*, Mr. Stavros, do you know what day it is? Or the month? Or even the year?"

"No. But then, neither do you."

He liberated that smile. A very broad, toothy, razor-sharp smile.

He was loving this—so far.

"And why would that be?" he said.

"Because *I* don't know. Don't you see? *You* don't know because *I* don't know."

The smile burgeoned. He simply could not suppress his glee at the psychotic hole he perceived me to be digging.

He moved to the front of his seat, anxious to help with the dirt work.

"So if I have this correct," he said, "it's your belief that I can only know what you know?"

"Or what I *believe* that I know. Or," I added, "what I believe that you know that I believe I *don't* know—but only, of course, to the extent that I subconsciously do know or believe that I do."

"I'll have to give that one some thought," he chuckled, thoroughly condescending. "In any event, if I understand this, you are saying that I am merely a conduit through which your own knowledge and beliefs are somehow manifested. Is that it?"

"Precisely."

"But Mr. Stavros . . ." He laughed again. "Why do you think that such an *egocentric construct*, let us call it, has even the slightest validity?"

My orderly, still blocking the door, actually seemed more interested in my response than the doctor.

"Because," I told the doctor, "to put this in no uncertain terms, I am you." I pointed at the orderly: "And I am *you*. . . . And *you* and *you*," I said to Ed and the Judge. "I am *all* of you. And by the same token, you are me."

"I think there was a song that went something like that," the orderly cracked.

He and the doctor laughed in unison.

"I'll take The Rolling Stones for a thousand, Alex!" Ed threw in. "Oh, no, wait, it was the other . . ."

"Shut up," the Judge commanded. "This is about to get serious."

"So," the doctor went on, "you believe that everyone here—*everything* here—is just a projection of your own thoughts?"

"That's it," I said.

The doctor slowly shook his head in a manner meant to emphasize the supposed absurdity of my theory.

"And how, pray tell, do you believe this came about?" he said.

"I don't know exactly. It's not a dream. Not quite. It's some other form of altered consciousness. Or at least, that's what I've been told."

"By whom?"

"That is none of your business. But I do believe that she was telling me the truth. Which is that you are working against me. That you never intend to release me from this place. That the Paisley Codex is real . . ."

The doctor threw up his hands. "Oh, good lord! I thought we were through with that!"

". . . And that this stuff about Carlo Marino, and working at a bar, and gambling problems, and on and on, is all crap. It never happened. And I will never again believe such total bullshit!"

His mood having changed, the doctor rejoined with a smirk of indifference that all too obviously masked a far less agreeable sentiment.

"You know, I think we've had enough for today," he said, rising from the chair. "I'll see you tomorrow."

"Don't count on it."

He shot me a look plainly meant to answer my threat with one of his own.

The orderly gave way as the doctor moved to the door.

"Hey, doc," I said, "before you go, one more thing."

He stopped. I heard him groan.

"What sort of drugs did you use on me when you tied me to that gurney? You know, that time I supposedly went nuts over the computer?"

He turned back to me, his suspicions grinding away as he contemplated the motive for my question.

"Just standard protocol," he said.

"Yeah, but *what?*"

"A sedative and an anti-psychotic."

I knew that. I knew that was what they did. Generically.

"But the drugs themselves," I pressed. "What are their brand names?"

"That is immaterial."

I was convinced: *He did not know.*

Because neither did I.

"Well, if you say. But if I went, you know, bonkers like I did before, would you use the same drug combination?"

"Why are you asking?"

"Because I'm the guy you would shoot up, and I think I have the right to know what you'd be doing to me. Don't you agree?"

He looked into the hall, answering curtly: "It would be the same."

For a second time, he started to leave.

"So I suppose the *effect* of those drugs would also be the same as before?" I said.

Once more, he stopped. He kept his back to me.

"Why wouldn't it?" he snapped. "Now, as I have said, we are done here."

As he stepped into the hall, I sprang from the bed, toward him. The orderly moved between us.

"I've had enough of this shit," I said. "I want my flash drive!"

As if it existed in this world. But my demand had served its purpose.

Wearing a look of disgust, the doctor reentered the room.

"Another delusion of which I thought you were cured," he said.

"Now listen . . ."

"*Non, vous écoutez! Je veux ma propriété. Et si vous ne me le donnez pas, vous serez vraiment désolé.*"[1]

The words had left my mouth almost reflexively.

They had all but spoken themselves.

And in that instant, I thought the doctor might pass out. His jaw fell open. His eyes grew wide.

The Judge was equally astonished.

As was I—in virtual disbelief at the restoration of my faculties.

"*Oh oiu, je parle français,*" I said. "*Et je le parle très bien.*"[2]

The doctor stood speechless, shaking his head in tiny, rapid jerks.

"*Watashi wa hoka no gengo mo hanashimasu,*" I said in Japanese. "*Ikutsu ka kikitaidesu ka?*"[3]

Locked in stupor, he didn't seem to.

Nonetheless, I switched to Danish: "*Så du forstår, du røvhul, du er ikke så klog.*"[4]

He appeared to agree.

I then addressed both the doctor and his hairless attendant:

"*Xiànzài, xiānshēngmen,*" I concluded in Chinese, "*wǒ bìxū xiàng nǐmen gàobié.*"[5]

They looked at one another, dumbfounded.

---

1. "No, you listen! I want my property. And if you do not give it to me, you will be really sorry."

2. "Oh yes, I speak French," . . . "And I speak it very well."

3. "I speak other languages too," . . . "Do you want to hear some?"

4. "So you see, you asshole, you are not so smart."

5. "Now, gentlemen," . . . "I must bid you farewell."

I glanced at Ed. He gave me two thumbs up.

Facing the orderly, I initiated a cock of my right leg—but swiftly changing course, made a short pivot and, with a sweeping soccer kick, planted my foot in the doctor's groin.

Promptly folding to ninety degrees, the doctor made a sound like a braying donkey, then, unable to find another breath, continued his descent in silence, his purpled and vein-bulging face convulsed in the throes of a muted scream. The orderly, meanwhile, stood frozen in a kind of daze, a shocked and passive observer to both my unexpected attack and its immediate aftermath—the latter of which saw the doctor at last sink fully to the tile floor, a jackknifed puddle of agony.

And in the midst of that spectacle of pain and perplexity—all of which I had proudly authored—I was out the door.

"Stavros!" the orderly called, first starting after me, but at once returning to kneel beside his wounded chief. "Somebody stop him!"

I ran down the hall and into the dayroom, where another orderly took up the chase. I reached the nursing station ahead of him and slammed my face into the thick, unbreakable glass.

And damn, that hurt. But then, the crazier the better.

"I want my fucking flash drive!" I raged, blood running from my lips and nose.

The orderly who was tailing me caught up. I spun to confront him.

"I will tear your throat out!" I said, brandishing a claw-like set of fingers as I assumed the sort of Kung Fu posture I had seen in films.

Unsure of my level of martial arts training, he took a step back.

"This is the end!" I announced, blood sliming my face and neck as if I had gorged myself on the flesh of a living animal. "For every last one of you! You're all gonna die . . . *bitches!"*

(And yeah, that last part was definitely Ed talking.)

I heard shrieks and screams. Some from patients. Others from nurses and techs.

And I'm not just talking about the women.

I stuck my tongue out, wagging its bloody tip around like a hungry, disgusting beast. It was all so perfect.

A multitude of staff poured into the day room, joining those already there. Together, as a single body, they grouped about me, keeping their distance.

But all the while slowly moving in.

I retreated, backing into the main hall. The door through which I had once escaped lay to my right. And though the code was no longer what it had been, it occurred to me that I knew the new one as if I had reset it myself.

Which, in effect, I had.

Yet I had no intention of taking that route. There was a much better way.

Several tense moments passed that heard only the sounds—from both myself and the crowd—of heavy breathing and shuffling feet. I went ever in reverse, and they toward me, until at last my back met the wall.

I looked from person to person, ready for whoever might be the first to increase the stakes of this standoff. No one volunteered. But then, from behind the mass of my encirclers, I heard an almost comical moaning and saw, through the gathering, the doctor, glassy-eyed and bent at the waist, stumble onto the scene doing a very fine Quasimodo impression. He was being hauled along by my orderly, and it was evident from the yellow stream running the length of his sport coat that the bold physician had puked himself.

"Ready the injection," he muttered, as if directing an execution.

I smeared the blood about my face like warpaint.

"Don't mess with me, doc. I'm a bad man."

"And you are about to be a very sleepy one," he said, limping on while managing, with extreme discomfort, to straighten himself.

Bearing a ghastly scowl—the cold sweat of his misery spouting from his every pore—he cast off the orderly's helping hand and staggered toward me. The nurse with snakes for hair handed him a loaded syringe.

And like the splitting of a seam, the horde of hospital personnel began parting before him.

"Now," he said, "if you will please go quietly."

I let loose a maniacal laugh—a blood-spattering farewell to this house of pain and its many ghostly residents, all unsuspecting of their imminent demise.

The doctor continued on, raising the needle. My orderly, the dutiful henchman, at his side, gunning for me. The swarm of others around us moving back further and further, allowing them passage. Forming an ever-widening lane of attack.

And with a rebel yell, I charged into the breach.

SCRIPTOR LIBRI

The Tale
of the Nine Years

THE STAIRWAY SEEMED HIGHER than before. Impossibly high. And steeper. Less stable. On all sides I heard the grating of wood, the weight of my every upward stride risking the integrity of the rickety framework. Threatening to hasten its collapse into the shadows that lay below the last discernible step. A chasm from which this towering span appeared to spring without a starting point. And just as its base stood veiled in darkness, its summit was likewise obscured, the visible, winding tendril between the extremes wagging in a slow serpentine wave.

All of it, I felt, ready to topple at the least further disturbance.

I tread more gently with the scaling of every riser. The climb wore on me. My legs ached. My lungs heaved. But in the dark ahead, my objective came into view. And in a burst brought on by the proximity of the finish line, I bounded over the last few steps—only to find, as my leading leg swung to the landing, that my trailing foot was suddenly bereft of underpinning. In that same moment there came from below a multitude of pops and snaps and, nearly simultaneous, the cacophonous sound of complete structural failure; the stairs fell away. And as the greater part of me did likewise, I dove and clung to the platform that remained, the fractured remnants of the staircase plunging, strangely noiseless, into what seemed a bottomless depth.

I pulled myself onto the landing, gasping, dizzy, trying to process the seconds that had just proceeded—then, lacking all but the smallest semblance of composure, rose to face the door—the closed door—that now presented as my only viable option.

I was about to knock.

"Come in, Leonard."

I swung the door open. The pastor, as before, sat at his desk in cleric regalia. The room, as before, was well lit.

I wobbled in, wild-eyed, "Your stairs . . . They're gone."

He calmly closed the book he had been reading and lowered his glasses. "Gone?"

I made a sweeping sign with my hands. "Completely!"

He put down the book and shrugged. "No surprise, I suppose. They were quite old and feeble."

"Yeah, but I barely . . . I mean, I almost . . ."

"Now, Leonard, didn't I tell you last time that if you left, it would be difficult to return?"

"Yeah, but . . ." I looked around the windowless room, its single means of egress now useless. "So how do we . . .?"

He smiled warmly. "Do you wish to leave again so soon?"

"No, I'm just . . ."

I could not finish a sentence.

"Then you'll concern yourself with that later," he said. "There is always a way." He removed his glasses and motioned to the chair in front of his desk. "Please. Sit."

As I did, I noticed things I did not recall from my previous visit: On the wall to my left, a copy of Hofmann's Portrait in White. On a small stand in the corner, a bust of Martin Luther. And behind the pastor, on a polished and otherwise bare wooden credenza, set in a gilded frame, a photograph of a young girl with dark hair.

A service of piping hot tea sat on the desk to one side. The pastor poured a cup and set it down in a saucer near the desk's edge where I could reach it.

"Thank you, pastor."

"As I recall," he said, "no cream or sugar."

"Correct."

He poured himself a cup—like mine, unsweetened—and took a sip.

"It's quite nice to see you again," he said. "I don't get many visitors here."

I took a long look toward the door. "And I doubt there'll be many more."

"Yes, well, it's an arduous trip in any event. But I think so much of the difficulty lies in the aversion people have toward speaking with the departed. We pass on with so much baggage. Regrets for things done and undone, things spoken and unspoken. Resentment. Guilt. Fear. We bring it all with us—and yet also, somehow, leave so much of it behind. And the finality of death—the permanent separation from the living world—makes it all seem so much worse. So much more tragic. Which is why, of course, those to whom we were most close choose to remember us in cheery, fanciful ways that bear no relationship to the lives we genuinely lived. For them, that is the way of convenience. Easier for them than to deal with us as we really are—or were."

"*Us?*" I said.

"You know. The dead."

"Wait. You're saying that *you're* dead?"

"Yes, Leonard. I have been for some time. I thought that was established. I thought you knew."

Come to think of it, maybe I did.

"So am I dead too?"

"I don't know. Do you feel dead?"

"I don't think so."

"Then you probably aren't. On the other hand, despite all of this," he said, waving a hand along his clerical vestments, "I'm no expert." He pointed to my cup. "Try your tea, Leonard. It's quite good."

I did as he suggested. "Yes, it's very . . . refreshing."

"And soothing?"

"Yes, soothing." That was the word I had wanted.

He picked up his cup and saucer and took a series of small swallows, for a time intent only upon the tea. The act of consuming it. Tasting it. Experiencing it.

He set down the saucer and, with great care and a scarcely audible *clink*, placed the cup on top.

"Well, whatever the case may be," he said, "you are here again, and that is good. Leonard, you are as much a son to me as any I might have actually had. You know that, don't you?"

"Yes, sir."

"And as I always told you, I am here for you whenever you need my help."

"I know."

What had been a friendly, fatherly look turned then to a penetrating stare.

"I have a feeling you need my help now," he said.

Flustered, I looked around the room. At the bust of Martin Luther. At Hofmann's painting. At the picture of the dark-haired girl on the credenza, her soft, adolescent features suggesting a promise of womanly beauty.

"Your instincts may be correct," I said, as politely as possible. "And I don't mean to refuse your assistance. But right now, if you don't mind, I am more interested in something else."

He was clearly displeased with my response. Just as clearly, though, it was what he had expected.

"What is it, then, you wish to discuss?" he said.

"The last time I was here, you spoke of a book. The kind of book, you said, that was, generally speaking, not meant to be read."

"Yes, I recall that. And I also recall that the mere mention of it left you quite upset. I would hate to see that happen again."

"It won't."

There was a brief interim in which I could not read his thoughts, but in the next moment he appeared resigned to my choice of topic.

He took another sip of tea.

"Then we shall talk of the book," he said.

In a sort of celebration, I drained my cup.

"But any discourse on the subject would be incomplete without also further discussing a certain man of Italian descent, now long deceased. Do you remember his name?"

"I do. Ferrante da Rimini."

"And there was a woman, as well. Do you remember her?"

"Bellamente," I said. *"Beautiful mind."*

"Yes. Beautiful she was. In both mind and body."

He refreshed his tea and, extending the pot, offered me another cup, which I accepted with a whispered thanks.

"Now, we spoke before of their escape from Italy," he said, "and of how they fled to the west. But I do not believe we discussed precisely where they went—which was quite far from their starting point. Ultimately, they left the continent entirely, crossing the North Sea on a trade ship, which put them in Scotland. Fortunately for them, the Scottish king, Robert Bruce, had little care for anything that was happening in Italy, and in return for their considerable intellectual services, gave them sanctuary at Rothesay Castle, which Bruce had recently recaptured from the English. There they remained for the better part of a year. They were married there, and as I said before, they were exceedingly happy, each content in the belief that, in all the world, there existed no suitable partner for either of them save the other. But as I also said, circumstances would intervene. Circumstances, in fact, that had been set in motion some years earlier.

"You see, back when Ferrante was in the employ of King Philip the Fair of France, Philip had done a very dastardly thing involving the destruction of a Catholic monastic order known as the Poor Fellow-Soldiers of Christ and the Temple of Solomon. We know this order better today by their shortened moniker: the Knights Templar. The Templars were rumored to have a vast treasure of gold and priceless artifacts. Certainly, though, they had tremendous financial resources. And because of that, they essentially became bankers to some of the most powerful people in Europe—which is what got them into trouble with Philip. He borrowed money he could not repay. So he simply cancelled his debt by putting an end to the Templars. He had them rounded up by the scores all over France and, after little or no legal procedure—and a good deal of torture to obtain false confessions—had a great many of them publicly executed, burned at the stake, under fabricated charges of heresy. But then, I'm sure I haven't told you a thing you didn't already know."

He hadn't. However, I felt it rude to say as much.

"No, pastor, that was all quite informative. But I'm wondering . . . the book?"

He took a sip of tea. "We're getting there." He took another sip. "You know, I've more or less come to believe that it was Ferrante's revulsion at Philip's persecution of the Templars that prompted him to leave France and return to Italy. But I suppose we'll never really know what his motivation was. Anyway, the fact is, Philip failed to make a clean sweep of the Templars. A good many of them caught wind of the coming purge and escaped in advance to various havens beyond Philip's reach. And though several years had passed since the purge, it was only a number of months after Ferrante and Bellamente arrived in Scotland that three Templar knights, seeking favor, surfaced in the court of Robert Bruce with a particular item that Bruce quickly deemed to be of enormous value."

"The book," I surmised.

"Yes, the book."

I felt a chill across my shoulders. "My god! It originated with the Templars?"

"It would seem so. Though perhaps not with any of the three Templars who appeared before Robert."

"Why is that?"

"Because, as the story goes, none of them knew how to read it," he said. "The book was supposedly written in an elaborate code—or perhaps one should call it a cipher—of a type not even Ferrante or Bellamente had ever encountered. Nevertheless, they were, naturally, charged by Robert with the decryption process. And the stakes were high because, you see, the one thing the Templars *did* profess to know about the book was its subject matter, which, they alleged, concerned an accounting of items loaded aboard a cadre of Templar ships at the French port of La Rochelle only days ahead of Philip's assault on the order. And it concerned, too, they claimed, the saga of the voyage of those ships—and the disclosure of their ultimate destination. The secret resting place of the greatest fortune in all of Christendom."

I was hit with such a sense of wonder, I could not hold back.

"The Templar treasure!"

He gave a nod. "None of which has ever been found—although Philip the Fair spent a considerable amount of time looking for it. And it vexed him to no end that somehow his plan to dispose of the Templars had leaked before he could secure their riches for himself."

I shook my head in disbelief. "A treasure map." I looked at the pastor with something of a loss for words. "The book is basically a treasure map! I would never have guessed."

Neither confirming nor denying my conclusion, he slid his cup and saucer aside and leaned forward, solemnly clasping his hands and resting them, as a unit, on his desk.

"Ferrante worked day and night to decrypt the cipher, and after some time, he claimed—and believed—that he had cracked it. Bellamente, however, assured him he had not. In fact, she had, at the outset, declared the cipher unbreakable. Either that or the book was sheer gibberish, she said. A monumental hoax to which the king of Scotland was in danger of falling victim. But I don't have to tell you who Robert Bruce sided with. He was in the midst of a war with England. He had an army to feed. He needed money to buy the loyalties of the Scottish nobles who would otherwise have favored his adversary. And he needed any number of other things: horses, wagons, siege machines—the latter of which, at the time, he did not have a single one. So the prospect, however unlikely, of locating an outrageous fortune was quite appealing to Bruce, and he promptly organized an expedition to sail from Aberdeen. He put Ferrante in charge. And he pledged to Ferrante that should he locate the prize, he would be rewarded with a generous share of the take."

The pastor held up three fingers. "Three weeks. That is what Ferrante swore to Bellamente. Three weeks—twenty-one days—and he would return. The cipher was clear, he said: The ships from La Rochelle had not sailed far; the treasure lay relatively close by. And he knew just the place. Again, Bellamente distrusted all of this. Nonetheless, she promised to count the days. And on an unusually calm morning, the expedition left port in a single ship. A ship of the cog variety. Do you know of it?"

"Somewhat," I said. "A small medieval vessel."

"Yes, small and with only a single mast. The ship was also fitted with oars for times of adverse wind conditions. And though the hold was large for its time, it would certainly not have been anywhere big enough to accommodate the entirety of the treasure they sought. At least, not in anything like a single trip. But it was the best the fourteenth century had available, and with Scotland at war, Robert dared not risk any of the rest of his meager fleet. And so, limited as their resources were, Ferrante and some two dozen others put sail on a mission as strange and speculative as has ever been launched.

"Now, as I've said, Ferrante was given responsibility for the voyage. He did not, however, officially captain the ship. He was not a seaman. As a practical matter, though, he did captain the fortunes of all on board—and the fortunes, too, of Bellamente, who stood on the dock and watched as all she loved or ever would love floated away into the North Sea. And she watched, I am sure, until the last bit of the mast fell below the curve of the Earth and Ferrante was gone."

The pastor presented a look—a rough frown—of discontent.

"The winds were favorable," he said, "and within three days, using coordinates Ferrante claimed to have taken from the book, the ship reached a barren island north of the Scottish coast. A cold, small, and uninhabited place. It was thoroughly combed for evidence of the treasure, buried or otherwise. Yet nothing was found, and Ferrante had to admit that he had been mistaken—but only slightly. He undertook a reinterpretation of the cipher and concluded that it actually referenced another small and desolate island nearby. The expedition sailed there directly. But the result was the same.

"Ferrante, of course, did not want to return to Robert Bruce empty-handed. However, there was yet another island in the vicinity that he thought to be a likely candidate. An effort was made to reach it. But the weather turned, and the tiny cog was blown far into the North Atlantic, into uncharted waters. Rough days passed on the open sea. And when the crew again sighted land, they saw a coastline none of them recognized."

I broke in: "I assume Ferrante didn't make it back in three weeks."

"He did not. Just as Bellamente had feared. Nonetheless, she had taken lodging near the port. She watched the harbor. She counted those twenty-one days as she had said she would. And after marking the last in that series, she began another. And another. Observing the progress of time in batches of twenty-one. And sometimes upon reaching twenty-one, as if to figuratively erase the passing of those days, she counted backwards. And so in time, it was always such: Twenty-one up, and twenty-one down."

"Sounds like she went a bit off her rocker."

The pastor nodded. "She was headed there. But then, so was Ferrante. For him, everything was at risk: His status with Robert Bruce. The trust of the crew. And most of all, his own self-respect. His ego. Because he had never in his life been so stupendously incorrect—and with such potentially dire consequences. He simply could not accept such an embarrassing and catastrophic personal failure.

"And thus he went back to the cipher. He reinterpreted once more. And soon he had convinced himself that this strange shore before them was the very place they sought. So, at Ferrante's insistence, they made landfall, where they were met by the local inhabitants—who, it turned out, were overtly hostile. There was a bloody fight. A number of the crew were killed. But there was no treasure.

"At this point it should come as no surprise that a mutiny was imminent. Ferrante claimed to have again reread the cipher and, again, ascertained a new destination—this time a place inconceivably far away. To the last man the crew stood against him. Threats were made. But Ferrante, with his persuasive powers, talked down the insurgents. He appealed first to their national loyalties, then to their fear of Robert Bruce, and then to their pocket books, pledging his entire share of the treasure to be divided equally among those who would continue the quest. And it was that last one that did it. They sailed on.

"The book led the way—or so Ferrante professed. And as his supposed readings of the cipher grew more and more erratic, the expedition journeyed to ever more exotic lands. To forests, jungles, deserts. Places where no civilized man had ever set foot. And as time passed, the search ceased in any way to be rational. And Ferrante and those who accompanied him—their numbers gradually dwindling through death and desertion—ceased to be rational as well. They had given their full measure of effort. They could have returned, without disgrace, to Scotland. And they knew that. Yet they continued their pursuit, the remaining crewmen driven by monetary desires. But Ferrante by something else: A refusal to concede his inability to conquer that which could not be conquered. To obtain that which could not be obtained. A blind denial of his own fragile and imperfect humanity."

"I'm afraid I know something of that," I said.

"Yes, Leonard, you do. And Ferrante would learn the same lesson. And with that lesson would come a moment of clarity. A day when he was at last able to separate himself from his noxious vanity and admit to his men—and to himself—that as Bellamente had warned, the book was at best indecipherable, and at worst a nonsensical hoax. Yet either way, a volume of deception that should never have been trusted."

He offered a droll smile. "To say the least, this was not well received by the crew, and Ferrante spent several days in chains, facing possible execution. But with their numbers so considerably reduced, it was decided that he should be spared if for no reason other than to help physically man the ship. Then too, both the captain and navigator were long dead, and Ferrante, with his analytical abilities, had kept the ship on course ever since. So to an even greater extent, his efforts were necessary on the charts and tiller. And indeed, after many further adversities—months of hard seas, thirst, starvation, numbing cold—it was by Ferrante's guidance that the ship at long last returned to Scotland. To the very place from which those few left on board had departed.

"They had been away nine years," the pastor said grimly.

Nine years.

The span of time itself seemed an abject indignity.

"You know," he said, "most people today live nearly eighty years. Some more. Some less. Yet in those days, a good deal less. Still, in any age . . . nine years? A wasted nine years! Think of it, Leonard. Both now and then, nine years embodies a considerable portion of a man's life. Or . . ." He raised his brow line. ". . . a woman's."

"Bellamente," I said.

"Yes." He took a deep breath and, at length, released it. "Nine years. And she had waited. Watching the port. Counting and uncounting the days. All others had given up on the expedition long before. But she had never wavered in her hope of again seeing Ferrante. Yet that hope had consumed her. She had, in her distraction, become useless to Robert Bruce. And in time she wanted for money. She was expelled from her lodgings. She became a thing of the street, taking handouts, mixing with the dregs of humanity. Babbling incoherently to anyone who would listen to her tales of her illustrious and long-lost husband who, she claimed, would one day return. And as I have said, he did."

From his expression I could see the pastor was, for a moment, occupied by an unrelated thought. He started to look behind him, toward the photo of the young girl—but stopped himself.

He continued:

"The cog neared Aberdeen on a horribly frigid winter's day. Only Ferrante and five others were left. They were utterly exhausted. Defeated. Wanting only to dock and end this torment they had almost wholly brought upon themselves. But they were met with a final challenge: The River Dee was frozen, choking the port entrance with ice. In some places very thick. In others, quite thin. Nonetheless, the short expanse between ship and land was clearly impassable and would be so for days.

"Ferrante and the crew debated what to do. And it was during this discussion that one of them noticed what appeared to be an old and ugly woman on the shore, near the pier, with matted gray hair and ragged clothes, waving to the ship as if she were hailing it. As if she recognized the vessel. Some of the men laughed at her." He paused, sad and pensive. "I wonder if Ferrante joined them. In any event, the woman persisted. She called out something in a hoarse and half-mad voice that none of the men could understand. And then, to their astonishment, she ventured onto the ice, toward the ship.

"I wish I could tell you that the men—or at least one of them—cautioned her to retreat. But history does not record such a thing. We know only that this woman continued toward the ship, oblivious to the danger underfoot. A danger that, with her every step, became more and more certain to manifest itself. And what, Leonard, do you think happened?"

"The ice," I said. "She fell through."

"Yes. And what happened then?"

"She died. She drowned. Or froze. No one could get to her."

"And no one tried." He put his elbows on the desk, propping up his clasped hands, his eyes peering out over the tops of his fingers. "Now, could she have been saved? Perhaps. Or perhaps not. And perhaps the attempt would have also taken the lives of all others who entered the water. But again, no one made the effort. The men—Ferrante among them—watched her flail amid the ice and disappear into the dark water. Yet the previous nine years had brought such tragedy, this was merely another. And a small one at that. Just a crazy old beggar-woman."

"She was obviously more," I said. "Much more."

"And very soon, Ferrante would learn that. And he would be driven to a despondency—and a guilt-ridden madness—far greater than you, Leonard, have ever known. By permission of Robert Bruce, he went back to Rothesay Castle to live out his days—which, it turned out, were few. For less than a year after his return, he threw himself from a tower window, presumably ending his suffering."

"And the book?"

"It had cost him everything. He destroyed it."

Just as I had done at my last visit, I sprang from my chair. But his time so quickly, I lost my balance.

I caught myself against his desk.

"Impossible!" I railed. "The book exists."

He leaned back, away from me—but in a manner that coolly rebuked my outburst. "You have assumed too much, Leonard. Ferrante had his book of demons, and you have yours. But they are not the same."

The enormity of my mistake landed like a sucker punch. I stood before him with nothing more to say. Feeling small and silly. The wretched successor to a long dead genius, the both of us shattered by the price of our ambitions.

The pastor twisted himself in his chair and looked at the girl in the photograph. "A brilliant young woman. Grown now." His lips held a proud smile. "My only child."

He gazed up at me.

My eyes went elsewhere.

"Let me ask you, Leonard: What do you think Ferrante would have done if he had proven himself the master of the Templar cipher? If he had found the treasure and sailed into that harbor with the greatest fortune known to the western world—then merely watched as the one thing he loved died in the icy water? What do you think would have changed for him?"

"Nothing."

"And what do you think would have changed for him if he had tried to save her? Even if it meant his own death?"

He did not seem to expect an answer.

I glanced at the door.

"Don't let me keep you," he said.

"But I told you. The stairs . . ."

"You'll think of something." He donned his glasses and opened his book. "Goodbye, Leonard. It was nice speaking with you again." He did not look up. "And Leonard?"

"Yes?"

"If you should see her, please tell her I send my love."

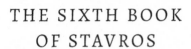

THE SIXTH BOOK
OF STAVROS

Symmetry

Doubtless, despite his suffering,
he had fallen asleep while walking,
for now he sees another scene—
perhaps he has merely recovered from a delirium.
He stands at the gate of his own home.

–Ambrose Bierce
"An Occurrence at Owl Creek Bridge"

-38-

THROUGH THE NIGHT SHADOWS and the soft light of streetlamps, I moved along a cobblestone sidewalk, slippery, in places, with compacted snow. Around and above, buildings that had stood centuries lay cloaked in the gloom and glistening damp as, before me, once and again, the fog of my breath turned the world to a hazy smudge.

My shoes beat a rhythm on the stones, the sole disturbance in the quiet air. The walk, the street, was mine alone. Yet someone, I thought (no, I *knew*) was coming my way. Or would be.

Or should be here already.

I slowed my pace, then came to a stop, looking behind me and, again, ahead. Waiting. Watching.

There was no one.

I told myself to go on.

But to *where?* Strange. I could not recall my destination.

Did I even have one?

I spent some time deliberating until, no closer to an answer, I decided it best to return from where I had come.

And where, I asked myself, was that?

With a shock, I felt at once like a drunk awakened from a blackout. Or rather, like a man—a quite sober man—who had simply *awakened*. A man pulled from sleep to find himself inexplicably cast into a place without purpose or starting point.

Yet these surroundings were not unfamiliar. I knew this street.

And hadn't it been just last evening, in almost this very spot . . .?

Or no. Not last evening. Not a day ago.

Not even so much as an hour.

In fact, it seemed it had been only . . .

I glanced back down the block, into the space I had occupied moments before. My actions there removed from the present only by the short time it had taken to arrive where I now stood. And beyond that? Farther down the street? Had I not been there too? Just several foggy breaths ago?

And seen a woman?

Or had I? I could not be sure. There was a vagueness about it. As if the memory of my trip from there to here were recorded on a strip of celluloid that had been cut and spliced back together, undergoing, in the process, the loss of several frames. Like missing pieces of a dream, never to be recollected.

But still, I knew that on this street, in *some* time past, I had seen her. Rushing toward me. And in my mind I saw her even now. Her face. Her hair.

A name arose in my thoughts and, just as quickly, fell from my lips as I called into the cold, empty dark. Hearing only an echo, I looked even farther back down the street, to that certain establishment near the corner. That place of once free goulash and the woman who had provided it.

Dim lights shone from within.

I hurried for the door and entered.

A lone man sat at a table in the shadows—the very table where I had once sat with her. From what I could see, though, in the entirety of the place, there was not another person present.

"What took you so long?"

The voice came from the table. And as my eyes adjusted to the weak light, I recognized Ed, sipping a bottle of beer.

"What are you doing here?" I said.

"Waitin' for you. We belong together."

"I seriously doubt that."

"Oh, really?" He chuckled. "Once upon a time you told a so-called doctor you didn't think you could live without me."

"I must have been crazy." I sampled a whiff of the room, hoping for a sign of her. "Was she here tonight?"

"Who?"

"You know. Nina."

"Oh, so *that's* her name," he said. "No, she doesn't work here anymore."

"Since when?"

He shrugged, indifferent. "I don't know. About a week ago some guy came in here and got her all upset, and no one's seen her since. At least, that's what I heard."

"From whom?"

"I can't remember."

Slowly, I came up to the table, looking down on him. "That's bullshit. She would never do that. Just disappear. She's not like that."

"So you think. But who's to say she's still the person you knew—or thought you knew. I mean, all those pills she takes . . ."

I was incredulous. "What pills?"

"Guess you forgot about that, huh?" He finished his beer in several gulps, violently planting the empty bottle on the table. "You want somethin'? Come on. Last call."

He started to get up.

I pushed him back in his chair. He had to grab the table to keep himself from falling over.

His temper flared. "Oh, tough guy."

"That's right. And I may just kick your ass."

"I'd like to see you try."

"Did you bring your gun?"

"I won't need it."

He moved higher in the chair. Jutting his chin out as I met his eyes. In every respect, *my* eyes. And his voice—its tone, its pace—mine as well.

I put a hand up, ready, if need be, to keep him in his place.

"Where do I find her?" I said.

"What do you care?"

"I mean it. Where is she?"

He smiled, showing his teeth. "Same place as always, dumbass. You go by there every night. You stand and look. But you never go in. You don't give a shit about her."

I wanted to slap him.

"And *you've* never given a shit about *anyone*," I said. "All you care about is yourself. About what makes you feel good."

He appeared as if he had swallowed a mouthful of vinegar. "Wrong, bitch! It's about what makes *us* feel good. What makes *you* feel good. Just like that book. I never gave a damn about that book. But *you*—Mister Fancy-Pants!—wanted to be famous. And rich. And show ever'body how smart you were."

"And you *made* me want that! The Paisley should have been a diversion. But you made it an *obsession*."

"Oh, so blame me for all your problems, bunghole."

"You *are* the problem! You took nine years of my life. Everything I had. You ruined me!"

"*I* ruined you?" He came forward in the chair, laughing in my face. "For a guy who's supposed to have such a big brain, you just don't get it. And by the way . . ." He laughed again, slapping his knee. "You can't even count. Where'd you get that *nine years* shit? From that crazy story the preacher told you?"

"No."

"Oh, really? Well, genius-boy, you better think about that. 'Cause if you honestly believe you spent nine years on that stupid book—and that you're even close to bein' forty-two years old—then that fancy math degree you got ain't worth the butt-wipe it's printed on."

I backed away. "I'm through with you. I'm leaving."

"You'll take me along."

"I never want to see you again."

"You will, though. Every time you look in a mirror."

I started for the door.

"He's right, Stavros."

The voice, unmistakable, had come from the far end of the room, from the deepest shadows.

The Judge stepped forth.

"You've been here the whole time?"

"Of course," he said—still half-veiled in darkness. "Always."

"Then you know that I'm done with him," I said, shifting my eyes toward Ed. "And the same for you. I'm sick of you blaming me for his mistakes. I'm finished with both of you."

"You might as well be finished with life itself."

"That's just what you want, isn't it? You'd have me die of guilt. Of regret. Of self-loathing."

"I want no such thing," he said. "I never have." Through the dark he smiled in a way (an almost gentle way) I had never seen before. "The price of redemption is high, Stavros. But misery is a useless currency."

I let my head fall and threw up my hands.

"Then what would you have me do?"

"Only what you would have yourself do."

He took several steps toward me, into the light of the streetlamp shining through the front window, his face, to one side, assuming the gleam of a quarter moon.

"Stavros," he said, "could there be some possibility that of all you believe yourself to have lost, something remains?"

"Why do you ask me that?"

"Because for some time you have been asking yourself the same question. Yet you deny yourself any answer but the most dispiriting."

"That is absurd. Why would I do that?"

"For the reason that you find it easier to behave as if all you had is gone rather than face the reality of what you must do to salvage that which may be left."

I was indignant. "Another accusation!"

"No, an *observation*. And as you well know, an accurate one."

He advanced further into the room and spoke something else—though not aloud. A silent, encoded message to which I felt I had the key, but could not decrypt. An incomprehensible call to action.

"I'm not sure what I'm supposed to do," I said. "Just tell me."

The Judge shook his head in the way of a forlorn apology. "How can I tell you that which you refuse to tell yourself?" He looked to the door. "In any case, you will soon understand. But time is short. You must be on your way."

"To where?"

"Go back where you came from, Stavros," he said. "And go now."

"Don't listen to that old man!" Ed cried. "You'll regret it! We both will!"

I looked from one to the other, hesitant.

"*Go*," the Judge said firmly.

I went to the door.

Ed shouted after me: "Don't be an idiot! You're gonna kill us all!"

I jerked the door open as Ed's craven warning became eclipsed by that familiar and solemn voice of authority:

"Good luck, boy."

I was about to look back, but sensing a sudden emptiness in the room, did not.

I let the door shut behind me and started up the cobblestone walk. Ahead, a faint glow rose above the skyline.

-39-

I WALKED WITH MY SHOULDERS HUNCHED, my hands deep in the pockets of my jacket. It felt colder now than when I had entered the bar. But here, it was always cold. The sun, the sky, forever clouded over. Never a glimpse of blue by day or stars by night.

As I went further, I glanced at the church tower clock. But the hands—the entire face of the clock—lay obscured in darkness. I should ask someone for the time, I thought, if someone should come along. Yet as before, both the way ahead and behind were deserted.

With my every step, what had initially appeared as a mere glimmer on the horizon grew in size and brilliance. And soon I perceived a kind of flickering about it. Its source, for certain, was not far off. But the many structures that stood in front of it hindered what better view I might have had.

I crossed the street to the park without spotting a single vehicle and quickly strode the grounds among the many metallic heroes—observing, casually, the prominent dent in the ass of a certain steed made, I knew, by a bullet. This had always been a place youngsters would hang out, even on cold nights. Smoking cigarettes and doing whatever else they were inclined to. A smattering of others—lovers and loners—would come here too. But the lights of the park, bright as they were, revealed not a soul on the green.

And ahead, in the west, the mysterious radiance continued ever more in bloom. Ever widening. Ever brightening. As if the sun were about to rise in the wrong hemisphere.

I left the park, venturing down a familiar alleyway and into an equally familiar neighborhood of old stone buildings. There, as I headed south, the close proximity of the three- and four-story structures blocked all sight of the western sky and, accordingly, the peculiar light that threatened to fill it. But as I turned down the street that led to Ed's apartment, I was met by a wave of warm air. And above Ed's building, originating from no more than a block further distant, I could see, through a fog of smoke, the tips of flames lashing up toward low-lying clouds. Billowy folds of cumulus hued with a luster of fiery red.

The street, like those before, was vacant. I ran its length, feeling, as I did, the full loss of the evening's chill. And as I came to its end and veered toward the river, I was hit by a blast of heat as hot as the hottest summer's day.

At the river's edge, abutting the promenade, an old and elegant three-story stone apartment building stood ablaze, deep orange torrents of fire spewing from its upper-level windows and breaching its wood-shingled roof. Gray and black smoke rose and gathered above the flames, hanging like a filthy, suffocating wreath over the aged façade and gables.

I felt the night grow hotter still. I slowed to a jog, and then a shuffling walk, entranced by the sight of the building's ongoing destruction. I started to cross the street, but at its midpoint was stopped, halted by the scorching air. And there, from within the blaze, I heard cracklings and strange whistlings and the roar of the heat-driven wind, impelling the fire to greater devastation.

But there were also things I did *not* hear. Things I expected: The cry of human voices. Voices of panic and desperation. And sirens. And the bustle of firemen hauling hoses to hydrants.

I heard none of it.

I looked around me. To every side. Up the street. Down the promenade.

Everywhere.

There was no one. Not a person.

Anywhere.

Where, I wondered, had the world gone?

But just then, I had the feeling that someone was behind me. I turned to find a tall young man with long blonde hair standing barefoot and shirtless in boxer shorts and a leather jacket. He spoke in a loud, excited voice: *"Did everyone get out?"*

He was answered by a woman, not far away: *"I don't know. What about Mr. Alberti?"*

Another woman answered her: *"He's out of town."*

"Oh, thank god."

They spoke as if I were, to them, unseen. And just as the second ringing of a bell sounds as a mere replica of the first, their voices bore the quality of perfect echoes—the exact words stated in the exact tenor precisely as I remembered from some other time.

And then came the chatter of others, all taking sight as their voices took sound. Another scene, just as the one before, playing itself for an encore:

"It's an old building."

"Up like a damn tinderbox."

"Everything I own."

"I always said this would happen."

"Where the hell is the fire department?"

In the next instant, I saw a throng of onlookers coming from the promenade. Others approaching from the north. All rushing to the calamity. And from the north, too, came the sirens of police cars, and lights flashing red and blue and throwing a whirling strobe effect onto the fiery street and the thickening smoke that covered it. This, also—every element of it—unfolding as a now twice-played drama.

And as the blare of the sirens rang against the surrounding buildings, the barefoot young man in the leather jacket spoke again: *"Hey, I'm still not seeing everybody. What about the Hannemanns?"*

From down the way, an older man with a weeping woman in his arms gave a short wave. *"Over here!"*

"And where's Nina?"

"Who?"

"Nina Stavros. On the second floor."

Another man's voice came in reply: *"I went to her door. I knocked. No answer."*

The woman who had asked about Alberti spoke again: *"Maybe she's gone too."*

"She's not gone," said the man in the jacket. *"She hasn't been out of there for days."*

"Hey," the other man said, *"I tried. I yelled. I pounded on that door."*

"You should have kicked the damn thing in!"

"There wasn't time! Man, I had to get out!"

A woman who had not yet spoken—an elderly woman—balled her hands together, churning her fingers. Her face quivering. *"Oh, God. Nina. She's in there."*

She was going to cross herself, I thought. She had done it before.

She did it again.

And I knew what she would say next: *"God save her."* But then she said something else: *"Or someone."*

Or someone?

It was my first time to hear that. It jolted me like the sound of an alarm clock. And I felt at once as if I had been roused from the depths of an almost fathomless sleep.

But yet not a sleep. Not a real sleep. More of a waking sleep.

A waking *dream.*

A dream that had at last reached its intersection with reality.

How long, I wondered, had I been away? Clearly, only seconds—the fleeting stretch between that old woman's invocation and her two words spoken after. Yet in that interval it seemed I had nevertheless lived many days. Days that had passed in the capsule of a moment. But a moment disposed to such subjectively extended length that one caught in its grip might sense in a mere instant the flow of almost infinite time. The measure of all existence bound up in the span of a lightning strike.

I remained facing the burning pyre as men lamented, women wailed. "It's hopeless," the young man in the leather coat said.

I closed my eyes, giving myself a respite from the glare; I took a step in retreat. But still the heat slapped at me, and I began to feel something like the sting of a worsening sunburn. And a fever. A boiling sweat. Blisters on my cheeks.

Though why was I here if not for some measure of penance?

I reopened my eyes and recaptured the stride I had surrendered—then added several more. Moving close enough to the conflagration that, over and over, flames from the upper stories shot out above my head. Great arcs of light in tangles, each a hovering, transitory crown of fire.

Then, from behind me, for the first time, came a recognition of my presence:

"Hey there, get back!"

"You're too close!"

"Who is that guy?"

"Jesus Christ, it's Leonard!"

I stared into the heart of the furnace, held fast by its destructive pulse. I stared until, as before, its flames grew as blinding as the sun, and all sight of the building—and with it, all grasp of my surroundings: the scalding heat, the snap and rumble of the fire, the cowering crowd—was lost, and before me lay only flitters of orange and yellow melding to a single orb of white. A silent ball of light burning into my eyes and brain. Supplanting all semblance of temporal thought and feeling, and leaving my mind to wander once more into places of its own creation. Places of refuge. Places of torment. Places from which I might never return, and where the sum of myself would stay locked for eternity in conflict with those parts that comprised it.

But then, she spoke:

Leonard, it is time.

With the soft air of her voice, the great globe of fire gradually fragmented to the elements of its former self. And I saw again those sparks of orange and yellow, then watched as they became, once more, a host of slithering, consumptive flames that lit the building, the street, the sky. The sounds of my environs returned as well—the sound of the inferno, and of the scorching wind that swirled the unremitting smoke and embers and hoisted them aloft.

All of it seeming insurmountable to human flesh.

I don't know what to do.

You cannot be serious. Leonard, I have already told you twice.

In my dreams, you mean?

In our *dreams.*

I felt a tug on my arm. A clasp and a quick release. I turned to see a police officer recoiling from the heat. Shielding his face.

"You need to move back," he said.

He stretched out to retake my arm.

Am I dreaming now?

No, Leonard. This is not a dream. And you have always known that. Now, come on. Get going.

I tore loose from the man and took another step toward the building. He stayed put. "Sir, please. Get back."

Nina, I'm sorry. I can't do this.

Of course you can.

I took another step.

"Sir!"

I teetered on the beginning of yet another pace forward. My foot, though, feeling mired by a tremendous weight.

Nina, it's impossible.

No, it is not. It is simple.

How?

You know how. Come home to me, Leonard. Just come home.

My foot rose from the pavement. I took a long and steady stride. I straightened myself.

Just come home.

I gave the officer a nod of farewell.

And with that, ran into the fire.

-40-

NEAR THE BOTTOM OF THE STOOP I met dark smoke rolling from the front entrance. Things grew blurred, and as I continued to the top of the steps was engulfed in a blinding, fiery, airborne mass of soot that seared my nose and throat. I fell to my hands and knees, gagging and retching from the hot insult. My eyes stinging and tearing and shut tight against the further onslaught of carbon shards. Awash in this misery, I felt, rising inside me, a spontaneous cry of pain—but it was a cry that, for lack of breath, could not escape my lips.

I'm dying, I thought. Right here. Right now.

She spoke to me sternly: *Leonard, for goodness' sake, you are not even in the building yet.*

I can't breathe.

That makes two of us.

Too weak to even stay on all fours, my arms began to buckle and I sank further until my chest and face were flat to the concrete—which led to a discovery of the obvious: The smoke was thinner here. A lesser version of the poison above. Nevertheless, I needed some way to screen out the lingering miasma. A gas mask of some kind.

Remaining as low as possible, I wiggled worm-like as I peeled off my jacket, then clumped it into a ball and shoved it to my face. Within a half dozen breaths I felt a resetting of my faculties, and a deep cough produced a wad of throat-clearing, smoke-flavored glue. A perfect filter, this was not, but it was a stark improvement over the alternative.

With my left hand, I kept the jacket to my mouth and nose as, with my right, I reached out to find the threshold of the entrance. Then, staying prone, I pulled myself across the doorstep onto the granite tiles of the foyer. I could no more than squint into the onrush of fumes. Nonetheless, in the light of fire ahead, I was able to see the main hallway and, to its left, the foot of one of two stairways that led to the upper stories. The hall appeared largely aflame, impassable. But the stairs seemed, from my perspective, untouched.

Hugging the floor, I dragged myself onward, heading for the stairs. Yet within a short distance, I saw I had been mistaken: The bottom two steps—all that had previously been visible to me—had indeed, so far, escaped the fire. Above that, however, the carpet runner shone red through the smoke, striking a wide, bright line all the way to the mid-landing. And as I drew closer, I noted that on either side of the runner, the steps themselves—old and wooden—were smoldering in a way that suggested their ignition, too, was imminent. I thought there was still time, though, to ascend in relative safety. And if the stairs went up after me, a retreat by way of the other staircase might be a possibility.

But there could be no more of this crawling.

Keeping the jacket hard to my face, I got to my feet and made for the stairway, parting my eyes in the heavy smoke just long enough to see my foot land squarely on the right side of the first step in the space between the bannister and the burning carpet runner. From there, I went on sheer faith and memory, eyes closed and climbing in a near sprint. Staying aside the burning carpet. Counting steps—twelve, I recalled—to the mid-landing.

I stopped. I took a peek. I had made the landing. At a loss for breath in the putrid air, I grabbed, with my right hand, the bannister to steady myself—and felt as if I had touched a scorching stove.

I recoiled to see both the bannister and the cuff of my shirt afire, my hand likewise covered in flames. In a desperate, reckless panic, I flapped my hand wildly about before burying it in the jacket, smothering the fire. But in my frenzy I had taken on lungfuls of toxic sludge. I reeled, nearly overcome. My wrist and hand roasted, all but useless.

And around my feet, something I had just noticed: The entire landing was aflame.

I danced in the fire, uttering the silly shrieks of a man in a hopeless place. A man burning to death while dancing. Burning in a silly and hopeless way.

I heard her over my squawking: *Leonard! Leonard!*

I did not answer. I danced. The lower part of my pants had caught fire.

Leonard, you have done your best. You have. But you were right. You cannot make it. No one could.

I can!

You cannot.

I will!

Then Leonard, please ... please ...

Please what? I sprang about at random. A human pogo stick. *WHAT?*

Hurry. Please hurry.

My lower legs were literally being incinerated. I smacked them with the jacket. But no good.

Fire. Everywhere.

And pain.

Run, I thought. Run-Run.

I was up the next flight of stairs as if I had levitated. Twelve more fiery steps. At the top, I fell. I rolled. I spanked at my legs. The skin below my knees, perhaps the deep tissue, ravaged. But the flames, through some miracle, were snuffed out.

It was the worst pain I had ever felt. I bawled like a child.

Yet within moments, on charred legs—legs that should not have functioned—I forced myself to stand and meet the hallway.

And my god, the hallway.

Four doors on the left. Four on the right.

And all of it a veritable crematorium.

The fire was global. A vise of flames from every direction. A thing so hot, its very smoke devoured by its heat.

But again it came. That soft and pleading voice: *Leonard ... hurry ...*
No time for the jacket. No time for pain.

Once more, I ran into the fire—but now becoming, it seemed, the fire itself. Parts of me starting ablaze even as I maintained full stride to the second door on the left. The door from which I had made my exit all those months ago, thinking myself never to return.

The door that was mine.

And I did not knock. I did not yell.

I kicked the damn thing in.

I leapt through the entrance and onto the floor of the main room of the flat, rolling and swatting myself and my burning clothes until the flames that had again attached themselves to me were gone. My arms, shoulders, and back raged as if my skin had been flayed with a knife. I put a hand—my good hand—to my head and found the bulk of my hair missing, singed away.

But suddenly, curiously, it seemed needless to assess myself at all. For despite my trauma, I began to perceive an odd sort of numbness. An almost divine loss of physical sensation that rendered me, at least for the time being, impervious to my injuries.

I promptly stood and called her name.

There came nothing in return.

Where are you?

Not even a voice in my head.

The fire had not entered here, and it was dark save for the shifting light from the flames in the hall. But smoke seeping in from the vents and around the door had nevertheless accumulated to the degree of a lethal vapor. No worse, really, than I had already been through. Yet it added to the aggregate effect, and the heavy fumes at last brought me to the point where the thing above my shoulders became little more than a large cumbersome ball, drooping from its own weight.

In air-starved confusion, I staggered about, bumping into furniture, searching for her in the haze. Repeating her name with a hoarseness that sounded at first desperate, then frail and half-hearted. No, she was not here. He had been wrong, that guy in the jacket.

But why, then, had she coaxed me into this slice of hell?

Or had she? Rather, had that sweet voice in my mind instead been nothing but fantasy? A final psychotic fabrication through which I might lead myself to a severe and deserving end?

It was becoming ever more difficult to process my situation. Feeling dull and anesthetized, I looked down the short hall that led to the bedroom on one side and the bath on the other. Appreciating nothing of what I observed, I saw that the door to the former was shut—and I saw that because the room around me was growing brighter, and had been for some time.

And then I saw why.

Through the open door of the flat's entry, the fire had gained access. The doorframe, caved in from my own arrival, was alight—as was the wall on either side, the couch, a lamp shade.

The ceiling.

In the next instant, like the flaring of a giant match head, the room gained in heat and brilliance. The fire feeding on every available source. The smoke thickening and running in advance of the flames. My mind adrift, I thought of simply closing the door. Of finding some way to prop it shut against the splintered frame. But it was too late. From top to bottom, the door had become a fiery mass, and even had I been able to secure it to the frame, the room itself was too far gone for that to have done the least good.

Clearly, to stay here, in this room, meant death. And that, seconds away.

But I could not go back the way I had come. Outside, in the hall, the fire had reached its zenith. An invitation to self-immolation.

I watched as the fire embraced the room, rapt in its power and menace—but in my stupor, I watched, strangely, without the slightest sense of dread.

Surely, I thought, there was a way out. Wasn't there always?

In apparent retort to my question, a portion of the ceiling collapsed.

All right, then, I thought. So there wasn't.

Shit.

Leonard?

Her call came so feeble, it was, even within my head, barely audible.

Nina? No response. *Are you there? Talk to me.*

The effort seemed almost too much for her: *There is.*

Is what?

A way.

Out?

Yes.

How?

The bedroom.

Of course. The closed door. I had seen it. Only seconds before. But my disordered thoughts had been of the fire. Only the fire.

And in its swift encroachment, it reached out for me, eager to take me into its amorphous, killing arms.

But I had broken, already, for the bedroom. I ran with the flames in chase, replacing my every former step. And in my final stride, I grabbed the hot metal knob, turned it, and swung the door inward—but less than halfway open, it stopped abruptly, jammed against something on the other side. I had space, though—just enough—to shoot the gap. Which I did.

And slammed the door.

The sudden shift from the glare of the fire to the unlit room left me momentarily sightless. However, I soon recognized a faint illumination from each of the room's double casement windows, the curtains of the one closest to me fully parted to reveal, through the pervading smoke, a dim, gray sky.

Night becoming day.

The wooden flooring under the door had ignited, and in the flickering, the state of the room itself grew discernible. The bed was unmade—and unoccupied. On the night stand stood a bottle of her sedatives with the cap off.

And on the floor, in a long-sleeved nightshirt, lying prone—one arm angled toward the door, the other extended toward the nearest set of windows, as if reaching for a thing unattainable—I found her.

It appeared as if she had crawled out of bed and shoved the door shut, trying to protect herself. To buy herself time.

To buy *me* time.

I knelt next to her, but, with my head spinning, almost fell over. Righting myself, I grabbed her under the far shoulder and rolled her toward me, onto her back, as a loss of equilibrium again left me tipping to one side.

I put my hands to the floor, bracing myself as I hovered above her. Her nightshirt was soaked from the heat. Her short hair damp and tousled and, like her face, covered with a grimy film from the smoke. With the fingers of my unburned left hand, I stroked her arm, then moved the hand to her shoulder and into her thick hair, cradling her head. I could not tell if she was breathing.

"Nina?" I shook her gently. Then with a violence. *"Nina!"*

A kind of grinding, guttural noise came from her lungs and throat. Her chest rose and fell in a single, rapid gasp. More, it seemed, an imitation of breathing than an actual respiration.

Her soft features tightened to a hard, wrinkled grimace. She coughed and convulsed as though she were about to be sick.

But as she heaved for another breath, her eyes opened.

There was a recognition. Almost a smile.

"Leonard?"

"It's me."

"You came home." At once, her face again constricted. "Oh, Leonard . . ."

She rolled away from me and threw up. I held her steady even as I saw that the fire had spread from beneath the door to the border of the area rug, a mere foot away. A hot yellow glow outlined the door, and from the gaps between the door and its frame, folds of smoke bled into the room, amplifying the density of the already noxious air.

There was no time to waste.

She was still sick to herself as, from behind her, I looped my arms under hers, fastened my hands together at her front, and lugged her toward the closest set of windows. Such a small woman. Always so light.

And now, for me, a thousand pounds.

I found just enough wind to speak.

"Can you stand?" I said stupidly, knowing the impossibility of it.

She lay limp in my arms. Eyes closed. The image of a lifeless doll.

I peered through the drifting grunge, examining the length of the nearest set of windows. They were well shorter than me. Shorter, even, than her. But the opening was nevertheless wide enough for both of us—if not for the damn wooden post running down the middle of the casements.

A problem which I could think of only one way to solve.

Leaving her for the moment, I took the wooden desk chair by its back with both hands and tried to lift it. My burnt hand, as numb as the rest of me, did as well as the other. But I had so little strength, I could scarcely get the legs of the chair off the floor.

I saw then that even in the dearth of oxygen, the fire had meandered across the rug and found the bed. It had crept up the sagging top sheet and spread over the mattress, lighting the bedding with a host of innocuous, low burning flames, like candles on a birthday cake. And in a brief cognitive lapse, I thought perhaps I could just blow them out and everything would be all right.

But the flames were dying on their own. Dying just as I was. As Nina. And for the same reason.

And very soon—well before the final advance of the fire outside—we would all be gone.

I tried once more, in the same way, to lift the chair. But with the same result.

I could hear Ed: *You better think of somethin' else, brainiac. And you better think fast.*

The point was hard to argue.

I turned the chair so that it was facing me and tilted it toward me, on its front legs, then half-squatted and put the top of my head to the chair's back. I grabbed the seat on both sides. From there, my thighs struggling under the load, I pushed myself to a standing position with the chair legs facing the windows, and, wasting no time, threw myself ahead. Charging with full force.

Then, shattering glass. The post giving way. The chair, with its momentum, tearing loose of my hold and trailing the debris downward.

The world outside opened itself to me. The sky, lighter than before. Almost blue. And the river below, not quite frozen. A channel of open water running its middle. Chunks and floes of ice covering the rest, all in motion, a slowly churning mass of puzzle pieces.

In the next moment, a rush of frigid air filled the vacuum of the room. The bed erupted in the backdraft. I was swallowed in a whirlwind of smoke. The closed door behind me rattling under the hot pressure of the newly fed fire.

I took her, as before, under the arms, dragging her to the window, her tiny form unwieldy, resisting. I sat myself on the frame and, in stages—heaving, groaning—pulled her up to me. Feeling, in the process, barbs of glass, rooted in the window's lower rail, puncturing my pants and skin, their points driving deeper as her weight pressed me hard to the bottom of the fractured casement.

I worked my shoulder under her and managed to turn her just enough, putting her atop me in something like a fireman's carry.

While behind us, the bed had become a bonfire. And above, the ceiling too was aflame.

I stood up, wobbling and teetering, my legs threatening to buckle. The curtains on either side of us caught fire as I fought with both hands to stabilize her. I put my left foot on the window ledge. A height of less than two feet. Yet under the crushing weight on my shoulder, my leading leg, by itself, lacked the power to raise us further.

More was needed.

Leaving my foot on the ledge, I held my body stiff, using one arm to balance her on my shoulder. With my free hand, I grabbed the outside of the window frame and pulled myself forward as, in the same motion, I pushed with my leading leg and hopped from the floor with the one behind. The effort brought with it an agonizing strain that slackened only as I made a sound like the cry of a wounded animal.

But it had been enough. I stood, now, on the ledge.

Though still more in the room than out.

I hunched over to fit the opening—and in doing so, gazed down. My eyes falling upon the thin strip of concrete promenade that ran past the building's foot. A small but seemingly impossible hurdle.

I kept my hand on the window frame, steadying myself. But she was slipping from me. I could not hold both her and my position. I took my hand from the frame and braced her against my chest and shoulder, locking my arms around her.

Nina, this is it.

I know. I trust you.

There was an instant in which we were neither fixed nor falling. A kind of floating between the extremes. Descent, though, was certain. Gravity was master.

I held her ever closer and, as we dropped, pushed with my legs. With all I had. The fire from the curtains following. The flames taking me. Lighting me from behind.

I became a shooting star. A spent, failing firework.

I saw the river. The ice. The strip of promenade. All coming fast.

I shut my eyes.

-41-

I OPENED MY EYES. I stood at the entrance to a faintly lit room, its walls covered in white plaster and shadowed tapestries, its wood floor unvarnished. Beside me was a canopied bed with linen curtains, and to its other side, along a rounded wall, were three windows—the one nearest the bed with its sash thrown outward, allowing the entrance of a breeze that rustled the bed curtains enough to reveal, within their enclosure, the bed itself—unmade and unoccupied. Three large floor-standing wrought-iron candleholders burned next to the bed, while across the room, on a long wooden table, two more candles, melting in a three-light candelabra, supplied the remainder of the room's illumination.

I went to the open window and looked into the night to find a starry sky and a gibbous moon. I saw too, in the moonlight, that the earth lay far below. To my left, a castle battlement stretched into the distance to meet a rounded tower, the pinnacle of which appeared to reach a height just above that of my own. And at the base of the castle wall, running its length and lapping against it, sat the glistening water of a moat.

Nina crossed the room to the long table. She glanced back and forth along its top.

"Leonard, come here."

"What?"

There was a tone of shock in her voice: "This."

She pointed from one end of the table to the other. It was an unpolished, battered old thing. If set for dining, it would have accommodated ten or more.

But no one had been eating here. Not recently.

This was a work station.

Across the table, in three rows, lay stacks of vellum sheets. Three sheets to each stack. Seven stacks in each row.

Twenty-one in all.

And all covered in script. The pages of a book ready for assembly.

A penknife and an open inkwell rested on the table's far right end, a feathery quill protruding from the small container. A simple four-legged stool stood on the floor nearby. And within reach of the stool lay what I took to be the most recently composed of the vellum piles, the candelabra, set next to the parchment, casting sparkles of light on the text of the topmost sheet.

The ink there not yet dry.

"Can it be?" Nina said.

I sat on the stool and pulled myself closer to the table, my eyes racing over the newly written lines. Marveling at the hand that had so faultlessly shaped this seemingly incompressible mix of alphabetic characters—Latin, Arabic, and Greek.

"What do you think you're doing?" I heard.

In tandem, we turned to look behind us.

Near the bed stood a tall, olive-skinned woman. One of the most beautiful women I had ever seen. With high cheeks and soft angles along her nose and jaw. Her thick long hair, as dark as the sky outside, parted down the middle and hanging unbound down her back. She wore a long-sleeved, bright red gown that reached to the floor and fit snugly from the waist up, the upper spheres of her cleaving breasts showing above the white lace of a low-cut neckline.

"That book," she said, glaring at me, "is not for you."

Nina stiffened. "It is for whomever can read it."

From the woman came the hint of a smile—or perhaps a smirk. Something Da Vinci might have painted. "Thus the thrust of my previous statement."

Nina took a step toward her. "Now, listen! You have no idea . . ."

I rose and took her arm.

The woman uttered a muted, derisive laugh, becoming, it seemed, even more enchanting than before.

Yet at the same time, there was a continuing austerity about her. An unyielding air of authority.

I glanced to the table and back to her, mustering the nerve to speak: "Are you the author?"

"No." She looked to the open window. "Sadly, he has left us."

I moved toward her through the shadows, Nina at my side, moving with me, her arm clutching mine. Our feet shuffling on the dusty wooden floor.

The woman watched our approach, giving no ground. We stopped close enough to touch her.

"I know who you are," I said.

"And who are *you?*"

"Leonard Stavros."

"I have never heard of you."

"He is the greatest cryptanalyst in the world," Nina said.

The woman tipped her head back and laughed again—this time loudly. "*Vere? Et artes cum linguis habes?*"[1]

Latin, articulated to perfection.

"*Multas linguas loquor,*" I said.[2]

"*Kum al`adad?*" she asked in Arabic.[3]

"*Oi perissóteroi apó aftoús,*" I answered in Greek. "*Pollés me efchéreia. Ta ypóloipa me elafrós ligótero.*"[4]

---

1. "Really? And do you have skills with languages?"

2. "I speak many languages," . . .

3. "How many?"

4. "Most of them," . . . "Many with fluency. The rest with slightly less."

She scoffed at my arrogance and, in a slow and regal manner, strode past us to the table, looking over the stacks of quires.

She spoke with her back to us.

"What you say may be true. Or not. It does not matter. Whoever you are—or *think* you are—you are wasting your time here. No man possesses the skills to read these pages."

"Does a woman?"

She wheeled about, facing me. "Do you think I am going to help you?"

I shook my head. "I don't need your help."

I felt an increase in the pressure around my arm, Nina tightening her hold as she took a deep, expectant breath. "Leonard, what are you saying?"

I looked into her dark eyes and smiled.

There is a certain phenomenon we have all encountered: that singular experience where a thing once learned and engraved upon the mind—a thought, a phrase, a word, a name—has become stuck in the brain's hard drive, refusing all attempts at recall, and then, in a flash—unprompted, involuntary—makes itself known again. Such events are most generally minor epiphanies, marveled over and dismissed as quickly as the thing forgotten is remembered.

Yet I can now say that far more notable varieties of this sort of breakthrough may occur.

Think, for instance, of an entire Shakespearean play committed to memory, every syllable and nuanced expression flowing effortlessly from the mind to the tongue and lips, one after the next, precisely as the Bard intended—but then, mysteriously, gone. All recollection of it ostensibly wiped clean from the intellect by which it was held.

Only, just as mysteriously, to reappear.

Such are the vagaries of the subconscious and its oftentimes inclination, however misguided, to deprive us of the very things we most consciously require.

I put my arm around Nina, pulling her closer to me. Running my cheek against her short, thick hair.

"Where is the first quire?" I asked.

With a mocking grin, the woman pointed to the far and all but light-less end of the table.

She appeared ready to laugh once more.

"Shall I fetch it for you, oh great cryptanalyst?"

I gently pulled away from Nina. "That won't be necessary."

I approached the table.

I caught the woman squarely in her eyes.

"This," I said, "is how it starts . . ."

The woman's grin—a grin that might have matched the laughter I had once heard from the book—remained only a moment longer, fading as I drew near. As though she sensed the prospect of something unpleasant.

And the seemingly absurd amalgam of letters, all mentally assembling themselves before me, at once fell prey to the labyrinthine solution that I had buried so deeply within myself, never meant to be found.

But now rediscovered.

And then, as if from a man possessed of the very words he uttered, came this:

"*I, Ferrante Bonifacio da Rimini, master of languages and secret writings, advisor to the highest courts of the West, mathematician, diplomat, and poet, hereby set forth the account of my life, all telling of my deeds and triumphs, my regretful travels of nine years, and the tragic loss of my only love. So that through Our Lord's grace I might atone for my pride, my avarice, my selfish ways, and my conceit, I offer also, in these pages, my true and last confession. God have mercy upon my soul.*'"

There was no need to go on. I knew it word for word.

So did she.

And she knew that I knew.

She lowered herself to the stool at the table, hiding her eyes from me as the candelabra led a shimmering dance of light in her ebony hair. It was some time before she spoke.

"You are what your woman claims you to be," she said.

"But no greater than he," I replied, glancing at the open window.

"No, no greater."

"Nor than you."

"If you say."

"I do say."

She gave me a reserved but grateful dip of her head, her striking looks now mellowed to a sad and tender elegance. A countenance that appeared somehow, if only slightly, less youthful than before.

"May I ask you something?" I said.

She stared at me, impassive, neither authorizing nor forbidding my inquiry.

I went on.

"He—the author—" I looked again to the window. "He states that the negotiations in Naples, where you met, began in the sixth month on the Feast of Saint Clotildis, in the fourth year of the reign of King Robert—which I know from other events in the manuscript to be the year 1312."

She raised her head in a way that invited me to continue.

"And please excuse my ignorance—I am not a religious man—but on what day is—or was—this Feast of Clotildis?"

Her face took on something resembling the da Vincian smirk I had seen previously—albeit a strangely and steadily maturing version.

"Hard to fathom that a man as yourself could suffer from such a failure of reasoning," she chided—then put her own question: "What day do you think?"

I felt like a fool.

"The third of June," I said, straightaway.

"And there is your answer. Just as you supposed."

For the moment, this ended our exchange. Her eyes fell upon the open window, and despite the room's pale light, I could see her lips moving at a regular cadence. There was an accompanying murmur, like the chanting of a prayer.

With fascination, Nina watched the woman, her own lips moving in empathetic unison.

Twenty-one up. Twenty-one down.

At length, the woman ceased her numeric exercise. But her focus remained on the aperture, the timber frame of its sash swinging on the breeze, hinges creaking.

"A symmetrical compulsion born of hope," she reflected. "And desire. And dreams. But there is a symmetry to everything. Numbers that tell of the day lovers met: *six, three,* and *twelve.* Becoming, together, a score and one. And that same number, a score and one—*twenty-one*—forming the last thought of earthly life."

I noticed, then, for the first time, streaks of gray in her hair. Lines on her face. A slumping of her shoulders.

A trembling of her hands and arms.

"We should go," Nina said.

A brisk wind entered the chamber, dousing two of the candles near the bed and both of those afire in the candelabra. The woman's thinning, sinking form became nearly one with the tapestry on the wall behind her. A patch of almost nothing in the virtual black.

"Did you read," she said, her voice quavering in the void, *"all"* of the book?"

"Yes."

"Are you *quite* sure?"

I thought.

I thought again.

"No, *signora,* I did not. There are forty-two pages, each page with forty-two lines, which were impenetrable. A different cipher used there, more complex, even, than the other."

"And you could not read those pages?"

"No, none of it."

"Truly?"

Another hard gust took the room. Beside the bed, the flame of the last lit candle died in the rush.

"Signora," I called into the Stygian dark. "I swear I could not. And even if I had . . ."

"Then?"

"I would forget those words."

"And you must," she said, frail and trailing off. "Some words are for two people only."

-42-

I FELT MANY HANDS ON ME, pulling and pushing me up to the
promenade. To the light of day. As I reached the landing, I looked
back to see half a dozen men in the cold water, ice bobbing around
them—our rescuers.

I lay on the hard concrete, and beside me, on a gurney, lay Nina,
wrapped in blankets. Limp and white. Appearing no more alive—even
less—than she had as we leapt from the building. One of two attending
paramedics was placing an oxygen mask over her face, carefully working
the elastic support strap behind her head.

There was a crowd around us. Some of them—a small collection of
men and woman—were wet about the front of their clothing and had,
I assumed, helped haul us from the river. Others were at the shoreline,
pulling up the men who remained in the water.

A young man's voice came from far away: "That was fucking awe-
some!"

I raised myself to my knees and saw, running up, the long-haired and
barefoot young man in the leather jacket and boxers. He looked at me
with a kind of reverence—and also, I thought, a bit of repulsion. The
latter, no doubt, due to my appearance, which, I was sure, resembled a
burnt piece of toast.

The one paramedic continued with Nina. The other, sporting a thick
beard, bent down and touched me on the shoulder.

"Please lie back," he said. "We've got more blankets coming. And
another gurney,"

I rose to my feet.

"No, please don't." he said. "You're hypothermic. You're burned. You're in shock."

"Bullshit. I've never felt better."

I looked around at the persons in the crowd, all of them staring back as me as they would a circus freak.

"Is she okay?" I asked the paramedic assisting Nina.

"She's breathing. She's stable."

"Does that mean she'll live?"

He gave a hesitant nod. "But we need to get her out of here."

Some thirty meters away, an EMS vehicle sat on the promenade, its rear facing us, its back doors open. A second, identical vehicle was in the process of parking beside it, and as it stopped, a three-person crew burst out, one of them carrying several blankets and the two others handling a gurney. All of it, obviously, for me.

"No, no, no!"

"Hey, now come on," said the bearded paramedic. The other one left Nina's side and stepped toward me, both of them clearly intent on caging me into some form of medical assistance.

But I felt fine. I really did. And not the least bit cold.

Nearby, fire and smoke spewed from the collapsing shell of stone. Sending hot air over the promenade. Warming even the pavement as the barefoot young man in the leather coat stood before me without the slightest apparent discomfort. Along the street above, fire trucks, having arrived at last, shot streams of water into the dying, blazing structure, not to save it, but to salvage those properties yet undamaged to the north.

And to the east, down the promenade, I saw what seemed an almost foreign fire: The sun. Crowning the horizon. Orange-red in a cloudless sky.

Nina stirred, a pale hand emerging from her blankets, brushing my burnt fingers. Through her oxygen mask, I could see her lips moving.

"What?" I said, taking her hand.

I knelt beside her and pulled her mask up. The paramedic attending her touched my arm as a warning, but the bearded one intervened, allowing me to go on.

Her eyes parted, but only barely. Becoming dark slits.

"Leonard," she said. "This time. Remember."

I nodded and squeezed her hand.

She closed her eyes. "Will you leave me again?"

"I will not," I said, emphasizing each word. "Ever."

"You mean you *won't*," she said through a fading smile.

At once she was whisked toward the emergency vehicles. At the same time, the two newly-arrived paramedics with the gurney attempted to usher me onto their stretcher.

"Get away!" I flailed my arms. "All of you, get the hell away. I can walk on my own." I looked around, shouting to every onlooker: "And I can say that any way you like. *Fluently.*"

The EMS staff—and all the crowd—stepped away from the madman, giving him leeway.

But I paused. Something was amiss in my pants pocket, poking at my thigh. I ran my one good hand into the opening to find the cause—and pulled out a simple black and red flash drive.

I tossed it in the river.

I followed Nina to the ambulance. Ahead, the sun grew ever brighter. And in the welcome light—the now soft blush of morning becoming gold—the city, the world, lay before me like sheets of virgin vellum. The pages of another book—a better book—waiting to be written.

Vince Wheeler

Vince Wheeler is the author of *The Things of Man,* his debut novel, which was presented a silver medal at the 2017 Independent Publisher Book Awards. He is also an attorney with many years of litigation, trial, and appellate experience. *The Stavros Manuscript* is his second novel. For more about Vince Wheeler, please visit his website at vince-wheeler.com.

THE THINGS OF MAN

Brad Manford—successful attorney, and loving husband and father—has a dire secret: He used to be someone else. But his memories of that former life? Gone. Replaced, inexplicably, by false recollections from a life he never lived. Who, really, is Brad Manford? And what was he doing during those forgotten years? Through a frightening journey of surreal self-discovery, Brad learns an unimaginable truth about not only himself, but the entire world around him.

"Hints of Stephen King . . . The Twilight Zone."

SEATTLE BOOK REVIEW

"A surprisingly captivating novel . . . mixing general fiction with science fiction in an unexpected and wonderful way."

PORTLAND BOOK REVIEW

Made in the USA
Coppell, TX
03 December 2023